DARE *to* DREAM

Content Warning

Books in the *Desert of Dreams Series* address many sensitive but important topics which may include bullying and peer pressure; troubled sibling relationships; struggling friendships and romantic relationships; divorce; religion; historical events of the late 1980s and 1990s; racism and classism; death; neglect and abuse (physical, emotional, and/or sexual); trauma (generational and situational); drugs, alcohol, and sex; teen pregnancy; abortion; and mental illness including depression, suicidal ideation, PTSD, and anxiety.

If you or someone you know is struggling with their mental health or is in crisis, please reach out for help. In the US, you can call or text the National Suicide and Crisis Lifeline at 988.

DARE *to* DREAM

Desert of Dreams Series Book 1

AMANDA LAPERA

ADAMO PRESS

Aliso Viejo, Calif.

Dare to Dream
(Desert of Dreams Series Book 1)

This is a work of fiction. References to historical events and places are used fictitiously. Names, characters, places, and events portrayed in this book are products of the author's imagination. Any resemblance to actual persons, living or dead, events, or locales is entirely coincidental.

Copyright © 2025 by Amanda LaPera. All rights reserved.

First edition.

Published by Adamo Press, 27068 La Paz Rd, Suite 102, Aliso Viejo, California 92656. Printed in the United States of America. No part of this book may be used or stored in any electronic form or reproduced in any manner whatsoever without prior written permission except in the case of brief quotations embodied in critical articles and reviews. Scanning, uploading, or distributing this book without permission is theft. No permission is granted for use with any AI system or program. Thank you for supporting the author by buying an authorized copy of this book. To schedule an event with the author, or to inquire about discounts for bulk purchases, contact us at info@adamopress.com or www.adamopress.com.

Library of Congress Control Number: 2025935408

Publisher's Cataloging-in-Publication Data
Names: LaPera, Amanda, 1978- author.
Title: Dare to dream / Amanda LaPera.
Description: Aliso Viejo, Calif. : Adamo Press, [2025] | Series: Desert of dreams series ; book 1. | Audience: Young adult.
Identifiers: LCCN: 2025935408 | ISBN: 9780986247194 (hardcover) | 9781965660010 (paperback) | 9781965660003 (eBook)
Subjects: LCSH: Teenage girls--Psychology--Fiction. | Children of divorced parents--Fiction. | Single mothers--Fiction. | Small cities--Fiction. | Lake Los Angeles (Calif.)--Fiction. | Mojave Desert--Fiction. | Teenagers--Family relationships--Fiction. | Friendship--Fiction. | Bullying--Fiction. | Self-esteem--Fiction | Self-reliance--Fiction. | Generational trauma--Fiction. | Gifted children--Fiction. | Bildungsromans. | BISAC: YOUNG ADULT FICTION / Coming of Age. | YOUNG ADULT FICTION / Girls & Women. | YOUNG ADULT FICTION / Social Themes / Self-Esteem & Self-Reliance.
Classification: LCC: PS3612.A5894 D37 2025 | DDC: 813/.6--dc23

Cover design by Fiona Jayde Media

Dedicated to Mom:

You were one of the good ones

Table of Contents

The Beginning

1 Desert Welcome 1
2 Out There 7
3 A Fresh Start 14
4 Sugar Cube Igloos 23
5 Joshua Trees 33
6 Adapting 37
7 Grandma 43
8 The Disaster 51
9 Snow Globe 57
10 So Lucky 62
11 Things Fall Apart 68
12 Lovejoy Buttes 75
13 Eruption 85
14 Trouble 93
15 Deceived 98
16 The Outsider 107
17 Patches 113
18 Camping 123
19 Burn Day 128

The Middle Years

20 Impressions 135
21 Dodgeball 145
22 Perspective 153
23 Reconnected 158
24 Shifting Ground 167
25 On the Air 174
26 A Darker Turn 181
27 Silent Night 189
28 Uncertainty 195
29 Barbed Wire 199
30 Building Bridges 209

31 Halloween 213
32 The Freak 218
33 The Dance 226
34 Hypocrisy 235
35 Promotion 241
36 Bright Stars 247
37 St. Andrew's Abbey 253

High School

38 Left Behind 261
39 Big Rock Creek 270
40 Trauma 275
41 Playing the Part 282
42 Climbing Trees 291
43 The Outsider 300
44 Innocence Lost 310
45 Suffocation 323
46 No Direction 329
47 Wild Night 338
48 Things Left Unsaid 343
49 Giving Up 350
50 Poison 354
51 The Poppy Fields 361
52 Powerful Silence 367
53 Alpha and Omega 374
54 Distance Between Us 386

Author's Note 393
Acknowledgements 394
Discussion Questions 396
About the Author 397
Also by the Author 398

The Beginning

Desert Welcome

Southern California, April 1984

TWO FACTS ABOUT LAKE LOS ANGELES: one, there's no lake, and two, it's nowhere near Los Angeles.

To find the place, look real hard while driving 70 in a 55 on a two-lane highway leading away from the city. There's a little green population sign that never seems to change, the informal *Welcome to Lake Los Angeles*. Don't blink, or the sign disappears and so does the town.

Six-year-old Kiara lay in bed and cringed as her mom downstairs yelled, "Go to hell!" at her dad. Kiara waited for him to yell back. This time, he didn't. Her mom screamed, "I'm leaving!" and slammed the front door shut, which shook the upstairs windows.

Her little brother Tommy crept into her bed, or at least tried to. The king-size waterbed rocked back and forth while he pawed at her. She reached over, grabbed his little hands, and lifted him up. She squeezed him like a teddy bear and drew the covers over their heads. They lay still, cheek to cheek, until the bed stopped swaying. He whimpered, so she sang him lullabies.

After that, the screaming ended. So did the marriage. Words got thrown around: *divorce* and *sell the damn house.*

Dad never returned. Every night at dinner, while Kiara choked down her fish sticks and mushy peas, the phone rang. Her mom didn't answer. Eventually, the phone stopped ringing.

<hr>

The first night in their new house was a sign of things to come: the movers got lost somewhere between the coast and Lake Los Angeles, the electricity company hadn't flipped on the power, and the mercury plunged below freezing. Wind whistled and rattled the windows. The three of them—Kiara, Tommy, and her mom—shivered, fending off hypothermia together under a single blanket on their brown shag carpet. The desert had laid out the welcome mat.

Kiara lay there with teeth chattering and stared into the darkness. She imagined her old life, her two-story home in a neighborhood of tree-lined streets and sidewalks. A life before Dad left them, for what her mom called *the whore down the street.*

This was their "fresh start"—a new wood and stucco Craftsman single-story on a dirt road in the middle of nowhere. Her mom called it "affordable housing"—Kiara called it hell.

Newly built didn't mean well-built.

She rubbed the goosebumps on her arms and snuggled closer to Tommy. His hair, scented with baby shampoo, tickled her nose.

"Mom," Kiara whispered. "Are you awake?"

"Go to sleep."

It wasn't as if Kiara could flip off a switch in her brain. "I'm trying. I was thinking, maybe me and Tommy could visit the lake—"

"—there isn't a lake."

"Isn't it called—"

"I said, go to sleep."

Kiara squeezed her eyes shut. "Where's Skittles?"

"Your dad took the damn dog."

All the muscles in Kiara's body tightened. "When do we see Dad?"

"Hopefully, never." Her mom growled. "Damn it, Kiara. Go. To. Sleep."

Kiara bristled at the tone of her mom's voice—the same tone she took during cussing competitions with her dad which often ended with her mom hurling any portable object across the room, always barely missing her dad's head. Regardless of her mom's poor aim, every shot struck Kiara in the heart. It hurt. All their yelling and insults hurt.

The way her mom spoke now reeked with that same anger and disgust.

Kiara balled up her fists and dug her fingernails into her palms. Maybe her mom was lying. Maybe Dad and Skittles would come back. Kiara would find the lake by herself.

Most of Lake LA was mapped on a grid with straight lines. People lived on dirt or roughly paved roads like 160th Street

East or Avenue Q-1. Because everything looked the same, residents figured out where they were headed based on things like the collapsed Joshua tree, the reflector nailed to the wooden electric pole, or the rocks piled up by that sign.

At night, it was desert dark. Unlike city dwellers who relied on the manufactured glow of lighting to ease their fear of the unknown, folks of this community insisted on darkness.

Stars are brighter that way.

Didn't matter the reason. Kiara missed seeing where she was walking at night without tripping over her own damn feet.

A month after moving in, Kiara stood on the dirt corner of two of these letter-number streets, 158th Street East and Avenue Q-8, on the southern tip of town. Back at her old house, her friends lived two blocks away. Here, she had none. Her mom said that if she tried to make friends, she would. Be nice and others will like you. So far, the advice had proven to be useless.

Kiara hovered near a bunch of kids waiting for the school bus. Wind swept around her bare legs, coating them in a layer of dirt.

The sun beat down. She took off her pink sweatshirt and tied it around her waist. After dealing with below-freezing temperatures the month before, her mom said to dress in warm clothes even though it had been a solid week of hundred-degree-plus heat with dry, gusty winds.

With her backpack pressed against her sweaty back, Kiara approached a couple of girls. She lingered nearby in a slice of shade afforded by a massive Joshua tree, which wasn't a tree in the traditional sense—more of a cactus with spiky pom-poms at the end of each gnarled branch.

Kiara waved to the girls.

They rolled their eyes and whispered to each other.

Kiara cringed. She kicked at the ground, flinging loose rocks in all directions. Her sweatshirt dropped.

A boy twice her size ran over, grabbed it, and smacked her with it.

"Give it back," Kiara said. She stomped her foot.

"Give it back," the boy taunted.

Kiara considered her options. Was it worth fighting for? The sweatshirt was too big and too pink, like most gifts from her grandma.

Nearby, a dust devil gathered up the loose top layer of sediment and swirled it around into an impressive funnel that lifted scraps of paper and tumbleweeds. It turned and twisted. The kids, used to the spectacle, laughed and pointed.

Kiara squinted through her fingers trying to protect her eyes. The wind pulled strands of hair out of her ponytail and whipped them in her face.

It was over as quick as it started. Weeds tumbled back to the earth, papers flew away, and her hair settled down. She spat out the grit in her teeth. Though her chapped lips were sealed tight, dirt found a way in.

In the chaos, the boy dropped her sweatshirt. She shook off the dirt and stuffed the sweatshirt in her backpack.

Her old home, the big house at the end of the cul-de-sac, had grass, not dirt, where she used to play fetch with Skittles; they had a rock waterfall that streamed down into their hot tub then into the pool; her huge upstairs bedroom, with the king-size waterbed, had curtains that billowed in the cool breeze—all gone and replaced by a dusty, barren landscape.

The bus would arrive soon. Even though her bare thighs would stick to the vinyl seats for the sixty-minute ride to school, Kiara couldn't wait to be out of the sun.

A couple of boys threw a baseball back and forth across the road a few houses down from the bus stop. She used to play ball with her dad; he was patient every time she missed a catch or botched a throw.

The girls under the Joshua tree glanced her way and giggled.

Behind her rang out a loud shriek. Over by the boys, her little brother, Tommy, not yet three, sat in the middle of the street, screaming.

Oh my God. Kiara marched over there. What was *he* doing out of the house? He should be getting ready to go to the babysitter's so Mom could get to work on time.

Kiara had half a mind to scold him for being where he shouldn't have been.

She bent down beside him. That's when she saw it—blood trailed down Tommy's scalp, his brown hair soaked with it.

2

Out There

KIARA TOUCHED TOMMY'S FACE. He flinched and cried. By his feet, a baseball rolled away. Kiara's fingers were bloody. Her stomach sank, and anger rose to her cheeks.

Sure, she punched Tommy when he tore pages out of her favorite coloring books, cut the tails and manes of her My Little Ponies, and ripped the heads off of her Barbie and Ken dolls. None of that mattered though, because this time someone *else* had hurt Tommy.

"Stay put," she said to him. He groaned.

She scrambled to her feet, grabbed the baseball, and hurled it at the boys. She missed. If she could kill them, she would. She ran over to the boys, twice her size.

"Why did you do it?" she screamed.

The boy who'd taken her sweatshirt held up his hands. "It was an accident."

The others laughed and high-fived him. Someone said, "Good shot."

"Liar!" Kiara shoved the boy.

He shoved her harder. She stumbled backwards.

In between sobs, she yelled every cuss word she'd heard from her parents.

The boy wiped the baseball on his jeans and tossed it back to the others.

Kiara sprinted back to Tommy. His face and hands were now bright red.

"Don't worry," she said. "It'll be okay." She wasn't so sure.

She rubbed the snot and tears from her face and lifted Tommy to his feet. She squatted. "Hold on," she said, carrying him piggyback down the road.

The front door was ajar. She kicked it open. Huffing and puffing, she set Tommy down. His crying had stopped. He crumpled to the floor and curled up.

Kiara panted and wiped her sticky brown hair from her face.

Her mom, in a pale-blue work dress, string of pearls, white pantyhose, and high-heeled pumps, came down the hallway and caught sight of them. She narrowed her brown eyes and wagged her finger at Kiara.

"What's wrong with you?" she said. "You should be at school."

Still too out of breath to say anything, Kiara pointed to Tommy.

"Answer me," her mom said. She pushed in her pearl earrings and dabbed her finger at her blue eye shadow. Then she seemed to understand the situation. She bent down next to Tommy and stared up at Kiara. "What have you done this time?"

"I didn't do it," Kiara said.

Her mom picked up Tommy, who roused and scanned the room with confusion. She carried him into the kitchen, set him on the counter, and grabbed a dish towel.

"Call for help," she said to Kiara. "Now! Are you listening?"

In school they mentioned some brand-new phone number to call in case of emergencies. Kiara didn't remember. Was it 9-9-1? In a panic, she stuck her finger in the rotary dial at the nine, and waited for it to spin back into place. She repeated the motion. The nines took too long to dial.

She hung up and dialed zero for the operator. She was connected to an impatient man who said it'd be faster if they drove Tommy to the hospital themselves on account of the town having nothing but a fire department, and it didn't sound like anyone was on fire.

"You tell them we need an ambulance," her mom yelled, and Kiara repeated it.

The man on the line scoffed. Kiara relayed his message, "If it's so bad, why would you waste forty minutes waiting for an ambulance to drive all the way out there?"

Exasperated, Kiara's mom loaded Tommy in the front passenger seat of her old Dodge Colt, seat-belted him in, and told him to hold the towel on his head.

Kiara jumped into the backseat.

When they reached the main road leading out of the neighborhood, her mom pulled over. The school bus had arrived at the stop, and kids were lining up.

"Get out," her mom said.

Kiara crossed her arms. "I'm not going."

"Don't you back-talk me. Get out and get on the bus before it leaves."

"What about Tommy?" Kiara sniffled.

"What do you think I'm doing? Get out so I can get him to the hospital."

"I'm coming, too."

"No, you're not. I can't deal with you right now."

Kiara protested.

"Traffic is getting worse every second," her mom said. "I need to get going. Get out. Now."

Kiara stumbled out of the door. She stepped back as her mom's car squealed off, kicking up dirt in her face. Her eyes stung, either from the dirt or unshed tears.

Kids on the bus yelled out the windows at her. The bus driver motioned for her to hurry on up.

Kiara grabbed her backpack from the ground where she'd left it. The pink fabric had gained a couple of dirty shoe prints.

She growled and ascended the steps.

The bus snaked through the town of Littlerock into the town of Pearblossom along Highway 138. All Kiara could think about was poor Tommy, how freckles dotted his nose, how his cowlick stuck up even when she combed it down, and how much it annoyed him when she squeezed his pudgy cheeks.

At last, the bus idled alongside the curb at Alpine Elementary.

Kiara stared out the window during class. Had her mom gotten Tommy to the hospital in time? Could the doctors save him?

At recess, Kiara stood near a circle of girls from her class who were clapping hands and singing, "Mailman, mailman, do your duty. Here comes Miss American Beauty."

"What are you doing over here?" a blonde girl with pigtails asked Kiara.

"Nothing," Kiara said. The truth was she didn't want to be alone.

"Eww." Another one scrunched up her nose. "Why's your T-shirt bloody?"

"And your hair's gross," a third added.

Kiara touched her hair, matted from dirt, sweat, and Tommy's blood. She didn't have the energy to explain. It wouldn't do any good anyways. She went to the restroom to wash the mess out of her hair over the sink, which didn't work. Water dripped onto her T-shirt and spread the dirt and blood stains bigger.

She went outside and sat under a tree. The girls approached her, pointed and snickered.

"Look. It's little Miss Know-it-all."

Whenever Kiara raised her hand in class to answer the teacher's questions when no one else could, these girls mocked her.

Kiara folded her arms and turned the other direction.

"Too good for us?" a girl asked.

"Leave me alone," Kiara said.

"Why don't you go change your clothes?" the girl with pigtails asked.

So, Kiara said the worst word of all, the *f* word. The girl told her to say it to her face, so Kiara said it again. Twice. The girls stood in shock. One ran to the yard lady who hurried over.

"Come with me." The yard lady grabbed Kiara's hand and escorted her up to the office. "Where did you learn that language?"

Kiara could've said she'd heard the words from her mom and dad countless times and knew she used it the right way, but it was better to say nothing.

The principal sat at his desk and shook his head. "Look, sweetie, even if you're having a bad day, don't take it out on others. And don't use that language. Do you understand?"

Kiara nodded. Apparently, it was better to be a jerk like those girls.

"I called home. No one answered, so I left a message," he said. "I'll mark this as a warning, since you've never been in trouble. Your teacher says you're such a nice and well-mannered girl in class. Why don't you try being that way during recess, too?"

"Okay." Kiara walked away. Under her breath, she added, "Asshole."

After that, Kiara kept her mouth shut. She didn't eat her lunch, which she'd made herself—peanut butter and jelly sandwich on stale bread with a mushy red apple. Other kids bought lunch, but Kiara's mom said they had to apply for the free lunch program. Until then, her lunch was the same every day—not ham sandwiches with chips, grapes, and a Twinkie, which her dad used to give her.

Didn't matter. She was too worried about Tommy to eat.

Turns out, all the blood made the head injury look worse than it was; the doctor closed it up with a few stitches. Tommy had a miserable headache and a big goose egg. The doctor said to give him aspirin for pain and watch for signs of a concussion.

Her mom was livid that she missed work. She was exhausted and yelled at Kiara to take care of Tommy.

"And feed him dinner," her mom said, before retreating to her room.

Kiara kicked and mumbled at the wall.

"I'm hungry." Tommy whined.

Considering that he did end up with a hole in the head, Kiara dragged a chair over to the microwave, climbed up and cooked two hot dogs. She set paper plates into two wicker paper plate holders, laid a slice of bread on each, and squirted out ketchup, as red and runny as a stream of blood. Her throat constricted. She might hurl.

"Here, have them both." She gave them to Tommy.

Kiara escaped outside to sit on their concrete front porch, held her knees and stared at the dirt road in front of her house, the newly poured concrete pads up and down the street, and the tumbleweeds that rolled by.

Whenever a car passed, dust in its wake settled on the partially built houses and on Kiara. Still, she didn't move.

The sun lowered and the temperature plummeted.

A tear dropped down her cheek and, through clenched teeth, she said, "I hate it here. I hate it. I hate it. I hate it."

3

A Fresh Start

KIARA'S LIFE DIDN'T IMPROVE in first grade, with one notable exception: Her mom promised her and Tommy a surprise and drove them into town. That's when Kiara first stepped into the dank and glorious building of possibilities—the Palmdale City Library.

With its spiral staircase—a daring adventure—and its second-floor balcony of books—a magical space to hide from Tommy—the library became Kiara's best friend.

Because of their monthly visits there, Kiara had books to comfort her when girls in school ignored her. Each time she opened another book, Kiara was transported to a new reality, one of dragons and queens, spirits and hauntings, or magical cupboards and cowboys. She voraciously read everything and checked out books by the armful.

Eventually, though, there were strings attached.

"Read to your brother," her mom said.

"Why can't you?" Kiara sat up in bed and slipped her bookmark into her *Choose Your Own Adventure* book. "Why do I have to?" She pulled her lumpy flowered comforter up and tucked it around her waist.

"Come on, Kiara." Her mom crossed her arms. "I work all day. I'm tired. What don't you understand?"

"Tommy can read. I know, because I taught him." Kiara opened up her book, and moved her finger down to where she left off. "Besides, you never read to me. Only Dad did."

Her mom yanked the book from Kiara's hands and threw it across the room. It hit the wall with a thud and slid to the floor. Pages folded over themselves.

"Mom! I have to pay for it if it gets ruined."

"Guess you should've thought of that before you argued with me." Her mom left and slammed the door shut.

Kiara fingered the pages and straightened them, trying not to let her tears soak the paper. She gave up and laid the book on her dresser.

Kiara grabbed her pillow and smacked it against the wall until her shoulders hurt and her tears ran dry.

Lake Los Angeles, an unincorporated community, was split down the middle; one zip code tied to the city of Palmdale, the other to the city of Lancaster.

Kids on the Lancaster side had a school, Wilsona Elementary.

Kids on the Palmdale side, Kiara's side, had none. As the population increased, the school district added more buses instead of what everyone kept asking for—a new school. Nobody had time or money to drive their kids to town, and with each additional bus stop, the rides, and the school day, got longer.

Kiara trudged to the bus stop in pre-dawn darkness and added one more item to the list of things she despised—alarm clocks.

When June rolled around, Kiara celebrated. Finally, she could sleep in late and read books in bed—an ideal summer vacation.

While she and Tommy sat on bar stools at the kitchen counter eating off-brand cereal for breakfast, her mom joined them. She didn't often do that; Kiara and Tommy usually ate alone.

"Tommy turns four next week," her mom said. "Old enough for you both to go to the summer program at church in town."

"What?" Kiara dropped her spoon, which clanked in her bowl. "Why?"

"It'll be good for you." Her mom glared. "We'll attend Mass there, too."

No, no, no. Please, no. "Come on, Mom," Kiara said. "We haven't gone to church since… our old house." She knew better than to say *since Dad.*

"Exactly," her mom said, "It's time we go back."

Why couldn't her mom go alone? Why drag the unwilling?

When Kiara's parents were married, they attended Mass every Sunday morning. Kiara hated waking up early for something that brought her no joy. Her dad felt the same, so they had a special understanding. He rolled his eyes at her every time they had to kneel, sit on the pews, then kneel, which made her giggle. That was the only redeeming part. Without Dad, going to Mass meant misery.

Kiara swirled the soggy cereal O's around in her bowl. Great. There went her whole summer. Between religious classes and church, every day except Saturdays would suck.

She asked her mom why they went to the Catholic church instead of the other Christian ones. Her mom said Catholic was a type of Christian because they all believed in Christ. Kiara couldn't understand why they had so many types of Christianity except maybe it was like the grocery stores up in town—they all had food, but everyone had their favorite market.

"Any more questions?" Her mom put her hands on her hips.

Kiara held her tongue. Another word and she'd be found guilty of back-talk and sent to a timeout in the corner, which would make her cereal soggier.

Tommy flung a spoonful of milk at her, and her mom shook her head and left the kitchen.

Kiara narrowed her eyes at him. What would be the penalty if she beat him to a pulp? For that, she'd be willing to deal with a long timeout.

The summer church program separated Kiara and Tommy into different classrooms based on age. Kiara slouched at her desk in the dark room and stared out the window at a huge oak tree. Its leaves danced shadows on the ceiling.

"Kiara." The nun tapped on her desk. "Pay attention. God is watching."

Kiara sat up straighter and rested her elbows on the desk. Perhaps the lesson would be more interesting if God Himself read the Bible to them in a bellowing voice. Kiara smirked.

The nun frowned. By the third day, she left Kiara alone.

Maybe that's because nuns couldn't smack kids with rulers anymore, which meant the teacher had nothing to hold over Kiara's head except heaven.

In the afternoon, Kiara sat on a bench in the suffocating sun and sang songs about Jesus with kids she didn't know. Some girls smiled and tried to talk to her. Kiara had no interest in befriending anyone who enjoyed being there.

As far as she could tell, Jesus hadn't made her life any better.

The Tuesday after Labor Day in 1985, past the Lake LA fire station, Kiara finally found the lake. Or rather, a hole in the ground where the gloriously failed attempt at a lake once stood.

Her new school, Lake LA Elementary, took root in the former lake's clubhouse.

Accordion dividers transformed the building into two combo-classrooms, a kitchen, and an office. Mrs. Wright, the new principal, took charge, along with the school secretary, and the school's unofficial mascot, an orange tabby named Fred.

Ready for second grade, Kiara waited at the bottom of the porch steps for the bell to ring. She kicked the dirt with her brown Mary Janes.

"Stop it," her mom said. "You're going to scuff them up. I can't afford new ones."

"It's stupid to make me wear white stockings in the dirt." Sticky sweat accumulated between the nylon fabric and her legs—even September mornings knew no reprieve from the brutal summer sun.

"Watch your mouth, young lady. They go with the dress."

Kiara pulled at the hem of the red velvet Calico. "You only forced me to wear it because you like dresses. It doesn't even fit me right." Her mom, to present a professional appearance, bought herself half a dozen new dresses and pantsuits, while Kiara and Tommy had hand-me-downs of questionable size and condition.

"Isn't this nice being closer to home?" Her mom smiled.

Kiara examined her surroundings—a one-room schoolhouse with wood shingles, a couple of out-of-place pine trees fighting for life in the hard-packed dirt, a flag pole, and a hastily thrown together playground: a metal slide, a couple of swings, and a metal jungle gym, all anchored in hot sand.

"How is this better than my old school?" Kiara fanned out her hand. "At least Alpine had grass, a huge playground, and actual classrooms."

Her mom pursed her lips. "This is only a fifteen-minute bus ride."

"Fifteen?" Kiara crossed her arms. "You said five—"

"Which is better than an hour up the 138—"

"Death Alley—"

"Highway 138." Her mom sighed. "We fought hard to get a school here. Be thankful."

"For this?" Kiara said. "It isn't even a real school."

"Don't be dramatic. It's temporary, until they find a bigger place."

Kiara nibbled the inside of her cheek. "I'll be stuck here in the desert forever."

"You want out? Get good grades. That's your way out. If I had finished college, maybe I..." Her mom looked at her then drifted off in thought.

Kiara ignored her mom and counted the forty-seven other kids dragged out to the dry lakebed. Any prospects for friends?

Her eyes settled on one boy. With thick black hair that curled tightly and a more tanned face than any kid she'd ever seen, he was at least six inches taller than her. He stood next to a very pregnant mom who had an arm linked in his, maybe to steady herself. The boy buried his hands into his brown corduroy pants and stared at his shoes—not new, but clean.

When he lifted his chin, his striking green eyes locked on hers. How long had she been staring? She blinked and averted her gaze.

A bell clanged and jolted Kiara from her headspace. Mrs. Wright, a tall, lanky woman with shoulder-length hair and a pronounced nose, shook a hand bell—a brass *hand* bell like something out of the TV series *Little House on the Prairie*.

Nobody had to be told twice. Kids raced up the wooden porch steps and herded into the correct "classroom"— kindergarteners and first-graders in the smaller area and second and third-graders in the larger space. A welcoming blast of air conditioning hit Kiara in the face and whipped strands of her long brown hair that had escaped her ponytail into her face.

The teacher introduced herself as Ms. Gilespie. "Sorry, desks weren't delivered until last night. I didn't have a chance to assign seats, so for today, sit wherever you want."

Kiara preferred the front, not to be a kiss-up but to see the board without it being a blurry mess. By the time she got halfway there, a cluster of chatty girls had laid claim to the desks. She groaned. Behind them remained an open seat amidst a group of guys, two of whom were making fart sounds in their armpits, so Kiara circled back around.

She slipped into a seat next to a window that faced out back, towards Lovejoy Buttes.

Kiara squinted at the brightness of the blue sky and gazed at the rocky cluster of boulders and brittle rocks, which blended into bland brown. Under careful examination, they were a mosaic of peaches and tans, mixed with the fool's gold sparkle of quartz.

Ms. Gilespie cleared her throat. Kiara twisted to find her teacher there with a smile.

"Good morning. Are you Kara, or is it Kerra?"

Kiara's cheeks reddened. "It's key-are-ah." She sank a little lower. Why did Tommy get a normal name? Thomas easily shortened to Tom or Tommy. *Kiara*? Oh, the kids loved to taunt her with the word *key*, or *k-k-key-ra, rhymes with She-Ra*. Being compared to a *Masters of the Universe* Superheroine wasn't bad, but the "key" thing had to go. Hopefully the girls here would, at best, ignore her.

"Lovely name, Kiara." Ms. Gilespie squatted to her level. She had optimistic brown eyes, black hair tied back in a bun, and a youthful face, free of makeup and full of warmth. "When I make the seating chart, would you like to stay here by the window?"

An actual *choice*? Kiara nodded.

"All right, as long as you can pay attention. We have lots to learn this year."

Ms. Gilespie continued down the row to talk to every student. Kiara returned her attention to the buttes and Joshua Trees when something hit her in the back of the head. A paper airplane crash-landed onto the floor. A group of boys jeered. Kiara narrowed her eyes at them.

"What's the problem?" The boy nearest her looked way too old to be in the same classroom. "Trying to fly it out the window."

She rolled her eyes. "The window isn't even open."

"Duh." He and the others laughed.

They'd been waiting for her to say that. Why did she always fall for these stupid traps?

The girls in the front row turned to face the commotion. They quickly bored of it and resumed their conversation.

If Kiara could sit by the window, maybe this could be the best year yet—even if she didn't make friends. After all, she didn't have to wake up as early this year, and she still had her books from the library. What more did she need?

4

Sugar Cube Igloos

TRUE TO HER WORD, when Ms. Gilespie completed the seating chart, Kiara kept her seat.

While Ms. Gilespie reviewed how to add and subtract double-digits—something Kiara figured even Tommy could learn how to do, Kiara fiddled with her pencil.

She doodled mountains, lakes, and trees on the corner of her completed multiplication worksheet and stared out the window daydreaming. Buttes became mountains, Joshua trees became fir trees, and dirt…well, the dirt was still dirt.

Kiara tilted her head towards the sky. Bright blue, it became a lake, pristine and clear. White clouds transformed into swans gliding across the surface. A larger cloud, stretched thin in the wind, became a dragon twisting and curling across the lake.

"Does that one look like a dragon to you, too?" a voice behind her whispered.

Kiara jumped in her seat and turned around. It was the dark-skinned boy with the bright-green eyes. She blushed and looked away. "Yeah." She focused on the swans which broke up into puffs of clouds lined in a row. "Do you see the ducklings?"

"Yep," he said. "I'm Cole. Are you Kiara?"

She nodded, her cheeks turning crimson.

"That's a pretty name," he said.

Where were her manners? Kiara faced him and whispered, "Thank you. I like your eyes."

"Yours are turquoise like the sky." He smiled. "Do you spend a lot of time finding animals in clouds?"

"Well, this lesson is boring," she said.

Cole's math worksheet was already filled out, too. A sketched train made its way through a forest at the bottom of his paper.

"Agreed," he said. "If we could escape on this train right now, I would."

"Or at least run outside and climb the buttes," she said.

"We should do it."

"Now?" She raised her eyebrows.

He shrugged. "I'll say I have to go to the bathroom. Then you do the same."

"I can't. I don't want to get in trouble."

Cole opened his mouth, then froze as his eyes glanced up.

Kiara swiveled in her seat to find herself face-to-face with Ms. Gilespie.

"Are you two done talking? You're missing the lesson." Ms. Gilespie pointed to their worksheets. "We haven't started on those yet. You're done already?" She picked up their papers and checked both sides. "They're all correct." She grimaced. "Great."

She stopped by her desk and returned with two papers. "Here. Can you do these?"

Kiara took her copy—multiplication up to nine times nine. Kiara scrunched her nose and scribbled answers frantically. She flipped the paper over. The numbers went up to twelve times twelve. She gripped her pencil tighter and wrote as fast as she could. "Done."

"Done," Cole said at the same time and held his paper up in the air.

Ms. Gilespie took their worksheets and scanned the answers on the front and back. "A hundred percent. Oh jeez." She mumbled and dropped her shoulders. Her expression said *what the hell am I going to do with these two?* "See those books over there in the bookcase? Why don't you pick something to read? And please stay quiet while I'm trying to teach."

Ms. Gilespie returned to the front of the room while Kiara and Cole perused the titles on the bookshelves in the back.

Cole held up *The Cat in the Hat*. "Let's challenge ourselves with Dr. Seuss."

For the first time in a while, Kiara laughed. The muscles in her face were stiff. "Right."

He opened the book. "On this cat was a hat, and when the roof fell flat, he went splat."

"Not bad." She motioned to the rows of books. "I've read all of these."

"Same. Maybe we should go back to Dr. Seuss." Cole turned to another random page. "Hey, Sam, you're the man. Get us out of here if you can."

Kiara grinned. "Sam, I hate dirt and I hate sand. Take us from this hellish land."

They burst out in laughter.

When Kiara caught her breath and wiped the tears from her eyes, she found Ms. Gilespie there, arms crossed, tapping her foot.

Ms. Gilespie made a change to the seating chart and put Cole on the other side of the class.

Damn it. Kiara had made a friend and managed to screw it up all in the same day.

During class, she searched for animals in the clouds. When there weren't any clouds, she gazed at the rocky buttes and Joshua trees.

During recess, while other kids played on the swings, slide, and jungle gym, Kiara sat by herself near a scraggly pine tree. It must've looked nicer when there was actually a lake. She ate her lunch at the empty end of a table and kept to herself.

Kiara glanced around until she caught sight of Cole's curly hair. Whatever he was saying made all the boys around him smile and laugh. This hurt. Why couldn't she join them and listen to his jokes? She looked away lest he find her staring.

A group of girls giggled and chatted on the front porch steps. One girl brushed another one's hair and braided it.

Kiara had an emptiness in her stomach. What was she doing wrong?

She turned to the sky and focused on a puffy cloud until it changed into a bird and its wings spread out, carrying it across the desert sky.

On Saturday morning, Kiara's mom was in a better mood than usual and agreed to play a game with Kiara and Tommy. Finally, quality time. Maybe they'd all get along better and fight less if they could do something fun together.

Kiara and Tommy set up Monopoly on the coffee table.

"I'll be the banker," Kiara said. "Let's wait for Mom, first."

They waited. And waited. Twenty minutes went by.

Kiara knocked on her mom's bedroom door. "You said you'd come play."

"Give me a minute." Her mom's voice was muffled by the locked door.

"We set everything up." Kiara leaned her head on the wall.

"I said, I'll be out in a minute."

Yeah, right. Her minutes became hours. Same thing happened last month when Kiara and Tommy set up Mousetrap. Her mom said she'd be out of her room in a minute. Two hours later, they played without her until a fight ensued and Tommy threw a plastic mouse at Kiara's head.

Kiara returned to the living room. "Mom's not coming, so let's play. I'll let you go first."

After three circles around the board, Kiara landed on Boardwalk. She paid for the prime property.

"I don't want to play anymore." Tommy picked up his game money and threw it at her.

"Stop being a brat," she said. "Pick it up."

"Stop being bossy. You pick it up." He stuck out his tongue, ran to his room, and slammed the door shut before she could chase him down.

"Damn you," she said under her breath. She cleaned up the game, shoved the box in the hallway cabinet, and slammed the cabinet door shut. It didn't elicit a satisfying sound.

Kiara took a deep breath, curled up on the couch, and escaped in a book.

At Lake LA School, nobody knew what to do with kids like Kiara and Cole who tested into GATE, Gifted and Talented Education. Ms. Gilespie tried different methods. If they finished an assignment early, they got an extra math worksheet. More math? Other kids snickered—even at that age they figured less was more.

Not Kiara or Cole. They raced to the front of the class, grabbed a worksheet, finished it, then grabbed another. Ms. Gilespie got tired of making so many copies for them.

Instead, she offered them wordsearch puzzles.

"Can we find extra words?" Kiara asked.

Ms. Gilespie said, yes, so Kiara filled it out front and back. She dropped her shoulders when she observed Cole had done the same. They raced up to get another wordsearch puzzle.

Ms. Gilespie complained that she had others to focus on. Mrs. Wright arranged for the district to send a teacher's assistant once a week to work with them.

Even though Mrs. Jodie, the teacher's assistant, wasn't there yet on her first scheduled day, Ms. Gilespie directed Kiara and Cole to a long table behind the accordion divider.

"You two are going to get a special lesson when Mrs. Jodie arrives. In the meantime, can you manage to keep your voices down while I'm teaching?"

Kiara and Cole nodded.

Ms. Gilespie returned to class and dragged the accordion divider shut.

Kiara and Cole sat on little yellow plastic chairs and stared off into space.

She had so many questions to ask him. Every time she opened her mouth, nothing came out. The longer it was quiet, the less she wanted to speak.

Cole cleared his throat. "Knock, knock."

She grinned. "Who's there?"

"Wood."

"Wood who?"

"Would you be willing to talk to me again after I got us in trouble?"

Kiara wished to give him a big hug and tell him they could be friends forever but worried that would ruin things.

"It's not your fault," she said. "I was too loud. My brother says I talk too much."

"I don't think so. I enjoy talking to you. At home, I usually get blamed for everything."

"By your mom?"

"No, my dad's the problem." Cole sighed. "I wish he was gone. What about your dad?"

Kiara twirled her finger around a loose string on her jean shorts. "He's not around."

"Oh." Cole made eye contact. "I'm sorry."

"Don't be."

He leaned forward. "Why did the chicken cross the road?"

"Why?"

"Because the lizard crossed the road." He paused. "Why did the lizard cross the road?"

"I don't know. Why?"

"To get away from the chicken." He shook his head. "It wasn't the funniest. I was trying to make you laugh."

Kiara smiled. "I like your jokes." They were quiet for a few minutes before she broke the silence. "I'm not used to getting in trouble. Teachers used to be proud of me for getting work done fast. Here, I feel like they're mad at me."

"Me, too," he said. "Did you grow up out here?"

"In the desert? No. I hate it here. We moved at the end of kindergarten." Kiara described her old house with the pool and waterfall and strawberry patch. "You?"

"Moved here a few months ago from Santa Monica, what you call 'down below.' That's a funny term." Cole smirked. "Then again, we are at three-thousand-foot elevation."

"I don't think it matters where you're from as long as you know what it's like to not be here." Kiara wondered when Mrs. Jodie would arrive. "What are we supposed to be doing?"

On the table lay a pink and white box with a perforated lid that had been separated open. Cole peaked inside. There were rows of perfectly shaped white granulated cubes. His eyes widened and he grinned as he handed one to Kiara. She turned it over in her hands. She had never seen sugar in little squares. How did it stick together? Would it taste the same?

The front door opened and shut. The teacher's assistant, an older woman with tight curls and a flowery muumuu walked in. She squinted as her eyes adjusted from the sun. She wiped her arm across her brow and rubbed the sweat from her arm onto her dress.

Kiara and Cole, each with a mouthful of sugar cubes, froze. They smiled without moving their jaws, letting the sugar dissolve on their tongues—torn between avoiding a reprimand and impeding their joy of this most unusual delicacy.

"I'm Mrs. Jodie. You must be Cole and Kiara." She pulled up the largest of the chairs and sat. "You're going to learn about structures made by different Native Americans, including dome-shaped houses covered with reeds or grass used by AV tribes. At the end of this unit, I have a treat for you. After we study teepees, we're going to have a real one set up outside." She paused. "Today, we'll start with igloos."

She removed a jar of Elmer's glue from her bag.

Kiara glanced at Cole. Not glue. It'd desecrate the treat. There had to be a better way.

There wasn't, Mrs. Jodie explained. These were blocks of ice, not sugar. She modeled the activity by gluing a circular bottom layer together. She explained the difficult task the Eskimos faced in not having the structure collapse while it was being built.

"Now excuse me for a minute," she said. "I'll be right back. Just get in a good start."

After she went to the restroom, Kiara and Cole popped a few more "ice cubes" into their mouths and got to work. Turns out "be right back" was a term not meant in the way it was said.

Cole and Kiara sat there swinging their legs under the table, each with a completed igloo in front of them. They used as few cubes as they could, and sucked down as many as they figured wouldn't be missed from the box. For a while they giggled and created stories about polar bears eating Eskimos and penguins moving into the igloos.

They quieted. How could she keep the conversation going?

"Want to play hide-and-seek?" Kiara asked.

Cole didn't respond right away, and she looked down. Maybe she shouldn't have suggested it.

"It'd be fun," she added. Maybe it was a stupid idea.

"Where?" Cole rocked back in his chair.

"Anywhere. Under this table, or the one on the other side, in the kitchen, or wherever, as long as it's not in class. You go first. I'll close my eyes and count to ten."

Cole crawled around the corner. She shouldn't have, but she peeked as he tucked himself under a table. Kiara closed her eyes and continued to count.

"Okay, ten." She opened her eyes, surprised she hadn't heard the heavy footsteps of Mrs. Jodie because, sure as anything, there she was.

"Where's Cole?" Mrs. Jodie was less than amused.

Rather than admit it was her idea, Kiara panicked and shrugged. "I don't know. I told him we should stay put."

"Go get him. Now."

Kiara had no choice. She led the way to Cole who was in the kitchen underneath a table. He had his eyes closed as if wishing that if he didn't see them, they couldn't see him.

"Get up and get over here, you two troublemakers." Mrs. Jodie narrowed her gaze. "They warned me about you. I live forty minutes away. Why do you think I drove out here?"

"Because they told you to." Kiara bit her lip when she realized she said that part aloud.

Mrs. Jodie shook her head. "No, because I want you to succeed, to be challenged. I'll give you both another chance. I'll only call home if you lie or are disrespectful."

"Please don't," Cole said. "I'm sorry."

"It's not my fault. I wasn't the one on the floor." Kiara's hand flew to her mouth. The damage was done. It was a shitty thing to say, and she knew it. Cole avoided her gaze.

"Don't blame others for the trouble you get yourself into," Mrs. Jodie said. "Got it?"

Kiara nodded and bowed her head.

Mrs. Jodie took Kiara's hand. "Honey, nobody is perfect. But think before you speak and be honest."

"I'm sorry," Kiara said. She knew she had messed up.

"Apology accepted," Mrs. Jodie said. "At least from me. However, I'm calling home."

Cole scowled at Kiara. After Mrs. Jodie left, Cole returned to his seat in silence. His smile disappeared. He wouldn't even glance in her direction.

Kiara felt horrible. He must hate her, like everyone else. This time, she deserved it.

5

Joshua Trees

DESERTS ARE HARSH. Nature can be cruel, but not everything dies. To thrive in the arid region of the desert, life hardens and adapts like the Joshua trees, which can grow for a hundred years with little to no rain by storing water inside themselves. In this way, the end goal isn't elimination of life but rather a toughening up in preparation to survive.

No one said the process was easy.

At the end of the day, Kiara got on the school bus and sat up front. When Cole stepped on, she caught his eye and mouthed the words, "I'm sorry," and truly she was.

He lowered his gaze and walked right past her. He didn't even glance in her direction.

Kiara stared out the window at the Joshua trees in the fields. She was mesmerized by them. Dusk turned their silhouettes into fuzzy pom poms at the end of a multitude of interconnected snakes, each reaching out and up for the sky. Sunshine revealed green spikes at the end of each branch, like a handful of sharp daggers gathered on crudely cut fence posts.

Kiara knew better than to touch the sharp thorns or rough trunk that was doing its best to grow up straight. She also knew better than to lie.

What could she do? Obviously, she couldn't keep her mouth shut.

Now both she and Cole were going to get in trouble for it.

Or maybe not. She could beat her mom home and delete the message like she did last time, back when the principal at Alpine called regarding her cussing.

When Cole exited the bus, only four stops before hers, he didn't say goodbye.

Kiara pressed her face against the glass and watched him disappear.

At her stop, she stepped off and turned away from the sitter's house. She hurried down the road towards hers. She'd delete the message and get out of there. No one at the sitter's would realize she was late, not with the chaos of fourteen kids running around (twelve when the inspector came).

Dust kicked up around her feet.

How could she make it up to Cole? Would he trust her again? She wouldn't.

Kiara had been lost in thought and raised her eyes too late. She winced and recoiled at the sharp pain as she brushed against a Joshua tree. Half a dozen scratches on her arm swelled and gave way to jagged lines of red. Her arm throbbed.

Kiara sprinted the rest of the way home. She opened the chain link fence side gate and went around back where she was pretty sure the back door to the garage would be open, and it was. Fortunately, so was the door to the house.

Thin trails of blood ran down from underneath her t-shirt sleeve. In the bathroom, she hopped up on the counter to reach the medicine cabinet and searched for a Band-Aid. What else did her mom use when they got hurt? Was it rubbing alcohol or hydrogen peroxide?

The brown bottle looked familiar. She jumped down and opened up cabinets for cotton balls. She couldn't find any. She held her arm over the sink and poured peroxide on the wound.

The fluid foamed and searing pain shot out. Kiara screamed and dropped the bottle. Liquid flew everywhere, creating a layer that fizzed over the sink and sprayed up onto the mirror. The remainder puddled on the floor.

It felt like claws were shredding her skin. She dropped to the ground in tears, squeezed her arm and prayed for the stinging to stop.

The six scratch lines grew to ten and puffed up around the edges. The sting gave way to a cool numbness. The wound was too big for a bandage, so Kiara let it be and examined the mess in the bathroom. She couldn't leave it like that. With hand towels, she wiped everything down—the sink, the mirror, the toilet, and the linoleum floor.

There's no way she was going to the sitter's house now. She'd have to tell her mom.

"Hello, accounting, how can I help you?" her mom cheerfully answered on the first ring.

"Mom—"

Her mom lowered her voice. "Why are you calling me at work?"

"I got hurt," Kiara said. "I'm at home."

"What do you mean you're at home? Why aren't you at the sitter's?"

"I ran into a Joshua tree and got cut up."

"Geez, Kiara. You never watch where you're going. Why don't you open your eyes for once? I'm sure the tree didn't jump out at you. Where's your brother?"

"At the sitter's."

Her mom grunted. "At least someone's behaving."

"Mom…"

"What?"

"I spilled all the hydrogen peroxide. I'm sorry."

"Damn it, Kiara. I don't have time to stop by the store tonight. Can you manage not to hurt yourself again until I get more?"

"Yes, Mom. I love you." Kiara held her breath. Could her mom ask her how she was, to show some sympathy, to care?

"Love you." There was no softness in those words. "Bye."

Click. The line went dead.

Kiara washed off all the blood before bed but the stinging lingered into the night.

6

Adapting

KIARA SCRATCHED AT THE CRUST left from her tears and opened her eyes. Her mom was standing in the doorway with arms crossed.

"Your grandma is moving in," her mom said.

"What the f—I mean..." Kiara sat up. "Why?"

"So, I can work and not worry about you both."

"Tommy and I can take care of ourselves," Kiara pleaded.

"I doubt that." Her mom frowned. "Especially after what happened with him getting his head cracked open—"

"—so, this is Tommy's fault?"

"—and you running into a Joshua Tree."

"—an accident."

Her mom narrowed her eyes. "Was misbehaving in school an accident, too?"

Oh, no. The message on the machine.

That was the end of that. Another change Kiara couldn't prevent.

Kiara dreaded her grandma's impending move. All she could remember about her grandma was that she looked like a toad, wore huge flowery dresses, and used a nasal cannula attached to an oxygen tank. She didn't come bearing chocolate chip cookies in a wicker basket, nor did she knit sweaters, or have heaps of cats.

Her grandma grunted and yelled, coughed and cleared her throat, and exuded scents of outdated lotion and hair removal cream, which she used on her upper lip. Half the time she didn't have her dentures in, and, while puffy at the cheeks, her face sunk in a little near the mouth.

At dinnertime, when Kiara had her macaroni and cheese fork midair, her mom stopped her. "Put that down," she said. "We need to say grace."

"What for?" Kiara asked. "We only do that on holidays."

"Not true, young lady."

Yes, it was. Kiara dropped her fork onto her paper plate and rolled her eyes.

"You both know what to do," her mom said. "Put your hands together and say it with me."

Kiara groaned. Her mom didn't hear. Tommy did and laughed.

"Both of you. Knock it off. Or so help me—"

"Is this because Grandma's moving in?" Kiara plastered on her best innocent face.

Her mom took a slow, measured breath, which meant she was restraining herself from screaming or smacking them.

Kiara figured God wouldn't look too kindly on that. She needed to get the prayer out of the way, because her macaroni and cheese was getting cold. Kiara made the sign of the cross, bowed her head and clasped her hands together.

The three of them recited the prayer together. "Bless us, O Lord, and these Thy gifts, which we are about to receive from Thy bounty. Through Christ, our Lord. Amen."

Kiara made another sign of the cross and gave her mom an angelic smile.

Finally, she was permitted to eat. Great. Yet another reason she wasn't looking forward to her grandma's move.

At school the next week, Mrs. Jodie taught Kiara and Cole how to make acorn paste, which, she explained, early people sustained themselves with and was still enjoyed at special events. Ms. Jodie was a lot nicer to them. Kiara wondered if maybe she felt like she overreacted by calling parents over a game of hide-and-seek. Maybe it was a guilty kind of nice.

Mrs. Jodie showed them how to use stone tools to grind acorns against a rock bowl. She handed Kiara the tools to try.

Kiara hit an acorn with the rock, and the acorn launched across the room; Cole dodged just in time. Mrs. Jodie shook her head and relocated them outside.

"Take your time," Mrs. Jodie said. "You'll get it. Here, try again."

Kiara struck the acorn and chipped a speck. A fragment shot up and hit her in the face. She flinched, and shoved the grinding stone and rock bowl over to Cole.

"Good luck." She snickered.

Cole cracked the acorn on his first try.

Kiara narrowed her eyes at him. "How the hell—"

"Native Americans worked together," Mrs. Jodie interrupted. "Helping each other is not just about survival. It's an important part of living in a community."

Mrs. Jodie wiped sweat from the nape of her neck and ushered Kiara and Cole back inside, to the table behind the accordion divider. She motioned them closer.

"Do you know who lived here, before the town was built, the ones who used the acorns?"

"Native Americans?" Cole said.

"Yes," she said, "Which ones?"

Cole shrugged.

She continued, "The Kitanemuk and other Shoshonean speakers survived on these lands for over two thousand years, making alliances and trading with their neighbors to the north and south, the east and west. They adapted to life in the desert by using the land around them, including something only found here in the Mojave Desert: Joshua trees. They made baskets from the roots, textiles from the fibers, and food from the fruit and flowers."

She pointed to three Joshua trees huddled together outside the window. "Nineteenth century Mormons named them after the biblical figure Joshua because of the appearance of outstretched arms." She demonstrated with her arms. "It's illegal to cut them down. It's too bad that people destroy things that take so long to grow. They don't always consider consequences."

Kiara didn't have a chance to talk to Cole until the bus ride home. To her surprise, he paused at her seat.

"Mind if I sit here?" Cole asked.

Kiara nodded and slid over. "I'm so sorry. It was stupid. I wasn't thinking."

"I know." Cole held his backpack on his lap while the bus jostled them along.

Hot air blew in through the windows and whipped Kiara's hair into her face. The strands stuck to her sweaty forehead.

"I'm not mad at you," Cole said.

"I don't believe you." Kiara stared straight ahead.

"Mrs. Jodie did call home, you know."

"I know." How much should she say? Oh, just tell him. "My mom is so mad that now my grandma's moving in and I can't stand her. She bosses me around. My brother blames me for everything, and she babies him. So, kind of like my mom, only worse."

"Damn. I thought that my dad finding out was bad, but..." Cole rubbed his upper arm.

"Did he hurt you?" Kiara gripped the seat in front as the bus bumped down the road. She turned to him. "Are you okay?"

"Anyways, it doesn't matter," Cole said. "It was my fault as much as yours. Besides, it's a stupid reason to get in trouble, don't you think? I mean, we could ditch class and climb the buttes, right? At least then they'd have a reason to be mad."

She smiled. "Or chase Fred the cat through the classroom."

He grinned. "Or catch that Garter snake they keep mentioning and let it loose in class."

"Yeah, or push Mrs. Jodie off the porch and watch her roll away."

Cole laughed. "These are great ideas."

During the rest of the short ride home, they agreed that the free school lunches were the best: Bologna or turkey sandwiches—with cheese! —syrupy pears, apple juice, cold milk, and a cookie—much better than what either of them usually had at home.

Before long, it was Cole's stop. The bus pulled over onto the side of the road, kicking up a cloud of dust. The brakes squealed and the suspension bounced as it came to a halt. The door swooshed open. Cole grabbed his backpack and got off.

Kiara watched him cross the street. He turned, smiled, and waved.

She waved back. Her heart fluttered in her chest.

Cole didn't laugh at her or call her mean names. He wasn't like the kids at her last school. He was smart, interested in what she had to say, and as impressed by her as she was by him. By the time the bus pulled to the side of her street, she felt like she was on those clouds she always watched.

Kiara headed down to the sitter's house where Tommy would be watching TV and trying to avoid getting punched by the older boys when the sitter wasn't paying attention.

Her mom was working late, again, and would be tired, so Kiara would make dinner for Tommy who wouldn't help with dishes. She'd scream at him; he'd tattle on her. It wouldn't matter. Her mom would be locked inside her room, and all the rest ... even Grandma moving in ... well, none of it mattered.

Everything was going to be alright. She hadn't lost her new friend, at least not yet.

7

Grandma

KIARA SAT ON HER BEDROOM FLOOR reading about witches and spirits haunting and hunting children. She jumped, screamed, and tossed down her book when her mom swung open the door.

"Geez, Mom, you scared me."

Her mom entered with boxes. "Because your grandma is coming, you're moving into Tommy's room, so Grandma can have your room. Pack up your things. We'll see how much we can fit in there."

"*My* room? Why?"

"Close that jaw, young lady. It'll only be for a little while." Another pause. "Until you two can stay home alone without killing each other."

That was never going to happen. Everything kept changing. Kiara lost her old house, her dad, and her room. And what was she getting for everything she lost?

Nothing as far as she could figure. She'd heard that when something bad happened, something good was bound to happen. Maybe she'd make a lot of new friends, nice ones like the kids described in her books.

Or, what if Kiara could find her dad? Maybe she could move in with him and *the whore.* Asking her mom would be like throwing herself to half-starved sharks.

Or, perhaps life would get even more miserable, like in some of the books she read. She hoped not.

Despite Kiara's daily chanting—*please don't let her move in, please don't let her move in*—her grandma moved in. She was exactly as Kiara remembered. She acted sweet, in the same fake nice way her mom did when they had guests over. She smiled and asked how everyone's day was during meals. Kiara called bullshit in her head, but she played along.

Her grandma offered to make dinner and put away dishes. She didn't lift more than a few things before getting winded and sitting down to rest.

She took over Kiara's room. Kiara and Tom shared a bunk bed in his. Tommy took the top bunk because he was smaller and Kiara kept hitting her head on the popcorn ceiling.

While her grandma slept on a queen-sized four-poster bed, they slept on cheap twin mattresses, more spring and less cushion. Kiara awoke with a sore back most mornings.

Kiara cringed when her grandma fell asleep on her recliner in the living room and snored, all while wearing an oxygen cannula attached via a long tube to a green tank in the bedroom.

Kiara's grandma spoke kindly to her when she read Bible scriptures. Then she'd get bossy. Neither Kiara nor Tommy was used to being told what to do.

When Kiara got home from school, her grandma started up right away. "Kiara, go fetch me some ice water." Her grandma held out the large Tupperware pitcher that she sipped out of all day. "Tommy, come here. Take this to the trash."

Kiara returned with water sloshing in the pitcher.

"I said ice water," her grandma said. "Clean out your ears."

"Well—"

"Is a hole in the ground. Here." Her grandma held out the pitcher. "Put some ice in it."

Kiara added ice and returned. She wanted to watch *Full House*, but her grandma had commandeered the Zenith TV in the living room with her soap operas.

Kiara lingered by the side of her grandma's recliner. "Hey, Grandma—"

"Hay is for horses." Her grandma's eyes were focused on the screen. "What is it now?"

"I was wondering if we could watch something else on TV."

Unless her grandma was napping, the answer was no, even if delivered with a toothless smile.

It didn't take long before the niceish act was over.

Kiara's mom came home from work, went to her bedroom and left Kiara and Tommy with their grandma who pressure-cooked pot roast, peas, and potatoes for dinner ... again.

Her grandma was used to feeding eight people—Kiara's mom was the oldest of six kids and the only girl. As a result, everything her grandma cooked, even if it didn't taste good—which meant everything except her tacos—was prepared in a ridiculous quantity. This assured they'd eat the same slop every day until even the leftovers wanted to walk themselves out of the house.

Kiara sat there chewing her last bite of meat thirty times until it was soft enough to swallow. She stood to throw away her paper plate.

"Where do you think you're going?" her grandma yelled. "Sit back down. There are starving children in this world. You will eat every single pea on your plate." She held her hand up to spank her. "Do you hear me? If you don't, you've got another thing coming."

Kiara's mom reappeared from around the corner. She raised her voice. "You will *not* spank my children." She pursed her lips, narrowed her eyes, and retreated to her room.

Kiara didn't want to risk it, so she finished the pea mush by gagging it down with a glass of milk.

When she moved in, her grandma had brought an upright freezer which they stored in the garage. It saved them from having to take so many trips to the market in town. Instead, they bought more food and froze it. The problem was that it froze *too* well. Maybe on account of the heat in the garage, the freezer pumped out so much cold air that ice escaped out around the sides and froze the door shut. Kiara had to bring a screwdriver and hammer to icepick the door open, chisel out a package of meat, and take a little extra ice off the door so it'd close again.

Struggling to get meat out was still better than eating leftover spaghetti with jarred sauce that had been mixed together and reheated in the microwave so many times that the sauce dried and the noodles practically liquified.

Kiara complained about her limited meal options to Cole.

"Honestly," Kiara said, "I'd prefer hot dogs and mac 'n cheese."

"Doesn't your mom cook?" Cole asked.

"No. Yours?"

"Well, yeah. She doesn't work." Cole shrugged. "Maybe your mom's tired."

"Not sure if she's tired so much as sad."

Cole cocked his head. "Why do you think she's sad?"

"She's always crying. Or screaming and angry. Or both. Maybe she wishes she didn't have to deal with me and Tommy and Grandma. Maybe she misses my dad, but she never talks about him. Maybe she's losing her mind."

"My mom says that my dad's not usually in his right mind."

"What do you mean?"

Cole took two fingers and held up an imaginary cigarette and blew fake smoke. He opened an imaginary can of beer and drank it. Then Cole shook his fist and raised his eyebrows.

Kiara couldn't think of a good response to that.

One upside to having Grandma there was that Kiara got to stay up late to watch *Wheel of Fortune* and *Jeopardy,* on one condition: Kiara had to use her feet to give her grandma a backrub while they lay on the floor by the TV, until her grandma fell asleep.

One downside to having Grandma there was that Kiara had no privacy. She had to go to the bathroom to change her panties.

"When I was your age," Kiara's mom said. "I never had my own room. I always shared a room with at least two or three of my five brothers in a little house in the valley."

Kiara was glad that she didn't live in *that* house. In *her* old house, before the divorce, she had a king-sized bed in her own bedroom double the size of Tommy's, so she guessed she and her mom had a different perspective.

The next week, after accompanying her grandma to one of her many doctor's appointments, Kiara got yelled at for *not being ladylike.* She hadn't kept her hands folded in her lap and had uncrossed her ankles while wearing a dress.

When her mom heard about it, she shouted at her grandma, "You leave my daughter alone!" She slammed her bedroom door for emphasis.

Although Kiara's grandma could occupy the toilet for an hour, she threatened to take a belt to Kiara for taking a fifteen-minute shower. Kiara got dressed and ran into her room to hide.

Her mom screamed about positive reinforcement and I'll raise them the way I want to, while her grandma came back with, your spoiled brat is wasting water, and she should be doing more work around the house.

Honestly, Kiara did everything around the house including their own laundry and now their grandma's laundry, too. So, yeah, having Grandma at home pretty much sucked.

After a particularly loud yelling match—louder than anything Kiara remembered between her parents, her mom got on the phone and spoke in a hushed tone. Her mom rarely talked on the phone, so whenever she did, Kiara paid attention.

Kiara snuck up close to her mom's bedroom door and listened as her mom whispered plans to ship her grandma off to live with one of Kiara's uncles in Ohio.

Kiara could only hope.

When her mom came home from work the next week, downtrodden, any mention of Grandma leaving stopped. Rather than scream and yell with her grandma, her mom retreated to her room and sobbed.

Kiara couldn't understand. Maybe her mom couldn't find another babysitter, or maybe they were too expensive. Or maybe it was because the last sitter had put duct tape over another boy's mouth as punishment. The boy *was* annoying as all hell, but still....

Maybe Kiara could convince her mom that she was old enough to take care of herself and Tommy. After all, she was nearly eight. Plenty of other kids her age were left home alone while both parents worked. The kids had a house key and let themselves in.

One night, while her grandma was snoring loudly in her room, the phone rang.

Kiara's mom said, "You and Tommy go to your room and stay quiet. I have to take an important call from an attorney." She shut her bedroom door.

Kiara made it her personal mission to do reconnaissance. She got down on the carpet and pressed her ear against her mom's bedroom door. Her heart thumped in her chest.

She found out why her grandma wasn't going anywhere— her mom got fired.

Something happened where her mom's boss had her "clean up the books." Her mom discovered something illegal. When she said something, he fired her and brought in a friend, to presumably continue doing illegal things. Problem is she didn't have access to the evidence.

At school, she told Cole. He didn't say much, only that he hoped everything would be okay. She hoped so, too. A little knot of anxiety now resided permanently in her stomach.

⁕

Kiara usually counted down the days to winter break. She loved how her mom decorated the house for the holidays. She blasted Christmas carols and staple-gunned so many strings of colored lights to the roof that people could see the dazzling glow from the next street over.

This year, though, Kiara begged for the holidays to be over.

While her mom wrapped the garage door in golden wrapping paper and attached a huge red bow, her grandma grumbled they were *wasting money on electricity*. Her mom retorted with *you wouldn't know what holiday spirit was if it bit you in the ass.*

Her grandma yelled about *screwed up priorities* and screamed, *Jesus is the only reason for the season.* After that, her mom set up two nativity sets, a small one inside and a giant illuminated one outside.

Oh God, how Kiara hated the fighting. She couldn't wait for the New Year and to return to school. She hated alarm clocks, but her options were to either stay at home and sleep in until the yelling started, or wake up early and sit through the drudgery of school.

At least at school, there was Cole. What's the worst that could happen there?

8

The Disaster

WINTER WEATHER BROUGHT A DUSTING of snow and below freezing temperatures. Everyone at school wrapped themselves in big coats and huddled together for warmth. They no longer desired to go outside for recess and instead lingered near the drafty but heated schoolhouse.

On a cold Tuesday morning, January 28, 1986, Kiara sat at her desk reading a book about castles and dragons. She had finished the assignment everyone else was still working on. She felt a flick on her leg. There was Fred, the secretary's orange tabby, weaving between the rows and columns of desks and chairs. Kiara set down her book and reached over. Fred rubbed his furry head against her palm and tickled her wrist with his whiskers.

The other students took notice and beckoned him. Ms. Gilespie was usually okay with it, but Fred lingered too long.

She shooed him away to the other end of the classroom. He stuck his tail up, glanced back at them, and strode outside in the chilly air to presumably hunt field mice.

Ms. Gilespie rolled the TV cart to the front of the classroom. She, along with Mrs. Wright, and later the secretary, fiddled with cables and antennae, to get the station on the tube television to come into focus.

Morning and a movie already? Maybe Ms. Gilespie wasn't feeling well.

Perfect. It'd be a fun day, everyone exclaimed in loud whispers.

No, Ms. Gilespie quieted them down. Today, she said, was a special day, a historic one.

Lake LA, out in the middle of nowhere, happened to be the nearest town to Edwards Air Force Base, where the Space Shuttles landed whenever weather conditions weren't ideal in Cape Canaveral, Florida. After completing space missions, the Space Shuttles landed at Rogers Dry Lake bed at Edwards Air Force Base quite often.

Hearing the crack when they broke the sound barrier and watching the shuttle streak across the sky to land was a rare treat. Whenever the shuttle piggybacked on a giant 747 on its return to the Kennedy Space Center in Florida, everyone ran outside to witness the spectacle.

Even though the Space Shuttles were built in California and landed at Edwards, they didn't launch from there. The best the kids could do was to watch the launch on TV.

"Today is even more special." Ms. Gilespie smiled. "A teacher will be on board, the first American civilian astronaut. She was chosen out of thousands of other teachers."

Chatter broke out and students shouted questions.

Ms. Gilespie answered that no, she hadn't applied, because she was scared of heights. She quieted the class.

The rocket booster ignited; the shuttle's nose directed up toward the sky. Static flickered across the TV screen. Ms. Gilespie wiggled a cord and the TV came back into focus.

Kiara leaned forward and squinted at the screen—everything had become blurry lately.

Cole leaned over to Kiara—Mrs. Gilespie had finally allowed them to sit together again, in the back row. "I bet Christa McAuliffe's class is watching."

"Who?" Kiara asked.

"The astronaut. She teaches high school in New Hampshire."

"How do you know all this?"

"My parents get the AV Press. My dad only reads the comics and dumps the rest in a stack near the fireplace. I hide out in the backyard and read them cover to cover. I also watch the news whenever I can."

"I'm stuck watching Disney movies to keep Tommy happy."

"Shush," Ms. Gilespie scolded the class. "This is history in the making." She sat down to avoid blocking the screen.

"Are they going to the moon?" a boy shouted.

"No," Ms. Gilespie said, "They're going to release a satellite into space."

Disappointment. But they'll be up in space. That's still amazing, everyone agreed.

The countdown started. 5-4-3 ... everyone sat on the edge of their chairs, elbows on desks, heads on hands, not blinking. Huge clouds of water condensation expanded violently from the bottom and rolled up and out from the ground. Rockets spewed flames of jet fuel that burned yellow and orange and white hot ... 2-1.

A boy in front of Kiara turned around to face her. "Look at the fire. It's way hotter than you." He high-fived the boys next to him.

Kiara wanted to punch him. Instead, she focused on the shuttle as it lifted off, shot up through the atmosphere, and headed to space. The camera shook as it followed the flight path.

Ten seconds, twenty seconds, thirty.

"It's going to be too far to see soon," Kiara whispered to Cole.

"Know how much power is needed to launch a shuttle?"

"How much?" she asked.

"Over seven million pounds of thrust."

"That's a lot." Kiara had no idea what that meant but was proud of Cole's intimate knowledge of these technical details and honored that he shared them with her.

After a minute, Ms. Gilespie headed to the TV to turn it off, when, 73 seconds after liftoff—an explosion of light in the sky.

"What's happening?" Kiara asked.

"No." Cole didn't move.

Voices on the TV station grew silent, then somber. Something was wrong, very wrong.

Kiara peered at Ms. Gilespie; terror was written across her face.

It took a moment for the tragedy to be realized: the Challenger had exploded, the shuttle burned and broken into millions of little pieces. And the astronauts, and the teacher along with it.

"She had two kids," Mrs. Gilespie muttered.

The thought chilled Kiara. The astronaut, a mom, was dead, while her students watched.

Ms. Gilespie sat in silence before breaking into tears and turning off the TV. The class didn't dare speak for a moment.

Then the boys, the same ones who harassed her on occasion, turned to face Kiara.

"Did you see that?" The boy in front of her stared at her to watch her reaction. "Boom!" He spread his arms wide to emulate the bursting into flames.

Kiara cried and ran outside. She huddled on the porch steps shivering. The astronauts had burned alive. She lay her head on her arms. The boys at school. Mom at home. Grandma. Life. Why did everything hurt so much?

A hand rested on her shoulder. She glanced up. Tears obstructed her view.

Cole wrapped his arms around her and let her cry onto his shoulder.

After a while, Kiara pulled away.

"I hope they all went to heaven," she said. Surprised at the words, she blushed. "I mean if you believe in that sort of thing."

"My dad's Catholic," Cole said. "My mom's not. I don't know what I believe."

"In church they teach if you're good, good things will happen. I don't think that's true," she said.

"Good people don't deserve to be blown up in space."

After that, things changed. Every time Kiara heard a sonic boom or saw a Blackbird or Air Force jet streak by, she held her breath. She faced the sky and followed their flight paths until they disappeared safely into the smudge of horizon.

On Sundays, Kiara spent her time in church pondering death. People spoke of *God's Will* and the *Will of God* to explain tragedy. God was pretty horrible if he willed the death of the Challenger crew. If that's what happened, Kiara didn't want any part of it, which she told her mom after Mass.

"It doesn't work that way," her mom said. She sat down on a bench beside Kiara. "We don't pretend to know everything. God works in mysterious ways. He loves us so much that he gave us free will to make mistakes."

Kiara gave this some consideration. Clearly someone who built that shuttle or maintained it had made a mistake. "If God doesn't save people, doesn't make things better, or protect them, what good is he? He killed them."

Rather than be aghast, her mom patted her knee. "God didn't kill them. It's the devil who tempts people to murder."

"If God lets people kill each other, how's he any better than the devil who tempts them to do it?" Kiara said. "God didn't save the astronauts."

Her mom hung her head, her lips moving in prayer. She looked at Kiara. "God saves your soul. It's not rewards in this life; it's rewards in the afterlife."

Kiara hated to argue with her mom who was clearly trying her best to counter Kiara's points, but there was more to be said. "What's the point of that?" Kiara asked. "How can you enjoy rewards if you're dead?"

"In heaven ..." her mom explained. She'd already lost Kiara who had zoned out, far away in thought. "... these are the promises God has made to us."

Why should Kiara trust promises made by a God who let people burn to death?

After more consideration, Kiara decided people didn't have the power to control their fate, and neither did God. Sometimes bad things happened, and no one could prevent it. Percentages of survival mattered, and she was sure Cole could figure out the odds if she asked.

9

Snow Globe

BY MAY, THE WEATHER WARMED. While her classmates played outdoors during recess, Kiara isolated herself under a tree to read. She finished a book about friends who discovered a magical world on the other side of a waterfall, a land encircled by mysterious mountains.

Kiara wished for a group of girls to adventure with. How could she make friends, as her mom said, if she didn't try? She contemplated the girls hopscotching on the blacktop. After working up the nerve to approach them, she stood a few feet to the side and waited. She mumbled an inaudible hello.

No one invited her to play. She stepped forward and got in line. Nobody objected.

The girl in front made it halfway across the hopscotch boxes before losing her balance; the others groaned and laughed and high-fived. When Kiara failed, no one said anything at all.

Kiara felt invisible. She resumed her spot under the tree.

She scraped at the dirt with a stick. At the sight of scuffed up tennis shoes, she raised her gaze, and there was Cole.

"Everything okay?" he asked.

She shrugged. "Just bored."

"Hmm." He tilted his head. "Want to come play at my house sometime?"

"Sure." Her heart fluttered.

Cole returned her smile. He reached to retrieve a ball that she hadn't noticed had rolled there. He waved and ran back to his friends.

Did Cole want to hang out? Or had he only talked to her because he had to get the ball? She hoped he meant it but wasn't going to bring it up unless he did.

Kiara went back to drawing in the dirt. She felt better when Cole was near. She smiled at the thought of her friend.

Kiara's mom stopped driving them to the library. Gas had gotten too expensive for the half-hour drive to town. Kiara kept herself busy at home sketching pictures of the San Gabriel Mountains beyond her window. Tommy even let her sketch a portrait of him and said he liked it. Coming from him, that made her prouder than any compliment she'd gotten before.

At school under her tree, Kiara attempted to reread a book. It wasn't fun to already know how it ended. She opened her notebook and sketched the ocean, which she hadn't seen in years. She added a sunset over the horizon, flipped the page and gazed at the sky. A few remnants of clouds remained. Kiara took her pencil and wrote:

The valley floor, flat under a dome of blue, encircled by mountains and buttes I can view. Shake the globe of snow. Watch it swirl. Watch it flow. Powder floats through the air, melts, and leaves the earth bare. Tilt the globe upside down. Swirl it around. The snow is gone. It's been dirt all along. You're trapped in the desert under a dome of blue. How to escape? I wish I knew.

"What are you writing?" a voice asked.

Kiara raised her head. There was Cole.

"Nothing." She covered her hand over the paper.

"Let me see." He sat next to her. "Come on. Please."

She removed her fingers reluctantly.

Cole leaned closer to read and glanced at the sky. "It does look like a snow globe." He smiled. "I hope you keep writing. It's good. When you write a book, I'll be the first to buy it."

Kiara laughed. "Not much else to do. I'm out of books."

"Me too. Let's trade books until we get a hold of new ones."

This idea thrilled her. To not appear too eager, she changed the subject. "My mom used to take me to the library."

"Doubt my dad knows what a library is," Cole said. "He's not nice. Nothing I ever do is good enough for him."

Kiara sighed. "Same. My mom babies Tommy and hates me. Mostly, she locks herself in her room and ignores us."

"Being ignored is good at my place." Cole dug at the dirt with the heel of his shoe.

"Instead of trading books," Kiara said, "maybe we should trade houses for a while."

Cole laughed. "I don't think you'd like mine. My dad throws things when he's drunk and angry. I've learned it's best to keep my mouth shut and safer to keep out of sight."

Kiara remembered how Cole rubbed his arm after the phone call home. Did his dad beat him? She couldn't fathom how to broach that topic.

"My mom throws things and slams doors without drinking," Kiara said. "She's always stressed about money."

Cole shook his head. "Dad says we never have enough money although he buys himself cigarettes by the case, the ones in the red and white boxes. And twelve packs of beer."

Kiara paused. "My uncles have scratchy beards and smell like Coors Light and cigarettes. One uncle used to give me hugs that lasted a long time and made me feel gross. We don't visit him anymore."

"That's weird."

Cole got quiet. Kiara worried maybe she said something she shouldn't have. She didn't want it to get awkward. The hand bell rang, so she didn't get a chance to ask.

The next day at recess, Cole handed Kiara a couple of books by R.L. Stine. "I figure these can't be scarier than your creepy uncle." He grinned.

She promised to bring him books the next day. As she walked back to class, she traced the spines with her fingers and flipped through the pages. Cole's fingers had flipped through these same pages. Her stomach tingled.

Cole got in the habit of telling her jokes, mostly one-liners. He seemed pleased every time she laughed.

"My parents say we're getting a pool this summer," he said. "It probably won't happen, but if it does, you should come over to swim."

Kiara stared at him incredulously. "All I can do with my swimsuit is sit in a kiddie pool."

Cole laughed. "The little, blue plastic ones?"

"Yeah, or Tommy and I spray each other with ice-cold water from the hose. Most times the hose gets pretty strong for him, and he ends up spraying himself in the face. It's hilarious." She demonstrated by jumping around and mocking Tommy's voice, "Ahh. Make it stop."

Cole giggled so much that it brought tears to his eyes.

She laughed, seeing him laugh. It made her proud. It was the first time she got such a reaction out of him. She decided she'd keep telling him stories whenever he told her jokes.

Cole asked for her phone number and promised they'd talk and get together at his house. She didn't get her hopes up. Even if it didn't happen, she was glad he asked for her number.

Kiara's mom got hired at the local real estate sales office, working for the company that built their home. She said it'd take a while to make commissions. When she did, she'd buy Kiara and Tommy nice new clothes and toys. In the meantime, her grandma paid bills with her social security checks. Occasionally, they'd get a box of food from the church.

While they lined up for lunch at school, Kiara updated Cole with the news. "At least my mom is working again. Less time for her to scream and cry."

"That's a relief." He smiled. "Right?"

"I don't know what to think of her selling houses out here."

"What do you mean?" he asked.

"Don't you think it's a bad idea to sell more homes in the desert? A lot of us hate it here."

"It's not all bad." Cole gave her a sideways glance. "Right?" He nudged her shoulder. "At least if you have good friends."

Kiara smiled and blushed. "I mean if I had to be trapped out here in the desert, at least I'm trapped here with you."

Cole grinned.

10

So Lucky

AT THE START OF SUMMER BREAK, Cole phoned Kiara—
her first call from a friend. She wasn't sure what to say.

"Tommy is a pain in the butt," Kiara said. "I try to play
Trouble, or Chutes and Ladders, or Sorry with him. All he does
is throw pieces at me."

Cole laughed. "My sisters are brats, too. They throw pieces
instead of playing the game."

"Please, Mom," Kiara pestered for the third time that
week. "You can meet his mom."

"Fine." Her mom relented. "You can play at Cole's house as
long as his mom is there and you stay out of trouble."

When Kiara got to his place, Cole opened the front door
and she was greeted with a rush of air-conditioning and the

aroma of fried oil. Built by the same company, his house layout was identical to hers.

The curtains were parted and filled the room with sunshine, unlike the darkness of Kiara's home—her grandma kept the curtains shut to keep it cooler without having to run the AC all day; at night when the desert temperatures plummeted, they opened windows and balanced box fans precariously on window sills to pull in the outside air; in the morning, they shut everything up and plunged the house back into darkness.

"The baby's taking a nap," Cole whispered, motioning at the first door down the hallway. "We're lucky my other sisters are at the neighbor's. Come meet my mom."

In the kitchen, Cole's mom, tall with long, black curly hair, stood gracefully at the stove. She turned and smiled.

"I've heard many good things about you, Kiara." She pronounced Kiara's name correctly on the first try. "So nice to finally meet you. I made you both grilled cheese sandwiches." She had the softest, sweetest tone of voice. Kiara's mom never said Kiara's name with such kindness. "Honey, do you like fruit?" Cole's mom pointed to a plate of freshly sliced peaches.

Kiara thanked her profusely. A mom who cooked dinner *and* lunch? With fresh fruit! And she wasn't yelling. She even called her "honey." Cole was so lucky.

After lunch, Kiara and Cole relaxed on the shag carpet in the living room where he unveiled a massive game board with a million tiny plastic pieces: Risk. There was a world map and little soldiers and tanks in different colors.

"The goal is world domination," Cole said.

Clearly, he had played the game a bunch; it was a lot for Kiara to get the hang of. Although she had lots of games at home, this one was more complicated.

They played for hours until a car pulled into the driveway. Kiara heard it before she saw it—the engine rattled and brakes squealed, until it lurched to a stop.

Cole's mom was feeding his baby sister in a high chair in the kitchen. Everyone, including Cole, got still. Cole's mother ceased midway, a spoon halfway to her daughter's lips. The car door slammed and a few moments later, Cole's dad entered.

Lanky with a mustache, he strutted in like the commander of a ship. He paused when he noticed Kiara and strained his face into a smile. "Hello there. You must be Kiara. Cole told us about you. Hopefully you can be a good influence on this knucklehead."

Kiara hardly had a chance to wave at him before he disappeared down the hallway.

Cole's mom peeked around the corner. "Sweetie, maybe it's better if you clean up the game and walk your friend home. It was nice meeting you, Kiara. I hope you come back soon."

When Cole walked her home, he didn't mention his dad, so she didn't ask and instead discussed the upcoming school year.

"Another year at the dry lakebed, now with Tommy," she said.

"Can only get better from here." Cole gave her a cheesy smile and a double thumbs up.

"I heard they're bringing in trailers, or where are they going to put us all?"

"If they have to do lap seating..." Cole smirked. "I'd be happy to share my seat with you."

"You're so kind." She rolled her eyes.

"I am. Look at what a gentleman I am, walking the lady to her door."

"Because your mom made you."

"Minor detail." He paused at her driveway. "See you soon?"

"I hope so."

Even though Cole's family didn't get a pool that summer, he and Kiara talked on the phone, hung out to play games, and he always walked her back home.

She loved spending time with him—the worst part was saying goodbye.

The following week, Cole walked her home but detoured up the road and kept going. They passed the last houses and the road dead-ended near the buttes.

"Where are we going?" Kiara asked.

"To the water towers." Cole said.

Without asking why, she followed him up the steep, rocky path up the buttes. Beyond the neighborhoods, at the top of Lovejoy Buttes, water towers nestled partway into the ground.

She paused, panting. "How high up are we going?"

"3,340-foot elevation."

"You've got to be kidding me." Kiara stopped. "I'm not going up that far."

"We're not going to the peak of Lovejoy." Cole turned and held out his hand. "Come on, it's only 500 feet higher than your house."

Kiara waved away the help but soon lost her footing in the loose gravel and grabbed his hand to steady herself, until she regained her balance. "Why are we up here?"

A trail on either side of the water tanks led downhill. From the peak, one direction overlooked the Palmdale side of Lake LA, their neighborhoods, and beyond that, the majestic purple-hued San Gabriel Mountains. The opposite direction commanded a view of the other half of Lake LA, where the vastness of the Mojave Desert extended out to Edwards Air Force Base.

Kiara slowly spun around. It was as if the entire world was laid out in front of them. She could see forever in every direction—the desert was endless.

Quartz in the rocks sparkled. Kiara ran her fingers along the rocky edges.

"The buttes are prettier up close," she said.

Cole sat against a boulder facing the Lancaster side. "They're mountains of granite, from 70 million years ago, back when there were dinosaurs."

"My grandma might remember that." Kiara smirked.

Cole slumped his shoulders and stared into the distance.

Kiara settled down next to him. "Is something wrong?"

Cole bowed his head and mumbled. "My dad hates me."

"What? Why?" Kiara couldn't imagine anyone not loving this boy.

"Don't know." He shrugged. "I run up here to hide from him whenever he throws a fit."

Kiara had never considered simply running out of her house and hiding up in the buttes when things got tough.

Cole continued, "He hates a lot of things. When he gets home from work, he yells that his work sucks and life sucks. Maybe he wants a different job. Or a different kid."

"Can you ask him?" Not like she would ever ask her mom that unless she wanted her head to make impact with a wall.

Cole's face blanched. "No. It's better I keep my mouth shut if I want to live." The corner of his mouth upturned. "He likes you though, so he's nicer when you come over."

Kiara smiled at him.

"Come on." Cole stood, reached for her hand, and pulled her up. "Time to get you home."

What happened at Cole's house behind closed doors? Kiara didn't ask. She'd listen when he was ready to talk.

Kiara's mom took her and Tommy to Kmart in town and bought them each a few outfits for school. She told them to be careful with the jeans because she couldn't afford to get them new pairs if they ripped at the knees.

Tommy declared he'd decided to go by the name Tom. He was handsome, even though his hair had gotten as long as Shaggy's in Scooby Doo.

Their neighbor Mrs. Helvan across the street was now "doing hair" and offered to cut his. Kiara sat in the neighbor's dining room and observed as the neighbor snipped Tom's hair.

Kiara's hair had gotten long. Perhaps she could ask for a spiral perm like Farrah Fawcett. She didn't interrupt while Mrs. Helvan and her mom were chatting.

The two women laughed. Mrs. Helvan made a few more snips. They talked some more, then a couple more snips. Kiara peered around their backs, but her view was blocked.

"That should do it." Mrs. Helvan stepped back.

Kiara's eyes widened. It was a bowl cut, without the bowl.

"I cut it short," Mrs. Helvan said, "but it'll grow out quick."

Kiara was embarrassed for Tom. Better he didn't hear it from her. She figured he'd hear about it at school.

It didn't matter. By the time September rolled around, it became apparent that Tom didn't have the same friend deficiency as Kiara. Within weeks, everyone in his class knew his name, and invited him over to play. Not so for Kiara.

Did the number of friends matter though? Having one friend like Cole was luckier than having ten of the others.

11

Things Fall Apart

AUTUMN DAYS WERE UNPREDICTABLE. Weather could feel like the last of summer with smothering heat, or leap ahead to winter and cast a below-freezing chill. At home, cold days were the worst for the electricity to go out, something that happened not infrequently. Sometimes the lights went out for only a few minutes. Other times it stayed dark for hours.

Her grandma brought kerosene lanterns with her when she moved in, which Kiara used to do her homework.

If the power went out on a cold night, wrapping up in blankets wasn't enough; Kiara's mom lit a fire in the fireplace to keep warm. She showed Kiara how to use fireplace tools to turn the logs, to shove newspaper underneath, and to fan the flame to keep the fire going. Kiara tried to read. With the flickering firelight, the words jumped around, so she gave up.

Even when power outages weren't a problem, lack of money was. It meant no heat.

Kiara shivered in the shower. Hot water streamed down her back while condensation from her breath stayed suspended in the frigid air.

She wrapped herself in a robe and knocked on her mom's bedroom door. With teeth chattering and numb fingers, she asked, "Can I turn on the heat?"

"No," her mom said.

"It's freezing."

"Get into jammies and get a blanket."

Kiara's hands shook as she zipped up her pink pajama onesie. She scratched at the itchy polyester neckline, which pulled down on her shoulders since she had gotten too tall for it. Her feet got sweaty, which only made her colder. She complained to her mom who cut the feet off of the jammies, which now slid up Kiara's shins. Her toes tingled.

"Put on some socks and get to bed," her mom said.

Kiara grabbed a book and snuggled underneath a pile of blankets.

"Lights out," her mom said. "Go to sleep."

After her mom locked herself in her room for the night, Kiara hid underneath her comforter, stacked heavy with blankets, flipped on a flashlight, and opened a scary book Cole had lent her. She ignored the howls of the coyotes in the fields outside, and read. She stayed up late most nights reading books she traded with Cole, or that her teacher loaned her out of her personal library, until Kiara had read every book that she could get a hold of.

Kiara wasn't the only one reading books. Her grandma, like her mom, read romance novels with covers of half-clothed men hugging women whose dresses were off their shoulders.

Unlike her mom, her grandma read religious books, too—*Our Lady of Fátima* was Kiara's favorite. When her mom came home from work and heard her grandma telling Kiara stories of the young girls who saw visions of the Virgin Mary, she was furious.

"Don't read that garbage to the kids," her mom said.

"Why not?" her grandma said. "It's the truth, and she likes hearing it."

Her mom ground her teeth and left the room.

Kiara and her grandma exchanged a smirk. They had won that one. This time they were on the same team.

By the spring of 1987, the Palmdale side of Lake LA had grown, largely because of all of the homes purchased from her mom's company—many sold by her mom! With that came more kids. People talked about building a school, one with a cafeteria so that kids wouldn't have to eat outside in the cold or the heat. Nobody could agree on where to put it though.

Kiara sat on the couch watching reruns of *The Brady Bunch* while Tom played with Hot Wheels on the floor. Her mom exited her room and sat next to Kiara, despite having three couches—they had absorbed her grandma's furniture, too. Kiara wasn't sure what to make of the close contact and scooted away. This, thankfully, was missed by her mom.

"Are you going to Cole's this weekend?" her mom asked.

"No, his dad will be home and he doesn't want a lot of noise." The real reason was that the last time Kiara went over to play, Cole's dad drank too much and cussed Cole out, despite Kiara's presence. Everyone decided it was best if Kiara didn't witness that again.

"Why not invite Cole here?" her mom asked. "Your brother is having friends over. I'll get pizza."

"Really?" Kiara scrutinized her mom's face to judge her sincerity. Before her mom could change her mind, Kiara ran to the kitchen to call Cole.

Kiara's mom insisted that Kiara and Cole play their game on the formal dining room table—leftover from the divorce. They slid the papers and junk to the other end of the table and set up Scrabble. Kiara felt like a stranger sitting on the high-backed chairs at the inlaid table that they never used. Her grandma was kind enough to stay in her bedroom.

"It's nice Kiara finally has a friend over." Her mom laughed with a snarky tone.

Kiara gritted her teeth and glared at her mom, telepathically telling her to shut up.

"Tom has no problem making friends," her mom said. "Who knows what her issue is."

Kiara stared intently at her Scrabble pieces, no longer interested in the game. She didn't want to yell and fight with her mom in front of Cole, so she sank a little lower in her seat.

"Sweetie," her mom said. "Earth to Kiara. Do you and Cole want some pizza?"

"Sure." Kiara balled up her fists on her lap. Hearing her mom call her "sweetie" made her skin crawl, because her mom was faking it—only Tom got that title. She looked at Cole, who avoided eye contact.

Kiara gnawed on her slice of pepperoni pizza with its dry sauce and scant cheese. Her mom returned to offer more pizza, sounding sweet as sugar. Kiara eyed her mom with distrust.

Her mom allowing Cole over was too good to be true.

"They're building the new Lake LA School around the corner, down on 160th," her mom said. "You'll start fourth grade there."

"That'll be close to both of us," Cole said. He and Kiara exchanged a glance.

"There will be several hundred students," her mom said. "It's going to be a K-8."

"A what?" Kiara asked.

"It means you'll be there until high school," her mom said.

If she stayed at Lake LA School through eighth grade, Kiara wouldn't deal with lockers and changing classes in middle school. Instead, she'd get an extra couple of years to build up the anxiety of facing all those things in high school. Like Joshua trees, she'd have to adapt.

"You'll walk to school." Kiara's mom pointed at her. "Tom will be in first grade for full days, so you'll walk him, too, and help him with his homework."

"Why do I have to? I have my own homework."

"Because I said so." Her mom left the room.

Kiara looked at Cole who was focused intently on forming a word with his Scrabble tiles. She ground her teeth. Why did her mom embarrass her while Cole was there?

Although Cole was kind enough not to rehash what had happened, neither of them invited each other over again—him, because of his dad, and her, because of her mom.

Kiara felt more miserable and alone, especially after experiencing the joy of playing with a friend outside of school, and having that opportunity yanked from her.

One evening, her mom's attorney phoned. Kiara's mom said she was going to take the call in her bedroom.

That meant it was important.

Kiara's grandma was distracted by an episode of *The Love Boat*. Kiara crept up to her mom's door. Her mom was crying and whispering. Kiara leaned in closer to the door. Not that she needed to, because her mom raised her voice.

"We could lose the house," her mom said. "If that happens, I don't know where we'll go… I was hoping for some better news … Well, nothing I can do."

The last time Kiara heard her mom cry that she didn't know what to do or where to go was the night her dad left.

If they couldn't survive in the desert, where would they end up? Kiara felt an itch on her nose and turned to scratch it. She bumped the back of her head into Tom. "What are you doing here?" She scowled.

Tom grabbed at Kiara's shirt. "What's wrong? What does 'lose the house' mean?" It was clear he was worried.

"Everything's okay," she said.

"I don't believe you."

She stared into his bright blue eyes. She hadn't realized Tom was mature enough to understand anything beyond toys and tattling. Here he was, as old as she was when they had to move the first time.

"Come here." Kiara patted her lap. He climbed up. She wrapped her arms around him and he let her like when they were younger, when he used to climb up into her waterbed, when she'd rock him and sing him lullabies to drown out the sound of their parents screaming. "You were too little to remember before the divorce. Things are better now," she lied.

He leaned against her. She kissed the top of his head like when he was a toddler.

"I don't know," he said. "It sounds pretty bad."

"Tommy," Kiara said softly. "You and I fight. A lot. But I'll never let anything bad happen to you. I promise." She held him tighter. "Everything will be okay."

Being close to her brother gave Kiara hope that even if things fell apart, they'd at least have each other.

12

Lovejoy Buttes

WITH KIARA'S HOUSE BELOW LOVEJOY BUTTES, the surrounding fields and her backyard were littered with rocks. She collected pretty ones that sparkled in the sun. It didn't matter if quartz wasn't worth much—it might as well have been diamonds to her. She kept a bunch in an old dented metal lunchbox.

When she wasn't reading, sketching, or writing, Kiara took out her rocks and rotated them until they shimmered. Then she tucked them back in the lunchbox and hid it in the corner of her backyard under a bush where Tom wouldn't find them.

In between her house and Cole's, amidst the backdrop of Lovejoy Buttes, the new school took root. Kiara had a short fifteen-minute walk to school, unless she and the other kids on her street fooled around in the fields on the way there, or unless Tom slowed her down.

Sure, it wasn't a one-room schoolhouse anymore; however, there wasn't a permanent building onsite. The basketball courts on the blacktop and playground equipment bore more semblance to a typical school than the double rows of trailer classrooms.

The bottom of each trailer was bordered with wooden planks painted to match the trailers, which formed the façade of a foundation. They each had air conditioning units and windows, a ramp and stairs in front, and the hitch still visible from the side.

The bathroom trailer was patrolled by a yard-lady with long, greasy hair who explained to the girls that it wasn't healthy to shampoo hair every day; she was "deep-conditioning" hers.

In the middle of the school stood a small plot of grass, still more than what most children had in their neighborhoods. On the grassy plot was a single sad pine tree. It was scrawny, scruffy and hardened and, much like the children, determined to keep growing, which eventually it did, albeit at a slight angle from the wind.

Near the tree, a flag pole was cemented into the ground, evidence that the school, like the people, was here to stay. To be chosen to raise or lower the flags was a special honor for any kid, except on the windy days when the rope pulley got ripped out of their palms.

Most days you could hear the flap of the stars-and-stripes being whipped back and forth and the clanking of the rivets against the steel. The constant clinking created a comfortable noise, broken by gusts of wind that scraped up dirt and swirled it around before flinging it against the side of the buildings or the children's heads and legs. On other days, it was silent.

In front stood the office, a trailer with two entrances and ramps at both ends, one for the public, one for the teachers. A simple hand-painted "Office" sign was nailed across the top, below the hand-painted name of the school, Lake Los Angeles, with the word "School" crudely attached in a different font at the end like an afterthought.

Since there weren't many college-educated teachers in the area, the district recruited young, unsuspecting graduates from Minnesota or other northern states, lured by the idea of sunny California beaches and palm trees. Many of the teachers didn't stay long after they found endless sand without the ocean and Joshua trees rather than tropical palm trees. The San Gabriel Mountain range separated them from the beach and this high-desert rural plateau was a dot in the vastness of the Mojave Desert. At close to 3,000 feet above sea level, this meant occasional snow.

Kiara and Cole joked that if the San Andreas Fault line, which ran right through the Antelope Valley, finally caused "The Big One," California would separate along the fault line and the western section would sink, creating new shorelines up and down the state. They'd all have beachfront property— except that wasn't going to happen.

There was no river, no ocean, only the refreshing ice-cold stream that flowed from the school's water fountains to be lapped up several times a day.

With a bigger school and more kids, there were fewer combo classes. Kiara and Cole were placed together in a fourth-grade class—Ms. Lawrence's class.

Ms. Lawrence had the appearance of a woman too young to teach but trying hard to prove she could. She tied her hair back in a bun, applied eye makeup and deep red lipstick, and wore pencil skirts more suited for an office than a classroom.

In the end, she reminded Kiara of a teenager playing dress-up in her mother's clothes. Kiara liked her, because she was nice enough to be helpful and firm enough to prevent chaos.

Except for the outliers, Kiara's school had an ethnic makeup of thirds: third black, third white, third Hispanic. Even though no one directed them to, many kids separated themselves out into those groups, especially if their parents were friends.

Girls created a social hierarchy: the popular girls, the cliques, and the loners who were often called "loser," "dork," and "uncool." The former had spiral perms and teased bangs held in place with Aqua Net hairspray, Guess and Jordache jeans, and Reebok shoes, and decided they were prettier; the latter had ratty clothes and struggled with appropriate social interactions, and were therefore deemed less desirable as friends.

The "it" girls commanded the attention of the boys. Nobody made you join a group, so you could float until you found where you fit. Kiara was a floater. If she didn't make friends soon, it was going to be a long five years until high school.

During lunch recess, Kiara sat on the dirt against a wall near the playground while everyone else played. Cole easily slipped in and out of many groups of boys. Sometimes she wished she was a boy, because they didn't have to deal with stupid cliques.

Kiara envied Tomika, Rochelle, Shavonne, Lakisha, and other girls who had the balance and rhythm to play double Dutch. Two girls, one on each end, held two of these long jump ropes and swung them in alternate directions. The red, white, and blue beads smacked against the blacktop, keeping a steady beat.

"Why don't you come try?" Tomika called out to her.

"I don't know how," Kiara said.

"We'll show you."

Kiara didn't want to appear ungrateful for the invitation, so she went.

"All about the timing," Tomika said. "Duck your head until you're in."

It wasn't regular jump rope where you jumped with both feet; this was a dance, each foot danced with one jump rope at a time. Kiara stood behind Tomika and copied her swaying in time.

Kiara collided with the jump ropes. She wasn't hurt, so the girls laughed, and so did she.

"Take the ropes from Lakisha," Rochelle said. "You'll feel the beat."

Kiara tried. The ropes knocked into each other and landed limp on the ground as did her spirit. She felt like a total failure at double Dutch and making friends.

Rochelle stood beside her. "Sway your body each time you swing the rope."

"Relax," Tomika said. "Don't be stiff."

"You got it," Rochelle said. "Come try and jump in."

Kiara jumped in successfully. All the girls cheered. She was so happy that she forgot what she was doing and tripped on the rope and fell, and before the girls could stop it, the second rope came down on her head.

"You all right?" Tomika asked. "Need help?"

"I'm okay." Kiara stood up and brushed off. She had skinned up both knees and elbows.

Rochelle and Lakisha went to the bathroom to wet some brown paper towels, and handed them to Kiara so she could clean the gravel off her skin. They all said they were proud of her, because they had done it—they taught the girl with no rhythm to double Dutch.

Kiara finally felt included, but it was clear that she couldn't double Dutch without getting hurt, and that's all they wanted to play. She resumed her lonely spot out by the wall, albeit with a little more hope. Maybe there was another group for her to join. Maybe she could make friends after all.

Over the next few days, while her knees and elbows scabbed over, Kiara watched another group of girls: Loretta, Anita, and Josephina rubbed handfuls of sand between their fingers and palms before swinging across the monkey bars.

Anita made it across. Loretta dropped halfway, dismounting like the gymnasts on TV that her grandma watched. Josephina swung long from every other bar and quickly made it across. Kiara stared in awe.

The girls waved Kiara over to join them. She felt honored to be noticed.

"Use sand," Josephina said. "Sweat makes your hands slippery."

Kiara gripped the rails and stepped up the ladder. She jumped onto the second monkey bar but couldn't get momentum to keep going. She hung there, her hands hurting, until she let go. Her landing wasn't so graceful.

"Don't put both hands on the same bar," Josephina said. "Use your body weight to swing across, one arm at a time."

Kiara did and her hands blistered.

"Happens until you get calluses," Josephina said.

"I can't do this." Kiara's arms were shaking and her palms throbbed.

Josephina shrugged. "Try again later if you want."

Kiara, crestfallen, sat by herself, and stared across the playground.

The girls playing double Dutch leveled up with two girls jumping in simultaneously.

Kiara felt an empty spot in her stomach. She didn't have a place and it was her fault. She didn't have rhythm for the ropes or calluses for the bars.

She ate lunch by herself then searched for Cole. He was in the field playing flag football.

The boys didn't invite her to play like the girls did, so she summoned the courage to ask if she could play. No one gave her a second glance, too absorbed in their catching, throwing, and running to hear her.

She waved at Cole. He didn't notice. When the guys took a break to get some water from the drinking fountains, she waved at Cole again and this time, he waved back.

"Is it hard to play?" Kiara jogged over to him.

"Not if you can throw," Cole said. "Here."

He tossed her the football. It bounced right through her open arms. He laughed, told her to keep her eye on the ball, and tossed it again. She flinched and closed her eyes. It was no use.

"Toss it back," he said.

She tried. It bounced off the ground a few feet away.

"You toss like a girl."

"Yeah, well, how am I going to learn if no one teaches me? And what's that supposed to mean?"

"Can you run?" Cole asked.

She raced him a couple yards down. Being smaller and shorter than the others had a benefit: she could run fast. She was out of breath.

When the guys started another game, Cole told them Kiara would play one time. Some grumbled but Cole said if a girl asked to play, she should get to try.

Cole passed her the ball. She ran and swerved around people and sprinted across the field. She did pretty well, they all agreed, even though she had run the touchdown in the wrong direction.

Panting for air after a few other attempts, she thanked Cole for getting her in the game and returned to the shade by the playground.

Eventually, three girls approached Kiara. The most self-assured of the group, Stephanie had dark blonde hair, wore silver hoop earrings, and had a penchant for raising an eyebrow and aggressively crossing her arms whenever she made a point.

Next to her, Jessica had an infectious giggle, narrow shoulders, and golden curls that cascaded halfway down her back.

Heidi, petite with a voice that conveyed a calm confidence, had delicate features, long eyelashes, and beautiful auburn hair. The trio told Kiara that they liked her hair, which was down her mid-back, and complimented her dirty blonde highlights—whatever that meant.

They said they loved Kiara's eyes even though Jessica's were a deeper blue. Stephanie had brown eyes she called hazel, and Heidi's were a mixture between blue and green and she called hers hazel, too, so Kiara had no idea what the term meant.

"Dang, you're so pale." Stephanie pointed at Kiara's legs.

Puzzled, Kiara glanced down.

"Yeah, look." Heidi held her arm alongside Kiara's arm. Jessica did the same.

"You need a tan," Stephanie said.

They spoke with an attitude that didn't sound as friendly as the other groups of girls. Despite that, Kiara was happy to tag along, because they had come up to her when she had no other good option.

Stephanie proceeded to the pullup bars. It was hot, so Kiara wasn't sure why they all had sweatshirts. The three girls each threw a sweatshirt over a pullup bar, and hoisted themselves up.

Heidi dropped back down to explain and let Kiara borrow her sweatshirt.

"Put your hands on both sides of the bar, not on the sweater or you'll fall on your face," Stephanie said. "Swing one of your legs over the bar and bend your knee over the sweater. That's what the sweater is for, so you don't rip off your skin." She jumped up and demonstrated.

They may as well have been explaining how babies were made, because it was confusing. The three girls each sat atop their own pullup bar holding on, with one leg hooked over the top, and the other leg hanging down behind.

"They're called cherry pickers," Stephanie said. "Tuck your arms under the bar and wrap them around your knee to lock in place and hold on. Fingers together. Then get yourself going."

On cue, the other two followed suit. They tucked their bodies tight to their knees like cannonballing into a pool and spun rotations around the bar.

Kiara stared in awe of their gymnastics. She could barely do a summersault. A cartwheel? No. Flipping around a bar? Impossible.

Kiara hung out with the girls for recess. It was obvious she couldn't master swinging around a pullup bar. She did a single rotation, hardly worth the additional blisters.

"Well, if you can't do this, are you going to run back over to do double Dutch?" Stephanie asked. It wasn't in a nice way.

"What do you mean?" Kiara asked.

"She meant, do you wish you were Double-Dutching instead with *them*?" Jessica's tone was something ugly that Kiara didn't like.

All three girls laughed and jumped down.

"Come on." Heidi motioned. "We're messing with you. You can still hang with us."

Kiara, deep in her heart, knew she didn't like them, and she didn't trust them.

Still, she was tired of being alone.

So, she followed them off the playground and they said she could be *their* friend.

Even if they were no better than the quartz in Kiara's rock collection, the sparkle of their friendship was alluring.

13

Eruption

KIARA'S NEW SCHOOL DIDN'T HAVE A LIBRARY. She was beyond disappointed, until a Bookmobile—*hope on wheels* as Kiara called it—showed up at school. Kiara overheard teachers say that merciful people at the library in town sent books to spare the Lake LA kids from vices—whatever that meant. The Bookmobile returned every other week.

Kiara eagerly anticipated the days when the white vehicle—perhaps the carved-out shell had housed a food truck in its previous life—drifted into her dusty school parking lot. Stepping through the hanging flaps of thick, yellowed plastic thrilled her. When the air conditioning hit her face, she smelled the damp and dank glory of books, old and new.

A lady with short bobbed hair, glasses resting precariously at the end of her nose, reminded all of the kids, "You can only check out two."

The shelves built into both sides of the Bookmobile were mostly bare, sparse books tied down with bungee cords. Kiara eyed four books of her new favorite series, *The Babysitters Club*.

The lady smiled. "I brought them for you. And, yes, you can check out all four."

Kiara wished she could get more. Unlike most of her classmates, she read everything she checked out. Kiara stepped off the truck with her four books. She was frustrated that she'd have to wait two Tuesdays for the Bookmobile to return to her school—the school without a library, the school on wheels.

Stephanie, Jessica, and Heidi each exited with a single book—the minimum their teacher required they check out.

"What's all that?" Stephanie pointed to the stack in Kiara's arms. "How come they let you check out four?"

Kiara wasn't sure how to respond. Would they make fun of her for reading?

"Let me see." Jessica leaned closer.

"*The Babysitters Club*," Kiara said. "I think it'd be a good way to make money."

"Oh," Heidi said, "My cousin makes money babysitting. That's cool. Maybe with the extra money, you can buy better clothes."

That stung.

Kiara and her new friends—the *three witches* as she and Cole secretly nicknamed them—hung out during lunch recess and gossiped about other girls, especially the social outcasts who loosely gathered together.

Stephanie, the ringleader, remarked how these *other* girls were nerds who couldn't even match their clothes. Jessica nodded and laughed.

"Right?" Heidi said. "Look what a tangled mess their hair is."

"They're so ugly." Stephanie raised an eyebrow. "I'm sure the boys would agree." She smirked. "Should we ask them?"

"That's messed up," Kiara said. Her stomach sank. Why did she open her big mouth?

"Oh really?" Stephanie asked. She pointed down at Kiara's feet and scoffed. "Do your socks even match? Oh my God, are you wearing one pink sock and one white sock?"

Jessica and Heidi snickered.

Kiara blushed. She had made herself a target. They were right. She had to do her own laundry and forgot to separate the whites from the colors and one of her white socks got tinted pink. She laughed at herself to get them to change topics.

Kiara hadn't paid much attention to socks or shoes before. She realized her friends each wore two pairs of socks, one color layered atop the other, scrunched down, with their jeans tucked inside their socks.

While Kiara had scuffed up sneakers, the other girls wore fancy new ones, Reeboks and L.A. Gear. Shoes were expensive. Her mom couldn't afford another pair.

Cutting through the desert field on the way home, Tom ten steps behind her, Kiara kicked rocks with her already dirty shoes, which created a cloud of dust around them. She cussed the whole way, using the worst words in every way possible.

Getting picked on felt terrible. She stared at her white sock and her pink sock. How could she be so stupid as to not check to see if they matched? She shuffled her feet to kick up more dirt.

"Stop," Tom said. "You're getting dirt in my face."

"Then don't walk so close to me."

Tom scowled. He lingered a few steps back.

By the time Kiara got home, neither of her socks were white or pink. Good.

After taking a bath, Kiara wiped down the ring of grime in the bathtub and went to her room, opened her dresser drawer, and dumped all of her socks on the floor. She put the white pairs back in, and set aside the unmatched socks, the ones that had turned pinkish or bluish.

While Tom took his bath, her grandma watched TV, and her mom locked herself in her room, Kiara took a pair of scissors and jabbed holes in the tainted socks, over and over again. She pulled out threads and piled the socks in the corner to justify why she needed new ones.

She resolved to separate her whites and colors next time she did her laundry.

The next morning, she inspected Tom's feet before they left for school. One sock was longer than the other. She ground her teeth. She wasn't going to let anyone make fun of Tom.

"Go change your socks," Kiara told him.

"Why?" Tom lifted up his backpack.

"Because they don't match."

"Whatever. It's fine."

"It's not fine. That's so embarrassing. Go change." She blocked the front door.

"Stop being bossy. No one cares about my socks." Tom stormed to his room. He emerged with matching socks.

They barely made it to school on time. By the time they did, Kiara's white socks were streaked with dirt at the creases where she scrunched them down. It was okay, because neither one was pink.

Kiara sat in her living room groaning audibly while her grandma watched one of her soaps, *Days of Our Lives,* on TV.

"Can we please watch something else?" Kiara asked. "I'll give you a back rub."

Her grandma grunted. "Don't you have homework or something to work on?"

"I have a science project on volcanoes, but I have to wait for the Bookmobile to bring me the books I need." She couldn't use their encyclopedias at home; her mom ran out of money before Encyclopedia Britannica could send the last few volumes, which included the letter V.

"Don't you have clothes in the dryer?" her grandma asked. "Go put those away. While you're at it, do your grandma a favor and put mine in the wash."

Kiara moped as she filled the machine with clothes. Her mom said her grandma moved in to help. Kiara was taking care of her grandma, rather than the other way around, which is not what her mom had intended.

On the next Bookmobile Day, Kiara checked out books for her project. She wrote her report in neat cursive. That should get her a decent enough grade.

She read how to make a paper mâché volcano and simulate an eruption using baking soda, vinegar, and food coloring. Even the *three witches* at school would be impressed. Instead of being made fun of, she could be admired for being cool.

Ms. Lawrence said Kiara could show it explode—not a real explosion of course.

Kiara wrote a list of what she needed and handed it to her mom who agreed to help her make the model. They gathered old newspapers from the stack near the fireplace, and a thick telephone book, one with both the Yellow and White Pages.

Next-door neighbors on one side had chickens, and neighbors on the other side had what appeared to be a developing junkyard, so getting chicken wire and plywood wasn't difficult.

Kiara and her mom retreated into the garage, which was so full of her grandma's stuff you practically had to climb over everything by hanging from the rafters like a monkey.

Kiara mixed flour and water in a bucket. She reached for the chicken wire.

"Stand back," her mom said. "It's sharp. I'll do it."

Kiara observed the mountain take shape. "Maybe a little lower on the right?"

Her mom adjusted it. She stepped back and frowned. "Now it's crooked. It was fine the way I had it the first time."

Kiara didn't agree. Her stomach tightened at the criticism.

"I'll put the can in the middle," Kiara said. After their lunch, she had washed the Spaghetti-O's can—the real deal, a special treat! —and tore off the label.

"Give it to me before you mess it up." Her mom grabbed the can from her hands.

Kiara ground her teeth. She dunked a strip of paper in the paste until it was sopping wet, and pulled it through her fingers to wipe away the extra goop. She laid it across the wire mountain.

"That's got too much paste," her mom said. "It's never going to dry. I'll fix it."

When the model was done, rather than feel accomplished, Kiara felt awful, same as when her mom flaked on playing board games.

"Can I paint it now?" Kiara asked.

"How on Earth would you do that when it's wet?" Her mom put her hands on her hips and rolled her eyes. "Well?"

Kiara wished she could hide in her bed under her blankets. "Maybe you should do the whole thing by yourself."

"So, now you're being ungrateful?" Her mom raised her voice. "After all the work I've done?" While she spoke, her eyes flashed with anger. She might be seconds away from flinging the entire project across the garage. "And here you are—"

"Mom, no, wait, I'm sorry." Kiara wasn't sorry. "I appreciate your help, Mom." She planted her best fake smile across her face. "Hug?" She opened her arms wide.

Her mom relaxed. "Not with paste all over your hands."

Crisis averted. Her mom set the model outside. The desert sun took care of the drying.

"Now you can paint," her mom said. "No one will know if you mess up."

Her mom arranged to go in to work late. She brought the model to school and sat in the back of the classroom while Kiara presented her report.

Kiara mixed the baking soda and vinegar in the soup can. The kids gathered and waited. A cloudy mixture bubbled up and slid down the sides of the volcano like fog. The kids cheered. Ms. Lawrence was impressed.

It had worked even better than Kiara had hoped. She figured her cool factor had jumped. Her friends would brag about her to everyone. She smiled at the class.

Before her mom left with the model, she whispered, "See? Didn't I say it would work?"

Kiara's stomach tightened. The volcano had been *her* idea, not her mom's. Couldn't she get credit for something? It didn't matter though. Kiara had achieved social status success. She collected her report, double the length of anyone else's. Ms. Lawrence had written 'A+ Super!' across the top. Kiara headed back to her desk.

When she walked past her friends, Stephanie snickered and said, "Little miss showoff thinks she's better than us," loud enough for her to hear.

Kiara's cheeks reddened. She slunk down in her seat and glanced over at Cole. His earthquake model consisted of brown grocery paper bags taped over a shoe box. He had drawn jagged lines across the top with a black marker.

Cole beamed with pride and gave her a thumbs up.

The *three witches* giggled and sneered back at Kiara.

Kiara kept her head down and slunk deeper into her seat.

While walking Tom home from school, Kiara wondered why she didn't fit in. What was she doing wrong? She wasn't *trying* to show off.

Her foot caught on a rock. She stumbled head first into a tumbleweed. Thistles scratched at her arms and face. She brushed herself off, picked up her books, and reached for her volcano report, now covered in a layer of dirt.

She rolled up the report and smashed it against the rock over and over again.

"What are you doing?" Tom stopped her. "What's your problem?"

"Having to walk you home is my problem. Go away, Tommy!" she screamed.

He took off running.

Kiara ripped up her report and shoved the pieces into the bottom of her backpack.

What would happen if she stopped trying? Would anyone even notice?

14

Trouble

AFTER THAT DAY, KIARA STOPPED checking out books from the Bookmobile. She stopped raising her hand in class to volunteer answers. Why make herself a target?

Ms. Lawrence kept looking in her direction and eventually called on her after getting frustrated that the previous five students couldn't answer correctly.

"Kiara, what is photosynthesis?" Ms. Lawrence asked.

"I don't know." Kiara shrugged. Plants need sunlight to synthesize food from carbon dioxide and water, but why did it matter if *she* gave the answer?

Ms. Lawrence glared at her with suspicion. She let it go and called on Cole instead.

"Chlorophyll," Cole said, "which is the reason plants are green, absorbs light which provides the energy…"

Kiara glanced at Stephanie and rolled her eyes. Stephanie smirked back.

Kiara felt guilty. She stared at the ceiling and wished she were somewhere else.

At recess, Stephanie led the group to the pullup bars. Kiara stood in the shade. Heidi and Jessica encouraged her to try.

What did she have to lose? Surprisingly, she mounted the high bar on the first try.

Kiara sat atop straddling the bar, satisfied to stay put.

"You're already up there," Jessica said. "You might as well do cherry pickers."

"Here," Heidi said, "I'll count." She moved to get a better vantage point to verify the rotations. "Okay, go."

Well, why not try? Kiara tucked her arms under the bar and around her shins. She held on tight and swung her body forward to get the momentum to do another turn, then another one. Each time, her ponytail whipped around after her.

"3... 4... 5..." Heidi counted.

After the fifth time, Kiara felt queasy. Her leg throbbed from rubbing against the bar, so she stopped.

"Why'd you stop?" Stephanie asked. "You were actually doing it right."

Kiara's couldn't focus with the world spinning. She had gone faster than she had ever seen the others go. Her stomach was so unsettled, she feared she'd lose her lunch.

The bell rang for them to go to class. Kiara peered down at the ground, which made her dizzy. Stephanie, Heidi, and Jessica stood to leave.

"Wait," Kiara yelled. "I don't feel so good."

It didn't help that it had been another triple-digit day.

Stephanie rolled her eyes. "I don't feel so good," she mocked. Her posse laughed as if this was the funniest joke ever.

Kiara might puke. Her arms shook. Maybe she'd fall and hit her head. Her muscles weakened. She screamed to her friends who stopped and huddled.

Stephanie glanced back at Kiara and said, "Wait there. We'll get someone."

The three witches ran to class. At least help would come fast.

A minute went by and no one came. Kiara gripped the bar. Her leg cramped and her muscles turned to jelly. The sun bore down on her.

The playground cleared out and maybe because of her small size—or maybe an oversight—the yard ladies had left the yard.

Still perched on top of the bar, Kiara's center of gravity caused her to roll forward until she was hanging upside down. The ground got closer and farther and closer and farther. Her head pounded. Noises faded. The bright day dimmed.

No one came. If Kiara didn't get down soon, gravity was going to pull her down. With shaky arms, sweaty skin, and achy legs, Kiara, as best as she could, unlatched her stiff leg. She half jumped and half fell off the bar onto the hard, hot sand. She didn't land on her head. She landed on her side, back, elbow, and knee. Like a gut punch, it knocked the wind out of her.

The sky shook; her vision wasn't right. It was nauseating.

Kiara pushed off from the ground to sit up. She leaned against the hot metal sides of the playground to catch her breath. She scanned the area where her friends had gone. It was quiet, other than the flag's metal rivets clanking against the flagpole as the flag whipped in the breeze.

She doubted the witches had gotten help. She'd be more surprised if they had.

Dizziness and nausea overtook her. How would she make it back to class? She wished she had someone to lean on, to carry her back into the air-conditioning.

Hot wind flung dirt across the ground. Her skin stung when the sand smacked her legs, arms, and face. The sun blinded her. Although hot, she stopped sweating. Her throat parched.

Didn't anybody wonder where she was? Wasn't someone going to search for her?

She couldn't stay out there forever in the heat.

The shaky vision passed, but the lightheadedness did not. She gripped a scorching metal bar to pull herself up. Her class was too far. She needed water.

Focus on the ground, not the sky, she repeated, until she made it to the bathroom. Inside, she held her wrists under the cold stream of water until her blood cooled. She bent over, turned her head sideways, and drank gulps, the rest splashing in her face, a welcome respite.

Grits of sand had dried into the blood on her knees and arms. She soaked a brown paper towel in water and diluted pink powder soap, and dabbed at her stinging wounds until the skin around her injuries was haloed white with a ring of dirt. She examined herself in the mirror. Her hair was messy, her cheeks streaked with tears. She washed her face. Her hair was hopeless.

Her reflection reminded her of that day when Tommy got hit by the baseball, when the bitchy girls at Alpine teased her. Her *friends* weren't any better. *Fuck them.*

Kiara headed to class. When she entered, everyone stared at her but remained silent until Stephanie, Heidi, and Jessica—her *friends*—pointed and laughed. The others followed suit.

Ms. Lawrence didn't find it funny at all. "So, you thought you'd get some extra time at the playground, young lady?"

Kiara held back tears. She shook her head. Luckily her hair was so messy, it hid her eyes.

Stephanie blurted out, "We tried to get her to come back in, but she wouldn't."

"Is that right?" Ms. Lawrence said. "You've been acting out quite a bit lately. Guess you'll be staying after class with me."

The kids' eyes all widened—the-glad-it's-not-me expression. An "ooooh" refrained around the room. Stephanie had thrown her under the bus. Kiara watched as the girl, with her head held high, haughtily shared an invisible high-five with Heidi and Jessica.

These weren't three witches. They were three bitches.

15

Deceived

OVER THE NEXT FEW WEEKS, Kiara spent recess outside in the shadow of a trailer, sketching by herself. The pencil and pad kept her company. She observed trains of clouds drift across the sky while her paper flapped in the wind.

Heidi and Jessica approached. Kiara focused intently on outlining a winding road that disappeared into the horizon.

Jessica cleared her throat. "Stephanie didn't mean it. She says things she doesn't mean."

"You guys are messed up." Kiara added a fence alongside her road. "Go away."

"We were just kidding." Heidi flipped her auburn hair. "Can't you take a joke? We told you Stephanie is sorry."

"We miss hanging out," Jessica said.

Despite the sting of bitter betrayal, Kiara figured she should forgive them, because that's what had been drilled into her. Forgive. While not one of the Ten Commandments, she figured it must fall under the Golden Rule: "Do unto others as you would have them do unto you." Then again, Kiara wouldn't have done half the mean things they did. Why didn't the rule work both ways?

"Fine." Kiara closed her notebook and followed them back. Stephanie was nicer. Nobody brought up the incident.

Kiara figured if there was a God, she had racked up a few points by forgiving them. Perhaps she'd have enough to get out of the burning purgatory her grandma kept threatening.

The more her grandma read her religious stories, the more preoccupied Kiara became with heaven and hell—how to get into the former and avoid the latter. Mary and Jesus paintings and religious statuettes assumed prominent positions in the house.

One night, after reading a scary book, Kiara got up to use the restroom. With her eyes half shut, she bumped into the wall and opened them to find a bloody picture of a crucified Jesus.

"Jesus Christ!" she screamed. She covered her mouth.

Her mom rushed out to yell at her for cussing. Kiara pointed to Jesus, so she got away with it that time. She figured she'd tell the priest in confession—she had used the "Lord's name in vain," which was supposedly terrible. If it was so bad, why did it relieve frustration, hurt, and anger? Was it said to be "in vain" if it served a purpose? Seemed right to her, so no confession needed.

Kiara's grandma made them attend church every Sunday morning. Her mom drove them up to the Catholic church in Palmdale. The church, built of wood and stone, had stained glass windows, an upstairs choir room, private booths for confession, and many rows of pews with padded kneelers for use during the prayers. Kiara missed her dad every time they had to kneel.

After church, the parish hall hosted breakfast, where Kiara first tried O'Brien potatoes, tasty little squares of potatoes with diced onions and peppers. Unlike the donut station that had a donation box nearby, or the donation baskets they passed around during Mass, the breakfast price wasn't optional. Kiara's mom only let them buy it once.

It didn't take long until her mom and grandma fought about going to church. Kiara and Tom were watching reruns of *Gilligan's Island* when the yelling started.

"We can't afford the gas to drive up to town every Sunday," her mom said.

"What am I giving you money for?" her grandma said.

"To pay the bills, so we can keep the house."

Her grandma raised her voice. "If I can't have a daughter who follows the faith, at least I can have grandkids who do."

"What's that supposed to mean? I've always gone to church and—"

"Until your shameful situation—"

"This has nothing to do with that!" her mom screamed.

Everything went quiet for a moment.

Her grandma cleared her throat. "Then we go to church. Pray on it."

"How's that going to help if we can't afford the gas to get there?"

"Then find something closer." Her grandma ended the conversation, went to her room, and slammed the door shut.

Kiara's mom found a closer church, halfway between Palmdale and Lake LA. Services were held in a stone building, perhaps a poorly designed house or bomb shelter in its former life. The large dark room had no windows and a tile floor covered with a layer of dust.

They used battered metal folding chairs, no pews. There wasn't a parish hall that served breakfast and they offered stale two-day old donuts, for a donation of course. Mass was in Spanish. Kiara got used to saying her prayers "*Padre Nuestro*" and "*Ave Maria*" in Spanish.

Her mom said the gas still cost too much money, so they stopped going.

Her grandma put up a fight. Kiara didn't care. She was happy to sleep in on Sundays.

Her joy didn't last long. Her mom made an announcement over dinner.

"Good news," her mom said. "They're offering 7:30 AM services in the cafeteria trailer at your school. That's much more convenient. Isn't that great?"

No. Nothing about that was great. Not the waking up early part. Not spending more time in a school trailer. And definitely not hanging out with kids she didn't know singing the kind of songs that would get you beat up at school. She already had enough trouble making friends. She didn't need to lose the few questionable ones she had. Kiara hoped nobody would find out.

Sunshine and heat hit early that spring. By May, Stephanie and their posse gave up on the metal playground bars and instead sat and discussed clothes and hair and boys, none of which meant much to Kiara. Still, she appreciated not being alone.

Stephanie had permed her blonde hair and Jessica and Heidi said they would, too. They debated how to tease out their bangs with Aqua Net hairspray and curling irons. They told Kiara they wished their hair was as healthy as hers.

Finally, a compliment. Kiara could get used to that.

The school nurse called kids up to the office for hearing and vision tests. The nurse told Kiara she was as blind as a bat. She couldn't understand how Kiara wasn't failing school on account of not being able to see the board at all.

Kiara had been squinting for a while now. She begged the nurse not to call home. How was her mom going to afford glasses? Plus, she didn't want to be called four-eyes. The nurse called anyway.

Her mom took her to her first eye doctor appointment. Sure enough, the optometrist prescribed glasses. Her mom said their insurance would cover it. The only catch was that Kiara had to pick out a frame from a very limited section of the store.

There were no frames for a small face, so Kiara ended up with a thick pair of maroon ones that blocked out her pretty eyes, and her eyebrows, and half her cheek bones, too.

She hadn't realized how bad her vision was because it had happened so gradually. When she stepped outside the doctor's office, she stared up at the trees. She had never noticed so many leaves, each dancing individually in the wind, their edges in sharp detail.

The sidewalk was clear, not blurry, and faces, too. A new world opened to her. She was amazed by every part of it—until she got home and met her reflection in the mirror. She was more four-eyed than the kids in class who wore glasses—the ones the three witches made fun of. The longer she stared at herself, the more hideous she became.

She couldn't go to school looking like this. She'd rather be blind.

Her mom seemed to sense the darkening of her mood.

"Do you want to get your hair permed?" her mom asked.

Kiara's eyes widened. "Yes, but that's too expensive." She had never gotten her hair done—her mom trimmed her bangs and the ends, and used an electric clipper on Tom's hair.

"Not to a fancy salon," her mom said. "Mrs. Helvan said she can do perms."

Kiara was skeptical, but agreed to try. She was in shock—she was going to get a real, professional perm. She spent hours flipping through magazines to study the spiral perms that Madonna, Brooke Shields, and Farrah Fawcett all had. And with Kiara's hair falling to the small of her back, she imagined how gorgeous her hair would look. Maybe they wouldn't ridicule her glasses if she had a tight spiral perm.

Tom wasn't interested in the field trip across the street, so he went to stay the night with one of his many friends. Kiara's grandma was praying the rosary at someone's house.

When her mom said it was time to head over, Kiara brought a magazine with her to point out the pictures. Mrs. Helvan sat Kiara on a chair in the kitchen. She wrapped a towel around her shoulders and laid newspaper on the floor. She said, yes, she could give Kiara that style.

It took forever. Mrs. Helvan said it was turning out great. After perming Kiara's hair, she gave her a trim. Then she trimmed a little bit more to make it even. Not too much, Kiara asked softly; she didn't want to sound demanding because she was pretty sure the neighbor wasn't charging them much.

The curls would shorten her hair, but Kiara was hoping the ends would still reach her mid-back. She shifted in the chair. Clips of curls fluttered to the ground. She got excited.

More snip-snips of the scissors and more clips of hair spread out onto the floor. Kiara asked for a mirror. The two women were oohing and aahing and telling her not to worry, they didn't want her to peek until it was done, and that it was almost perfect.

Why so much hair on the floor? Kiara silently willed them to stop cutting.

Her mom had threatened her to be polite. Kiara folded her hands in her lap, and listened to the snips and watched the curls float down. She imagined her beautiful new hairstyle.

Finally, Mrs. Helvan finished and handed Kiara a mirror, and her glasses so she could see. Her long hair was gone. Completely gone.

The reflection was Orphan Annie—a character Kiara detested. She couldn't quite explain her uncomfortable hatred for Annie's short frizzy hair.

Her mom and the neighbor were all smiles and Mom said she looked adorable.

Kiara gasped.

Mrs. Helvan told Kiara to use a special comb called a hair pick and not to use a regular brush or the curls would come out.

Her mom made her say thanks, which she did, then Kiara ran home across the street. Tears streamed down her cheeks. Her chest heaved.

Her mom's bathroom had a big mirror. She grabbed a brush, and pulled on the curls, hoping they'd get longer with each stroke. It was no use. She was ruined. Ruined forever.

Her mom came home a little bit later, proudly, and confirmed it was her idea to cut Kiara's hair to copy Orphan Annie's, because she believed Annie was the cutest little girl.

Kiara didn't want to make her mad so she wiped her tears away, which her mom didn't see, and pretended it was okay. Ultimately, she couldn't.

She burst out into dry heaving sobs and screamed, "I'm ugly. I hate it! My life is ruined."

Her mom's eyes widened and her jaw stiffened. "Get out of my room and go to bed, you horrible, ungrateful, little brat."

Kiara ran out, threw her glasses across her bedroom, and flung herself onto her bed. She soaked her sheets with tears, pounded her fists into the bed, and screamed into her pillow.

Kiara didn't get dinner that night and she didn't care because she wasn't hungry at all.

The next day, she tried to be sick—truth was she felt sick—but her mom made her go to school. She couldn't get out of it.

Kiara hid behind the trailers. When the bell rang, she had no choice. She rounded the corner. The kids had lined up for class. Everybody saw. A few gasped wide-eyed. Kiara kept her head down as she passed by the row.

"Wow."

"Is that Kiara?"

"What happened to her hair?"

Most kids stayed quiet and kept their opinions to themselves, which was kinder than she expected.

Then the three witches gasped. Kiara peered at them. Their faces twisted at her grotesque appearance. They laughed until they cried.

Kiara's lower lip quivered. She balled up her fists.

"Oh my God," Stephanie said. "Someone got hit with an ugly stick."

"No way I'd be caught dead around her," Jessica said.

"Why would she do that to herself?" Heidi said. "And glasses, too?"

Kiara got to the end of the line, behind Cole. She stood a few feet back. She stared intently at her sneakers with their frayed laces and tried her best not to cry.

"Hey, Kiara," Cole said softly. "Now your hair is curly like mine. We match."

One of the guys in front of him said, "Dude, she looks weird."

Kiara's stomach tightened. Maybe she'd throw up and get to go home.

"Knock it off," Cole said. He turned back to her. "Don't listen to them."

Kiara crossed her arms. "It's fine. Just leave me alone. I don't want to be friends with you, either."

"What did I do to you?" Cole said.

"You're not standing up for me."

He lowered his voice and leaned closer to her. "What do you want me to do?"

"Leave me alone. Go away."

Cole stood with his mouth open. "You don't mean that."

"You heard me," she said. "You're not my friend anymore. I don't need you."

She narrowed her eyes at him, huffed, and ran off.

After that, Cole was polite but kept his distance.

When he did try to approach her, Kiara turned the other way and hurried off. She couldn't stand the sadness in his eyes, so she avoided his gaze.

Kiara hated herself for pushing him away. She was too proud to tell him. Maybe she deserved to be alone after that. Plus, it's not as if he *really* defended her. He probably felt the same as the rest of them.

Kiara's heart stung worse than ever before—worse than when her mom ignored her, worse than when her grandma was mean to her, and worse than when her dad took Skittles and disappeared. Kiara felt awful and empty and so completely alone.

16

The Outsider

THICK GLASSES AND SHORT, CURLY HAIR: social exclusion wrapped up all nice and neat. On top of her banishment from schoolyard society, Kiara didn't have an easy last month of school.

Her mom got more involved in the school and the community. With her bookkeeping background, her mom ran for PTA treasurer—unopposed—and accepted the position, which meant a mess of boxes and papers piled in her bedroom. Then when no one ran for PTA president, she took that job instead. Kiara pleaded with her not to.

She became known not as Kiara's mom, but as Ms. Marcy Leneghan, PTA President and community volunteer, friendly all-American single mom.

During lunch, one of the lunch ladies stopped Kiara at the cash register. Kiara froze. What if she wasn't getting free lunches anymore? How was she going to pay for everything on her tray? She'd give it back and run out of the cafeteria.

"Hello," the woman with the hairnet said. "Aren't you Marcy Leneghan's daughter?"

Kiara exhaled and nodded.

"Tell her I said 'hi.'"

Same thing happened when Kiara passed the crossing guard, and the secretary in the front office, and the yard lady with greasy hair. "Tell Marcy I said hi."

It happened overnight: Kiara lost her identity.

She was no longer Kiara; no, now she was Marcy Leneghan's daughter. In this way, Kiara lost her name, too. She became invisible and yet had a spotlight on her all the same.

She was relieved when the school year ended.

The neighbors got to know Marcy and she got to know them, especially the new ones who she introduced herself to, and she made some friends for Kiara. That's how Kiara, Ms. Marcy Leneghan's daughter, met Melissa and her family who moved in around the corner. Kiara's mom had sold them their house.

They moved in next to one of the only older houses in the neighborhood with towering trees—somehow planted decades before. Melissa's family planted grass, actual grass, in the front yard, probably able to survive because of the tree shade and the rotating sprinkler they attached to the hose, which the neighborhood kids, those lucky enough to be invited over, ran through.

Melissa was a year older and a grade ahead of Kiara. She had gone to a private Christian elementary school which didn't go past fifth grade, so she was going to start sixth grade at Lake LA School.

Kiara hid behind her mom when she got introduced, intimidated by Melissa's poofy spiral permed hair—the style Kiara wanted, except much longer—perfectly teased bangs, trendy outfits, poise and confidence. Her room was spotless. She had a white wooden bedroom set, her flowered bedspread was pulled taut, and dirty clothes tucked into a wicker hamper, unlike the floor pile at Kiara's house. In her bedroom, she had her own telephone with a clear plastic case that showcased the pink, blue, green, and yellow components inside.

Kiara's mom and Melissa's mom said the girls could go over to each other's houses and play whenever they wanted as long as they said where they were going and returned before dark.

"It's wonderful how close we live to each other," Melissa said.

"Do you want to come over to play at my place?" Kiara said.

"I'd rather we play here. We can listen to music and sing." Her brown eyes smiled.

With houses around the corner from each other, Kiara hopped over two fences, when that in-between neighbor wasn't home, and cut through a ditch to make it there faster. Melissa's mom loved having Kiara over, because she was so polite, saying please and thank you.

Kiara was relieved by this warm welcome and that they had Oreo cookies stocked in the kitchen and cold milk to dip them in. They had chips and snacks Kiara didn't have at home, including Twinkies and foil-wrapped Ding Dongs.

One summer afternoon, Melissa and her mom handed Kiara two knitting needles and some colorful yarn. They demonstrated how to knit a pot holder. It was tougher than it seemed. Kiara kept having to pull the yarn back out when she messed up. Hers came out crooked.

Melissa's mom stayed home to take care of Melissa and the house; her dad was an aerospace engineer for Boeing, Northrop Grumman, the manufacturer of the black triangle B-2 Bomber which boomed whenever it broke the sound barrier. He explained to Kiara that other engineers out there worked for Rockwell who built the Space Shuttles (Kiara cringed), or for Lockheed-Martin and Skunk Works who built top-secret aircraft test-flown overhead.

Melissa's dad said some other dads, and a few moms, too, had top security clearances for NASA and worked out at Edwards Air Force Base, too. He wasn't one of them. Those were the highly-educated families and Kiara figured that's why Melissa's family had more stuff. They didn't treat Kiara, in her raggedy, worn-out clothes any differently.

Melissa's mom offered Melissa's hand-me-downs to Kiara who, much like her mom, didn't want charity. Embarrassed, Kiara thanked them and accepted the clothes. She tried them on at home and realized that she didn't mind wearing them.

They had a new Nintendo video game system with Mario Bros. Kiara loved playing even though her character kept dying from everything—falling off cliffs or clouds, getting destroyed by the Venus flytraps in the green pipes, drowning and ricocheting turtle shells. She spent more time dying than moving across the screen. Melissa got tired of Nintendo, which was fine because Kiara's thumbs and fingers throbbed from pushing buttons on the controller.

Kiara proposed they play with Barbies. Melissa declined. She jumped on her bed, handed Kiara a hairbrush "microphone" and blasted Madonna, Debbie Gibson, Tiffany, and Cindy Lauper. Without a stereo of her own, Kiara didn't know many lyrics, so she faked it.

Halfway through the summer, Melissa's mom invited Kiara to a big sleepover party Melissa was having for her birthday. Strange that Melissa didn't mention it.

When Kiara went over the next time, Melissa led her into her bedroom.

"Hey," Kiara said. "Your mom said you're having a birthday sleepover. She said it was going to be a big backyard campout."

Melissa's jaw dropped.

"Did you forget to tell me?" Kiara asked.

"No," Melissa said. "She wasn't supposed to tell you. You wouldn't know anyone. They're all older than you. I thought you'd be bored and didn't want you to be miserable."

"That's okay. I don't mind."

Melissa smiled. "You're not mad?"

"No, but can I borrow a sleeping bag? I don't have one to bring."

Melissa ground her teeth together. "You're not coming. I'm only friends with you because my mom said I had to, because she's friends with your mom. I wasn't inviting you."

"Oh." Kiara's chest heaved a little. She held back the tears. She sat there for a moment in stunned silence. "I want to go home."

Melissa didn't stop her.

Kiara walked back in the heat in silence. Great. So, she was ugly with glasses and curly hair and was a stupid, annoying embarrassment to everyone.

It was a terrible, rotten, mean thing to say. How had Melissa been okay with hanging out so much? It seemed as if she'd been having fun. Maybe Melissa was not the same

Melissa when her mom was home as she was around her friends.

And if this were true, neither of them had much in common really.

Kiara decided it best she stick to her own backyard and stop going over there, even if it meant no more Oreos and milk. It also meant no more Nintendo, or talking with Melissa's nice mom, or having a friend named Melissa, or having any girlfriends, nice or not.

17

Patches

WHEN HER MOM ASKED WHY she wasn't going over to Melissa's anymore, Kiara avoided answering. She was getting good at avoiding things. She hid in her bottom bunk and pretended to be asleep whenever her mom and grandma fought. Often, Tom wasn't home because he'd been invited to spend the night at a friend's house.

Lucky him. She was jealous that he escaped the fighting at home, had so many friends, and no longer needed her. Kiara missed having him around.

One night, while Tom was at yet another sleepover, Kiara couldn't stand the screaming. She quietly closed the door and hid under her blankets. After the screaming stopped, her mom came into Kiara's room and squatted down next to her.

"Melissa's mom said you're not visiting anymore," her mom said. "Why not?"

"Because she doesn't like me." Kiara pulled her pillow over her head. "No one does."

Her mom paused for a moment. She lifted the pillow off of Kiara's head. "Look at me."

Kiara obliged. She crossed her arms.

Her mom sighed. "Kiara, I'm sorry, sweetie. It must be frustrating."

Kiara didn't say anything. Her chest felt a little lighter.

"When I was your age," her mom said, "I didn't have friends, either. I was always so busy raising my brothers. It's hurtful not having girlfriends."

Kiara blinked back tears. Was her mom actually opening up to her?

Kiara's mom reached over to brush Kiara's hair from her face. "I've been thinking that it might be nice if we do more things together as a family. Would you like that?"

Kiara nodded, too emotional to speak. If she opened her mouth, she might cry.

"How about this?" her mom said. "Until I buy what I'm going to buy, which is a surprise, I'll bring home stuff for you and Tom to play with outside."

Kiara shook her head, confused. "What? Why? It's too hot outside."

"I'm tired of the fighting. Your grandma says you're both too loud in the house and, regardless of how hot it is, that kids should play outside during the day."

"And you agree with that?" Kiara looked up, wide-eyed.

Her mom didn't answer. She sighed and left the room. This time, instead of slamming her bedroom door shut, her mom closed it quietly. Even with two closed doors and a hallway between them, Kiara heard her mom crying, big, ugly sobs.

In mid-summer, someone broke into Kiara's house, or rather, opened up their front door—no one locked front doors out there, except maybe at night. The thief stole her grandma's purse. They found the purse and a trail of debris along the street, including her empty wallet—she had a couple dollars that weren't there anymore. No one was caught.

Her grandma was relieved that her driver's license and social security card were still there. A credit card was missing. "To hell with them," her grandma said. "It's over the limit." She called and cancelled the card. After that, she decided to get a dog for protection.

That's when Patches came. A huge mutt with long legs, small ears, and a short white coat with brown splotches, Patches also had the longest, sharpest teeth.

Their house, like every other tract home out in Lake LA, was set on a rectangular one-acre plot separated by chain-link fences. This meant Patches had plenty of space to run around.

Kiara's grandma grew up on a dairy farm in South Dakota, so she didn't have any real emotional attachment to animals. Patches turned ferocious, especially after her grandma rolled up a newspaper and smacked him on the nose whenever he did something she didn't like, mostly digging, which he did a lot.

After losing Skittles, Kiara always wanted another dog. She pitied Patches because he got hit with a newspaper and yelled at so much—she figured they had that in common. So, she went out to pet him. As soon as she raised her hand over his nose, he snarled and lunged at her hand. She pulled back just in time. He tackled her to the ground. She screamed.

Lucky for her, her grandma heard and came out with a newspaper raised over her head. Patches retreated. The next day, he got tied to a long metal chain attached to a stake in the ground. He lay his head down on his paws in resignation.

"Poor Patches. Mom, it's mean." Kiara examined the triple scratches on her arms and legs from his claws. "Even if he maybe deserved it."

"He's fine," her mom said. "The chain is long enough for him to reach the covered patio where his food and water is. On the leash, he can't dig as much, either."

The long chain meant two things to Kiara and Tom: one, the dog controlled the radius around the ground stake, which meant most of the yard—he could chase them down and destroy them before they could run out of his range—and two, if Patches made up his mind to go somewhere, he could jerk the chain so hard it would cut their legs or trip them if they were within the circle of death.

Owning a dog should be fun, but Patches wasn't there for fun. He terrified Kiara. When her grandma forced her and Tom outside to play, they tried to avoid his reach.

To make things worse, her grandma locked the sliding door. They had to knock to get let in. Did her mom condone this? Kiara didn't ask, because she kept getting in trouble for saying too much.

Her grandma pointed out there was a hose for them to drink out of if they got thirsty, and they shouldn't complain because the water was cold and they were lucky to have a big backyard to play in—even if the yard was nothing but rock-hard dirt with a few sad attempts at fruit trees and sprouting tumbleweeds.

Kiara and Tom created games. They collected a few quartz rocks scattered across the yard and drew hopscotch squares in the hard dirt, making straightish, but mostly squiggly lines. When the sharp edges of the rocks dug into their hands leaving bumpy indentations, that quit being fun and they moved on to something else.

At least her mom came through on her promise. One day, vehicle tires, all different sizes, some sheets of rough plywood, and a pile of red bricks appeared in the backyard. With all that, Kiara and Tom set out to make an obstacle course.

Kiara spread out the tires. Too heavy to carry, she put them on their sides and rolled them around. She had to watch out, because black rubber burned hot under the sun.

She took the bricks and made a row, longwise, to create a sort of balance beam between two tires. They were uneven though and Kiara almost twisted her ankle twice, so she separated them into two rows and placed the plywood on top.

She and Tom took turns running through the course—one foot in each tire, tiptoe across the bouncy plywood, weave in between the last couple of tires and jump over the last sheet of plywood to the finish line, drawn on the ground.

"Two points for me," Kiara said. "Two points for you. Want to go again?"

Tom fanned his red face with his hand. "It's too hot."

"Let's play with the hose. Come on. We'll make mud pies." Having Tom as a playmate rather than a wrestling opponent was a welcome change. She wanted to keep the fun going and led him back to the house. The chain rattled. Patches lunged.

"Run!" she yelled.

She and Tom darted in opposite directions until they were outside the danger zone. The chain choked Patches's neck, stopping him. He raced back and forth between them and barked.

"Now how are we going to get to the hose?" Tom asked.

"Distract him. Throw a stick. Maybe he'll fetch. I'll get to the spigot."

"Where am I going to get a stick from?"

Kiara scanned the yard. "The fruit trees."

"Mom planted those," he said. "I'm not touching them."

"Have you ever seen any fruit?" Kiara jogged to the middle of their huge lot, to the six scrawny saplings—two peach, two apple, and two pear.

That was one of her chores—water each tree until the earth stopped drinking it up and a small ring of mud remained around the trunk. It was futile. Every time she watered the next tree, the one before it dried and cracked.

A few trees had blossomed. They never bore any fruit. It was a useless chore, so she either conned Tom into helping or didn't do it every day. If her mom had put in sprinklers as she said she would, maybe the trees would have grown.

Kiara pulled off a lower branch and it snapped off with a crack. Inside it was brown—no sign of green life at all.

"Here." She handed it to Tom. "Distract him. When I get the hose, he'll leave us alone."

Tom whistled. Patches ran towards him, stopping short where he couldn't go any further with the chain tugging at his collar. Tom waved the stick around. Patches cocked his head and followed the motions.

Kiara sprinted for the hose. She was almost there when Tom screamed.

"Kiara, run," he said. "Patches ate the stick. He's coming for you."

Paws pounded the ground and the chain rattled. She focused on the spigot and pumped her legs as hard as she could. She reached the hose, but had yet to get to the spigot. His bark got closer and Patches snarled. Tom whistled, but Kiara's movements must have been more appealing because Patches kept after her.

Kiara twisted the hot metal spigot and hot water thrust through the hose. She turned around with her finger on the trigger and shot Patches, only inches from her, in the face.

Her heart pounded. She kept spraying. Patches shook his head. His ears flopped side to side, and he retreated to the shady patio.

Tom took a roundabout way to reach Kiara to avoid the ring of terror—anywhere within the monster's reach. Tom's face was bright red from the sun and pale at the same time.

"I don't want to make mud pies. It's too hot." He stumbled. "I want to go inside."

He wobbled in place; her heart fluttered in panic.

Kiara considered spraying Tom in the face. She stopped herself and handed him the hose. "Here hold this. Keep Patches away until I can get us in. Stay in the shade."

Kiara yanked at the handle of the sliding glass door. It was locked. She pounded on it. She had to protect Tom.

Earlier, her grandma told them to stay outside until lunchtime. By the growl in her stomach and the sun's place in the sky, it was clearly past lunchtime. Why wasn't she opening the door?

"Kiara," Tom said. "I don't feel good."

"Me, neither, but she's not letting us in." What were her options?

Tom was getting worse by the second. He swayed with the hose in his hand.

"Come on," she said. "We'll try the front. Spray Patches so he leaves us alone."

Tom did so. She unlatched the side gate of their chain link fence. Was Tom well enough to stand on his own two feet? She considered carrying him piggyback like when he got hit with the baseball, but he was too big now.

"Quick," she said. "Watch where you walk." She held Tom's clammy hand in hers and maneuvered around the holes that Patches had dug out along the fence. Luckily the dirt was so hard he hadn't been able to dig himself out completely.

After they were safely on the other side of the fence, Kiara turned off the nozzle, threw it down, and relatched the gate.

The front door was unlocked, so apparently her grandma hadn't learned her lesson. How did it make sense to lock the sliding door where Patches would kill any intruder, but leave the front door unlocked? Might as well hang a sign saying, "come and rob us."

Kiara led Tom inside. Cool air blew the sweat off her skin. She instantly felt better.

"Go get water while I fix us something to eat," she said.

Tom shuffled down the hallway while Kiara shut the door. Her eyes had trouble adjusting to the darkness. Her grandma was in a reclining chair with a fan blowing on her face.

"Why are you coming in the front?" her grandma asked.

"Why didn't you open the back door? I pounded."

"You listen to me young lady," her grandma scolded, taking deep breaths on account of the oxygen tube.

Kiara, hot and hungry, had had enough. "No, you listen to me—"

"Don't you dare backtalk to me. I told you and your brother to stay outside."

"Why don't *you* go outside if you think that's such a great idea?" Kiara squinted in the darkness. Now that her eyes adjusted, she saw a bowl of cherries—cherries! Those were so expensive! —and some chocolates next to her grandma. "I'm telling Mom."

"Don't use that tone of voice. I'll give you something to tell." She raised her hand threatening a spanking. "Get over here."

"No. You want me? Come get me." Kiara stood her ground.

Her grandma, heavier than her legs could handle, took her time standing up. When she did, she found a burst of energy to charge at Kiara. Tom had returned and, too shocked to say anything, jumped up on the couch to watch it all play out.

Kiara dashed to the dining room, and took a position across the long formal table next to the ornate China cabinet and hutch—another leftover from the divorce.

She glanced up at the crystal chandelier and all the Princess House crystal in the cabinet—recent purchases of her mom's, which made no sense in a house like this in the desert. Besides which, they never used the formal table to eat on, except twice a year on Christmas and Easter, and the rest of the time, the table held stacks of papers.

Kiara grabbed hold of one of the high backs of the chairs and watched her opponent on the other end. Her grandma headed right; she pivoted left. Her grandma changed directions and headed left; Kiara went right.

By this time, her grandma was red in the face and steaming mad, and swearing under her breath. Kiara would be hunted down and it wouldn't be good, so as soon as she had a clear path, she ran out the front door and down the street, around the corner, and into the fields to hide. She wasn't hungry anymore and figured she'd wait it out until her mom got home to see if her odds of survival improved.

Kiara glanced over her shoulder then settled down in a coyote trail, a ditch that wound through the fields, run down so much by kids and coyotes and bikes that it was a full three feet deep or more in some parts.

She nestled into a deep part of the trail, her back against the wall of the trench, much cooler than the dirt above. She tucked her legs, and bowed her head to catch the shade of the creosote bushes and Joshua trees above, not that there was much. God, she hated it here.

One day, she'd buy a huge house near the beach with 70-degree weather year-round. She'd plant shade trees and grass around her home and have two strawberry patches.

Maybe she'd get married, and she and her husband would have kids and raise them together. They'd get two dogs—nice dogs—and two cats.

Kiara couldn't wait. If she could, she'd run away and never return. Except for Tommy. She couldn't leave without Tommy. What if her grandma was giving him a hard time right now? Even if so, what could Kiara do? Nothing.

Kiara sat in the trench and watched the shadows shift as the sun continued its path west.

At her *old* house, Kiara had giant sunflowers with seeds she chewed on, even if they weren't tasty and she had to spit them back out. She used to help her dad water the fruit trees on the slope—those trees actually produced fruit, albeit small and bitter.

Her bedroom curtains used to billow when the window was open, the smoky scent of meat lingered in the air from the neighbor's BBQ. She used to lounge alongside the pool and dangle her feet in the cool water, even though she couldn't swim—the sound of the waterfall drowned out by her parents screaming and her baby brother crying.

What had changed? Location, family members ...

Why wish her way out of the desert? Sure, if Kiara escaped, she wouldn't be burned by the heat, but would it matter? The joy of perfect families and happy endings portrayed in Disney movies and sitcoms and books was fake. The concept of everlasting happiness—noble but impractical. Nothing would change. Misery was inevitable. Acceptance was peace.

18

Camping

WHEN KIARA'S MOM HEARD the whole story from all three witnesses, she was livid that Kiara's grandma had locked them outside and tried to spank Kiara.

Her mom threatened, in front of them all, to ship her grandma out to Kiara's uncle in Ohio for violating the conditions they had agreed to when she moved in.

Kiara and Tom exchanged smug glances and crossed their fingers.

After a few days, everyone calmed down. Grandma apologized and suggested that instead of spanking Kiara, they should go to church *every* Sunday.

Kiara and Tom rolled their eyes and moped to their room.

Her mom opened their bedroom door. "We're going to dinner to celebrate."

"Celebrate what?" Kiara asked. Under her breath, she added, "Not killing each other?"

Before her mom could answer, her grandma yelled, "It's a waste of money."

Her mom shot her grandma a nasty look. Her grandma didn't say another word other than to declare she wasn't going.

Kiara's mom took her and Tom to a Chinese restaurant in town.

Guilt gnawed at Kiara when her mom placed their order with the waiter: foil wrapped chicken, cream-cheese wontons, eggrolls, egg drop soup, sweet and sour chicken, beef and broccoli, pork fried rice, and chicken chow mein.

Tom scarfed down his serving and piled on a second helping.

After the waiter refilled their hot jasmine tea and left, Kiara's mom pointed to the untouched food stacked on Kiara's plate.

"Go ahead and eat," her mom said.

Kiara shook her head and crossed her arms. She leaned towards her mom. Barely above a whisper, Kiara said, "This is too much money, Mom. We can't afford this."

"Kiara, stop worrying about everything. Things are great at work. I'm getting some big commission checks. Aren't we allowed to celebrate?"

Kiara begrudgingly ate the soup and unwrapped the chicken, which was warm and moist and delicious. Her mom demonstrated how to use chopsticks. She and Tom laughed while Kiara tried and failed to get the noodles from her plate to her mouth. She heaped another portion of sweet and sour chicken. An explosion of flavors burst in her mouth with every bite. The crunchy bell peppers, crispy fried chicken, tangy sauce—a far cry from the mush at home.

At the end of the meal, they each got a fortune cookie.

"What's yours say?" Tom asked. "Mine says, 'You will always be surrounded by good friends.' Which is like, duh, of course. Who wouldn't want to be my friend?"

He ducked when Kiara flicked a wad of foil at him.

Her mom pulled the strip of paper from her cookie. "'Goodness is the only investment that never fails.' Hmm ..." She stared into the distance while she ate her cookie.

Tom reached for Kiara's cookie. She snatched it back.

"What does it say?" he asked.

Kiara cracked open her cookie. She placed a piece of cookie in her mouth and unfolded the paper. "What's this supposed to mean? It says, 'Dare to dream.'"

"It means eat the rest of your cookie before I do." Tom smirked.

"What am I going to do with you two?" Kiara's mom shook her head and smiled.

At home, they kept the peace for a while—her grandma said it was thanks to God.

When she came home from work, Kiara's mom told them all to come outside. On the driveway was a huge camping trailer, the kind you pull behind a truck, and a new pickup truck.

"Who's visiting?" Kiara said.

"No one." Her mom laughed. "I got another big commission check and bought a trailer so we can spend time together camping."

"Camping?" Kiara said. "In the desert?"

"No, in the mountains. I bought a Thousand Trails Club membership."

Neither Kiara nor Tom had camped before. All of them squished together in a trailer didn't sound fun. Sure enough, the following weekend, her mom drove them and the trailer up a nauseatingly winding mountain road to a campsite in the woods.

"Isn't it beautiful up here?" her mom said. She breathed in the crisp forest air.

Pine trees towered in the sky. Birds chirped and swooped overhead. When the sun set, the night sky filled with bright stars like in the desert except trees obscured part of the view.

"We'll do a campfire and s'mores tomorrow," her mom said. "Now it's time for bed."

Kiara and Tom got in their footed pajamas—her mom bought them new ones that fit—and brushed their teeth in the trailer bathroom, which felt smaller than a port-o-potty.

"You and your brother sleep here." Her mom converted the dining table and benches into a bed. "Your grandma and I will sleep on the bed at the other end."

"Mom." Underneath a blanket, Kiara's teeth chattered and she shivered. "I can't sleep. It's too cold."

"Put on your jacket."

"I did. Tom keeps putting his icy hands on my neck."

Tom stuck his tongue out at her. "Can I sleep with you, Mom?"

"There's no room up here."

Tom went up there anyhow. That woke up their grandma who shouted at them to give her space, so Kiara's mom switched places and let Tom stay up there.

"This is too firm." Her mom tapped on the converted bed she and Kiara were lying on. "We'll get a sleeping pad for next time."

Kiara had goosebumps. Her back hurt. She stared up the ceiling.

Tom came back and crawled on top of them. "I'm cold."

"For God's sake, will the two of you let me get some sleep?" her mom said.

"Quit your yelling," her grandma called out. "You're going to wake up the whole forest."

In the morning, because everyone was exhausted, they cut the trip short and drove home.

A couple weeks later, they packed more blankets and sweaters and tried camping in the trailer again. Again, they ended up cold and uncomfortable and arguing.

The trailer moved into the backyard where it provided shade for Patches and collected dust. The truck, however, had two bucket seats in the extended cab for Kiara and Tom and held more groceries in the bed which meant fewer trips to town. That saved gas.

Kiara doubted the savings offset the cost of the trailer. She kept her mouth shut.

19

Burn Day

PARCHED FROM DRY SPELLS, invasive bushes—Salsola tragus, known as Russian thistle or wind witch, and to the desert folk known only as tumbleweeds—brown and dry up.

Winds pile tumbleweeds against houses and fences, blocking garages, doors, and windows. Scrape them away with rakes and shovels and pitchforks; unravel them, layer by layer. Scoop and stack. The piles grow. In backyards, people whack and smash them down until thistles intertwine, binding them together with piles taller than cars.

Any green or succulent juices must dry to a toasty brown. Green doesn't burn like brown. Those roots stubbornly grip into hard dirt, but when they dry, they must burn.

"Go to sleep," Kiara's mom said. "I'm waking you at dawn."

"For what?" Kiara sat up in her bed and set her book down.

"I told you. Tomorrow is Burn Day."

"That's what you said last week," Kiara said. "Then they canceled it."

"Well, the winds dictate that, don't they?"

"Can't I sleep in?" Kiara yawned.

"We have to burn before the winds pick up." Her mom flicked off the light.

A gray sliver of light appeared on the horizon. Kiara rubbed her eyes and leaned against a shovel. She tied a handkerchief around her nose and mouth.

Her mom handed her the hose. "Take this and stand back."

"Better not burn the dead fruit trees." Kiara rolled her eyes.

Her mom glared at her. "They're not dead." She struck a match and lit some crumpled newspaper on fire. She pushed it underneath the edge of the stack of tumbleweeds. The flame licked at the brush. The fire ignited.

Kiara wore jeans, a long-sleeved sweatshirt, and work gloves, same as her mom. She had her hair tied back and, even though it was early, her body warmed from the flames. Red and yellow embers danced into the sky. Billows of black smoke and rolling clusters of white smoke rose above their heads. Kiara's face heated uncomfortably, so she turned away.

"Keep your eyes on the flame," her mom said. She pushed in at the edges of the pile with a rake whenever the weeds spread out. "Be ready with the hose."

"It's too close. I can't." Kiara squinted at the flames. Her eyeballs were drying.

"Pay attention." Her mom stepped back, stretched her hands into the small of her back, and massaged her neck and shoulders.

Within minutes, the mountain of weeds had been reduced to an imprint of scorched earth.

"Are we done?" Kiara asked. "Can I go back inside?"

"It's not done. Give me the hose. I'll show you." Her mom sprayed the black soot.

The water sizzled and smoke rose.

"See?" her mom said. "Nature fooled you. Remember, burn then hose it down."

"What if you don't have a long enough hose, or you forgot to turn on the water?"

"Don't be stupid."

The next week, with the brush cleared, Kiara's mom dug four deep holes into the hard-packed earth. With a neighbor's help, she constructed a metal playset. She set each steel leg into a hole, poured in concrete powder, and mixed it with water until it hardened around the poles. She attached a metal slide to one end of the monkey bars, two swings on the other end.

"What do you think?" her mom asked.

"Cool." Tom gave her a hug. "Thanks, Mom."

"You two better appreciate it," she said. "Wait a few days for the cement to harden."

A swing set didn't excite Kiara. Maybe it would have if she had friends her age to play with, or if she were still friends with Cole. He had given up on her so easily. She didn't mean it when she said she didn't want to be friends. He should've known her well enough by now to figure that out. She could call him and invite him over but refused to make the first move.

After the cement hardened, Kiara and Tom spent hours playing. Both developed blisters from the monkey bars. Turns out desert dirt didn't work as well as playground sand in protecting hands and knees and elbows. The slide was too hot to the touch. They'd have to wait until dark to go use it, to avoid getting burned.

On occasion, Kiara's mom once again drove them to the library to check out books. Sometimes, they couldn't get back before the books were due and the librarians grew tired of waiving late fees. Visiting the library was a hardship, no longer because of the cost of gas, but because of the hour it took to drive there and back, now that her mom worked weekends.

"I'm sorry," her mom said. "I'm too busy this weekend."

Kiara nodded sadly. "I know you need to work, because we need the money. It's okay."

"I think you won't mind when you find what comes in the mail for you next week."

"What do you mean?" Kiara tilted her head.

"You'll see."

The mailman slid a brown package into their barn-shaped mailbox. Kiara jogged across the street to bring in the mail. A cardboard box was addressed to Kiara, from a company called the Weekly Reader Book Club.

Kiara pulled the perforated strip and voila! — two hardcover books fell out.

"The library delivered books to me," Kiara told her mom. "Look!" She held them up.

"No," her mom explained, "those aren't from the library. They're yours. You get to keep them. Every week you'll get two new books randomly selected and sent to our house."

Kiara couldn't believe it. What witchcraft was this? Magical at home delivery of books?

This was more incredible than the monthly Scholastic Book Sales with the colorful newspaper printed menu of books. These were *hardcovers.* They were hers.

Kiara disappeared into her room to read.

She raced to the mailbox every time the postman came. Sure enough, once a week, there it was—a glorious cardboard wrapped gift. With the books, the rest of the summer flashed by. She stacked them in a bookcase and on the floor. For now, these would be her friends.

What would she do when she finished reading them all? Would they sit there, taking up space? She imagined the books going up in flames on burn day. Like old friendships that had served their purpose, feed them to the fire.

She wouldn't, of course, do such a horrendous thing, although the idea of burning toxic links to the past brought a smile to her lips. Her attachment to what was, could no longer be.

The Middle Years

20

Impressions

FIFTH GRADE APPROACHED. Kiara's mind turned from books to her appearance. She stared in the mirror at her big glasses and ugly hair. The curls didn't hold up. Her hair had gotten darker and straighter, which added length so that it reached her shoulders, a definite improvement.

Kiara dreaded school. The three witches were awful, so if she didn't want to sit by herself, read, draw, and write all year, she needed new friends. She had hoped Melissa's friendship would've stuck, but it didn't.

The school posted the class lists outside the school office the night before the first day. There were enough kids that each grade had multiple classes. She skimmed the lists. She was assigned to Ms. Porter's class. Her stomach sank: Stephanie, Jessica, and Heidi would be in her class. On the bright side, so would Cole, as he had been every year since second grade.

Kiara missed hanging out with him, but the distance between them was her doing.

The three witches ignored her on the first day of school; they acted like they didn't know her. Kiara was glad. Cole didn't give her more than a smile and a wave hello. At least he acknowledged her.

Kiara reached out to the other girls, the ones the three witches made fun of. Most of the misfit girls eyed Kiara with distrust even when she smiled and said hi.

Tessa, a knock-kneed girl with a pointed nose and long hair with bangs, invited Kiara to sit next to her at lunch in the cafeteria, the double-wide trailer with linoleum flooring and long tables, the same place where her church met every Sunday.

"You hang out with the mean girls," Tessa said.

"Not anymore," Kiara said. "They're jerks." She toned down her swearing to make a good impression.

"To you, too?" Tessa tried to sip milk out of a straw even though the carton was empty. She tore her sandwich into little pieces and ate each chunk one at a time.

The slurping and tearing up of food irritated Kiara, but she let it go. "Yep. I want to be friends with nice people."

Tessa wiped her mouth with her shirt. "You can come over to my house sometime."

Kiara couldn't believe her luck. Before Tessa could change her mind, Kiara agreed. They made plans for Saturday. Tessa had to babysit and said Kiara could help.

By the end of the weekend, Kiara discovered several things about Tessa: she was a Jehovah's Witness, had five younger sisters who resembled her, and didn't have a mean bone in her body. Her house didn't have enough food, except nasty sprouted bread which only tasted slightly better with loads of butter, cinnamon, and sugar.

Within a month of hanging out, Tessa asked, "Do you want to be best friends?"

"Definitely," Kiara said, even though Tessa was starting to annoy her. It was the little things—the way she chewed gum with her mouth open, how her shoelaces were never tied, and that she occasionally wore her shirt inside out with the tag sticking out, until Kiara pointed it out and had her fix it.

Kiara was grateful Tessa liked her company though, so she stuck by her side, even when Tessa couldn't pronounce words correctly when called on to read aloud in class, or when she struggled to answer basic math questions.

At lunch Kiara sat next to Tessa at the table of loosely organized "loner" kids. Every once in a while, she glanced at Stephanie, Jessica, and Heidi, or at Cole who was surrounded by other boys, all laughing and joking. Even with Tessa by her side, Kiara felt alone.

The GATE pullout program restarted and this time Kiara and Cole were mixed with kids from different grades. They met once a week. Kiara finally had an excuse to communicate with Cole. She wanted to resume their friendship. She needed to apologize.

She sat next to him while they drew horses for an art lesson on proportion. Cole kept his mouth shut and his pencil moving.

Kiara leaned closer to him. He smelled like spicy citrus shampoo. She breathed him in and spoke. "I miss Ms. Jodie."

Cole didn't stop sketching. He said, "Do you remember the last thing she said to you?"

"Stop lying?"

"No. She said, 'stay away from people who aren't trying to become the best version of themselves. They make bad decisions. How can people who make bad decisions feel good about themselves? They don't. And don't have your best interests in mind.'"

"She had great advice." Kiara scrutinized her distorted horse. "What happened to her?"

"She retired."

"Retired, or got tired of us?"

Cole cracked a smile. He quickly regained his focus on the drawing.

Kiara slouched. "I wasn't nice to you the last time we talked."

"Great powers of observation, Captain Obvious."

Kiara drew a circle where the horse's head should be. "Do you like my horse?"

"That's a horse?" Cole glanced over. "More like you pulled a horse in two directions and stretched it like salt water taffy."

"Wow." She playfully knocked him in the arm. "You're so complimentary."

"You know you scrunch your nose when you smile? It's cute."

Kiara's cheeks warmed. "Your horse is better than mine."

Cole turned to her and raised an eyebrow. "Are you blind? It resembles a cow."

"Ouch." Kiara adjusted her glasses. "Not a cow. More like my grandma sat on it and squashed its legs short."

Cole turned to her. "How's it having your grandma there?"

"Oh, it's great. Just loads of fun. Wish you were there."

"Well, somebody..." He pushed his shoulder into hers. "Didn't want me there."

"Not true." Kiara erased and redrew the neck. "I do."

Even though Tessa got on her nerves, Kiara now had a place at school, especially because she and Cole were back on speaking terms. Their friendship was on the mend.

Life had improved at home, too, even though her grandma was still there. Her mom was getting commissions on the homes she sold, and she'd been selling a lot. She got promoted to top sales manager. Her boss invited them over to her fancy house in Apple Valley for Thanksgiving. Kiara's grandma opted to stay behind.

Kiara had never been inside a neighborhood of mansions in the desert. She followed her mom across a manicured front lawn and long front porch, and through a grand double-door entry—stained wood and etched glass.

A woman with big blonde hair, warm round face, and a gorgeous flowy dress said, "You can leave your coats in the foyer." She herself had a faux fur wrapped over her shoulders.

Kiara glanced back at Tom and mouthed the word "foyer." He was as puzzled as she. Kiara observed and copied what her mom did; she hung her coat on a hook along the wall.

"This is my boss," Kiara's mom whispered to them.

The boss and her husband (Kiara's mom whispered that he was also her boss), showed them around the backyard and "outdoor living space" which included a fireplace, mini bar, and furniture underneath a huge gazebo. Outdoor loungers and umbrellas surrounded the pool, twice the size of the one at Kiara's old house.

The bosses and her mom strategized upcoming sales and business expansion. Kiara stood by Tom and shivered; her coat was in the *foyer* and she didn't want to ask to get it. Instead, she rubbed her arms across her arms and hopped around.

Eventually, the couple guided them back indoors to watch a football game on the biggest TV Kiara had ever seen. A massive wraparound sectional couch took up most of the living room.

The lady boss glanced up and down at what Kiara and Tom were wearing, seeming to notice them for the first time.

Kiara grimaced at the pink corduroy pants she had on. They were a bit too short and the fabric was worn down at the knees so much that you couldn't make out the lines anymore. Kiara felt ashamed. Her mom was the only one with nice clothes, because of her job.

The lady boss told Kiara's mom that she would love to take Kiara and Tom on a school clothes shopping trip—her treat.

Rather than be excited, Kiara filled with dread. She didn't want to be alone with the boss lady who said words like *foyer* and *outdoor living space*. She didn't want to owe this woman anything, because there's no way she'd ever have money to repay it, and neither did her mom.

Kiara smiled and said, "thank you" and sat on the edge of the leather couch. Two adults—Kiara was told they were the boss's kids—yelled at the ref on TV for making "a bad call." Both the daughter and son were tall, beautiful, and imposing.

Kiara had to use the bathroom. Her mom was talking to her bosses. Kiara didn't interrupt. She crossed her legs and focused on the football game.

Before Kiara could ask where the restroom was, the boss lady announced dinner was ready. She directed them not to the huge formal dining room, but to the *kitchen nook*, which was grander than Kiara's kitchen. The casual table was as large as Kiara's formal one at home.

Kiara wiggled. She leaned towards her mom to ask about the restroom. Her mom flicked her hand at her to be quiet.

Before digging in to their delicious meal, the boss lady announced they'd all share what they were thankful for. The boss, his son, Kiara, her mom, and Tom kept it short: food, family, friends, and such.

"Thank God for this abundant feast," the boss lady said, "and for finally having our kids back home to share it with us."

The daughter snickered. "Really, Mom? Sorry if I'm at college. I didn't have to come."

"And you usually don't," the boss lady said.

"Well, I'm here, so let's get on with it."

"Yes, the princess has graced us with her presence," the son said. "It's always about you."

"Please don't start," the boss lady said. "It's Thanksgiving for God's sake."

Kiara glanced at her mom who intently focused on the eggnog in her glass. These people with the beautiful house and so much money still fought as a family. Perhaps money wasn't the magic wand of happiness.

Tom gave Kiara a wide-eyed stare then bowed his head.

The boss's husband glared at his daughter. "Let's thank God for this meal. In honor of the first Thanksgiving when the Indians—"

"You mean Native Americans?" the daughter said.

"Oh my God, really?" the son said. "Stop being so sensitive."

"This is not the time nor place." The dad slammed his fist on the table, which silenced both of them. After that, everyone calmed down, ate, and engaged in small talk.

How could the kids be so rude in front of company? With the feast before them, Kiara couldn't imagine being anything except appreciative. Kiara cut her turkey and ham. She shook her legs. She had to go to the bathroom. That's what her thoughts were on while she sipped their eggnog and placed carefully cut bites of ham in her mouth, trying to make herself invisible.

After dinner, they retreated to the commercial sized kitchen to put final touches on the massive amounts of food they were still cooking—they provided dinner at the local homeless shelter, their annual charitable tradition.

Kiara crossed her legs. She couldn't take it anymore and tugged on her mom's dress.

"Oh, honey," the boss lady said. "Do you need to use the bathroom? You could've asked. Use the one upstairs. It's the second door on the left."

Kiara nodded, hoping she hadn't made her mom look bad. She hurried over to the grand staircase, wood steps with carpet down the middle. She held the wooden rail and stepped up each one until she reached the landing.

The stairs dead-ended at a long hallway. To her left were rows of tall cabinets. On the right, there were many doors on both sides. Kiara froze. She had never seen so many doors in a house before.

Second door on the left.

She turned the handle. It didn't open. Maybe it was locked. Or maybe it was a bedroom. Terrified that she'd screwed up and gotten her mom in trouble, she ran downstairs.

"Did you find it okay?" the boss lady asked. Kiara shook her head. "Dear, please show Kiara to the restroom."

The daughter led Kiara up, grumbling the entire time about her mom. Kiara had to go so badly that she couldn't hear anything. They stopped in front of the door Kiara tried earlier.

"It gets stuck sometimes," the daughter said. She yanked the handle and pushed it open.

Never had Kiara been so glad to use the restroom. She felt so relieved that she hadn't messed up and ruined her mom's job, because without money, they could lose the house. Then where would they go?

Kiara ignored the boss lady's promise to get them new clothes. She was used to adults offering to do things that they didn't follow through on. The following weekend, though, the boss lady drove from Apple Valley to pick them up.

Kiara sat in shock, even after her mom told her and Tom to get ready. The trip was imminent. Her mom had to work, so Kiara and Tom would go alone in the woman's car.

A car pulled up into the driveway, and Kiara peered out the window at the shiny white Cadillac. Her grandma had to push them out the door.

What if Kiara said something wrong and got her mom fired? What if the boss lady didn't like them or was mean? How was she supposed to act? Rather than be excited, Kiara dreaded the trip. She sat in the front on squishy white leather while Tom settled in the back.

Kiara crossed her hands on her lap and crossed her ankles, careful not to let her shoes touch anything. Say thank you to everything. Remember to say please. Don't make a fuss. Her brain cycled through the stern advice that her grandma had given her the night before.

During the long drive through the nothingness of the desert, Kiara stared at the Joshua trees whirring by her window and imagined animals transforming in the clouds.

They pulled up to a strip mall and stepped inside the nicest clothing store Kiara had ever been in. She glimpsed a price tag on a shirt she liked and her hand recoiled as if it were on fire. There's no way they could afford that.

"I appreciate it," Kiara told the lady boss, "but we don't need much clothes."

"Even if you don't need any, will you allow me to buy you some?"

"I don't want you to have to spend so much money." Kiara glanced down at her tattered jeans. "Thank you though."

"Honey, don't worry about how much anything costs. I have the means to help others, and I enjoy doing it. Honestly, we can buy everything in this store if that's what you'd like. And I don't want you to feel bad. Allow others to do nice things for you. You and your brother are such wonderful, polite children. Let others show you kindness."

"Are you sure?" Kiara tilted her head. What was the catch?

"Absolutely honey. There's a lot of room in that trunk of mine. Let's fill it up. There's a back seat, too, if we need more space." She grinned. "That green shirt is gorgeous with your pretty eyes. Why don't you go try it on?"

Every time Kiara stepped out of the dressing room wearing a different shirt, skirt, or pants, the boss lady gushed how flattering it was and that she must get it. After Kiara had selected almost one of every article of clothing in the store, the boss lady had Kiara sit alongside her to join her in praising everything that Tommy tried on.

The salesperson helped them carry everything to the car. Bags and bags of clothes filled up the trunk. Afterward, they went shoe shopping. That's when Kiara got her first pair of LA Gear sneakers—shoes that would impress kids at school.

Sure enough, when Kiara got to school, Stephanie, Jessica, and Heidi approached her. They complimented everything from her LA Gear shoes to her jean skirt and jacket. Tessa stood beside her in shredded jean shorts, a faded t-shirt, and scuffed shoes, a hole forming at the toe.

Kiara saw through the three witches and their fake kindness. She walked away with Tessa, but, as she did so, she glanced back at the other girls longingly.

21

Dodgeball

FOR SCIENCE, MS. PORTER SAID they were going to grow plants out of seeds. She passed out a clear plastic cup to each of them and a paper towel with some seeds.

Kiara leaned to Cole and mouthed the words, "Something green growing from thin air?"

"Until the desert kills it," he whispered back.

They laughed.

Ms. Porter explained that they had to wrap up the seeds in the paper towel and keep it moist and give it some sunlight and plants would sprout from the seeds. They were going to do this for the science fair, and create boards, write a hypothesis, and diagram the plant life cycle and photosynthesis and so forth.

Sounded easy enough. Kiara brought her cup home and followed the directions mostly, until she came home from school one day to a sad scene. Despite daily watering, the sun had scorched the little plant and dried its baby leaves to a crisp brown.

Cole was right: the desert killed it.

Kiara and Cole agreed that they hadn't learned anything new in math for two years. For English, Ms. Porter had them write a two-page short story; Kiara wrote a ten-page story. No one except Cole volunteered to peer-edit, so Ms. Porter read it and said she'd done a good job. Kiara didn't get detailed feedback. She had hoped to learn how to improve, so maybe she could write a book one day like all the ones she was reading.

The school still didn't have a library; instead, the Bookmobile came more frequently. The selection was limited—Kiara had already read most of the ones they brought as had many of the other kids. Kiara got an idea: She'd start her own library.

Between the monthly Scholastic Book Clubs and Weekly Reader Book Club, Kiara had amassed over 100 books, paperbacks and hardcovers.

She spent hours at home making an alphabetized list on paper. Every time she got a new book, the handwritten list got messed up, so that didn't work. Instead, she listed each book title along with the author, and wrote a number in pen inside each front cover, along with her name.

It didn't take long before the boys and girls in her class, and some outside of her class, got wind of it, and asked to borrow books.

"I'm sorry. It's only for my classroom," she said to a stranger who approached her.

Kiara didn't want to be mean. She only loaned books to people she knew, not because collecting late fees would be a hassle, but because these were her babies. She cared about each one and wanted them returned like new. Kiara was proud to make other kids happy.

She noticed the three witches had been eying her for the last couple weeks every time she took her lending library list and handed books to someone. Kids chose from the list. Kiara brought the book the next day—quicker service than any Bookmobile.

Finally, one day Queen Stephanie approached, with Jessica and Heidi as her court. "What you got there? Can I see?"

Tessa stood nearby shaking her head and mouthing the words "don't show them."

"Well?" Stephanie asked. "Are you going to let me see?"

Kiara handed her the paper.

"Super cool," Heidi said. "Can I borrow some?"

Kiara nodded. "Which ones?"

"Me, too," said Stephanie.

Kiara promised to give them priority service and to bring their books for them tomorrow. The girls walked away. Tessa sneered at them.

On the way to lunch, Stephanie, Jessica, and Heidi waited outside. When Kiara and Tessa passed by, Stephanie called out to Kiara.

"Hey, want to eat lunch with us?" Stephanie asked.

Kiara tilted her head. "Can Tessa come?"

"Fine," Stephanie said. She, Jessica, and Heidi headed into the cafeteria.

"I don't want to eat lunch with them," Tessa said.

"We can hang out later," Kiara said.

"Yeah, right," Tessa said. "Whatever. You were using me."

"That's not fair to say."

"Why do you want to hang out with them? They're mean. You said you don't like them. They're a bunch of stuck-up jerks."

Kiara bristled. "Who are you to put down others?" She tugged at Tessa's shirt tag hanging out. "You can't even dress yourself."

"You're so mean."

"And you're annoying."

Tessa wiped her eyes. "Leave me alone."

"Fine. I will." Kiara held up her head, entered the cafeteria and sat down next to Stephanie, Jessica, and Heidi. She relayed the conversation she had with Tessa. The girls found it hilarious every time Kiara repeated the "you're so mean" in a mocking tone.

And like that, Stephanie, Jessica, Heidi, and Kiara were friends again. No one made fun of Kiara's curls, which were gone. The girls mad-dogged anyone who called Kiara four-eyes, because only they could tease her. Kiara figured this was okay.

Anytime she felt bad for Tessa, she remembered the annoying things Tessa did and so she felt justified. Or at least she could mostly ignore her guilty conscience.

By spring, the frost cleared and the weather warmed. PE class started up. This usually meant an hour a couple of times a week when Ms. Porter would take their class to join up with another class on the blacktop, and sometimes another teacher would lead it. Today they had a new PE teacher, one Kiara hadn't seen before; she had curly blonde hair, and a personality as strict as a drill sergeant one moment and as bubbly as her hair the next; she switched between the two modes as fast as the wind changed directions.

They did windmills by stretching and held their arms out to a T, palms down, while Ms. Drill Sergeant counted on her stopwatch; then she had them flip palms up and hold the pose some more. Kiara didn't see the point. Her biceps and triceps were on fire.

Ms. Bubbles cheered while they did jumping jacks. Kiara's arms wanted to fall off.

After everyone was done groaning—a few sat on the hot blacktop in protest—the teacher blew a loud whistle and dragged out an overflowing, colorful pile of fabric that Kiara hadn't seen in years—the parachute game.

Each kid grabbed an edge and spread out in a big circle, further and further back until the wheel of color was taut, alternating colors: blue, yellow, green and red, stitched together in slivers like a pie. The kids tried to contain their excitement—it had been a favorite game when they were younger—and instead painted a bored, pre-teen expression on their faces, with the joy cracking through. A couple of them—mostly boys—threw sideways glances at each other, a corner of their lips upturned in communicating a scheme—a lot of them were always scheming.

"Can we toss someone on top?" asked one and a wave of enthusiasm spread among them.

"No," Ms. Bubbles replied, "that's unsafe."

And it was. A few years ago, back at the dry lake bed when Kiara first played this game in PE—a kid went home with a broken arm. That's when the parachute game disappeared for quite a while.

First, they practiced synchronizing, lifting up and down, to mushroom out the fabric. When they had the hang of that, Ms. Bubbles called on some volunteers to run underneath the inflated dome and switch places with another kid who ran wildly underneath. They had until the mushroom deflated before getting eliminated.

When younger, the kids would lift it up high by the handles—as high as their little arms could reach—then bring it down real gentle. No longer the case, a few of the boys led the way in violently jerking it back down as hard and as fast as they could so that the parachute yanked out from smaller hands giving a rug burn. Ms. Sergeant told them to knock it off or they wouldn't play.

Even though it ballooned high, it was a huge circle to get under in time. A few kids tried to slide through as if they were sliding to first base, and ended up tearing holes in the knees of their jeans and skinning elbows because blacktop wasn't grass and grass wasn't much better.

After a few of these injuries, Ms. Sergeant said they'd try it a different way. She tossed a couple of red handballs on top, the type you'd hit against the outside of a classroom wall or against a garage door at home.

The kids lifted and lowered the parachute, launching the balls higher and higher until some went off course and kids got hit in the head real hard.

"Ouch," a boy said. "That rattled my brains."

The kids laughed.

Ms. Sergeant looked horrified. "All right everyone. Let's roll this up."

The next time they had PE, she told them about a new game. She pointed at several steel poles newly planted in the dirt: tetherball courts. She clipped yellow balls on rope to the top of the poles and demonstrated how two players could compete to wrap it around in the direction they were swinging; meanwhile, their opponent tried to smack it hard with a closed fist to stop it. This was a huge hit. Kiara enjoyed it. She wasn't coordinated and couldn't block well, so she was an easy opponent to score off of.

A few weeks later, red handballs came out and the PE teacher had them circle up on the blacktop. Kiara and the others looked around for the parachute. It was nowhere to be found.

Ms. Sergeant said they'd learn dodgeball. She said the goal was to hit each other with the ball to get them out and not to get hit yourself, or to catch it. In Kiara's mind this meant the goal was not to get knocked unconscious before you could get back to the circle's safety perimeter after having to run across.

Some of the boys had a pretty strong arm and good aim and took out the nerds and the kids they didn't like. The three witches—who no one tried to hit with the ball when they ran across—thought this was the funniest thing they'd ever seen and egged them on to keep eliminating their enemies—of which there were many.

One boy, quiet, sweet, and on the smaller side got knocked down particularly hard and hit his head on the blacktop, shielded only slightly by his small soft hand. He screamed a terrible scream, the kind that sends shivers down your spine, and sat up with tears in his eyes. Jessica tossed another ball and hit him in the back before Ms. Sergeant blew the whistle and marched over to him. He was in tears. She helped him to his feet and said she needed to walk him to the nurse and for the kids to put the balls back in the bag and stay put.

No sooner had she left than Stephanie high-fived Jessica and the boy who made the direct hit. Cheers and chants tore through the crowd. Kiara's stomach knotted up. She wanted to scream and cry at the same time. She thought of the astronauts and the cruelty of life and the unfairness and no-good meanness. She couldn't say anything or she'd have a target on her back, and so she sat down on the dirt in the shade of a building against the wall. She hugged her legs tight and stared at the scene playing out. She hated them all in a visceral way.

Stephanie, Jessica, Heidi, and some of the boys laughed and called the small frightened boy who bore the brunt of their meanness a crybaby and loser.

Cole, a head taller than most of the boys stood up and yelled out, "That's screwed up. Not cool, guys. Not cool."

A moment of silence passed while the troublemakers considered their options. Cole had a group of boys standing behind him. The others bit their lips and shut up. They didn't want any trouble, so, like hyenas, they backed away without conceding.

Kiara wiped the tears in her eyes. Cole spotted her and nodded. He said what she could not. He knew it and she knew it.

22

Perspective

THE NEXT TIME THEY WERE IN GATE CLASS, Kiara and Cole learned perspective in landscape sketching—an optical illusion. In the background, she drew a small winding fence and creek close together. As it approached the foreground, the fence and creek widened and lengthened and spread out to create a three-dimensional image.

Their teacher explained that this technique controls the point-of-view of the viewer. Three artists painting the same scene from different directions end up with three different paintings, each from their own perspective.

They were also given logic problems to work with, mainly math related: Sally has four brothers, three are older, one is younger. Together their ages add up to fifty, and so forth.

Kiara and Cole competed to figure it out first. They were pretty even on the score.

They studied light refraction and mirrors, concave and convex, and made periscopes out of milk cartons. Cole was better at taping and gluing his stuff together. Kiara was better at getting her fingers glued together.

In class, Stephanie, Jessica, and Heidi asked Kiara for help with math and writing. It was so easy for Kiara, and she explained it well enough. They increasingly came to her for more help. They asked her to do a couple more problems "so they could figure it out on their own."

Even though she saw through their ruse to get out of doing it, Kiara didn't mind. It didn't take her long at all. Besides, there were things Kiara didn't like doing, especially dishes and laundry, and if she could get out of doing them, she would.

Next time she was in GATE, Cole said something to her about it. "I see you've been giving answers to the three witches."

"They need my help."

"They don't need your help," he said. "You're doing it for them and that's not right."

"Who are you to tell me what's right or wrong?" Kiara bit her lip.

Cole threw her a sideways look. She knew he was right. He left it at that though.

Kiara backed off on the help a little, and instead encouraged her friends. They got a little irritated but didn't say anything. Maybe friends will take advantage of you if you let them, even if they don't intend to.

Kiara sat in the front row because of her poor vision. Whenever she and Cole finished their work early, Ms. Porter let them hang out at a small table in the back.

Kiara wondered if the three witches gossiped about her when she and Cole sat back there, because they glanced back at them and giggled. When Cole was near her, the three witches spoke in syrupy sweet voices and smiled at him. It was annoying. Kiara didn't say anything.

A few new students entered class throughout the year. One was Nelly, a shy girl with glossy black hair, long skinny legs, and glasses as big as Kiara's. She attended the GATE program with Kiara and Cole.

Kiara went out of her way to talk with Nelly. Eventually, Nelly opened up. She had just moved out there. Kiara offered to be friends. Nelly said that'd be great.

At lunch Kiara brought Nelly to where she and her friends ate in the cafeteria.

"Why's *she* here?" Stephanie asked.

Kiara narrowed her eyes at Stephanie. "Nelly is my friend, so she's going to sit here."

Jessica and Heidi laughed—and not in a nice way.

Nelly didn't say anything. She bowed her head.

"With those jeans, are you going to a flood?" Stephanie said. "Do you comb your hair at all? Maybe you should try it."

Nelly put down her sandwich and wrung her hands together.

"Leave her alone," Kiara said.

Nelly shook her head and whispered, "It's okay. I'm used to this."

Stephanie pointed to another table in the corner. "The dork table is over there."

Nelly grabbed her lunch, and hurried away.

"You guys are so fucked up," Kiara said. She stood there with her lunch.

"Are you going to eat with *them*?" Stephanie asked. "If so, you aren't hanging with us."

Kiara looked both ways, torn in the middle.

"Come on, sit down," Heidi turned to Stephanie. "Kiara's right. That was mean."

Stephanie rolled her eyes.

"What we're saying is that you're better than her," Jessica said. "Sit down, please."

Kiara turned to find Nelly sitting at the other table next to Tessa and some other girls who glared back at Kiara's table.

"Do you got a problem?" Stephanie asked. "If so, say it."

"I don't want to waste my breath," Kiara said and sat down. She pushed away her tray; she had lost her appetite. She glanced at the other end of the cafeteria at Cole and his friends. He stared at her, shook his head, and turned back to his group.

Kiara wished she had stood up for the new girl and wished she had stood up for herself, too. She heaved a sigh and slouched in her seat.

"Are you going to cry?" Stephanie said. "Seriously?"

"No," Kiara said. "I don't care. I don't even know her."

Nothing felt right. She couldn't understand how to make it better. Kiara decided she'd try to mind her own business. She couldn't be expected to protect everyone else, so she justified it to herself that way. Deep inside, she knew there wasn't any justification.

Regardless of how cruel they had been to Tessa and Nelly and others, Kiara couldn't work up the nerve to stand up to the witches. Although she didn't speak out, she shut up and shut everyone out—everyone except Cole. Later that day, a boy came up to Kiara in class and asked to borrow a book.

"The library is closed," Kiara announced loud enough for most of the kids to hear.

She closed her heart as well, because she'd been hurt and didn't realize how deeply until she stepped away from the witches—her *friends*—for a while to clear her mind.

For the next several days, Kiara thought and sometimes thought nothing at all. She sat apart from the others. The yard lady came over out of concern over her isolation and didn't believe Kiara when she dismissively claimed to be fine.

She wrote in her notebook. That was as a legitimate excuse for keeping to herself like Emily Dickinson. She wrote poems and short stories about murder.

Eventually, Stephanie, Jessica, and Heidi approached her.

"What's your problem?" Heidi asked.

Kiara narrowed her eyes at them. Through clenched teeth, she said, "I'm fine."

"Right," Jessica said. "Stop being a weirdo."

"What's wrong with you?" Stephanie said. "Did Tessa and the other nerds reject you?"

"Leave me alone." Kiara crossed her arms. "Go find someone else to annoy." She wanted to say more but bit her tongue. They weren't worth it.

The girls stepped back and exchanged surprised glances. They resumed their haughty act and, with an air of superiority, strode off.

From her vantage point on the outside, Kiara understood they added no value in her life.

That was that. Kiara had made her decision; she would be alone, and she would be alone on her own terms.

23

Reconnected

KIARA WAS SITTING BY HERSELF during recess when Cole approached.

"Do you want to play catch with me and my friends?" he asked.

"No, thank you," she said.

"I want you to know I'm not ignoring you, not like before when you told me to."

"I appreciate that."

He squatted and placed a hand on her shoulder. "I got to tell you that I'm so glad you're not hanging out with those popular girls. They're not nice."

She nodded.

"Let's try to get together soon," he said, "and play games like we used to."

"Just not around my grandma."

"Or my dad."

"Or my mom."

He smirked. "So, one day, then?"

"Maybe." She smiled.

That summer, Tom made his First Communion. Kiara's grandma insisted they celebrate with an expensive brunch at the Old Firehouse in Palmdale, a restaurant with rotating bamboo fans and a train that circled near the ceiling. Kiara wished they could go back, but didn't ask.

When Challenger Middle School, a new junior high on the Lancaster side of Lake LA, was built, their local Mass, which had been held at Lake LA School, relocated there.

Not having church in her school cafeteria trailer was welcome news. Having to wake up earlier to drive across Lake LA was not. With her increased community and church involvement, Kiara's mom forced Kiara and Tom to help set up sections of gray folding chairs before Mass. Afterward, Kiara's consolation prize was getting to choose from the day-old donuts in huge pink boxes: glazed, jelly-filled, chocolate, maple, or strawberry iced, or sprinkles.

Were donuts worth waking up at 6:30 AM? Kiara didn't think so.

The church group started out small until word spread in the community. By then, her mom had joined the church choir—consisting of a woman on a tambourine, her husband on a guitar, another couple, and Kiara's mom. They all huddled around a single microphone and sang. Kiara's mom lobbied hard for Kiara to join the choir.

Kiara said, "maybe later," to get her mom off her back.

Her mom signed up to do readings, and requested Kiara do, too. The lectern was too high, so Kiara got out of that. When her mom volunteered to host a rosary group at their house, Kiara started praying for the misery to stop.

In the back of her mind, she wondered if some of her mom's religious zealousness was, in a small part, networking for her real estate sales job. Even if it were true, she never heard her mom bring up real estate unless someone mentioned a friend was looking to move or buy a house.

"Aren't you Marcy Leneghan's daughter?" Kiara got asked every week, when setting up chairs, getting a donut, or taking down chairs. Kiara smiled and nodded politely and exited the conversation as quickly as possible, because those types of conversations centered around a lecture or trying to get Kiara involved in something else that she didn't want to do.

Kiara couldn't be rude, though, because Marcy Leneghan—not her mom—was sweet as sugar and helpful to everyone. Her daughter and son were expected to be the same.

One Sunday morning after Mass, near the donuts and coffee, Kiara's mom introduced her to another family who, like her mom, had enmeshed themselves into everything religious. Both the mom, Jess, and the dad, Peter, sang in the choir and did readings. They had a daughter and two sons. Kiara figured she might as well meet the girl who probably felt as unlucky as she.

Kiara's eyes widened when she saw the tall skinny girl in a t-shirt, jeans, and black combat boots.

"This is Carolyn," Jess said. "She's your age, starting sixth grade here."

Carolyn would go to Challenger Middle School, not Lake LA school. Kiara wanted to write her off for that, but something about that creature mesmerized her. Maybe it was

Carolyn's long, straight, dark brown hair parted down the middle or her brown eyes, or that her posture was straighter than a Joshua tree. She swayed when she spoke as if dancing with the wind.

Kiara and Carolyn stepped aside while Tom and the boys were being introduced.

Carolyn spoke first. "I've been going to church with you for the last few years."

"What?" Kiara asked. "Where?"

"At Lake LA School. And Palmdale."

"I never noticed you."

"I'm always in the back row."

Kiara blushed. "Sorry. I'm half-asleep this early."

"Lake LA is not that big of a church." Carolyn shrugged and gave a disarming laugh. "You don't have to impress me. I couldn't care less." She walked away and exited the building.

Kiara felt embarrassed. How could she have been so oblivious?

Carolyn wore beaded necklaces and colorful friendship bracelets tightly woven, and t-shirts over jeans, with a long-sleeve flannel tied around her waist. Kiara stole glances at her every week and eyed her with envy; Jess's daughter didn't have to dress up like Marcy's daughter did. Or maybe Carolyn did but didn't care. Kiara wished for a shred of that confidence.

Carolyn was nice enough, but didn't go out of her way to be friends, as if to say, I'm one with the desert, wild critters are my friends, you can come or go like the wind if you please, I'll be here either way.

Kiara wanted to befriend her but got the impression that she shouldn't try too hard. Let it happen naturally if it did at all. She hadn't met anyone else her age who wore combat boots, sometimes even with the laces untied.

After a few Sundays, Kiara, tired of stealing glances at Carolyn, decided she'd sit next to her. Before Mass, while their parents sat with the choir, Kiara paused at Carolyn's row. Carolyn didn't look up. Kiara stepped across empty folding metal chairs to slip into a seat next to her.

The first time, Carolyn didn't acknowledge her presence other than a one-word hello. She also didn't seem to mind. So, that became a thing.

By the third time, Carolyn actually smiled at her.

"Hey," Carolyn said. "I see you've decided to join me in the I-hate-it-here back row."

Kiara grinned. "Pretty much."

Carolyn rolled her eyes when she didn't like something, even if it was the priest's sermon. She'd been through the whole sacrament thing like Kiara.

"It's stupid my parents are making me go through Confirmation," Carolyn said. "I told them I don't believe in all this."

"You can say all that to them?" Kiara said. "I mean I don't want to do it, either."

"What would happen if you said so?"

"My mom would get mad. She's always disappointed in something I'm doing. I wish she were happy."

"Really? Your mom always seems happy."

"It's an act."

Carolyn grunted. "I know all about that." She raised an eyebrow. "But you're the Golden Girl."

"What do you mean?"

"Your mom always brags to my parents that 'Kiara gets straight A's, Kiara reads all the time,' Kiara this, Kiara that."

Kiara stared at her. "She's never said that to me." Her mom was proud of her? Was it part of the act, or was it for real?

"Don't get pissy. It means my parents might actually let me invite you over. They don't let anyone spend the night. They may let the Angelic Catholic Kiara."

Both girls giggled. An older lady in front of them turned, scowled, and shushed them.

Church wasn't so bad after that. Especially when Kiara found out that in 9th grade, she and Carolyn would go to Littlerock High School together.

Then Kiara's worlds collided. Who should show up the following Sunday, but Stephanie and Jessica; apparently their parents were Catholic, and the super-involved type, too (Heidi was a different type of Christian, one that sang Christian rock music in church). They had been going to a big, fancy Catholic church up in Lancaster every Sunday—Kiara mused that those two girls hadn't learned a damn thing from the "do unto thy neighbor as you wish done unto you" Golden Rule lessons or at least hadn't taken them to heart.

Why were *they* here at the Mass held in a school?

Evidently, their parents switched congregations to quit driving into town.

Marcy Leneghan and the parents of the two girls made friends, in the 'we go to the same church' kind of way and went to introduce their kids. They were delighted to hear their girls knew each other—in the same class, even! —and invited Kiara over anytime. Kiara's mom agreed. Stephanie's parents scheduled a time to host the families at their house.

The parents decided Kiara's fate. She couldn't object; Stephanie and Jessica smirked, conveying the message that she would again be theirs to toy with.

Kiara sat far away from them during church, next to Carolyn. Stephanie and Jessica eventually migrated closer to them. The witches giggled and gossiped throughout the Mass.

Carolyn glared, ready to explode, contrary to the chill vibe she normally conveyed. After the final song, everyone crowded back by the donuts. Kiara paused long enough to hear Carolyn, under her breath, say, "Those bitches are fucking obnoxious as all hell."

Kiara held her hand to her mouth. She couldn't help but laugh. Carolyn turned to her and laughed in her carefree way.

After that, there was an unspoken understanding. Kiara was being forced to befriend the evil twins by going with her mom to their homes. She and Carolyn mocked the girls whenever they got the chance. In this way, church did bring a little joy to Kiara's life.

There were potluck dinners with lots of families gathering together, and prayer groups rotating between Stephanie's house, Jessica's house, Kiara's house, and thank God— Carolyn's house. That was the best, because it wasn't on the evil twins' turf, so Kiara and Carolyn disappeared into her bedroom, because, as Carolyn informed her parents matter-of-factly, this is my room and I let in who I choose to.

When it wasn't at Carolyn's house, Carolyn stayed home, so Kiara was at the mercy of Queen Bee and her loyal follower. One such day, in Stephanie's bedroom, Stephanie brought up the topic of Carolyn and how weird she was and how odd her clothes were. Jessica agreed.

Kiara smirked. "Okay, I'll let her know that." By the fear in their eyes and grimaces, Kiara surmised they imagined Carolyn kicking in their faces with her steel-toed boots, so that was the last time they talked smack about her.

Kiara had at least one power point in her favor. Maybe the only one.

In sixth grade, Kiara was placed in the same class as the trio—Stephanie, Jessica, and Heidi. Thank God Cole would be there, too.

Without Carolyn, Kiara shrank into herself. She followed the girls around and observed the survival tactics she'd learned—laugh at their jokes or become the butt of them, nod when they picked on someone else, don't interject, or risk becoming the target of their wrath, dress well enough to not embarrass them—her iron-on knee patches that she still made with hearts and stars were up to their satisfaction because they were deemed cool enough—and help them with their homework whenever they asked.

Since Kiara rejoined the posse, other kids avoided her: they were nice but not too nice. Nobody wanted to piss off Stephanie.

Cole, like the lighthouse in the darkness, was there in class, and he grew taller every year. In GATE pullout classes, he called her out on her friend choice.

"I totally respected you for not hanging out with them," he said. "What happened?"

"My mom sucks. She's friends with their parents in church and forces us to hang out."

"I don't get you," he said. "Have a spine."

"Easy for you to say. Girls are horrible. It's either fight with them or against them."

"That's pretty shitty. Still, you have a choice."

"To hang out with who? The jerks, or the loners?"

"Why stop there? There are stoners you can smoke weed with or punks who fight."

"You're mocking me. The girl choices here are limited if you haven't noticed. They can make my life a living hell. Don't the guys do the same thing?"

"Guys take out aggression on the blacktop shooting hoops. We don't have a personal goal of creating daily agony." He softened his tone. "Isn't there *anyone* else you can hang out with?"

"Tessa, Nelly, and the others hate me with a passion, and I guess I deserve that. The Hispanic girls hang out and speak Spanish. The black girls talk about the Hispanic girls."

Cole shook his head. "Not a lot of options for a girl as pale as you—"

Kiara punched him in the arm.

"Hey," he said, "I'm only joking."

"The other girls make fun of me because I'm so white."

Cole paused for a moment. "Nah. You're blacker than me. You're so dark that you went all the way around the color wheel and landed back on white."

Kiara shook her head. "You're ridiculous."

"Only around you," he said with a grin.

24

Shifting Ground

KIARA TRIED TO BALANCE between her friends and her happiness, which constantly eluded her. In the meantime, she decided to make money. She'd been informally watching kids in the neighborhood for months. All she had to do was start charging fees. Nobody balked.

"Here, honey, we're running to the store in town. Be back in an hour or two."

And just like that, she'd be stuck babysitting a three-year-old and a five-year-old.

The following week it was a baby—she'd never even held a baby before other than her brother and that was eight years ago. When she voiced her concerns—in her meek way—the mom said, "Just leave him in the crib. He'll be fine."

The moms and dads on her street trusted her with their children. Kiara got good grades and was reliable, two deciding factors in her blossoming employment. Parents handed her a few dollars when they got back, and, on occasion, maybe even a five. All for keeping the kids alive.

Now almost twelve, she was a hot commodity in the local 'I need someone to watch these brats so I can do anything else for a couple hours' market. With her mom's guidance, she set up a rate schedule: $2.50 per hour for the first kid, $1.50 per hour for an extra kid, hopefully $1 more for the third, beyond that it got fuzzy, and she hoped for the best.

Minimum wage had gone up to $4.25 an hour, so with watching three kids, she could barely clear that amount. The money was under the table, she'd heard it said, so it was worth more somehow.

Kiara filled her old pink backpack with some of her old toys, Barbie dolls, coloring books, crayons, and toy cars. Inspired by *The Babysitters Club* book series, she treated it as a business. This is how she got kids to behave: the novelty of new toys—or at least new to them—motivated them to listen to her. She played the cleanup game. She was their cheerleader and convinced them to clean rooms and get in jammies.

Parents couldn't believe their eyes. They came home to a house more straightened up than when they left, kids happily in bed after having been read a bedtime story—many of the parents didn't have the time or energy to read to their children—and the babysitter calmly reading a book or writing in her journal in the living room—no parties, no boyfriends, no mess.

Word spread like desert wildfire and she booked up quickly. Parents went out for double-dates and she'd end up with two sets of kids, creating forts and mazes in the living rooms with pillows and blankets, making dinner and cleaning dishes, rotating the toys to keep the kids entertained so they didn't kill each other, or her.

And it was on one of these regular days after Kiara got home from babysitting that the ground shifted under her; her mom came home from work using words like "terminated without cause." She said her bosses—the nice lady and her husband—had a fight with their partner at the real estate company and the partner broke up the company.

Since her mom was loyal to the former bosses, the dishonest partner fired her and stole her commissions even though she had something like 10 homes in escrow. She spent hours calling the buyers to assure them purchasing a house was still a good idea, even if she wasn't there to shepherd it.

She spoke with her attorney because she had to fight the boss's partner for a while to get unemployment on account of them acting shady.

They needed money, her mom explained, and that's why she had to put on an orange vest to work as a crossing guard in front of Kiara's school. And that's why during lunch, one of the lunch ladies, who Kiara threatened not to so much as look at her or she'd run away never to be found, was her mom. This, to Kiara, meant social destruction. Her status was already on shaky ground.

At home, the tension continued.

Kiara's mom peeked her head inside her and Tom's bedroom. She wagged her finger at Kiara. "You left the lights on in the living room."

"It wasn't me," Kiara said.

"Well, it wasn't Tom since he's at his friend's house. You were the last one in there."

"No, I wasn't. Grandma was."

Her mom stepped into her room and scowled. "Don't you talk back to me, young lady."

"Stop blaming me for something I didn't do."

Her mom looked down at Kiara's metallic hot pink Barbie Corvette—a gift her mom gave her last Christmas after she had gotten another big commission.

"I said." Her mom kicked the car across the room into the wall. "To stop talking back."

Kiara screamed. She balled up her fists and, with tears streaming down her face, turned to her mom. "I *hate* you."

"Oh really?" Her mom kicked the Barbie dolls on the carpet across the room. She kicked Kiara's books which flew and scattered everywhere. "I'll give you something to complain about, you ungrateful little brat."

"Stop it!" Kiara screeched, hysterical.

Her mom left and slammed the door shut.

Kiara slumped to the ground. Her chest heaved as she cried. "I wish I could run away. I hate it here. I want to find my dad."

Her mom and grandma argued about who left the lights on and why the air conditioner was running nonstop.

"Money doesn't grow on trees," her mom screamed at her grandma.

The fight continued. Kiara put her hands over her ears, like she was a child.

"Who drank the last of the milk we were saving for breakfast?" "I told you not to run the AC. We can't afford it." And so forth. Something had to change, or the house would implode.

That's when it was decided: Kiara was old enough to take care of Tom. Her grandma packed her bags and headed East to stay with Kiara's uncle in Ohio.

And like that: Kiara had her room back with a big old lumpy queen size bed that carried the imprint of her grandma, and the massive antique dresser and mirror with the drawers that didn't open or close without strength of will.

It didn't matter. She and Tom didn't have to share a room anymore. No longer did she have to be careful when changing panties in her room.

Still, she worried their finances had shifted onto unpredictable ground.

Her mom couldn't make ends meet on the piecemeal jobs, and without help from her grandma's social security checks, had to figure out something quick. Taking inspiration from Kiara, her mom opened up her own daycare.

Her mom baby-proofed the house, set up a couple of play pens, and got herself licensed. There was never a shortage of families needing affordable daycare and so she maxed out pretty soon on the twelve-kid limit.

For Kiara, it was a mixed bag; not having her mom work at her school was a win; having little kids in her house waking her up early and encroaching on her space was a definite loss.

Her mom said it was good because she could keep a better eye on Kiara and Tom. That didn't happen because a person only has so many eyes. You've got to keep them on the paying customers. In a way, Kiara's mom was around more than ever before, yet no more present than before.

Dropoff and pickup from school was an adventure every day. Kiara's mom used her 4x4 white pickup truck with the cab's two bucket seats which she somehow got car seats hooked into for the little ones. Everyone older than that sat in the truck bed hanging on for dear life. The braver ones, like Kiara, sat near the wheel wells and gripped the sides as the truck drove along the bumpy half-assed paved road—with streaks, cracks, and patches over the numerous potholes, the usual way counties pave roads in unincorporated areas without a mayor or city manager to advocate otherwise.

Luckily for them all, the ride was only a couple minutes, or they might have lost a few good men every day.

After they survived the trek home, bumped up a bit from the ridges in the truck bed, they got started on homework; then it was movie mania. Over and over again they watched their favorites on chunky VHS tapes—Disney animated classics: *Dumbo, Cinderella, Robin Hood*; school-age-appropriate action films like *Super Fuzz* and *Tron*; and the raw violence of *Looney Toons* with that damn roadrunner who had it coming if only Wile E. Coyote could do it right.

The daycare closed at five, so the kids were in by 7 AM and most were out by 5 PM.

Kiara was glad to have silence. She leaned back on the couch and flipped through the TV channels searching for reruns. It was bliss not having her grandma there to boss her around.

On the evening of Thursday, November 9, 1989, while Kiara sat doing her homework in the living room, busy-work her sixth grade teacher Ms. Franklin had assigned, the phone rang.

"Kiara?" It was Cole. "Are you watching the news?"

He hadn't phoned her in a long time. Her heart fluttered.

"No, why?" Kiara asked.

"Go turn it on. NBC Nightly News with Tom Brokaw."

Since the twisted coiled receiver wasn't long enough to reach, she set the phone down. Tom was watching a movie on the VCR. She took the controller from him.

"Stop," he screamed. "Give it back."

"Just wait a minute." Kiara paused the movie and flipped on the news. On the screen, people lifted pieces of concrete. Kiara's heart sank. The month before there had been a hugely destructive earthquake in northern California that had crushed cars when a double-decker freeway came down. "Another earthquake? Great."

More death. Why did Cole want her to watch it?

"Here." She restarted the movie and threw the remote back at Tom. She picked up the phone. "Where did this earthquake happen? How many people died?"

"Earthquake?" Cole gasped. "Did you even watch it?"

"The concrete that fell apart?"

"That was the wall between East and West Germany." Cole sighed. "You should follow world events. I'll let you go—"

"Wait." Kiara hated to hear his disappointment. "I want to know. Tell me. Please."

"Okay." Cole perked up. He proceeded to give her the history of post-World War II.

She loved how his voice came alive with excitement. While he spoke, she closed her eyes and listened to his voice, which was deeper than she realized. When had that changed?

Her heart lifted when he explained that the collapsing wall meant the opposite of death and destruction—it meant freedom.

"Isn't that incredible?" Cole finished the history lesson.

You are incredible. "Yes, it is," she said. "We should get together to play Risk."

Cole laughed. "That's awesome. I'd love that."

She hugged herself, loving that she and Cole stood on solid ground.

25

On the Air

IN SCHOOL THE NEXT WEEK, teachers focused lessons around the East Berlin wall. Ms. Franklin showed them depressing documentaries of poor people stuck in East Germany, who had used homemade hot air balloons in the middle of the night to escape. Kiara was relieved the people were free of all that.

She and the other kids were also pleased that they had a field trip coming up in a couple weeks. Everyone turned in signed permission slips and were told to bring sack lunches. They were going to a science museum down below in Los Angeles, which Cole and Kiara eagerly anticipated; the others didn't care about the science part, just the no school part.

The morning of the field trip, Ms. Franklin came in with some bad news: they couldn't get the buses after all and so they'd have to cancel the field trip. She might as well have said that they'd all be starved to death based on the grumbling reaction and talk of mutiny.

Ms. Franklin said not to worry, they'd still do a field trip, just a different one.

She gave them a brief lecture on biodiversity and desert life. Kiara and the other kids in her sixth-grade class filed out in two rows, partnered up to keep an eye on each other. Each had a notebook in hand and a pencil as they headed out the front gate and to the left, in the direction of Kiara's house.

The field trip had been canceled due to lack of funds, according to what Kiara and Cole overheard. Ms. Franklin, optimistic they'd still have a great learning experience, led the class outside to the field next to the school—a literal field trip?

There were chaperones, too.

What was there to find in the desert that Kiara hadn't already seen a million times before?

"Stop right here," Ms. Franklin said. She had them reach out their arms to spread them all out from each other. Close enough to not get lost—where was there to get lost in this one-mile square plot of flat land? —but far enough away to not goof off and smack each other.

Ms. Franklin marked off the desert landscape into small separate plots; basically, students rotated around in a circle with arms outstretched and that was their assigned area.

"Now record every detail you see," Ms. Franklin said. "Every insect, every color and texture, animal prints, anything. Record your observations in your notebooks."

The midmorning heat bore down on the fields. A breeze blew and kicked up sand. The sun wasn't at the top of the sky yet, so Joshua trees left narrow shadows along the bushes and ground. Clouds floated overhead, unraveled and expanded in every direction then dissipated.

Kids grumbled and, despite the best cheerleading on the part of Ms. Franklin and chaperones, gathered at the edges of their areas and chatted every time the adults walked away.

Kiara had a single, short Joshua tree and some bushes in her area. She squatted and leaned in close to observe the difference in shades between the light and dark sides of the rough trunk. Black bugs flitted in and out of the bushes, a few creosote branches fluttered in the breeze, others remained unmoved. She sat on the dirt protected from the heat only by her jean shorts.

The rumble of a jet engine roared overhead. Kiara scanned the sky to find the source. In the distance, a black bird quickly approached—a triangular black silhouette in the sky. The compact B-2 stealth bomber climbed high, banked hard, and straightened out. Seen from the side, the narrow bird-of-prey accelerated and streaked over their heads, a black blur with oscillating jet fuel waves in its wake.

Everyone wrote it down in their notebooks, even though it wasn't plant and animal life; it was desert life. Here "top-secret" planes were test flown overhead before most of the country or world knew the aircraft even existed. After the B2 reached the other end of the sky, a crack as loud as thunder reverberated; it had broken the sound barrier.

The kids cheered and that was the end of the usefulness of this field trip.

On the way back, Cole, who was increasingly excited to share any facts with Kiara, walked alongside her. "The B2 goes at speeds more than 760 miles per hour. That's Mach 1."

"Wow," she said, even though she didn't understand the term 'Mach 1.' She was, however, enjoying the closeness she felt whenever Cole shared his knowledge with her. Even if she wasn't good enough for her mom, she was smart enough for Cole.

In early spring, excited chatter broke out in the GATE class. Kiara asked Cole what was going on. He grinned.

"We're going to be on TV," Cole said. "It's a show called *KidQuiz* that's filmed in Hollywood. Ms. Franklin asked me to be the team captain."

"For what?" Kiara had never heard of it. "Why you?"

"Because it's me." He laughed. "It airs at 7 AM on Saturday mornings on KCBS."

"First of all," she said. "There's no way I want to go down below to Hollywood at 7 AM on a Saturday for a show on a station that I can't tune in without static."

"It's not filmed at 7 AM, silly. That's when it airs."

Kiara felt foolish. "Well, what do we get if we win?"

"Bragging rights," he said. "And a trophy and a set of encyclopedias."

That didn't mean much to her. She had nearly a full set of encyclopedias on the bookcases at home—except for the last few books of the alphabet.

"I get to pick the team," Cole said. "Of course, you'll be on it."

They had to pick three more kids. Because Nelly had moved away, there were only two more students their grade level in the GATE program that year and they were both boys—Mikey who was new to the area and was cute enough that half the class had a crush on him—and Tristen who Cole and Kiara often made fun of because he had no social skills and picked his nose in class. For the last spot, Ms. Franklin picked another girl who did well enough in school, which, to Kiara's dismay, was Heidi.

The team had time to practice and found Trivial Pursuit to be a good training game. Kiara was almost as good as Cole on the arts and literature, and science and nature questions. She wasn't even close when it came to politics, history, geography, and sports.

Cole often won because he knew obscure facts and said it was because he read so much nonfiction at home—mostly to avoid his dad when he was drinking and smoking, which, as she knew, was usually.

Heidi was good with pop culture questions. When she wasn't answering trivia questions, she spent half the time drooling over Mikey and the other half flirting with Cole, which Kiara couldn't stand.

Stephanie and Jessica were excited that Heidi and Kiara would be on TV, and bragged to everyone. They wanted to go to Hollywood with them to meet the movie stars. Ms. Franklin said they needed kids to be in the audience, so Kiara's mom offered to drive the four girls up.

Heidi whispered to Kiara, "My mom's too busy whoring around to show interest in supporting me. Glad your mom can drive." Kiara's jaw dropped at this admission. Was Heidi's mom breaking up marriages? Because Kiara's dad abandoned them, she assumed that's what whores did.

Once they got to the studio lot, the kids in the audience got separated from the ones on the team. Stephanie and Jessica were disappointed.

A young employee with a clipboard gave the team blue t-shirts emblazoned with the *KidQuiz* logo and led them to the green room where there were snacks and drinks. Kiara didn't take anything even though they said it was free, because she figured there was probably a catch somewhere. She didn't want to get stuck paying for something she and her mom couldn't afford.

The guys grouped together. Heidi unsuccessfully tried to get Mikey or Cole's attention. Instead, Heidi zeroed in on Kiara and her hairstyle—or lack of one.

"Are you going on TV like that?" Heidi asked. She had her spiral-permed hair held in place with mousse and her bangs teased up and frozen in place with Aqua Net. "Can you take off your glasses?"

Kiara tried. She couldn't see past her hand. They decided it best to leave them on. Heidi fiddled with Kiara's hair, put it up in a side ponytail, and fluffed out the end to add more body.

They were told they'd be split up into two rounds. Before the cameras started rolling, the audience was given instructions on when to clap and so forth, and Kiara and the team met the host and weatherman, Maclovio Perez. The staff attached an acrylic sign saying Lake Los Angeles on their team's side of the set.

The game went by in a blur. Kiara knew most of the answers, but there was too much delay between her brain and her hand. She couldn't hit the buzzer fast enough. Cole, with his fast reflexes, answered most questions. Kiara tried to hide her frustration. Without getting the opportunity to answer, she was dead weight on the team.

Maclovio directed their attention to a video screen that played a clip of a cartoon. It only flashed on the screen for a split second before Kiara pounded on the blue buzzer in front of her. He called her name. She leaned close to the microphone and identified the character as Daisy Duck. Their team scored another point; unfortunately, it was Kiara's only point.

Heidi didn't answer a single question.

Kiara's team won the game and they advanced to the second bracket. That meant another trip to Hollywood. The second time, Kiara saved her reputation by answering "Mercury" when shown an image of planets aligned. Their team didn't win—not because they didn't have the answers, but because the other team's buzzers responded faster.

Kiara's mom drove her and the girls along Hollywood Boulevard to visit the golden stars inlaid in the sidewalks. The three witches hyper-focused on trying to spot movie celebrities.

Kiara and Heidi, and Mikey and Cole—not Tristen because he was a loner and nobody paid much attention to him—came back as classroom celebrities. Everyone commented that Mikey and Cole were hot (and Cole was smart), that Heidi's hair was stunning, and that Kiara, who was supposed to be smart, could only answer a single, simple cartoon question.

"What about Mercury?" Kiara said. "Did you even watch the show? I smacked the buzzer every time. I just wasn't fast enough." Nobody listened. Mocking her seemed more fun than the truth. Kiara couldn't get Stephanie and Jessica to stop.

It hurt. Maybe she wasn't smart enough to be cool, and not cool enough to be smart.

Heidi didn't get teased because nobody—herself included—pretended she was smart.

Kiara took a week off to herself to sit in the shade by the empty classrooms and sketch—practicing perspective with the fences and creeks.

Cole brought it up in GATE class. "Forget them," he said. "They're trying to make themselves feel better. They don't know the answers. We both know you're smart but slow."

He laughed and poked her in the side. She wasn't fast enough to stop him.

She smiled and looked away.

26

A Darker Turn

THE SUMMER BEFORE KIARA'S SEVENTH GRADE, Patches escaped from the yard. He chewed through his collar and dug a hole under the fence, which he had done before. This time he didn't return. Kiara's mom drove around for an hour searching for him before giving up. She said that he knew his way home and would be back if he decided to. Turns out he decided not to.

Nobody was sad. Patches was as mean and ornery as their grandma and now both were gone. The house was quieter without him barking at the other dogs on the street.

Kiara wondered if Patches had been helped in his escape, seeing as the day after he was gone, the daycare kids played outside on the swing set that she and Tom hadn't used in forever.

After Labor Day, Kiara's seventh grade year started the same as the others. She counted down the months until she could go to Littlerock High and get away from Stephanie, Jessica, and Heidi. With a much larger school population, she figured she'd be able to make new friends. Plus, she'd get to go to the same school as Carolyn. For that, she could hardly wait.

Kiara settled into her school routine: get Tom out the door on time to get to school, make herself invisible around the three witches, and hang out with Cole whenever she got the chance.

She had a home routine, too: avoid the daycare kids, confirm Tom's whereabouts—was he at another friend's house again? —figure out something to eat for dinner, pretend to go to sleep on time, then stay up reading books until she fell asleep.

Kiara's church held a couple of outreach events back at her school and they got to use different classrooms for the parents and different classrooms for the kids, separated by different ages. Maybe they were trying to reach out to the Palmdale-side Lake LA Catholics who had stopped going to church because of the drive to the Lancaster side of Lake LA.

Cole's dad dragged him to one of the church events, his first and last time. Cole played along, knowing his dad wouldn't stick with it; his dad paid tithings and prayed to a more down-to-earth God that brought him immediate comfort—one of nicotine and cheap liquor.

Kiara worried that Carolyn and her family wouldn't come to these events. She was glad when they did. On one of these events that lasted way too long, Carolyn whispered to Kiara that she needed fresh air. Glad to duck out to avoid Stephanie and Jessica, Kiara followed Carolyn and quietly slipped out the door.

Carolyn, dressed in her usual jeans with holes in the knees and an open flannel over her t-shirt, strolled through the middle of campus. Her hair had grown down to her low back and still blew a little wild in the wind.

Rather than the playground, Carolyn was more interested in the shady side of a classroom at the far end of campus, near the field. She leaned against the wall, reached into her pocket, and pulled out a lighter and a cigarette.

"What are you doing?" Kiara, wide-eyed, stared at her.

"Don't worry about it." She flicked the lighter, tipped the end of her cigarette, and took a long drag. She held her mouth closed then parted her lips letting the smoke exhale.

"Where did you get that?"

"None of your business."

Kiara shut up and slunk down to sit with her back against the wall. Every year in school, they showed pictures of a smoker's lungs and handed out red ribbons to celebrate being drug free. Although it seemed half the adults out there smoked—even when Kiara was in the backseat of their cars— she had never seen anyone her age smoking.

"Smoking is bad for you," Kiara said.

Carolyn shrugged and took another puff. "So are a lot of things." She took another deep drag, blew out the smoke, and coughed. "It's not like I'm asking you to do it. In fact, I wouldn't. It's bad for you." She laughed.

Kiara half wanted to leave her there, disappointed that the girl she had befriended was what she'd been taught to call a "bad apple," but torn, because she was a different kind of bad, a nicer one than the mean girls, but apparently a little self-destructive.

They existed in silence. Carolyn finished her cigarette, while Kiara sat far enough away to not absorb the smell.

When she was done, Carolyn dropped the butt, twisted her foot to put it out, then picked it back up and put it in her pocket. "I hate when people litter," she explained.

Kiara bit her lip. "How long have you been doing it?"

Carolyn contemplated this for a moment. "I guess I was nine or ten when I started putting the butts of my dad's cigarettes in my mouth to get a taste for it. He's a chain smoker." She paused, and stared Kiara in the eyes—brown meets blue. "Are you kidding me? You never noticed the ash trays every time you come over? He reeks."

"So, if you hate that he does it, why do you?"

"Sometimes we don't have a choice in the way things turn out."

"Does he know?" Kiara asked.

"No, but I think my mom does. She doesn't say anything because you probably haven't seen his temper, either." She shrugged. "I stay in my room and he leaves me alone."

Kiara didn't say much.

Carolyn continued. "He's really stressed. I guess there's a lot of defense spending cuts and he and my mom were both in the military. Even though he's retired, she still works for the government out in Edwards Air Force Base. Not sure what they do or did. They both have top security clearances. He says they'll be okay but worries a lot of their friends will lose jobs."

Kiara felt aware of her complete ignorance of the world around her. She didn't understand how people who worked in aerospace could lose their jobs because, according to Cole, the US was entering the Gulf War in the Middle East. It didn't sound good if a bunch of people were getting fired; it was never good when her mom got fired.

"I'm having a sleepover for my thirteenth birthday." Carolyn coughed. Kiara wondered if it was from smoking. "They usually only let me invite you over. This time they're letting me have several girls from school over. Do you want to come?"

"That would be awesome."

"I want to introduce you to my friends who aren't a bunch of superficial, bitchy airheads like Stephanie and Jessica."

"Like who?"

"Nicole and Jenny. Maybe Misty. You'll love them and I know they'll totally love you. They're super smart and overall cool people."

At home, Kiara asked her mom. "Can I spend the night at Carolyn's for her birthday?"

"Sure," her mom said, distracted by microwaving leftover spaghetti. With grandma gone, and no money for tasty frozen food, dinner choices hadn't improved. Kiara scrunched up her face. She hated the dried out red sauce mixed in with the soggy noodles.

"She's going to invite her friends from school."

"Oh, really?" Her mom's tone of voice changed. "Will Stephanie and Jessica be there? They're such nice girls."

"No. Why would they be?" Kiara rolled her eyes. Her mom had absolutely no idea.

"Then who are these other girls? Will they be drinking?"

"Mom, what are you talking about? Why would they?"

"I don't know these girls. They're not from church."

"It's fine, Mom. You know Carolyn's parents." As if going to church had anything to do with someone's good character. Exhibit A: Stephanie and Jessica. Kiara couldn't say this; her mom *loved* their parents and was so thrilled Kiara had them as friends.

"Carolyn is a little… rough around the edges."

"If you're referring to what she wears, that's not fair. She's super nice."

"All right."

Kiara took this as a yes, and told Carolyn. They both were super excited and made plans to watch scary movies and have popcorn. Kiara loved the idea of meeting new friends who she could hang out with later on at high school.

When Friday approached, her mom changed her mind like the desert wind changes direction.

"You're not going," she said.

"That's not fair. You said I could," Kiara protested. "Why not?"

"I never said you could. Why don't you go clean your room?"

"My room is clean. Even my laundry is put away and my bed is made. Tom's room is a mess. He's even got dirty underwear on the floor in the bathroom. And you let him go out with his friends all the time, even on school nights. He doesn't deserve that."

"Leave your brother out of this. Didn't you get a B on your last math test?"

"I shouldn't have told you that." Kiara balled up her fists. "I forgot to answer the questions on the back. It doesn't matter. I still have an A. I have straight As. Every year I have straight As. Tom doesn't. He gets Cs."

"Just because he has trouble with school sometimes does not give you a right to criticize him. At least he has a better attitude."

"He's smart, but he doesn't care. He's lazy. And he gets away with it because you like him better. You're always nicer to him. You love him more than me."

Her mom narrowed her eyes, clenched her jaw and smacked Kiara across the face. "Shut up. Stop being a bitch."

Kiara froze, stunned. Her mother had never called her that before. The slap didn't hurt as much as her words.

Kiara stared her down. "Well, I learn from the best." Then, before her mom could kill her, she ran to the bathroom, slammed the door shut, and locked it. She sat on the floor next to the bathtub and cried.

Her mom, surprisingly, left her alone for the rest of the night.

Kiara examined herself in the mirror and wiped away her tears. Her cheek was a little pink—no hand marks. She splashed on some cold water then went to bed. The spaghetti could rot in the microwave for all she cared.

How could Kiara escape that house and her mom?

She had nowhere to go if she ran away... unless she could find her dad.

Or maybe she could get married to someone and be happy and loved.

Or maybe if she got straight A's, she could get a good job and move out on her own.

First thing she'd do: Get out of the desert where everything dies. Everyone's hopes and dreams shrivel and die a slow death, like every one of her mom's jobs.

Until she could escape, Kiara made a promise to herself: She would never again share anything important with her mom who twisted words and threw them back at her. Her mom was kind to Tom, not to Kiara. Kiara didn't want to resent her brother but it was getting hard not to. He was never around anymore yet always praised.

All night, Kiara racked her brain to determine why her mom wasn't letting her go to Carolyn's—she had let her spend the night there plenty of times.

Maybe her mom didn't want to drive her. If that was the case, Kiara wished she'd say so. Carolyn's mom could've given her a ride.

She had half a mind to sneak out of her house and go anyway, but Carolyn lived too far. It'd take her over an hour and a half to get across town, especially since every yard was an acre and none of them could drive yet.

So, Kiara was stuck. She wanted to scream but that had only gotten her slapped.

Instead, she had a better idea.

27

Silent Night

KIARA GRABBED HER JACKET and crept down the hallway. She carefully turned the front door knob and closed it behind herself. The moon was out; the stars were bright.

Hidden in the shadows of night, Kiara hurried down her street and around the corner. Her eyes adjusted to the darkness. Across from her the fields, behind her the outlines of rooftops, to her right, a bright light in the distance reflected off the snow at the Mountain High Ski Resort. On her left, shadows of the buttes beckoned her.

She headed up the hill. Her shoes crunched on the loose gravel at the edge of the road.

Coyotes howled their horrid calls and crickets chirped in the bushes. Kiara kept an even pace. She pulled the hood over her head and tucked her cold hands in her pockets.

How could she escape her mom? She needed a plan.

At this hour, no cars were on the roads. Still, she glanced both ways before crossing the street. The shadows of the buttes loomed larger.

What if she found her dad? Maybe he'd let Kiara move in with him. Kiara ground her teeth together, not to keep them from chattering, but out of anger. Her dad probably didn't even know where they were. Her mom took them away from him. For that, Kiara couldn't forgive her.

Kiara puffed as the elevation climbed. She was almost there. Once off the road and on the trail, it became difficult to hike up without a light. Her feet kept slipping on the rocks and dirt so that she ended up half crawling her way up to the water towers.

The exertion pumped her blood and warmed her core, not her limbs which tingled in the windy air. At last, she reached the top. She turned in a 360. House lights twinkled on both sides of the buttes. The valley was silent.

She filled her lungs with the cold, crisp air. A heaviness lifted.

No wonder Cole found solace up there. Kiara felt removed from her problems, on a perch above them.

Winter break was a week away—the perfect time to push the issue. For now, she sought the warmth of her bed and headed home.

Days later, Kiara continued to consider why her mom was sabotaging her life: practically shaving off her hair three years ago in fourth grade and preventing her from making new friends. She bitterly stared out her bedroom window at the single scrawny tree in the hard-packed dirt that was bare of anything but twiggy arms.

A distraction came when snow fluttered from the dark sky and blanketed the ground. It covered the fields with a thin layer. The air turned frigid and the wind icy.

As Christmas neared, Kiara's mom got up on the roof to decorate the house which she did with over 5,000 lights—additional decorations she bought back when she was making money in real estate. It took her two full days. She hoisted a Santa and his sleigh pulled by reindeer all up onto the roof. She covered the garage in wrapping paper with a giant red ribbon and bow, which flipped around so much in the wind that going out and adjusting it became both a chore and part of the tradition.

In the front dirt yard, Kiara's mom installed three scenes, including a giant light-up plastic nativity set with three-foot tall figurines: Mary, Joseph, baby Jesus, angels, the Three Wise Men, and barn animals. She set up a Christmas morning scene complete with a decorated fake Christmas tree, around which life-sized dolls opened boxes wrapped as gifts.

At the edge of the dirt yard, her mom constructed a Mr. and Mrs. Tumbleweed Snowmen, both put together by actual tumbleweeds whose sharp edges helped to lock the layers in place. She strung white lights on both, then flocked them with white clumpy fluff that clung to the thorns. That was one way to give the tumbleweeds a useful purpose.

Every morning and afternoon, Kiara had to check for anything that might have been blown over and needed to be put back in place. One evening, she found the nativity scene and the outdoor Christmas tree and dolls had all been knocked to the ground from strong gusts that day.

"Go fix the tree and dolls," her mom said. She put the nativity scene back together.

Kiara tried to pound the stakes back in the ground. She couldn't get through the rock-hard dirt and the wind kept blowing the dolls over. Her hands were getting numb.

Kiara's mom returned and stood there watching, with her hands on her hips. "What are you doing? You're not putting those in at the right angle. Step back and let me do it."

Her mom pounded the stakes into the ground and tied the dolls to the stakes like Captain Hook in *Peter Pan* taking Wendy, her brothers, and the Lost Boys hostage.

Another gust of wind came through, whipping Kiara's hair across her face, stinging her nose, and knocking over Mary, Joseph, and the Three Wise Men.

"Go fix the nativity set," her mom said.

Kiara trudged over to Mary and Joseph and returned them to an upright position. Why did she have to fix stuff, when it wasn't her idea to put them up in the first place? She searched for baby Jesus and found him underneath her window. She dropped him back in the plastic manger.

"No," her mom said. "Put him underneath. He doesn't come out until Christmas morning on the day he was born."

"That's stupid," Kiara said under her breath. "I don't even believe in all this."

"What did you say?"

"Nothing."

Kiara picked up the Three Wise Men and shoved them further back in the stable. She readjusted Mary and Joseph. The wind blew the two figurines over again. The bulbs inside them went out.

"Great," her mom said. "Now they're unplugged. Can I trust you to fix them?"

"Why? They're going to fall over again."

"Don't argue with me. Stop being a brat." This time, she said *brat*, not *bitch,* but her tone was the same. "I'm going to check on your brother." Her mom went inside and shut the door, leaving Kiara out in the cold.

"Fuck this," Kiara kicked Joseph who knocked into Mary. She reached her foot back and kicked them both, harder.

The plastic cracked and splintered. Kiara kicked again and again. The plastic bodies broke apart under the force. She jumped up and down on both, on their hands folded in prayer, on their brown and blue robes, and their stiff torsos, enjoying every snap and crack. She picked up the top half of Joseph and swung down on Mary's head like a hammer.

Pretty soon, the only things left intact were the bulbs attached to the cords.

Kiara dragged all the pieces to the trash can and dumped them in.

"Guess the wind got to them." She smirked. She didn't care if her mom believed her or not. She turned to go into the house. On second thought, she picked up baby Jesus and threw him down onto the manger. "Sleep tight."

Kiara felt satisfied at last. It's not like any of them ever helped her before.

The next night, Kiara's mom, in her usual manner, acted as if nothing had happened. That was the way—pretend nothing ever happened. Tom wasn't home. Perhaps as a peace offering, Kiara couldn't be sure why, her mom made two cups of hot cocoa.

"I have a question." Kiara leaned on the kitchen counter and sipped on her cocoa.

Her mom held both hands around her mug. "What?"

Where's Dad? Why did he leave? Where is he? —None of these questions made it past Kiara's lips. Instead, she asked, "Why don't you love me?"

"I do, but you're difficult."

"To love?"

"To care for. I'm doing the best I can. Sorry if it's not good enough for you."

Kiara's stomach cramped. She grimaced.

"So, Dad is basically gone, right?" Kiara furrowed her brows and bit her lip.

"Yes."

"Is he never coming back? Does he know you took me and Tom away?"

"I didn't take you away." Her mom spun away. "He walked out on us. That's it. I pleaded for him to at least stay in contact with you and your brother, but..."

Kiara gulped hard. "But what?" She set down her cup.

"You'll understand when you're older."

"That people abandon their kids?"

"No," her mom said. She turned to face her. "That despite things being the worst ever, you can't give up. You've got to keep trying. Improve your life, protect your kids, or die trying."

Protect her kids? Or protect *Tommy*?

Her mom opened her arms and Kiara took the hug. Her mom held her tight, stroked her hair, and kissed the top of her head.

Even in her mom's embrace, Kiara couldn't, no matter how hard she tried, feel loved.

28

Uncertainty

KIARA'S MOM NEVER DID ASK about the nativity scene, and Kiara stopped asking about her dad. It was one thing she didn't share with Cole. She resolved that if Tom ever asked, she would tell him the truth, offer him the same hug her mom had, and hope it exuded more warmth.

On Thursday, January 17, 1991, when Kiara got home from school, the phone rang. It was Cole. He said to turn on the TV. She wondered what terrible or wonderful world event he called to share with her. Didn't matter. She felt at peace hearing his voice.

Her mom had replaced the rotary phone with a push button one with a much longer cord. Kiara untangled the coiled cord the best she could and brought the receiver into the living room where she turned off a movie Tom was watching—

he got mad and slugged her hard in the arm before he went to his room and slammed the door.

She turned on the news and saw a desert, deader than her desert, and flames burning from tall metal structures.

"That's the oil fields in Kuwait," Cole said.

She had no idea where Kuwait was, never heard of it before other than when Carolyn mentioned her older brother was fighting there in a war.

"In the Middle East," Cole said, "the Gulf War is no longer Operation Desert Shield."

Kiara felt far removed from the scene on the TV. "What's going to happen? Are they going to attack us?"

"No, not here. The US is leading a coalition against Iraq who lit the oil fields on fire when they retreated. President Bush ordered a strike. It's called Operation Desert Storm."

"What does that have to do with us?" She hoped, nothing.

"Oil. The war is about money. That's at least what the news reporters are saying."

"Who's going to fight it?" Kiara thought of Carolyn's brother.

"Don't worry. You're a girl, and girls don't get drafted."

Drafted? She had never heard the word. Cole explained.

Kiara figured she was safe, and maybe even the jobs for the engineers out in the AV—the Antelope Valley—would be safe.

Desert Storm ended a month later on February 28, 1991. Kiara was glad Cole would be safe from any draft even though he said it didn't affect someone until they were eighteen. Still, she didn't want to take any risks.

As it turned out, defense cutbacks continued, and evidence appeared everywhere in Lake LA. Oddly enough, engineers lived side-by-side with those without anything above a high school diploma who would be proud if their kids graduated high school in four or five years, or at least passed the GED high school equivalency exam. The streets became a checkerboard of poor families and educated families; and the educated ones' houses were becoming vacant. Plywood boards were nailed over windows because kids in the neighborhood threw rocks.

Kiara went up to one of the ones a few doors down. A sign posted out front said *foreclosure.* She asked her mom what it meant. The worrisome answer she got in return was, "What we're going to end up with if I don't make more money soon."

"Can't you raise your rates?" Kiara asked. She figured all the parents were happy with the daycare services.

"A bunch of parents are losing jobs. They can't pay more. And with the school year ending, not as many are going to need before and after school care or drop-offs and pick-ups from school. I hope more families need full-time daycare."

Kiara sensed that was unlikely, because many parents left their kids home alone whenever they had to. Her mom said she was getting a part-time job on the weekends cooking for people attending Christian retreats up in the foothills near Big Rock Creek at St. Andrew's Abbey. She applied to other jobs and considered getting back into bookkeeping.

"If I can figure out a way to make more money," her mom said, "I'm going to close the daycare when you get to high school."

Kiara didn't know what to think. She didn't respond other than to say, "Good luck."

She took a walk the next day, and, out of curiosity, turned onto Melissa's street. She hadn't seen her much since they stopped being friends. Kiara approached at a distance, not wanting to be accused of spying. She was disappointed that their beautiful green grass had turned brown—*can nothing survive out here?*

Kiara edged closer. Melissa's mom's car wasn't in the driveway. The shiny new bikes weren't on the front porch. She approached the house. A Foreclosure Notice had been attached to the front door.

She peered in the living room window—not yet boarded up. It was empty. Unlike other houses that were trashed inside or furniture left mid-move, Melissa's family had cleaned out everything. It was spotless.

The side gate was open. Kiara circled around back and peeked into Melissa's bedroom window; her bed, her dresser, the clear phone with the cord, the fancy stereo, gone—everything was gone.

Kiara sprinted back home and ran across her dirt front yard past the scrawny tree they had planted last spring. She cupped her hands and looked in her bedroom window. She sighed in relief; her bed was still there. Everything was still there. For now.

29

Barbed Wire

T OWARDS THE END of seventh grade, Kiara's GATE teacher, Mr. Jasper, said he had a special surprise for them. Last time she heard those words, her mom had come home with a trailer that still sat unused collecting dust in her backyard.

Mr. Jasper began a unit on solids, liquids, and gasses. He explained that when hot air expands, it rises; cool air descends as it contracts. He had them experiment with ice cubes and measure the mass.

One day, Kiara and Cole came to class and were surrounded by balloons and newspapers and colorful tissue paper. Cole figured it out first and told her they were going to make papier-mâché hot air balloons, and he was right.

She reminded Cole of the papier-mâché volcano and her mom's constant criticism.

Cole gave her a smile. "It'll probably be nice to do this one by yourself, you know?"

She nodded and returned the smile.

While they worked, Cole and Kiara complimented each other on everything—that's a perfect sized balloon, you got the perfect right amount of paste on that newspaper strip, those are pretty colors of tissue paper to cover the newspaper, and so on, until nobody else wanted to sit by them.

When everyone finished their balloons and everything dried, they popped the balloons and attached little baskets to the paper mâché balloon. Kiara was a little disappointed to learn that they weren't making ones that would actually fly.

Mr. Jasper told them all to get to school an hour early in the morning, and this request was beyond reasonable as far as she was concerned; there was no justification for it. She said she'd do her best to be there.

When she arrived ten minutes late, fifty minutes before the start of school, she headed out to the grassy field where they were told to meet. Not many students showed up, mostly a handful of younger GATE kids she didn't know. The corner of the schoolyard was cordoned off with yellow caution tape to keep the other students in school away from the area.

She got up for this? To be cold and tired and alone? Then she spotted Cole.

He stood in front of a life-size brown wicker basket with a cage attached and a contraption with a blue flame that lit up every time the stranger with a cowboy hat pulled on a cord.

Cole explained that the humongous hot air balloon, a real one with colorful striped fabric, blue and red and yellow, was being inflated by heating up the air inside it.

Kiara's eyes widened.

"Don't you wish you could go up there?" He motioned at the endless blue expanse of another crisp desert morning.

"Up in the sky? Can we?" She shielded her eyes from the bright morning sun with her hands.

"Mr. Jasper said this is just a demonstration. Wow, see the size of that?" he said. "I never considered the possibility of going up in one. If they'd let me, I'd do it."

She agreed and watched, mesmerized by the swishing sound of the flame each time it was fired up. The tufting fabric effortlessly rose from the ground with each spurt of fuel inflamed. It contracted a little then puffed up a little more until it rose up completely off the ground.

A hot air balloon could take her anywhere—over the buttes, beyond the mountains, towards the sea. She could escape far away from the desert, far away from everything. Would she take Tom with her? Maybe not. Maybe she'd go alone. Or, better yet, with Cole.

She imagined her and Cole floating up high above the clouds and drifting into the distance and never coming back.

She stole a glance at him. She wondered if he was imagining the same thing.

When school broke for summer, Kiara was glad. It meant only one more year at Lake LA School. Almost there. Just had to survive another twelve months.

During the summer, she was allowed to sleepover at Carolyn's house, so long as she was the only one spending the night. Or she could hang with Cole. Gossiping with Carolyn and playing games with Cole were two joys in her life.

Even if he did get away with everything, Kiara missed playing with Tom. Now he avoided her. He used to run to her for protection. Now she had transformed into an annoying mother figure to him—one who made sure he ate and nagged him to clean up after himself—since their mom wasn't doing a whole lot of mothering.

Maybe he'd appreciate her more if she bought a gift for him. Did he still play with Hot Wheels? She realized she didn't know him anymore.

One Saturday evening, after the sun got low and the dry desert air allowed the temperatures to plummet, Kiara put on her jacket and stood on the front porch waiting for Cole. He said he was going to come over so they could take a hike up the hill. She didn't want him to knock on the door or ring the doorbell, so Tom wouldn't get nosy. He had a friend over, his best friend David, the guy he spent most days and nights with.

At least the few kids that were left in her mom's daycare weren't there on the weekends. Her mom as usual was locked up in her bedroom watching the home shopping network, or old reruns of *M*A*S*H**, or reading, or crying—Kiara didn't much care which one it was this time.

Kiara and Cole had been getting together at each other's houses almost every other week over the summer playing board games, watching movies, and hanging out talking and telling jokes.

They had an understanding that her house was for the weekends as there was no real supervision, and his house was for the weekdays when his dad was at work. The other way around and it'd be chaos. So, they escaped the worst of their lives this way.

Kiara was glad not to have to be invited to the parties where the kids, including the holy three witches, were already starting to drink and smoke, even though most of them were only thirteen, getting ready for eighth grade. And Kiara felt uncomfortable at Heidi's house ever since she and the girls were over there at an end-of-the-year sleepover and got into Heidi's mom's and stepdad's—or boyfriends? —porn collection. That was a gnarly way to learn about sex. Kiara wanted to purge it from her memory.

According to their bragging, Kiara's friends were sneaking out at night and making out with different guys. Stephanie, Jessica, and Heidi were competing for whoever could get the most tramp stamps—hickeys on the nape of their neck underneath their hair, just low enough in so their parents wouldn't find them.

Kiara didn't have the same sexual interest in guys, yet, and wasn't sure if she ever would want more than a romantic friendship. Did all husbands and wives have sex?

She was happy to be free of the girls and their drama on account of school being out, except of course when she was stuck with them during church events.

The girls, especially Heidi, had been bothering Kiara to hook them up with Cole. Kiara didn't mention a word of it to Cole, because he was too good for them.

She was glad not to have to play dumb around him, like she did with the girls. She didn't dare point out when they got facts wrong or had flawed logic. They couldn't handle criticism without counterattacking.

As Kiara stood there on her front porch, she watched the street until she spotted Cole coming down her way. She waved and skipped up to meet him. She loved being able to say what she wanted and think freely around him.

"Where are we going?" she asked.

Cole shrugged his shoulders and smirked. "Guess you'll find out."

They strolled side-by-side out of the neighborhood and walked alongside the road leading up to the buttes. Up the paved road there were fields to their left. On the right, chain link fences wrapped around every acre-long backyard in the neighborhood. The road angled up towards the sky before disappearing over a crest.

"Are we going up to the water towers?" Kiara squinted at the horizon.

The water tower was closer to Cole's house than hers. Even though they were both on the west side, it appeared they were headed up that way.

"Nope," Cole said. "You'll see."

They topped the hill and the pavement of the road abruptly stopped, which would force cars to turn right into the last neighborhood. Cole didn't lead her to the right. He led her past the yellow Dead-End sign.

Kiara never noticed that the path continued, a rough and bumpy unofficial dirt road to nowhere. It wasn't traveled on much; there were huge dirt potholes that would tear up most suspensions. Only a few truck tread marks showed here and there.

Cole had gotten quiet and showed her the way with a pointed finger.

There, in the middle of tumbleweeds and Joshua trees was an old plaid couch, its cushions gone and springs poked out through the top. Over there, an old stove sat covered in dirt and missing a door. Some rusted out car parts looked older than the houses.

Cole led her further into the brush, away from all that. It was quiet up there, only a light breeze rustled through the brush. She couldn't see much on account of the vegetation that obscured her view of the low ground.

He came to a stop and she, staring around at the desert and not paying attention, bumped into him.

She stepped back and blushed. "Sorry."

He smiled. "Here's where we go in." He squatted down in front of a barbed wire fence. The fence ran the whole distance, short brown fence posts and double strings of barbed wire, menacingly strung taut across two rows, one on top of the other.

"Go in where?" she asked.

Cole squatted. Behind some sage brush, a big hole was dug deep for coyotes to crawl under the sharp wires—no sweatshirt would spare skin from that like it would over the top of the chain link fences.

"Under there?" she shook her head. "No way."

"The hole is deeper than it appears. Watch."

He got down on his hands and knees, and though he was twice her size, when he Army-crawled, he was able to clear the wires easily with a foot to spare above his head.

"See?" he said from the other side. "It's plenty deep."

Kiara sat down on the dirt and wiggled closer to the fence.

"I don't know," she said. "What if we get caught?"

"Who's going to catch us?"

"It's trespassing. There's a sign back there that says so."

Cole laughed and shook his head. "You're so funny. You're always trying to do the right thing, trying to please everyone else. Why don't you live a little and quit worrying?"

He patiently waited. She didn't move any closer.

Cole came closer to the fence and reached his arm underneath. "Come on. I'll help you."

Kiara stared into his green eyes and kind smile. She put her small hand into his; their dark and light skin tones contrasted making hers look lighter and his look darker.

"We both know you're not so coordinated," he said, "so take it easy."

That made her smile despite herself. She crawled underneath one knee and hand at a time, and didn't raise her head up until Cole said it was okay.

After they cleared that obstacle, they took to climbing their way up the butte. It was slow going and they had to use their hands to grip the flaky rocks, bits of sparkly quartz and sand scraping up their fingers and palms.

She didn't look down and kept following close to Cole's heels. At the peak of the butte, he reached over his hand to take hers and pulled her up.

He grinned. "You made it."

Kiara spun around and had a breathtaking 360-degree view of Lake Los Angeles. Unlike the water towers, she didn't have to walk a few feet in each direction to get the other half of the view. The expansive Mojave Desert stretched in all directions forever. Joshua trees sprinkled throughout were so tiny. Even the houses looked little and insignificant.

"Oh my gosh. It's beautiful."

Cole spread out his jacket and took a seat. He left a space for her.

"It's so windy up here." She shivered. "Hot with cold wind at the same time."

"Better down here," he said.

She nodded and took a seat close to him. She felt the heat of his body and it warmed her.

"How many times have you been up here?" she asked.

"Enough. Whenever my dad drinks too much, he screams, and mostly at me, so I bail out. Mom doesn't care either way, and probably thinks it's better I leave when he gets like that."

"How does he treat your sisters?"

"They're younger so he doesn't bother them much. He goes cussing off in the backyard. Sometimes he'll take a gun out there and try to shoot the heads off the gophers when they pop up out of the holes they've dug."

"That's horrible," Kiara said. "Aren't you scared of him?"

"Used to it."

The sun slipped closer to the edge of the Earth then dipped down below. The sky was streaked with color, aglow with flaming red and oranges, reflected across clouds even more vibrantly.

"Does he hit you?" she asked.

Cole shrugged. "Like I said, he must hate me."

"What's he so mad at? You don't do anything wrong." Kiara couldn't imagine anybody being angry at Cole. He got along with everyone.

"You mean I don't do anything right." Cole sighed and stared ahead at the setting sun which left a trail of rainbow colors. "Like you with your mom."

"At least she doesn't have a gun and isn't shooting heads off gophers."

They both laughed.

The light sank past the horizon and dragged the heat of the day with it, leaving a bone-cold chill in its wake. The temperature drop at night was like the rest of the desert weather—extreme. Overhead, a full moon was out, ready to take over the duty of night light.

As if he could read her mind, Cole pulled a flashlight out of his pocket. "Don't worry. We'll get back okay. I mean normally the moon is bright enough for me, but you and your balance are questionable."

"Going to get in trouble for staying out late?" she asked.

"My dad's probably drunk asleep. What about your mom?"

"Probably locked in her room asleep and assumes that Tom and I will have fed ourselves. I'm sure she doesn't even realize I'm gone. She hardly knows I'm there."

She thought of her dad. A sadness washed over her.

"Why do you worry so much about everything?" Cole asked.

"What do you mean?"

"Come on, I've known you since second grade and—"

"You probably know me better than I know myself." Kiara bowed her head. Dusk had wiped away the shadows of the day.

"I don't know everything. Do you have any dreams? What do you enjoy in life?"

She wiped her eyes with her sleeve. "I don't know. I mean this is nice."

"Yeah, I thought you'd like it." He paused. "Do you ever think about when we're adults, what we're going to do, where we're going to live, if we're going to be happy?"

Cole wasn't usually this talkative and definitely not about the future. The wild desert, being away from their families, seemed to give him the space to do so.

Kiara shrugged. "I guess getting out of the AV is success. What do you dream of?"

"Exactly. Getting out of here."

30

Building Bridges

THE RAGTAG COMMUNITY had been held together economically by the aerospace industry. Even that was unraveling.

Kiara's mom lost a few other families and so money got even tighter. She did, however, pick up a new client, one who wouldn't try to renegotiate the bill at the end of each week: Kiara's eighth grade teacher, Mrs. Cantrell and her redheaded toddler.

Mrs. Cantrell was old enough to be the little one's grandma. Kiara didn't say anything to her friends. She didn't want them to assume she could get special favors.

Her eighth-grade year was the first year she and Cole learned new math concepts; they switched classrooms during the day for the first time, and the two of them, along with a handful of others were taught Algebra by another teacher.

Having not been exposed to advanced math before, Kiara had a hard time figuring out why they were working with x and y when a and b were the first letters of the alphabet, therefore more logical to her. Her math teacher said they were in the Pythagorean Theorem. That meant nothing to Kiara.

She and Cole competed to finish assignments first, so math regained the fun factor.

Carolyn said that she switched classes six times a day over at Challenger Middle School. Kiara was glad she and Cole didn't have to do that yet.

She was terrified of high school, even though her mom and Mrs. Cantrell said they'd all be fine. What if she couldn't find her classes? What if she was late? What if other people bumped into her in the halls or bullied her? She'd read too many books about teenagers having a terrible time of it.

GATE class—she was told this would be their last year—had more surprises in store.

They got to create toothpick bridges. They formed teams and elected a team leader. Kiara led one team; Cole led another.

Each team went through the planning process, chose a bridge design, used their budget of fake money to purchase supplies and materials from the classroom store, and erected the structure. At the end would be a contest to determine whose bridge was strongest, which one could hold the most weight before breaking.

Of course, this meant design wasn't everything; workmanship played a big part.

"Which one are you going with?" Kiara asked Cole.

"The truss bridge." He held his head up with confidence and smirked at her. "You?"

"The one with the triangles? We're doing the arch bridge. It reminds me of the strength of the dam designs, like the Hoover Dam, that get stronger over time."

"Good luck with that." He didn't say it in a mean way, he just had to hurry up and get going because they all had a limited time.

Turned out that it wasn't so easy to make an arch bridge with straight toothpicks. Her team didn't have the time or money to start over, so they stayed the course. She modified the plan to shorten the span a bit to reinforce the support beams with additional mini lumber.

Each group had to record data, including span and mass, and run a Hot Wheel car across it. They calculated the bridge efficiency, materials cost, and whether they came in under or over budget. Soon it was time to test the strength.

Five groups had built five bridges in different designs.

After all construction was complete, Mrs. Cantrell tied a string to a little bucket and placed it across the center of a bridge. Gradually, a weight was added. She paused, then added another weight until the bridge cracked and splintered from the pressure. They recorded the results before they tested the next bridge.

Tension was high. Another group volunteered. Kiara and the others cheered each time another weight was placed in the bucket. They flinched when they heard the cracking of the tiny logs of wood. It didn't take long before their bridges snapped in two; one couldn't even hold more than a couple pounds.

Soon enough it was down to Cole and Kiara. Cole raised his hand first. Mrs. Cantrell stopped when the weight equaled the five-pound minimum for an A+ and said the bridge was a success. Cole pumped his fist and his group high-fived.

Kiara held her breath as Mrs. Cantrell added weights to her bridge. One pound. She took a breath. Two pounds. She breathed again. She squeezed her eyes shut when Mrs. Cantrell piled on the last weight to bring it up to five pounds. She listened for the crack. It didn't come.

The class cheered. Cole nodded at her and clapped at her success.

Both Kiara and Cole called out to Mrs. Cantrell, "Whose bridge is stronger?"

Mrs. Cantrell got a second bucket ready so the bridges could compete in real time.

Six pounds. Another couple ounces. Six and a half pounds. They kept going. Seven pounds. Kiara and Cole exchanged grins. She stuck her tongue out at him and it was in that moment that she heard the splintering. Toothpicks flew in the air as her bridge was demolished under the weight.

They put another weight and then another in Cole's before his, too, snapped in two.

The teams shook hands and congratulated each other.

Cole gave Kiara a hug. "It's okay if mine was better than yours."

She pulled back and raised her eyebrows at him. "Maybe you used more glue. We came in under budget."

He shook his head and they laughed.

31

Halloween

HALLOWEEN APPROACHED and Kiara and her friends were all at the age where they weren't sure if they were going to go trick o' treating, or not, because they were all technically teenagers. No one had any established rules or guidelines on that.

Stephanie, Jessica, and Heidi were going to a party hosted by one of their cousins who was already in high school. Kiara's mom said, "no way," and Kiara didn't argue since she heard there was going to be alcohol there and didn't want to get involved in that mess. She stayed home instead.

Her mom said that was fine and told Tom who was in fifth grade to get dressed in a costume. None of them ever had store bought costumes and mostly pieced together what they had. They scrounged around the house for something to wear.

Tom put on some Mickey Mouse ears—remnants from a trip to Disneyland so long ago. Their mom painted a nose and whiskers on him with eyeliner. Kiara helped him make a tail out of some felt and they safety-pinned it to a pair of red shorts that he had. He put on a black shirt and a black pullover hoodie on account of it being so cold out.

The sky and clouds were threatening to drizzle a little. Rain teased them on Halloween for as long as she could remember.

Tom got hold of his orange plastic jack o' lantern candy basket and sat on the living room couch, kicked his heels on the edge of the coffee table, and waited.

It was already dark outside. Kiara went to get her mom, who was getting into one of her moods and said 'just a minute,' which meant she wasn't coming out.

Kiara peeked out at Tom. She could tell that he was trying not to get sad. He was going to go with friends but their mom said she wanted to take him. Here he was, all dressed up, alone.

"I'll take you," Kiara said to him. "Just give me a minute."

Tom bounced around knowing that at least Halloween wouldn't get canceled on him—it was the best time of the year for free candy. Who wanted to turn that down, especially if some people gave out the good chocolate bars?

Cole had said he was going trick o' treating with his sisters. Kiara phoned him but was too late. They had already left.

Kiara realized she needed to figure out a costume, so she could get candy, too. She tore through her dresser drawers, piling clothes on the floor. Nothing much was speaking to her.

A short, flared out blue ruffled mini skirt with blue polka dots landed on the floor. She normally wore it over some black tights but ... what if? ... She'd heard her friends talk about getting jobs when they were older as cocktail waitresses to get tips, which would make them more money than a regular job.

Kiara decided that's what she'd do. She wasn't sure what a cocktail waitress wore but imagined it based on the movies she'd watched.

She didn't use the tights. She put on a white tank top. Her training bra showed through—she didn't have nearly as much up there as her friends did. She changed into a black tank top and, on second thought, added on a black sweater and tied the ends around her waist.

She pulled her hair back into a high ponytail—luckily it had finally grown out enough to hit her mid back.

She got into her mom's makeup—mom didn't even say a word while she lay in bed with her nose in a Christian romance novel—and wiped a streak of blue eyeshadow on each eye, and tried her best to put on some pink lipstick. Kiara hadn't done either one right. She didn't know how to. Not to mention it was hard to put on eyeshadow without her glasses on.

Kiara didn't own any of those high heeled pumps, so she put on a pair of flats. She found a pizza pan in the kitchen and decided that would be her tray. She had to balance that and a plastic candy basket in her other hand so she figured she was doing a bit of the cocktail waitress job already.

She was ready to leave when she heard Tom scream at the top of his lungs.

Surprised her mom hadn't been roused by this, Kiara ran to the living room.

Tom was standing on the coffee table and pointed to his shoes by the door.

Crawling out from his shoe was the biggest potato bug she had seen—bigger than the one she caught crawling across her bare legs when she was watching TV the previous week and it had grown bigger.

It was like a giant see-through spider-ant blend.

Kiara, terrified of bugs, wanted to protect Tom. She grabbed the pizza tray and used it to nudge the bug near the front door. Then she swung and smacked the bug outside, launching it up into the far distance.

She and Tom shivered away the creepy-crawly ickiness on their skin. Only one thing could motivate them to overcome the near-death experience, and that was candy.

She led Tom outside and they were on their way, and they both agreed to shake out their shoes in the future before slipping their feet inside.

Tom rang the doorbells and said, "trick o' treat" and got his candy before she stepped up to get hers. She always said, "Thank you. Happy Halloween" afterward and made Tom do it, too.

Whenever a dad or grandpa answered the door, his eyes lingered a little longer on her and it made her uncomfortable in the way it did back when her uncles used to give her the long, lingering hugs. Sometimes their eyes would travel down her bare legs and up to her barely developing breasts before smirking and handing her extra chocolate.

She shivered, and not because it was cold out.

Near the end of the night, when she figured they'd been out long enough, Kiara and Tom headed back. They were stopped by some other kids of Tom's age, a monster of some sorts and a pirate, who pointed at a lone house around the corner, and told them they were giving out full-sized chocolate bars. This was huge intel and she and Tom hurried up to the house.

A grandmother with dark skin and white curls opened the door and smiled at Tom. Sure enough, she held out a bowl with king-sized Snickers, Milky Way, Three Musketeers,

Butterfingers, and Baby Ruth, and told Tom he could pick one of them. He had a tough time deciding. He grabbed the Snickers.

Kiara stepped up to the door and said, "trick o' treat." The woman cocked her head to the side and looked Kiara up and down. It felt different than how men had gawked at her all night.

"Now, what, young lady, are you supposed to be?"

"A cocktail waitress." Kiara blushed.

"Mm-hmm." The woman paused. "Does your momma know you're dressed like that?"

Kiara didn't want to get into the whole 'my mom ignores us' kind of thing, so she just nodded.

"My, my." The woman shook her head in a sad way. "Here, child, have a chocolate bar. Maybe next year, you can be a princess, or better yet, a queen."

Kiara thanked her and backed away with Tom; the woman lingered at her doorway before going back inside.

Back at home, before she opened up a single candy, she ran to her room and changed. Her legs were freezing cold, her face was numb, and she was overcome with a creeping revulsion.

She set down her glasses, rubbed the makeup off in the sink and slipped into some pajamas and socks and felt a little better after that.

She and Tom laid out their spread and she checked to make sure there weren't any open wrappers like her mom used to do. Then she and Tom made trades.

Kiara couldn't stop thinking about that grandma's reaction and her disapproving stare and in spite of the sweet treats she felt awful.

32

The Freak

WHEN KIARA'S MOM TOOK HER BACK to the eye doctor for her annual exam, the optometrist came out to the waiting room to talk to them both together.

"Her vision is getting worse, much worse," he said. "The lenses are getting pretty thick for the frames we have for her small face. I recommend that you consider getting contact lenses."

Kiara's mom wore contact lenses. Whenever her mom reached in and touched her eyes to pull the little plastic cups off her eyes, Kiara got grossed out.

"You wear hard lenses, Ms. Leneghan. I'm recommending soft lenses for Kiara."

Kiara didn't want to do it. They both said it wouldn't be hard for her to learn. She finally relented but only if they could wait until Christmas break to give her at least a month to figure out how to put the darn things in and take them back out without clawing out her eyeballs.

She didn't tell anyone about the contacts, because she wasn't positive that she'd be able to get the hang of it.

Kiara's mom told her that it was time she learned how to apply makeup, especially since she'd be getting rid of her glasses soon. Well, it turned out that the school ran some after-school programs that were pretty cheap to sign up for—she had already tried gymnastics which didn't go so well; both she and the instructors gave up on teaching her how to do a cartwheel. It was obvious she wasn't destined for the Olympics. She was stuck doing somersaults, which was a waste of everyone's time.

Currently, there was a skin care course offered after school which promised to teach young ladies how to care for their faces and how to properly apply makeup, so they didn't leave the house looking like clowns, or sluts and whores—two words she'd been hearing more at and around school.

Kiara sat in the air-conditioned classroom around a large table—it must have been a primary grade class. There were a dozen other girls there, and she was the oldest. She wondered if maybe her friends had already taken the class. They had all been wearing makeup and fluffing up their hair for a couple years now.

Maybe her mom was nervous because Kiara would be starting high school next year and apparently wasn't very good at being a girl; Staphanie, Jessica, and Heidi criticized her for not dressing like a girl because she had gotten into the habit of wearing old jeans and oversized t-shirts. Her mom said she didn't act like a lady, whatever that meant, other than crossing her ankles when wearing a dress while sitting. That was super uncomfortable. And both her mom and her friends pointed out that she didn't do hair and makeup like the other girls.

It's not that Kiara was opposed to these things—she secretly read teen magazines to learn about fashion and complementary colors for different skin tones—but she couldn't grasp the concepts no matter how many times she reread the articles. She was too embarrassed to admit that terms like warm and cool undertones and summer and winter shades didn't make any sense.

Besides which, she wasn't comfortable in her own skin with her changing body, which is why she hid herself in baggy t-shirts and jeans and climbed trees whenever she was anywhere near them, rather than hang around a circle with girls all done up, showing off their developing breasts—Heidi had some huge ones already—with low-cut, tight shirts. Kiara still wore a training bra.

"This is eyeliner," the young woman instructed. "There are different types. You need to sharpen this one. Draw a straight line above and under your eyes."

Kiara tried. The line was squiggly and thick in spots and nonexistent in others. She wiped it off. Maybe she had to sharpen the pencil? The tip kept breaking off and the instructor had her move on to blush.

Kiara watched and tried to imitate it, but she ended up with two round circles on her cheeks like Raggedy Ann. They tried lipstick and lip liner. Kiara didn't like the dry texture on her lips and she bit and picked at her lips until they were worse than before.

Mascara application without good eyesight was less about perfection and more about trying not to jab herself in the eye or layer clumps on her eyelashes, which is what happened.

After the two weeks were up, Kiara would've said the whole class was a waste of time, except that she had learned to wash her face in warm water to open up her pores, and to splash cold water on her face when she was done to close them up, so she wouldn't have oily skin or get as many pimples as the other kids were getting. At least that's what she was told.

As far as makeup went, at least she could identify the basics: blush, mascara, eyeliner, eyeshadow, and lipstick, even if she couldn't use them. She had no idea what the heck foundation was or how anyone could smear paint all over their entire face and end up so pretty.

Her mom bought her some cheap makeup anyhow, and since Kiara had no interest in learning from her, her mom encouraged her to learn from her friends.

Stephanie, Jessica, and Heidi all wore makeup. They coordinated their blue or pink or purple eyeshadow based on what they were wearing. They read all the tricks and tips in the magazines and could transform their faces from blank canvases to a demonstration in skilled artwork. Even with their experience, Kiara chose not to ask for help.

That required far too much effort for Kiara whose idea of getting ready in the morning was to get out of bed, put on her glasses so she could see what she was doing, throw on something clean, brush her hair, and eat breakfast. That was it. That was all she could handle.

She valued sleep over frustration in failing to figure out how to contour with blush or how to apply eyeliner or mascara. She could admire her friends' faces and pretend she didn't care, even though deep inside, she did. They were far more glamorous than her. In contrast, she was an ugly duckling. Maybe after Kiara figured out the contacts, which she hadn't told anyone about, she might reconsider.

Even though it was still months away, in the spring was the eighth-grade school dance. Stephanie said Kiara needed an intervention before then—never too soon to prepare for it they joked—so Stephanie hosted a sleepover at her house; Jessica and Heidi of course would be there.

The agenda was a complete makeover for Kiara: try to teach her how to do hair and makeup, how to dress, and how to dance. It was overly ambitious she told them and rolled her eyes. They were all being nice to her, so she figured she'd play along and do her best.

They all gathered round Kiara and pulled out their bright plastic Caboodles, hot pink and turquoise makeup cases. Of course, she didn't have one. Her makeup was kept in a small cloth case with a broken zipper—leftover from her mom's stash. She wanted a Caboodle but didn't have the money for it, so she acted as if she didn't care.

Jessica pulled out a crimper, curling iron, and some Aqua Net. She'd be in charge of the hair tutorial.

Heidi brought out some cassette tapes. She opened the cassette player in Stephanie's boom box, and put in a tape by Technotronic. "Pump Up the Jam" and "Shake that Body" pounded a steady beat and the girls danced while working on Kiara. They discussed their favorite music videos on MTV. Kiara didn't have cable, so she didn't have MTV. They didn't make fun of her for that, because a lot of people out there besides her couldn't afford cable.

"We're going to teach you to freak," Heidi said, and the others squealed in agreement.

"What is a freak?" Kiara felt this was yet another secret she wasn't privy to.

"Oh my God." Heidi laughed. "You're so cool. Not." She shook her butt in front of Kiara and bumped it up against her legs.

Jessica set down the crimper. "Your hair is so frizzy and fine. It won't hold the curls."

Stephanie told her to quit moving so she could get the eyeliner on right. She drew the pencil across the top of her lashes, sat back to check out the progress. "What do you all think?"

"Needs more," Heidi said. "Why don't I paint her nails?" It wasn't a question so much as an announcement. She tapped a bottle of sparkly pink nail polish against her palm, grabbed one of Kiara's hands in hers and told her to stay real still. Kiara was trying to stay still. The more they reminded her, the more she was having trouble doing it and kept shaking.

After the umpteenth time of primping, the girls declared Kiara ready, or as ready as she could be.

"Wow, you're so pretty," Stephanie said, admiring her work. "You should wear makeup. And maybe lose the glasses."

That's when Kiara told them she was getting contacts.

Jessica squealed in excitement. "No way. That's so cool."

"That's going to help a lot," Stephanie said. "When are you going to wear them?"

"Hopefully before the dance," Kiara said.

Heidi gave her a hug. "Yes, you better. I'm so excited for you."

Jessica put her hair up in a high ponytail since it was weird with one side crimped, and the other straight; even the industrial power Aqua Net couldn't hold the curls.

They piled a bunch of clothes on Stephanie's bed and tried to choose an outfit for Kiara to wear to the dance. There were tight miniskirts like the ones the gorgeous models in the magazines wore. Kiara awkwardly tried one on. She couldn't move in it, so how was she going to dance in it? So, they narrowed it down to jeans with a cute top or a dress.

They circled around and gave her a crash course on all the latest dances: the Running Man, the Reebok, the Kid and Play, and the Freak. Surprisingly, she was able to figure out most of them. The Freak eluded her.

"Why do I need that one?" she asked.

"How are you going to dance up against the boys?" Heidi asked. "Duh."

The girls all sprang out in spontaneous freaking up against each other and against Kiara, who couldn't get the rhythm right. How would she be brave enough to do that with any guy anyhow?

After everyone settled down, they got down to serious talk—boys. After a couple of rounds of Truth or Dare, it came out that Kiara was the only one who hadn't kissed a guy before.

"Not even in Spin the Bottle?" Heidi asked and was even more surprised when Kiara said she'd never played Spin the Bottle before.

Where did they learn these things? Hadn't Kiara grown up in the same place? Why was she so clueless? Her cool factor was plummeting, so she changed the topic to ask who had a crush on who. Stephanie said a couple guys might sneak up to her window tonight because she asked them to, and if they came, she dared Kiara to make out with one.

Kiara's stomach cramped and the anxiety was back. "No, you do it. Or Heidi can do it."

Heidi turned to her. "I want you to hook me up with Cole. He's so hot—have you seen those eyes? And those curls? He's begging to have a girlfriend, I swear."

Everyone got quiet. Kiara froze. All eyes were on her.

"I don't know if he's already going with somebody," she lied.

"Then find out," Heidi said. "Let's call him."

"I don't know his number," she said quickly.

"Seriously?" Stephanie rolled her eyes. "You talk to him all the time."

"Maybe she wants to be his girlfriend," Jessica said. "So that's why she won't do it."

"No, I don't," Kiara insisted. She didn't want any of them to be his girlfriend but she couldn't tell them that; she'd be eaten alive and torn to shreds.

"Of course, she doesn't." Heidi looked her up and down. "She doesn't have any boobs, she's so not cool. Who would even want to date her?" Heidi jumped up and down showcasing her already size C, maybe even D, chest. "All the guys like these. I bet Cole would, too."

They all laughed, all except Kiara, who wanted very much to go home.

33

The Dance

KIARA'S MOM TOLD HER she was glad Kiara was planning to go to the eighth-grade school dance in the spring, which was a strange thing to say, considering she blocked her from going to Carolyn's birthday sleepover.

Kiara didn't want to argue and risk getting slapped again, so she didn't push. She did tell Carolyn.

"I'm sure she'll feel differently," Carolyn said, "after you're in high school and can have everyone over. Then she can meet all the girls."

"Yeah, and she can quit worrying."

"Your mom worries about the stupidest shit. Yet she adores those little whores."

Kiara laughed. Six more months at Lake LA School.

The day after Christmas, Cole phoned Kiara. Did he want to see her over winter break? Her stomach did somersaults.

"Kiara," Cole said, "Are you watching the news?"

A little disappointed, Kiara would at least have the chance to talk to Cole for hours on the phone. She took their new cordless phone to the living room and flipped on the TV.

She didn't have to take the remote from Tom because he was at Dave's.

"Remember the Soviet Union?" Cole reminded her of its spot on the Risk game board. "The Cold War ended as has the USSR." He explained it would be renamed Russia and that several other countries had broken away.

Kiara hadn't even realized there had been another war and felt foolish. The girls knew glamour; Cole knew international politics; she wished she was more knowledgeable about both.

"Like East Germany?" she said, hoping to sound smart.

"Exactly. That's so cool that you remember that." Cole's voice became more animated and he kept her on the phone for an hour talking about national security and nuclear weapons.

The entire time Kiara's heart swelled with pride listening to his voice. Every time she interjected with a fact, Cole spoke rapidly with more excitement. Kiara didn't understand half of what anything meant. She loved that Cole did, and, most of all, she loved that he shared everything important with her.

As spring approached, so did the eighth-grade dance.

The heavy weight on Kiara's shoulders was that she had put off learning how to use the contacts. Panic set in. She leaned over the bathroom sink with the drain plugged up in case she dropped them and practiced. Her mom tried to help but her patience was on a short fuse.

Kiara hopped up on the counter to get closer to the mirror. The contacts kept drying out and flipping onto themselves like tacos. She squirted contact lens solution to soften them and retried.

After several nights of trying, she finally got them in. She couldn't stand having them in for more than a few minutes. It felt like she had sand in her eyes. Her mom told her it was probably because she'd irritated her eyes from trying so much and to take a break for a few days.

Then it happened. She got them in and it didn't hurt. She was mesmerized by her eyes in the mirror. When was the last time she'd seen the color of her own eyes so clearly? It was a prettier version of herself staring back at her. She couldn't wait to show everyone at school.

She hadn't realized how long her hair had gotten. The destruction of four years ago was finally gone without a trace. Her hair was halfway to her elbows, lighter brown with highlights thanks to all the sunshine, which was a wave of relief.

Kiara asked Cole if he was going to the dance, and he said he was, that he would take any opportunity he could to get out of the house. She didn't ask if he had a girlfriend because she knew the answer. Not wanting to put ideas in his head, she didn't mention Heidi. She told Cole she'd see him at the dance.

Kiara stood in front of her bathroom mirror and put in her contact lenses. It would be the first time anyone would see her without the huge pink-framed glasses. She had butterflies in her stomach, the good kind.

She had the makeup her mom had gotten her. She examined the eyeshadow and eyeliner and felt overwhelmed. She was okay trying the mascara, so she brushed a few layers on her eyelashes and that made them stand out; it made her blue eyes stand out, too, and she, for what was the first time in a long time, didn't entirely hate the way she looked.

After telling herself she'd wear jeans, she instead reached for a light blue flowered dress which hung unused in her closet. Nobody had ever seen her in it and probably assumed she didn't own a dress. She had saved up babysitting money to buy it. She never felt comfortable enough to wear it.

She slipped it on over her head and it settled nicely on her hips—she hadn't realized her hips curved out so much from her small waist. It was flattering, even though from the waist up, she was straight. She slipped her feet into her flats, because she had told her mom she had terrible balance. She refused to try heels yet.

"You're beautiful," her mom said. "You did all right with the makeup."

Kiara smiled. "Thank you."

"See, didn't I tell you? You should listen to your mom more often. Wasn't I right?"

To Kiara, this no longer felt like a compliment. Her mom was complimenting herself. But this was not the time to focus on anything negative—it was her first dance and that's all she wanted to think about.

It was chilly out by the time her mom dropped her off at the school, so she rushed inside the cafeteria trailer, where the dance was held.

Inside, her eyes adjusted to the darkness. There were kids huddled into groups, the music, "Pump Up the Jam" was playing. She wondered if her friends had requested it.

There were balloons and streamers. Colored lights rotated around the room making sparkles of light on the ground. It didn't resemble a cafeteria anymore.

Boys in their nicest pants and shirts, a few with ties on, and girls mostly in dresses, turned towards the door when they realized someone new had arrived.

A bunch had puzzled expressions on their faces, heads cocked to the side, sizing up who it was that had entered. They didn't recognize Kiara in a dress without glasses.

Cole was the first one who did. He came up to her and gave her a big hug.

"You look pretty," he said. He gulped and smiled.

Did he mean it? Did he think she was pretty?

"Thanks," she said. "You, too." She wasn't used to seeing him in slacks with a belt and a button-up shirt. His green eyes shone. She stared into his eyes, then smiled and averted her gaze.

Kiara glanced around. Other guys were staring at her.

Had they decided they'd wrongly passed her over until now? Maybe that was wishful thinking.

Was her dress too short? It definitely wasn't as long as her jeans. Self-conscious, she tugged down at the hem.

One of the braver boys, a cute guy who goofed off in class, came up and asked her if she wanted to dance.

Kiara blushed. "No, thank you. I'm trying to find my friends."

"Tell me if you change your mind." He winked at her then rejoined his posse.

She smiled shyly at Cole who smiled back, his eyes warm with kindness.

That's when the three witches came out of nowhere and intervened.

"Hey, Cole," Heidi said. She glared at Kiara then back at him. "Let's go dance."

Cole wasn't the rude type, so he let her lead him over to the dark corner where some teens were already dancing. Kiara followed them with her eyes.

Jessica and Stephanie gave Kiara a hug and told her she was prettier in a dress and should wear more of them. They grabbed her hands and led her over to the center of the dance floor where they practiced all the dances that they had taught her. Kiara was having a good enough time until Heidi rejoined them, a big smirk painted across her face. She leaned in close to the three of them and giggled.

"I freaked him," she said and winked at them. Stephanie and Jessica said that was a success for the evening.

Kiara scanned the room. She couldn't find Cole.

Heidi snickered. "Who're you looking for?"

"There was a guy who asked me to dance and I was trying to find him," she lied.

This worked. The girls went on a mission to find him and brought him on over.

A slow song came on and he put his hands on Kiara's waist; she froze for a moment, having never had a boy put his hands on her before—her friends hadn't told her how to do a slow dance.

Other girls had their hands on their guys' shoulders and so she imitated them. There was a space of six inches between their bodies, and Kiara was thankful for that. She rocked back and forth like he was doing, and when he started moving his feet a little—slide one open, close it with the other—she copied it.

By the time the song finished, she was glad to be done.

Kiara and Cole didn't talk much about the dance when they returned to school until he brought it up in GATE class.

"What did you think?" He smiled and stared into her eyes.

The eye contact felt intense. She turned away and blushed. "It was fun. I liked the music and the decorations."

He nudged her arm with his. "Yeah, who knew some lights and streamers could hide the fact we were in a cafeteria trailer?"

She smiled, glanced at him and looked away. "Yeah, who knew."

After that, things got a little bit weird between them. There were glimpses of eye contact followed by looks away and sometimes a hint of blushing, even for Cole.

Kiara figured maybe it was because Heidi was throwing herself at him every chance she got and he didn't want to say so. Inside her stomach fluttered when he smiled at her.

Heidi gave up on Cole after a while; she said he told her that his parents wouldn't let him have a girlfriend and she said they wouldn't have to find out; he said she was nice and pretty and all, but it wasn't worth getting in trouble over. Heidi wasn't accustomed to rejection so she moved on to the train of guys waiting for her to hop on over.

In mid-April, in the wake of the arrest of four LAPD officers accused of beating Rodney King, a black man in South Central LA, some of the black and Mexican kids whose families had moved them out of LA complained the trial wasn't going to be fair because the cops were white.

Kiara talked it over with Cole. She acknowledged that with his black and brown relatives, he might know more than her. "Does this affect your family?"

"Yeah, my grandma in LA says everybody's getting edgy with the trial going on."

"I don't want you getting hurt." She blushed. "Or your family."

On Wednesday, April 29, 1992, Cole phoned. He didn't have to tell her to flip on the TV; it was already on. Sure enough, the jury—nine white people, one Latino, one Asian, and one mixed-race person—acquitted the four white officers. Not even hours later, horror unfolded before Kiara's eyes.

"Are you watching?" Cole asked.

"Yes." Buildings were ablaze, cars trashed, people beat. It was like the worst TV riot movie scene. "It's horrible. What's happening?"

"Can I come over?" he asked. "Now?"

"Yes, of course." This was a first. Normally, they just stayed on the phone during chaos.

Kiara stared at the news, unable to look away. Before long, Cole was sitting on the couch next to her. She felt his arm brush up against hers.

He pointed to the screen. "This is unreal."

She blinked. On the TV, a white semi-truck driver, caught in the middle of the city that had exploded in chaos, was dragged out of his big rig. Like a rag doll, he was yanked and beaten with a cinderblock. Even the newscasters were at a loss of words for the fear gripping everyone. There were no police anywhere to be seen.

Shop owners stood atop their buildings and pointed guns at the looters. Glass and trash and violence was everywhere.

"Are we safe?" Kiara asked.

Cole, not usually short of solutions, said, "I don't know."

She wished he'd put his arm around her and comfort her.

"My grandma lives near Watts," Cole said. "She moved from Virginia in the '50s to escape shit like this. She survived the Watts riots, and now here we go again." He shook his head. "We called to check on her. She said she's fine, staying safe behind her metal screen door."

That didn't put Kiara at ease.

"With all this going on, she gives me advice," he said. "She told me, 'Better to keep your mouth shut and be thought a fool than to open it and remove all doubt.' I guess she doesn't want me to talk about it with anyone." He looked at Kiara. "Except for you of course."

"I hope she's okay."

He nodded sadly.

Newscasters discussed whether Korean stores were being targeted.

"Why would they be?" Kiara asked.

Cole signed. "Last year, a Korean store owner shot and killed a fifteen-year-old black girl who he said was trying to steal orange juice. It was a lie. She had the money gripped in her dead hand. And the guy got away with it. He only had to pay a $500 fine."

"That's horrible." She pointed to the TV. "Look at the smoke. The stores are on fire."

"It's not just stores. People's homes are burning. The city is burning."

"I'm scared."

Cole wrapped an arm around her shoulder. She leaned her head against him. He didn't say it was going to be okay but no matter how scary everything got, she felt safer by his side.

At school, a few of the Hispanic kids in Kiara's class bragged they had family and friends going down to loot and get free stuff. Kiara wanted the details. She was afraid to ask, so she took Cole's grandmother's advice and kept her mouth shut.

34

Hypocrisy

A MONTH HAD PASSED since the LA Riots, or The Uprising, depending on who you talked to. People said it would take a long time to rebuild buildings, the cities, and trust; the latter which seemed to have never been built in the first place. Without witnessing the devastation first-hand, the chaos faded into the background for Kiara. She and Cole didn't bring it up.

In the desert, the heat was upon them. Under the sweltering desert sun, the 100+ degree temps were there to stay for the next six months with lows at night dropping into the 50s.

People were a little more short-tempered or too tired to deal with anything during most of these miserable days. Now that the chaos "down below" had calmed or at least tucked itself back into the shadows, the news stations moved on to other things.

Life out there resumed, albeit in the misery of brutal temperatures and bloated electric bills. Kiara's mom said they couldn't afford to run the air conditioning. Lately, her mom was on a rampage over something. Kiara escaped to Stephanie's house for a sleepover.

When she got there, after her mom finally was persuaded to drive her over, Kiara entered Stephanie's house and found her, Jessica, and Heidi on the couch eating crackers with Cheez Whiz. They passed the can around. Kiara took a bite and cringed. It was too salty.

Stephanie's parents weren't home; they were at some church thing at Jessica's house.

The girls complained about their periods—Kiara still hadn't gotten hers. They compared how many bases they'd gotten to with different guys. Kiara didn't understand the whole bases things. Everyone had different definitions of first, second, and third. Homerun, no matter what, meant the same thing, and she figured they were too young to be having sex.

She was wrong.

The three exchanged stories and brags about blow jobs— Kiara pretended to understand. She didn't want to sound stupid, so she sat there quietly and grabbed the can of Cheez Whiz to keep a constant flow of crackers and cheese spread in her mouth so she wouldn't have to talk.

She didn't know if they were making it up or not when they claimed to have lost their virginity or were on a mission to do so before high school. God, Kiara still hadn't even kissed a guy. She focused on the crackers, taking tiny bites to make them last longer.

The three girls were already partying with hot guys in high school. Usually, parents weren't home and even if they were, beer was readily available. Kiara hadn't tried anything more than a sip of her mom's champagne on New Year's Eve and she hated it.

The girls admitted they snuck out their windows at night, and Stephanie said her parents figured it out and put a lock on her window but it was easy to pick.

The conversation turned to high school girls at the parties and kids from their school.

"Damn reggins," Stephanie said. "Always ruining shit."

The girls laughed and repeated reggins.

"What's a reggin?" Kiara asked.

"Stupid. Spell it backwards." Stephanie mocked; the other two laughed.

"Are you fucking kidding me?" Kiara couldn't hide the horror on her face. The *N* word was offensive, forward or backward.

"What?" Jessica taunted. "They call themselves that all the time."

"You guys are seriously fucked up," Kiara said.

"What are you? A wigger?" Stephanie raised an eyebrow.

"A what?" Kiara asked.

"Oh my God," Jessica said. "Are you that dumb? A white person that's all confused and treats reggins better than white people."

"Yeah, I would never have sex with a stupid reggin," Heidi said and the other two agreed.

Kiara glared at them. Why did Heidi crush on Cole? Stupid bitches.

Surely, they were parroting what they heard. Kiara combed through her memory. Had she ever heard anything from their Christian parents to indicate this racist attitude? No, but who knows what's said behind closed doors.

At school, Kiara vented to Cole. She wasn't sure how he'd take it on account of him being part black and part Hispanic. He shrugged it off.

"You're just now figuring them out?" he said. "That's why I was mad when you went back to being friends with them."

Kiara's jaw dropped. "You were mad at me? I didn't want to be their friend. My mom—"

"They're not the only ones. I'm surprised you've never realized it."

She shook her head. His answer made her sad.

"You can't change some people," he said. "I mean look at the way we're living out here. We've both lived somewhere better. These people are stuck here. They can't get ahead so they're angry at the world and want someone to blame. Problem is they're blaming the wrong people."

She didn't ask what he meant by that, and who they should be blaming.

Three weeks before graduation, Heidi showed up at Kiara's door on a Saturday morning. She practically pushed her way inside and shut the door behind her.

"Shh," she said. "Is anyone home?"

No, Kiara said. Her mom was at her other job, and Tom was at Dave's.

"Are they going to be home soon?" Heidi scanned the room.

Kiara shook her head and eyed Heidi with suspicion.

"You got to promise not to tell anyone. I mean it. Not Stephanie, not Jessica, not anyone."

Kiara wasn't used to being asked to safeguard secrets like this but agreed.

"I mean it. If you say anything, I might have to hurt you."

Kiara didn't know what to say to that. "What do you want?"

"Can I use your bed?"

"My bed? For what?"

"I promise I'll clean it all up."

"Clean what?"

"You know your neighbor, Deshawn?"

"What about him?" Of course, Kiara did. He lived a couple doors down. He was nice to her and they waved at each other when they passed. Why was Heidi bringing him up? She hoped Heidi wasn't intending to hurt him or anything, because she, Jessica, and Stephanie apparently had something against people who weren't white.

"Well, he's coming over here in a minute." Heidi adjusted her low-cut top and pulled it down to show more cleavage. "And we're going to use your bed. I mean if that's okay."

Nobody in their right mind would want two teenagers doing it in their bed. But Kiara didn't feel like she had a choice. Heidi gushed thanks.

Sure enough, a couple minutes later, Deshawn knocked lightly on the door. When Kiara let him in, he smiled then headed straight for Heidi. As if she wasn't there at all, Kiara watched him take Heidi by the waist and pull her close. She wrapped her arms around his neck and they kissed. Then she grabbed his hand and pulled him into Kiara's room. She shut the door.

Kiara sat on the couch and stared at the wall. Her cheeks reddened. How dare Heidi and the others call people reggins and wiggers and then this?

Noises drifted from her room, like the ones she heard on porn videotapes that Heidi showed them a few years back.

Kiara turned on the radio in the living room. REM's "Losing My Religion" played loud and clear.

This was bullshit. Kiara made a decision: she was done with all three of them—Stephanie, Jessica, and Heidi—for good.

Kiara stormed down the hallway and pounded on her bedroom door. "My mom is on her way home."

She could hear panic on the other side. A couple minutes later, Deshawn ran out, dressed with his shirt off. Heidi was sitting in Kiara's bed, a sheet pulled up to her neck.

"You better not be lying," she said. "Or that's super messed up of you."

"Really? Like coming over here isn't messed up?" Kiara stomped her foot. "I want you out of here, now."

Heidi got dressed and left, but not before issuing another threat to keep quiet.

Kiara told Cole later, and he laughed. "And to think she tried to kiss me back at that dance. She's probably kissed everyone."

Are you fucking kidding me? She had to wait it out until high school. Then she'd be with Carolyn and there would be a lot more kids to meet from other towns like Littlerock and Pearblossom, and the other half of Lake LA.

She didn't need Stephanie, Jessica, or Heidi, or their twisted, racist friendship.

35

Promotion

AT THE END OF THE YEAR, Mrs. Cantrell, Mr. Jasper, and the other teachers decided Cole had earned Valedictorian and Kiara had earned Salutatorian of their eighth-grade class. That meant both had to give speeches at the promotion ceremony. Some parents of the kids hadn't even graduated from eighth grade, so everyone made a big deal for this milestone.

Kiara was a little miffed as to why Cole got the top spot, not her. She reasoned it came down to attendance and she had been gone for two weeks on account of getting pneumonia. Doctors said it wasn't contagious even though she and her mom both had it. The school didn't want her back around the others until she finished her antibiotics. Kiara was too exhausted to enjoy the home vacation, plus she had to finish her work on independent study.

"No, that's not why," Cole said. "It's because you only answered a Daisy Duck question on KidQuiz." He gave her a playful wink.

She lightly punched him in the arm. "That's not fair."

"Hey, life's not fair."

The promotion ceremony was held at Almondale Middle School in Littlerock. It had a real auditorium with a stage and podium. Cole and Kiara showed up early to do a sound check with the mics and understand their positions.

The mic on the podium was too high for Kiara. She couldn't see over it. So, they brought out a mic stand for her. The night passed by in a blur. Kiara, in a navy-blue dress with white polka dots, white pantyhose, and her first pair of heels—low white pumps, which made her ankles wobble a little—took slow, deliberate steps, especially when ascending the stage steps.

Her speech focused on memories of the dry lake bed and Fred the cat, and how far they'd come, while Cole's speech focused on the future and his hopes for them to do well in high school and beyond. She sat in the front row and cheered, proud to be friends with Cole. Afterward, he returned to sitting next to her.

The moment the ceremony was over, Cole leaned over and whispered, "Let's get cookies and punch and head outside."

With the sun down, it was cool and dark. Kiara and Cole leaned next to each other against a tree and nibbled on chocolate chip cookies. They both had trophies and award certificates in recognition of their grades and accomplishments.

No sooner had Kiara put the second cookie into her mouth than her mom appeared.

"There you are," her mom said. "I was searching all over for you. Come on. Let's go."

"Why? Can't we hang out for a little bit?" Kiara looked wistfully over at Cole.

"I ran into Stephanie's mom and she invited us over. We're going to take pictures at their house. Your other friends Jessica and Heidi will be there."

"They're not my friends." Kiara groaned. "I don't want to go."

"Don't be rude. Pick up your things and let's go."

Kiara threw Cole a helpless look.

In the car, Kiara's mom turned to her. "Did you make sure your brother got cookies and punch, too?"

"I didn't think it was my turn to babysit him."

"Watch your mouth." Her mom continued in an irritated tone. "We had to hurry up and get there early because of your speech, so he didn't get dinner."

Tom stuck his tongue out at her. She threw a cookie at him while her mom focused on driving.

"What did you think of my speech?" Kiara hoped her mom was proud of her.

"It was fine. Cole did a great job. His was entertaining and engaging."

Kiara sighed and stared out the window. Part of her wanted to throw her Salutatorian trophy out the window to see if her mom would notice, but Kiara didn't want to litter.

On Sunday, June 28, 1992, Kiara was jolted awake at 5 AM by her bed rocking back and forth. The house creaked and shook, everything on the shelves rattled. Her stuffed animals and books fell off her bookcase. It took her a moment to realize what was happening.

Her mom screamed at her and Tom to get into the doorway. They huddled there and braced themselves against the frame. Her mom kept the door from slamming into them.

They were too far from the dining room table, which would've been better, but it's not good to run across a house when the earth is throwing you around, and you have to avoid broken glass.

Five miles beneath the surface of a small town called Landers, several fault lines had come to life in a 7.3 magnitude quake.

Unlike most other earthquakes, this one didn't stop. Kiara felt like they were on a train barreling down the tracks. At first, she didn't mind it, being half asleep and all, there were a few seconds of fun. She got worried when it kept going for two to three minutes. It slowed and quickened and kept rolling.

"Is the house going to fall on us?" Tom panicked.

"The wood frame allows it to sway rather than crumble," her mom said.

When the earth settled, and the house stopped moving, they surveyed the damage—a few broken dishes and some things on the floor. Everything was mostly okay.

They turned on the TV and listened to the Caltech scientists reporting it was felt as far north as Sacramento and south into Mexico. Back in April, the 6.1 Joshua Tree earthquake struck. This one, they confirmed, was way bigger. They explained every single point higher on the Richter Scale, used for measuring earthquakes, was ten times as strong as the one before. This meant, a 7.0 was 100 times stronger than a 5.0.

Then came aftershocks. The largest one hit at 8:05 AM, a 6.4 magnitude centered in Big Bear, up in the mountains beyond their house.

She called to check on Cole. They were both rattled. She asked if he was watching the news. He admitted it was hard to view on a small screen.

"Small screen?" she asked. "What do you mean?"

"Last storm, lightning hit our house and the TV went out."

"Are you serious? Don't you have a lightning rod attached to your chimney?"

"My dad said our roof antennae got too close to the rod, so the voltage wasn't directed properly into the ground. He said the surge broke the TV, but nothing else got damaged. Now we're stuck with a five-inch black-and-white screen."

"The TV in our trailer is bigger than that. Did you feel the lightning hit?"

"No, but that's what Dad said happened. And we still don't have a real TV, which sucks because the Dream Team is going to the Barcelona Olympics in a couple weeks." He paused. "You know, basketball."

She invited him over to watch the news and he took her up on the offer.

They sat in front of the TV all day and waited for more aftershocks. They felt a few other little ones.

"Want to play a game?" Kiara asked.

"Absolutely. Monopoly?"

"As long as an earthquake doesn't knock the pieces all over the place."

"That's okay. My disaster relief company will come by and clean up. You do understand that we'll have to confiscate your property as payment."

"Only if you pay market value."

"Unnecessary. Your houses aren't up to code."

"You're ridiculous." She laughed.

Cole smiled a sheepish grin.

She realized he had pretty eyelashes. To distract herself, she changed the topic. "I loved the speech you gave at graduation. You did a great job."

"Thanks. We've been promoted. Would've been nice if my dad had been there."

She couldn't understand his dad's absence. For parents who claimed to be invested in his school and grades, they weren't supportive. Then again, neither was her mom. At least she came to hear her speech, for whatever that was worth.

36

Bright Stars

THE METAL RIDGES OF THE BED of her mom's parked pick-up truck dug into Kiara's back. She repositioned herself and stared at the stars, which glowed bright white amidst the black moonless night. Clusters of dots pulsated. Her cares floated away, leaving her in a state of calm. Wind raised the hairs on her bare arms and carried on through the desert fields across the street.

Crickets called and the round leaves on the neighbor's cottonwood trees jingled.

Slow and deliberate breaths escaped, each one bringing her further from reality, the reality of her impending high school transition, and a mom who slept inside her locked bedroom oblivious to her and Tom's whereabouts. And the fact that she and her brother, rather than cling to each other for support, had drifted apart.

Tom had been spending the night, school nights included, at his best friend Dave's house. Kiara's mom said Kiara couldn't spend the night at Carolyn's because she had a bad attitude and didn't clean her room, while Tom cussed in front of their mom and his room was a mess. How was that fair?

In silent protest, Kiara had slipped outside to clear her head.

The days of dust rising from dirt roads and the electricity going out so often that they ate dinner by kerosene lantern several times a month were gone; the power had gradually become more reliable.

Gone were the days of mud pies, metal slides in the scorching triple digit heat, and climbing chain link fences to play with her friends. Although she looked forward to a new school in September, she feared the transition to high school.

With eyelids shut, Kiara became one with the breeze. Her spirit swirled around in the mixture of desert heat and the chill of night that never blended completely, heightening sensations on her skin and cooling her cheeks. She opened her eyes in time to find a trail of light end in a burst of sparkles. Shooting stars were for making wishes. Trouble is that she didn't know what to wish for. Barbies and books were too trite, world peace and prosperity too grand. She settled for happiness, hopped down, and headed for bed.

Before she drifted off to sleep, she considered what made her happy, besides dreaming of a life outside the desert or getting married and having a family to love; she was happiest around Carolyn and Cole—two of the most genuine people she knew.

Maybe she'd ask Cole tomorrow to hang out.

She called him in the morning and her wish was granted. He had to help his mom during the day, but he could hang out later. She asked if he wanted to take a walk up to the water towers—she wasn't in the mood to crawl under barbed wire and Cole had gotten taller anyhow and might not fit.

Cole said he'd meet her up there.

In the late afternoon, right before the chilly night took hold, Kiara headed up the road towards the buttes.

She and Cole sat on top of the buttes overlooking the fields on the Lancaster side of Lake LA, houses in the far distance. With the huge, tan-painted metal water tower behind them, it was more secluded; no one from where they lived could see them.

Kiara nudged him on the arm. "Have you heard of bankruptcy?"

He shook his head.

"My mom said the bank is going to take our trailer."

Cole scrunched his forehead. "The one that's covered in dirt in your yard?"

"We used to go camping in it."

"What? Once?"

"Anyway, my mom said it means we don't have money."

"I'm sure everything's going to be okay."

"My old dog Patches chewed the wires underneath. That's what the bank gets."

Cole sat there quietly and didn't say much.

"And know what else?" Kiara said. "She closed the daycare. She lost too many kids because people keep moving away."

"Foreclosures. No choice."

They both understood that word. She explained that her mom worked two jobs to avoid that happening to them.

Cole discussed the declining aerospace jobs in the AV. He complained that families moving up from LA were bringing their gangster kids with them, along with more problems.

"Have you seen the graffiti lately?" Cole pointed to the water tower behind them.

Stars appeared before the sun fully disappeared. They walked around to view the sunset. Neither of them wanted to go home yet, so they returned to their spot on the other side and sat down. The temperature held steady without wind for once. Night stretched over the desert.

Cole took off his coat and spread it out on the ground and they lay down next to each other to search for constellations. After adjusting it twice to remove a few pointy rocks poking them in the back, they reclined back and traced the stars with their fingertips. She picked out the big dipper and the little dipper and Orion's belt. She tried to picture Ursa Major, the Great Bear, and Ursa Minor, the Little Bear, as Cole drew them in the sky. When she still couldn't find them, he took her hand in his and moved her finger along the outline.

"Did you see our yearbook picture?" Kiara asked. They had been voted *Most Likely to Succeed*. Their picture was funny, her the shortest in their grade, him the tallest. "The three witches must have been amused to find me at graduation in a dress with stockings."

"Yeah, not your usual jeans and t-shirt." Cole laughed. "Remember when you wore a jean miniskirt when it snowed?"

"I had on a big jacket."

"You're so stubborn." He smiled at her.

"Remember how we used to say that it's so hot we can fry an egg on the street? We never tried it."

"We talk about a lot of things we never end up doing," Cole said.

True. It was also true that she felt warmer lying alongside him.

"How do you deal with the heat?" she asked.

"What do you mean?"

"In the day. Sometimes I picture myself taking a hot bath until I break out in a sweat and that cools me off."

"You're so white," he said. "You need to stay out of the sun."

"My friends used to rub baby oil on their skin and go up on the roof to get a tan. I tried it once and lasted all of two minutes. I don't come in any color except white and red and I hate when my skin peels. It reminds me of a snake."

"Snakes are cool." He brushed his finger along her arm like a slithering snake.

It gave her goosebumps. "Remember drinking out of the hoses in our backyards?"

"Still do." He pulled his hand back.

"You know, we need a new couch. The springs are poking out. Tom and I put a sheet of plywood under the cushions to cover the springs so we don't get scraped up."

"You've had those couches for a long time."

"Neither of us get new furniture. Mom said no reason to get rid of a perfectly good set of couches, but I don't think they're so perfect." She leaned up on her elbow to face him. "Do you remember how we used to compete and race each other to get extra worksheets filled out?"

"Yes." He leaned up on his elbow, too, and smiled. Although everything was shadowy, she could still make out his face in the moonlight.

"Remember the igloos?" she asked.

"And you getting me in trouble for playing hide-and-seek." He gently knocked his forehead against hers.

Her skin tingled and she pulled back. "Not on purpose." She rolled back onto her back and he did the same. "Sorry for blaming you."

They were quiet. She could hear him breathing.

"Do you get tired of living out here?" she said. "I mean tired of dirt and tumbleweeds."

"Who doesn't? It's not all bad out here though." He leaned his head against hers.

She let it stay there. "I'm nervous about high school."

"Why?"

"Switching classes sounds scary."

"I'll be there to help you. Plus, we signed up for all the same classes so the teacher said we'll probably have the same schedule."

"I stopped being friends with the superficial, mean girls. If I don't make friends over there, I'll sit by myself and write poetry like Emily Dickinson until everyone thinks I'm a loner or hermit and leaves me alone."

"You've done that before. And I'm sure you'll make new friends." He added, "I'm glad you ditched all of them. You're too good for them. They're not going anywhere. You and I are going to get out of here one day."

"Maybe we can get a big fancy house on a street with sidewalks and lights."

"And grass and trees," he added. Even though it was dark, she could hear him smile.

"I'm so glad we're friends," she said.

"Is that all you want to be?" he asked.

Butterflies fluttered in her stomach. "What else would we be?" She stared at the stars and held her breath for a moment. She regretted saying it but couldn't take it back.

Cole was quiet for a moment. "Never mind. I'm ... I'm glad we're friends, too."

37

St. Andrew's Abbey

IN THE MOJAVE DESERT, tucked away in the foothills towards the base of the San Gabriel Mountains with a population under four hundred, is an unincorporated community called Valyermo. The name means barren valley in Spanish; it was anything but.

The main reason anyone ventured out to Valyermo was to visit Saint Andrew's Abbey, a Benedictine monastery, home to monks who traced their roots back to Chengtu, China, when, on Christmas Day in 1949, communists put them under house arrest; a few years later, Mao Zedong's government expelled them from China.

The monks relocated halfway around the world to Valyermo, California, on the edge of the desert in the Antelope Valley. Kiara's mom had told her that.

Saint Andrew's Abbey didn't resemble a desert, unless you climbed along the hillside to walk along the stations of the cross, where there were more Joshua trees and low vegetation.

Below that, the private property had been transformed into a spiritual oasis with trees and grass and a lake, alongside buildings and a chapel.

Kiara's mom worked there on weekends in a commercial sized kitchen cooking meals for the religious retreats. She had to go up to drop off some food and told Kiara to come along.

On the twenty-minute drive up to the Abbey along the two-lane road, they climbed in elevation and Kiara stared out the window at the changing vegetation. Fewer Joshua trees and scrubbier chaparral and Pinyon Pines.

They turned off the main road towards the entrance alongside a dry wash that would hold water when the snow in the mountains melted in spring.

They passed a wooden sign by the gate that announced "No Hunting, Except for Peace" and entered through the gates. Kiara rolled down her window; it was silent except the crunch of the tires on the gravel road.

It was Kiara's first time there. In the parking lot, she stared up at tall Maple trees nearby, they looked a century old and reached high towards the heavens. There were apple trees and grass and a working phone booth—randomly placed near the parking lot—more grass and trees, and pure unadulterated silence. This, a sanctuary in the desert.

Her mom said she had to take care of some things and told Kiara to explore the grounds and come back when she heard the dinner bell because they would be guests for dinner.

Kiara wandered through the grassy sections on cobblestone paths past meditation benches on patios, and along a brick pathway. Up ahead the ducks quacked, a sound unfamiliar to her. After walking around a clearing, she found the ducks in a beautiful peaceful pond.

She took a breath, paused and bent down near the edge of the water. There, in the murky green water, swam bright orange koi fish. Smaller fish scattered as she got closer. Turtles floated in the center of the water on branches; some sunned on the dirt shore. More ducks waddled by, quacking and pecking at the ground.

She wished she could share this with Cole, or maybe Carolyn—it was her type of place.

Kiara strolled past a simple red-painted archway, stone lions and statues, more red posts with curved roof tops— probably remnants of history carried over from China.

She approached a steep hill and climbed the dirt path. Wind rushed at her. A roadrunner with its long tail feathers ran by. At the top of the hill was a stone amphitheater. She hopped down to explore, imagining all the events that had taken place there.

She climbed back up and proceeded along a narrow trail up the ridge. At the next clearing, she discovered a grand view of the desert, higher than the one from the buttes. She strained her eyes to find her home. The distant desert blurred in the heat, a melding of beige and peachy tones. She could barely make out the buttes.

As she trekked up the dirt trail, her shoes slipped on loose rocks and dirt, and the heat intensified. There, high up on the hill, she came upon the Abbey Graveyard.

At the entrance stood a sculpture so big she was sure it could be seen for miles, a single slab of stone erected with no adornments other than a large oval opening in the middle, like the eye of a needle, and she remembered the Bible verse: it is easier for a camel to go through the eye of a needle than for a rich man to enter the kingdom of God.

Up there, she was surrounded by small stone crosses that stood neatly in rows.

Kiara observed the Abbey from her vantage point and considered where to explore next.

She returned back down under the canopy of trees, beyond the pond, where the air was cooler. That's when she realized there was no one else there; she hadn't seen anyone since the parking lot and first few buildings. A deeper peace washed over her.

Tucked away, a small path led up to a plot of land covered with grass and tall trees, perhaps junipers among the bigger ones with green and silvery, round leaves that shimmered in the light when shaken by a breeze.

Kiara circled the area and found small mint leaves growing by the base of a tree. She picked a couple to chew on and sat down on the grass under the trees. She stared up at the tree tops that swayed and, as they did, hid and exposed patches of the bright blue sky.

She decided this was where she would stay until the dinner bells rang. She lay down and contemplated life. What had happened between her and Cole?

She felt in her heart that she had said the wrong thing that night, and they both knew it.

She closed her eyes and listened to the gentle rustling of the leaves, and wished so much that he were there with her to share this moment.

Eventually the silence was broken by a monk ringing the tower bell. It seemed too early for dinner, but Kiara stretched, wiped the dirt and grass from her hair, and went down to where her mom said she'd find the dinner hall.

It was empty. She traversed the grounds towards the source of the sound. The chiming bell was coming instead from the Chapel. There, a couple people stood out in front in silence while the brown-robed monks entered.

An older woman, probably noticing the curiosity on Kiara's face, leaned close and spoke in a hushed tone. They were in for a special moment. The Sacred Chant of the Divine Office, sung in English and Latin; would be chanted a cappella during the evening Vigil.

The bells chimed and everyone made their way inside the small chapel, originally a barn, in reflective silence. There were wooden pews in three sections facing an altar. To the side was a beautiful stained-glass window.

Kiara sat in the back by the door, so she could exit without disturbing anyone. She wasn't sure what to expect and folded her hands in her lap and waited.

Then it started: the mystical Gregorian Chant, slowed down at a pace to create space for contemplative prayer and reflection. It took her breath away. She closed her eyes and the chant transported her centuries back to stone churches across Europe and Asia. She breathed in the melody and when it was over, opened her eyes.

She snuck out the door, found a bench secluded in a ring of trees and sat and pondered. There had to be more to life than the desert. There had to be.

When the dinner bell rang, she crossed the threshold into the dining hall. The room opened up high with a vaulted ceiling, a floor to ceiling glass window to observe nature, and beautiful murals on another wall. There were long wooden tables with wood chairs tucked in on both sides. The cool room was a comfortable respite from the summer heat.

She had never seen monks before that day, brothers dressed in long brown robes tied at the waist with a simple belt. Her mom was there and introduced her to a monk who welcomed Kiara with a warm smile.

He led them up to a serving table where, buffet style, they were served spaghetti in a red sauce, salad, and fresh brownies. She took a seat among the brothers and their guests eating side-by-side. Some who were there for retreats and others, like Kiara and her mom, were there for the day.

Her host explained the abbey's history. The monks there lived by *"ora et labora"* meaning offering to God through prayer and work, a Rule of Saint Benedict.

He invited them for Vespers, evening prayers at the Chapel; Vows taken by the monks meant no talking from evening prayer until breakfast in the morning.

Her mom said it was time to leave, and showed Kiara a beautiful ceramic angel created by the monks on site, which she'd be bringing home.

Kiara was changed by having spent the day there. She was at peace. The chaos and struggle of childhood were behind her. The future, high school and beyond, lay ahead of her. Her mind calmed. It would be okay. She didn't have to please everyone to be satisfied with herself. All she needed was the shade of some trees, a little silence, and the breeze on her cheek.

On the way home, Cole popped into her mind. She wished she could take him up there but didn't have the guts to invite him. She hated that—she always tried to be polite, never said what she wanted aloud. Taught to be considerate of others, not herself, she'd been trained to keep her mouth shut for so long that she wasn't sure if she knew how to open it. Yet another thing she wished she could change but doubted she ever would.

So much for the peace and serenity.

High School

38

Left Behind

KIARA STARTED HER PERIOD only a couple weeks before the start of high school, and at fourteen, she was the last of her friends to do so, not that it was anyone's business. She had been worrying something was wrong with her until it happened. When it did, she wished it hadn't. She hated the cramps and bulky pads. Still, she was relieved, especially because her cycle ended before Labor Day.

Kiara slipped on a pair of jeans and a ribbed t‑shirt. She clasped a necklace with a gold flower pendant around her neck—an 8th grade graduation gift from her mom. She gave one last glance in the mirror. Her bangs had gotten long. At least with the contacts, her blue‑green eyes were visible. She pulled back her hair into a ponytail and grabbed her new backpack—dark blue, nice enough but not bright enough to call too much attention to herself.

This school year had to be better than the last few.

No matter how anxious Kiara felt on the first day of school, she was exhausted at having to wake up so early. Her mom had gotten another job as a receptionist at a car dealership and had to drop Kiara off before work.

"I want to make a good impression, so I'm going to get there early," her mom said.

"Why 7 AM?" Kiara asked. With her hatred of mornings, it might as well be 4 AM.

Littlerock High School in Littlerock—one word, not two like the one in Arkansas—was ten lonely miles away. The route there consisted of a two-lane highway surrounded by desert fields of tumbleweeds and Joshua trees. Still far from the big city of Palmdale, it was like nothing she'd ever seen before in Lake LA—the school was massive.

The grand concrete structure loomed large from a block away. To drop Kiara off, her mom maneuvered around the ten buses idling alongside the curb.

Kiara lingered before getting out. To her left, a parking lot filled with students parking and piling out of cars. To her right stood ten blue gates, double doors, in a row welcoming the students. Which one was she supposed to go through?

"Hurry up, I need to get to work," her mom said. "Have a good day."

Kiara got caught up in the throngs of people who seemed twice her age and funneled through a gate. She felt small, like a kindergartener on a college campus. She scanned her surroundings, hoping for a familiar face—not the three witches—maybe Cole or Carolyn?

Her stomach cramped, but not from period cramps; this was overwhelming. As long as no one trashed her—dumped a lowly freshman into a trash can—she would make it through the day.

Kiara passed by raised planters with real trees. The school was an actual structure—not trailers—cemented into the ground, two stories high, connected together as one building, divided into four different quads, each open in the middle, so the warmth of sun shone on students as they ascended or descended the outdoor staircases.

Like moving into a cow corral, everyone meandered forward. Kiara was afraid of getting in anyone's way if she stopped, so she kept going. In the main square—the hang out or lunch area—the sky overhead was replaced by a massive concrete canopy. Students gathered in crowds. They talked and laughed in groups and shuffled by her. Kiara felt lost in a sea of strangers.

She found a large concrete column to lean against, where she could step back and observe the scene. This was nothing like Lake LA School, or the one-room schoolhouse that started with fewer than fifty students combined. Here fifteen hundred students spread out around her. Littlerock High School, built in 1990, served kids from Lake LA, Littlerock, Pearblossom, Llano, and the outskirts of these small towns.

Each year they expanded the number of grades and students until that fall of 1992 when they opened their doors to ninth graders. That meant that Kiara and Cole would be the first graduating class who would have had the opportunity to attend all four years at the high school where they started as freshmen. It also meant there were more students in one place than she had ever seen before.

Kiara took a deep breath. How could they fit so many people in one school? Bombarded by their chatter and movement, she still felt invisible.

Overhead, a loud buzzing bell—not the brass handbell—announced it was time to get to class. She hadn't oriented herself around campus. Kiara panicked.

Her first class, English 9 Honors was upstairs in the first quad; she had to ask an upperclassman to figure that out—a map would've been helpful. She tried to flag down three people before a tall guy in a leather jacket stopped to offer her guidance. She was too terrified to speak and stuttered. He smiled kindly and sent her off in the right direction.

Kiara filed in the door with a crowd of others. The desks were grouped in sets of five. She took a seat at a front table group along the wall and looked around. In the back, Cole waved to her and a sense of relief washed over her. She wanted to get up and move next to him, but he was preoccupied with other guys and all the seats towards the back were full.

At another table in the back was Carolyn who waved and blew her a kiss. She didn't dress up for the first day and was in her usual jeans, t-shirt, and combat boots.

Pretty soon all the seats had filled except one at Kiara's table, next to her, and two at another table, front and center.

A girl, tall and shapely with thick, flowing dark hair, olive skin lightly freckled, and a backpack slung over one shoulder, walked in, took a quick look around, rolled her eyes and, with an audible sigh, headed to Kiara's table.

When the girl got closer, Kiara couldn't help but notice the beauty of her shaped, dark eyebrows, pronounced cheekbones and chin, and large eyes framed by long lashes. She resembled the models in the teen fashion magazines. Kiara pictured this girl on the cover with the same perpetually bored expression on her face.

Her English teacher, an older woman who resembled a bird with short, tight curls and glasses, called out their names.

Of course, she butchered Kiara's. Kie-re-a, Kay-ra, and before she could try a third time, Kiara said, "here." The bored beauty said, "here" when the teacher called out, "Nicole."

The teacher, a bit scatterbrained and flustered, finished the roll call and had them talk to each other while she searched for her notes. She explained this was her first class of the day, so she had to find where everything was.

Kiara introduced herself to Nicole who politely responded to questions, without showing much interest in reflecting back the questions, so Kiara answered each one she asked.

Desperate to meet new girls, Kiara asked to see her schedule and realized she and Nicole had the same exact schedule all the way down to their drama elective, except instead of taking Spanish, Nicole was taking French— probably better for a model.

With exuberance, Kiara suggested they walk to their next class together, and Nicole shrugged.

"Fine," Nicole said. "I'm headed there anyway."

Kiara sat next to her in Geometry, too. Most of the students in that class were upperclassmen; there were only a few freshmen. Cole was there but more interested in a growing number of new acquaintances.

Their Geometry teacher, a woman who stood tall like a beanstalk with a short haircut and an attitude, was a no-nonsense former fighter pilot, both appropriate for the area and a curiosity to Kiara. Despite the grumblings of some students who whispered they wanted to drop the class—Kiara loved it. She would be learning new concepts from someone who knew what the hell she was talking about.

After second period, Kiara chose not to tag along with Nicole during their snack break, because she hadn't offered. Kiara followed behind at a short distance. She stopped when she reached the lunch area; she had passed through it in the morning, too nervous to pay attention to where she could sit.

The main quad was an expansive covered area on the bottom floor; the concrete ceiling with its opaque skylights was at least twenty feet high and the concrete floor kept it cool in the shade.

At one end of the main quad was an outdoor stage, behind which was the not-yet-finished indoor theater; on the other end, tall glass windows gave a view into the library. Individual lunch tables with benches lay scattered around huge support columns throughout the space. Most tables were already filled with groups of students who had claimed the space as their own.

Kiara, without a place to go, leaned against a support column and watched strangers hug hello. She listened to them compare their summers and new classes and how much they hated or liked their new teachers.

From her side appeared Carolyn who wrapped her in a tight embrace.

"This is so cool," Carolyn said. "We're finally at the same school."

"Where I don't know anyone," Kiara said.

"You would've if you came to my birthday sleepover." She winked. "Come and meet my friends. They're all super chill. We're all taking the same classes so we can help each other."

Kiara followed her to the far edge of a long lunch table—two different groups had laid claim to opposite ends of it.

There, in front of her, was the bored Nicole—her face glowed with a smile as she joked with a girl introduced as Jenny—a bubbly blonde with wavy hair and wispy bangs that she kept pushing from her fair face.

When Carolyn announced Kiara as the friend they never met, Nicole widened her eyes.

"Oh my God," Nicole said with a huge grin. "You're *that* Kiara. I had no idea. I thought you were just an annoying freshman who kept bugging me."

It wasn't said with malice, so Kiara didn't take it at that. Still, a flush settled over her cheeks.

They instantly clicked and swapped stories of life at Challenger Middle School versus Lake LA School, with Carolyn interjecting here and there about the bitchy girls Kiara had previously been hanging out with while Jenny and Nicole laughed.

Kiara spotted the three witches from across the quad hanging out with cheerleaders and football players—maybe that's who they'd been partying with.

After the end of the morning break, the girls split off to head to third period. They vowed to meet back at lunch—and hopefully claim more of the table.

This is what Kiara had been anticipating the most— distance from her former friends, not having to see them every day. Because they most definitely had different classes—they weren't in advanced classes—it was assured she'd be gifted with separation. And because Carolyn and her new friends would be in all the honors classes, Kiara finally felt free.

In the first week of high school, Kiara noticed four unusual things: One, there was a pregnant-minor program there with a daycare, although those girls stayed mostly separated from the general population.

Two, there were fifth year students—seniors who hadn't graduated in the standard four years and had returned. They were referred to as "super seniors" with an eye roll.

Three, there was a continuation high school on campus where students went if they couldn't finish high school in *five* years, or couldn't pass the regular classes. *How difficult are the classes?* Kiara wondered.

Four, the basketball courts and fields were where students, including Carolyn, could openly smoke, as long as it wasn't weed, or the adults couldn't tell that it was.

This was a microcosm of the Antelope Valley.

Even though they were taking the same classes, except for their elective, Kiara and Cole were only together in the same periods for Geometry, English, and P.E.

Cole had been more distant lately. In P.E., Kiara finally got to talk to him while they walked together around the "track," an oval area on the grass marked with orange cones.

Kiara and Cole debated how different high school was until he changed the subject.

"I may switch my schedule soon, because I'm going to try out for basketball in the fall and baseball in the summer."

"I'm sure you'll make the team with your fast reflexes, Mr. *KidQuiz* King. I'll be bummed we won't have P.E. together."

"It's one thing my dad supports," he said. "Sports. He says everything I enjoy—reading books, playing games, and studying history and politics—is a waste of time when I could be outside getting exercise." Cole shook his head. "He put a pool table in the garage and bought a set of weights. He wants me to start lifting. So…we can't afford new clothes or good food, but he can afford cigarettes and beer and a pool table."

"Seems like screwed up priorities to me," she said.

He shrugged. "Hey, I've been meaning to tell you something."

She blushed. "Yeah?"

"I can't hang out with you much now."

"Why not? I thought your parents liked me."

"They do. It's not that." He took a long pause as if finding the right words. "My girlfriend is jealous of you."

"Girlfriend?" She couldn't hide her shock. She stopped mid-step to face him.

"Yeah, I thought you might be mad. I told her we're just friends—best friends—but she said she didn't think it was right, and if Kelly and I keep going out, I need to prove I'm faithful." He paused then added, "You and I have been through a lot, together. I'm sure Kelly will come around then we can hang out again. For now, we can't."

"Prove? You don't need to prove anything to anyone." Kiara raised her voice.

"I know. We'll see if this works out. We've only been together for two weeks so far."

"When did you get a girlfriend? Kelly who?"

Cole got quiet. "I didn't think that's the part you'd be upset about."

Kiara turned back and continued along the track.

"Hey." Cole reached for her arm. "Please don't be mad."

She pulled away. "I'm not mad."

He didn't say anything and continued to walk by her side.

Kiara wasn't fooling anybody, especially not Cole who knew her better than anyone else in the world. How could somebody who knew everything about her toss her away for a girl he knew for two weeks? Was Kiara worth nothing?

She took a few deep breaths and asked, almost in a whisper. "Are you two doing it?" The words felt thick and heavy on her tongue.

"What? No way. It's not like that." He grimaced. "Come on, you know me better than that. We're fourteen, for God's sake."

"I thought I knew you." Kiara turned and walked away.

39

Big Rock Creek

CAROLYN OPENED UP A NEW WORLD to Kiara, heretofore invisible to her: desert, foothill, and canyon hikes. She offered to lead Kiara—Jenny and Nicole weren't the hiking type—on a hike along the Devil's Chair trail at a state park in Pearblossom called Devil's Punchbowl.

First, Kiara and Carolyn had to find a way to get there.

Before he was deployed overseas, Carolyn's older half-brother, Ben, had taught Carolyn to drive and gifted her his old Civic hatchback. She still had a while before she could legally get her license.

She reasoned to Kiara that as long as they stayed out of the city, kept to the rural areas, didn't go over the speed limit, and both wore seatbelts, then she was okay; not many cops patrolled the outer edges of the Los Angeles and San Bernardino County lines.

Early one morning, she picked up Kiara and headed for the Devil's Punchbowl.

"Thanks for driving," Kiara said. "I wish I had a car."

"Yeah, well, without a car," Carolyn said, "everyone's stranded out here."

"How do you pay for gas?" Kiara realized she didn't have any money.

"I babysit. I also make beaded rosaries with my mom. We sell them at the Swap Meet." She winked at Kiara. "Don't worry. I got it."

On the trails and in the desert, Carolyn explained which plants could be eaten and which were poisonous. She pointed out lizards, birds and mammals such as the Mojave Desert squirrel. She identified the woodsy fragrance of sage bushes, sprigs of which she said they could safely chew on. Like Carolyn instructed, Kiara ran her hand along the smooth, red manzanita trunks.

"How'd you learn all this?" Kiara asked, amazed.

Carolyn shrugged. "You would too, if you spent enough time out here. My brother got me a couple of botany books. I guess it started back at the field trip to the Indian Museum ... I think nature is more my home than my house is."

Devil's Punchbowl was lovely, no doubt, but after a couple of hours hiking, Kiara's legs burned and she ran out of water. Her lips were like sandpaper.

"Why did you only bring that little water bottle?" Carolyn asked. "On a long hike in the sun, you should have at least three liters of water."

Liters? Kiara imagined carrying a two-liter bottle of soda. She had never learned to bring a lot of water for a hike. She didn't even own a container big enough to carry that much. Her face flushed and she felt dizzy hiking along exposed trails without shade.

"Let's head back," Carolyn said. "It's hot. Next time, I have a better place to show you."

The following week, after school, the two of them drove past Littlerock, namesake of their high school. She explained that the town began as a small settlement called Alpine Springs Colony which morphed into Tierra Bonita before it became Littlerock.

"The first known settler built his adobe house there in the 1860s and he and his family lived there until he was killed by a grizzly bear in 1886," Carolyn said as they drove.

"A grizzly bear? In the desert?"

She gestured towards the mountains. "Must've come down from there."

Carolyn explained that the water that came to rest in Littlerock Dam started its path higher up as snowpack in the San Gabriel Mountains, which, as it melted, fed into different creeks, two on the north side of the range being Little Rock Creek and Big Rock Creek.

"Big Rock Creek," she said, "is where we're headed."

They drove through Pearblossom and wound through the foothills on a two-lane highway, Valyermo Road. They passed Saint Andrew's Abbey.

"Next time the Abbey has their annual festival," Carolyn said, "because both our moms will be there, we should slip away and hike along the riverbed."

Kiara smiled. If she couldn't share that special place with Cole, at least she could share it with Carolyn.

Carolyn turned off a side road, Big Rock Creek Road, that ran parallel to the creek. She said they could stop and pull over anywhere they could find a good spot to park. She found a wide shoulder in the road and parked further down, away from other cars.

"No sense in going to a secluded place and being mashed together with other people," Carolyn said.

Even though it was afternoon, the temperature was in the triple digits and Kiara was thrilled to hear the gurgling creek, which would soon be her respite from the heat. As the water traveled downhill, it formed small semi-private pools with calmer waters, each surrounded by bushes and trees.

She pointed to some tall, leafy trees high up in the branches where hefty bundles of green clung to branches.

"That's mistletoe," Carolyn said. "It's a pest, but the birds spread it to other trees."

"The Christmas type?"

Carolyn laughed. "I guess so. The berries and leaves are poisonous though."

"Can't wait to dip my legs into that water." Kiara sat on a boulder to untie her shoes.

"Well, about that...I wouldn't hop in so fast. The bottoms are covered with rocks, which will cut up your feet."

"Then I'll sit on the edge and dangle my feet in," Kiara said.

Carolyn smirked. She pulled out a cigarette and lit up.

Kiara got closer to the water, took off her shoes and socks— her feet were sweaty from the heat. She plunged them in, then screamed, and jumped up.

"Oh, holy hell, that's freezing," she yelled.

Carolyn laughed. "It's melted snow. What did you expect?"

"So, the options are, burn up from the heat, or numb your skin until you can't feel anything at all?"

"Pretty much." Carolyn took a long drag. "It's not as bad when you're not in the sun."

They strolled under the trees, Kiara far enough away to not get caught in the stench of smoke. Near an open clearing, they sat in the shade and listened to the birds chirping, leaves rustling in the wind, and the bubbling creek, along with the occasional car traveling up on the highway.

"I'm glad you know enough to warn me about poison oak and everything else," Kiara said. "I'd probably die up here on my own." She closed her eyes and lifted her face to the breeze. "I love it here."

"Good. I thought you would."

Kiara turned to Carolyn who took another drag on her cigarette.

"What are your dreams?" Kiara asked.

"My nightmares, you mean?" Carolyn shook her head. "I don't remember my dreams."

"No, I mean what do you want for the future?"

Carolyn took a drag on her cigarette, held it, then exhaled the smoke. "I guess moving out. Spending more time up here."

"Moving out of the AV?" Kiara asked.

"No, out of my parents' house so I don't have to hear my dad's Goddamn hissy fits."

"You don't want to get out of the desert?"

"Why?" Carolyn tilted her head.

Kiara considered this. "Everything out in the desert is so dead. Too hot, too cold, too windy, there's nothing here. Down below, there are big, beautiful houses. It's cooler and closer to the beach. It's so much nicer down there."

Carolyn dropped her cigarette stub, twisted her foot to put it out, and picked it back up.

"Down below, do you have this peace?" Carolyn asked. "Or do you have people everywhere, everyone going somewhere all the time, and nobody ever stopping to be where they are?" She shook her head. "I'll stay here. Do what makes you happy."

That's just it, Kiara didn't know what would make her happy.

40

Trauma

W HAT DIDN'T MAKE KIARA HAPPY was seeing Cole hold hands with his new girlfriend, Kelly, who was on the cheerleading squad. Because he never strove towards the limelight, Cole never struck Kiara as the type to date a popular cheerleader. Fortunately, it didn't last. Kiara didn't have to watch them kiss, because they got into a fight and broke up. Cole didn't tell Kiara, but she knew. So did the other girls, from all walks of life, who flirted with him.

Kiara minded her own business. She focused on her routine: go to class, hang out at the table with her friends, go home and do homework—boring but predictable.

Carolyn played an oboe in the marching band. Because of the long distance to get to other high schools, she had to miss school for games and competitions. When she was absent,

Kiara sat at their end of the lunch table and did her math homework while Nicole and Jenny chatted.

"You know how he is," Nicole said, referring to her dad, whom Kiara had never met. "Have you heard how he talks to me? If I want to model, then I'm a whore. He makes no sense. I'm a straight-A student and haven't even kissed a guy. Yet somehow, he thinks I want to be a hooker. He doesn't say shit to my sisters who dress skanky because they want to join him in the family business." Nicole twirled a strand of her dark hair. "My sisters are angels. Whatever. I'm over it."

"I don't even know if I have any sisters," Jenny said, "or brothers." She and Nicole stared at each other for a brief moment then burst out laughing. "My mom is so drugged out." Jenny wiped a tear of laughter from her eye. "But, hey, church is going great with my grandma."

Hooker? Drugged-out mom? Kiara was surprised her friends were such good students in spite of their home lives.

Even though Cole continued to be distracted by different girls vying for his attention—the nerdy girl who held the coveted top grade in science class, a shy girl in English class, an athletic softball player—he didn't do more than flirt, or hold hands if dating one. None of these relationships lasted long. They did end on good terms, because the girls waved hi and smiled when they passed. Kiara could see the appeal: tall, dark, handsome, sweet, smart, and funny.

In spring, when they had a sub in Geometry, Cole slid into an open seat next to Kiara.

"Oh, are you allowed to speak to me again?" Kiara didn't look up.

"Nice. I deserve that," he said. "In all fairness, you did it to me first. Remember when a bad haircut was justification for distancing yourself from me?"

She ignored him and doodled on her homework.

He bent down to be at eye level with her pencil. "You won't talk to me now that I'm on the baseball team?" He titled his head at her and smirked. "Is that not your sport?"

"You're such a dork. Even if you play sports, you'll never be a jock. That's a compliment by the way." She swiveled in her seat to face him. "Ms. Hellfire isn't here. Hope she's alive, because she's never absent."

Cole grinned. "She skewers people for not getting the right answers. Of course, that doesn't apply to either of us. She loves you. Tell me when the wedding is."

Kiara rolled her eyes. "It's only because I hate how she makes people feel stupid. If I explain the answer, someone else won't get picked on."

"I wish we had a sub more often." He winked. "Then we could hang out back here."

She blushed. "In drama, I always have a sub."

He cleared his throat. The pitch of his voice raised a notch. "Meet anyone new in there?"

"I hang out with Nicole and another girl in there named Misty. I wanted to learn how to act. I haven't learned anything. The theater isn't even finished yet."

"You're friends with Misty?" Cole relaxed. "She's pretty cool, right?"

Kiara bristled. "I didn't know you were taking drama."

"I'm not," he said. "Misty and the other drama kids hang out after school. I'm here late until I get picked up after practice." He paused. "We're not dating if that's what you're asking."

Kiara raised an eyebrow. "I didn't say you were." She felt relieved.

"Besides, I don't think Misty dates guys." He raised his eyebrows significantly.

"What do you mean?" Kiara pictured Misty—petite, lovely without makeup or frills, blue eyes that pierced your soul, and porcelain skin. She wore flowery, flowing skirts and braided a single ribbon in her long, brown hair. She hung out with drama kids at lunch. Beyond that, Kiara knew little about Misty other than her passion for all living creatures and the stage.

"Misty is one of those free-thinkers. She doesn't do things because society says you should." Cole paused. "She's dealt with a lot of shit. I admire her for that."

The bell rang. Students gathered books into backpacks and rushed out.

"I'm glad we got to catch up," Cole said. On the way out the door, he turned back. "Hey Kiara, K.I.T." Kiara threw him a puzzled look. He gave her a wide grin. "Keep in touch."

She laughed at the dumb yearbook reference—Cole jokingly added that line to the bottom of every one of the heartfelt messages he wrote in her yearbooks.

Several thoughts rattled around Kiara's head for the next several weeks. What was up with Cole? Was he flirting with her? She hoped so but was probably reading too much into it. He was being silly and friendly, like he'd always been. Nothing more.

Ignore the wishful thinking, she told herself. Focus on something real.

Her friendships were real. Kiara loved Carolyn, and Carolyn loved Nicole and Jenny. It didn't take long before Kiara loved them, too.

She invited the three of them over for a sleepover. Her mom was much more willing to host the girls than to allow Kiara over to their houses. She bought them 2-liter bottles of root beer and Pepsi, and breadsticks and cheap pizzas from Little Caesar's.

"Carolyn's friends are so nice," her mom said after the girls had gone home.

Kiara described all the drinking and partying that the so-called *Christian* girls, Stephanie, Jessica, and Heidi, did. Kiara's mom transformed into a wise person who knew it all along. Kiara didn't call her mom's bluff. All that mattered was that she approved of Kiara's new friends.

"Carolyn and her friends are all honors students at school?" her mom asked.

"Yes, all GATE students like me." *I told you so,* Kiara thought but held her tongue.

Her mom nodded and smiled. "You can have them over whenever you want."

With her mom's blessing, the weekend sleepovers became a regular thing, even when her mom wasn't home on account of her staying the weekend up at the Abbey, her third job.

One night, the four girls gathered on Kiara's queen-sized bed and stayed up chatting.

"I live my life protecting my little brothers from my dad," Carolyn said.

"Nobody's protecting you," Nicole said. "I wish you weren't scared shitless of him."

Kiara stared. What did that mean? Carolyn had never spoken of that to her.

Carolyn leaned back against the wall and massaged her neck. "He can go fuck himself."

"Same with my dad," Nicole said. "He never wanted girls. He got three. Serves him right that my mom had to have a hysterectomy. Now he'll never have a boy." She narrowed her eyes. "Pretty sure he's cheating on my mom."

"What do you mean?" Kiara asked. She observed each girl. The three of them shared a lot of secrets. Kiara didn't know what she didn't know.

Nicole raised an eyebrow. "It's a long story. Anyways, he's an asshole. He drinks too much. He's always screaming. Which is why I don't talk on the phone or have anyone over."

"Do you get along with your sisters?" Kiara asked. "Or your mom?"

"My sisters are kiss-ups. They help him with the business, so they're like the boys he didn't have. My mom doesn't care, either. I'm a big, fucking disappointment."

"That's awful," Kiara said. She thought of her and Cole. Why did parents treat their younger kids better? "I'm sorry."

"Yeah, well. It's reality." Nicole nodded towards Jenny. "She's got it worse."

Kiara watched Jenny pick at the thread on one of Kiara's teddy bears. Her normally blonde bubbly exterior was absent.

"I'm okay," Jenny said. She avoided eye contact. "It doesn't matter."

Carolyn and Nicole exchanged a look. They took turns filling Kiara in on the details.

"Her mom's been an addict for as long as anyone can remember," Carolyn said.

"She moves a lot, moves in with whoever gives them a place to stay... in exchange for *favors*." Nicole rolled her eyes. "Strangers, dealers, whoever, aren't the best *babysitters*." She glanced at Jenny.

"It's better now," Jenny said quietly. "I'm staying with my grandparents."

"Are they good people?" Kiara bit her lower lip.

"They're okay," Jenny said. "The people at their church are kind. Not that I'm religious, but I do like when we do community service—"

"At least it's not court-ordered community service," Nicole quipped. "Like your mom."

"I like helping out through church," Jenny continued. "We serve meals at the homeless shelter ... It's sad so many people end up on the streets." She had a vacant stare in her eyes. "My mom ... I ... I don't know whether to hate her or feel sorry for her."

"I don't understand how you have the emotional capacity." Nicole shook her head.

"Damn, this shit is heavy," Carolyn said. "I need a smoke. I'm going outside."

"I'll go, too." Nicole followed.

Kiara scooted over to Jenny and gave her a tight hug.

"You're always welcome here," Kiara said. "Anytime."

"I appreciate that." Jenny returned the hug. Despite everything, she didn't cry. Instead, she pulled away with a bright smile on her face. "Enough with the trauma train. Let's have fun. Should we watch a movie or play Uno? I'm up for anything."

What horrible cruelty had been inflicted on this sweet, blue-eyed blonde?

Kiara's problem with her mom—feeling unloved—felt insignificant.

41

Playing the Part

KIARA APPRECIATED THE DEEPER CONNECTION she had with her girlfriends, but she missed Cole. She missed playing Risk and Monopoly with him, missed talking on the phone for hours, and missed taking walks up to the buttes. Did he miss that, too?

The summer was a black hole of communication between the two of them. In all fairness, she didn't call or reach out to him, either. She figured he had plenty of guy friends and girls to keep him occupied.

By sophomore year, Kiara and Cole had the same schedule and were in most of the same periods: honors English, Algebra 2, world history, Spanish 2, and Biology class. The only difference was he was in sports, while she was in her last year of P.E. Sure, they said hi when they passed in the hall, and helped each other with homework occasionally over the phone.

But that was it. It wasn't enough.

To fill the void of missing him, Kiara spent more time with Carolyn, Nicole, and Jenny. That was until they started partnering up.

Carolyn's new boyfriend, Trevor, whom she met in horticulture class, wore a long black trench coat even on the hot days. They were both friends with Misty, the girl from Kiara's drama class who had hooked them up; otherwise, Kiara couldn't imagine how anyone would approach the tall, intimidating senior who stuck by himself, smoked, and shrugged more than he smiled.

In his defense, Trevor gave Carolyn space; other than sharing the occasional cigarette out in the fields, they hung out mostly outside of school. Carolyn didn't divulge details of their relationship or his background.

As the weeks went by, a few guys started hovering around their end of the table. Jenny, with her infectious giggle, and Nicole with her striking features, turned out to be a strong lure for the single guys. Both of them began to wear more of their short skirts and tight tops after the boys started flocking their table. By the time this became a daily thing, Carolyn had started to disappear to the fields with Trevor.

Kiara's heart sank without Carolyn by her side.

She eyed the other girls enviously. Kiara wore baggy t-shirts and jeans or jean shorts; it's all she could afford. She stared at their clothing and watched them giggle with the guys. Kiara sat at the table, head bowed, and stared at the ground. She felt like an ugly duckling and it stung.

She sat at their end of the lunch table and took out her notebook. She tried to write stories and poems, something she hadn't done in a long time. Everything came out cliché and lame. Instead, she sketched mountains, trees, and rivers and wished she were far away.

Nicole was the first to notice the change in her mood. "You're really pretty."

"Right." Coming from this model beauty, Kiara felt flattered but didn't believe it.

Nicole sighed and sat down next to her, booty bumping her over. She crossed her long tan legs, and nudged Kiara on the shoulder.

"What do you want?" Kiara didn't mean it to come out as rude as it must have sounded.

Nicole didn't seem to care. "Jenny and I want to take you out shopping."

"I can't afford that," Kiara said softly. She kept her eyes downcast.

"Listen up, shortie." Nicole nudged her.

Kiara was confused. Sure, she was the shortest of them, but what did that have to do with anything?

"You need a new look," Nicole said. "I have a lot of clothes that don't fit. Since you're smaller than me, the outfits would be perfect for you. They'd be super cute on you. Trust me." She smirked. "I have a pretty good sense of fashion. And obviously..." She motioned to Kiara's attire. "... you don't."

Nicole was right. Unlike the clothing from Melissa's family, the outfits Nicole gave Kiara didn't feel like charity, more like sharing clothes with sisters.

The outfits fit *too* perfectly. The way the fabric hugged her body embarrassed her and Kiara came to school with her arms crossed over her chest and tied a sweatshirt around her waist, which Nicole and Jenny promptly took away, encouraging her to *own it*.

Before long, Kiara stepped into school wearing short shorts that rode up her thighs, and tight tank tops. Sometimes, she wore flowery skirts that flared out above her knees and form-fitting blouses. Not long after her new style debuted, Kiara got lots of attention from the guys.

Kiara got butterflies whenever she stole glances at a tall, sandy haired guy. He was shy and sweet. When he finally approached her, she initially lost the ability to respond.

He said hi and introduced himself; she already knew his name—Luke. He pointed back at a friend of his, a slightly shorter guy with a thicker build who waved and smiled at her. Her crush asked her if she'd go out with his friend.

Kiara's heart sank. She told Luke she was sorry, but she was interested in someone else. She didn't feel it was right to admit it was him, so she kept quiet and watched the two walk away disappointed.

"Don't go after Luke," Jenny said. "He's a male slut."

"Yeah, you don't need that," Nicole said. "At least now you'll believe me when I say you look hot … in my clothes." Nicole smirked, apparently proud of her protégé.

Kiara shook her head and blushed. That's when she realized she totally loved her friends. They didn't denigrate others or view themselves as superior like the three witches had. They offered genuine support and honesty with kindness.

Not long after that, Mary, a pretty girl with dark eyes and straight black hair that reached the small of her back, approached Kiara.

"We have a couple classes together," Mary said. "I have a friend who wants to ask you out. First, I want to see if you're interested. He's a little shy."

Kiara peeked behind her shoulder to find an attractive guy with clean-cut, black hair; beautiful, bronze skin; and a mischievous smirk on his handsome face.

"I might be," Kiara said. "I want to get to know him first."

Juan took that as his chance to approach her table. "Hey, Kiara. Mind if I sit with you?"

"Sure." She slid over. Her cheeks were hot. She turned away so he wouldn't notice.

Juan gave her a smile. "We don't have any classes together because I'm a junior, and you're a sophomore." He scooted closer. "I've noticed you for several weeks before I asked Mary. You're so beautiful." He added, "Even when you wear baggy t-shirts and jeans."

Baggy t-shirts and jeans? That meant he'd been watching her for a while. Kiara couldn't come up with a better response than, "thank you."

He turned to face her. "Do you want to come over to my place to go rollerblading?"

"I've never done that." She tried not to panic.

"I can teach you."

"I have terrible balance," she said.

"I don't mind at all," Juan said.

She searched for an excuse. Why would she go over to this stranger's house?

He detected her hesitation. "Mary is dating my older brother, so she'll be there."

Kiara's friends encouraged her to go, so she got Mary's number and befriended her first.

The following Friday, she went over to Juan's house after school, and sure enough Mary was there. She soon disappeared into the house, leaving the two of them outside alone.

Juan helped her put on some rollerblades—he had extras that his cousins used when they came over. She immediately fell down. Juan helped her up and offered his arm for her to steady herself. He guided her to his front porch swing.

He showed off for her; he was an impressive skater, both forward and backward, and even while shooting hockey pucks into a net on his driveway.

Juan encouraged her to keep trying. They made it halfway down the street when her death grip on his arm almost brought them both down. They decided it best to relax on the porch, under the shade of the massive weeping willow in his front yard, and learn more about each other.

They covered the basics: family—he had an older brother, two younger sisters, and a younger brother, he lived with his mom and stepdad who fathered the younger three, he and his older brother didn't know their dads, and he had a lot of pets: dogs, cats, and a snake.

"I've never had a girlfriend before," Juan said.

She stared at him, incredulous. "Yeah, right."

"It's true. I'm too shy to ask anyone out."

They bonded over the missing dad commonality and her desire for pets, which he had. He brought a kitten out—one of their several cats had another litter—and handed the fluffy little furball to Kiara to hold.

"I wish I had a kitten," Kiara said. She nuzzled her face into its soft fur.

"Do you want that one?" Juan asked. "You can have it after it's done nursing. It's too little right now."

As the sun got nearer to setting, Mary kept peering out the window. Finally, she opened the front door and called Juan inside for a moment.

Juan came back out, a light blush to his cheeks, with something held behind his back.

He sat next to Kiara, and pulled a single red rose out from behind his back. "Kiara, would you be my girlfriend?"

Kiara flushed, her stomach dropped like on a rollercoaster, and she nodded yes, unable to think of anything else to say.

He leaned over to her and gently kissed her cheek.

"Was that okay?" Juan asked.

"Yes." Kiara nodded. She liked it but didn't say so. She thought of the teen magazines which advised girls to play "hard to get."

Juan reached up and gently held her face. "Close your eyes."

Kiara did and felt his lips press against hers.

Kiara pulled back. She was embarrassed and confused and excited that she could finally say she kissed a guy. Thank God he didn't try to French kiss her, because she would've freaked out if he tried to open-mouth kiss her. Even though Juan said he had never had a girlfriend before, he kissed her in a way that wasn't at all awkward, even asking her *to close her eyes.* Maybe he was getting better advice or reading better magazines than her.

Juan reached for her hand and intertwined their fingers together. Although it felt awkward, she thought it made her happy.

Over the next two months, Juan sat at the lunch table with her and held her hand and planted kisses on her cheek. When no one was paying attention, he brushed her hair to the side and kissed her neck, which made her all tingly.

One day, Mary told Kiara that all three of them were going to ditch school to hang out at Juan's house. Apparently, his older brother had already graduated high school and was enrolling in the army. Mary wanted to spend time with him, and Juan wanted Kiara to come over, too.

Kiara had never ditched school before, never had the desire or guts to do it, so she had to be talked into it. When they got to Juan's house, they each called the school and pretended to be their own parents to say their kids were sick and would be staying home that day.

Mary disappeared into Juan's brother's room, while Kiara and Juan sat together on the couch watching the Disney animated movie *Cinderella*.

Juan's mom was home—she was a stay-at-home mom whose husband worked long hours. She cooked torta sandwiches for lunch.

"It's too heavy for her delicate stomach," his mom warned. "Make her a ham sandwich."

"No, it's okay," Kiara said. "I want to try the torta." She sank her teeth into the thick bread and flavorful meat. "It's so good," she said in between mouthfuls.

"Slow down," his mom said. "You're eating too fast."

After a couple juicy, savory bites, Kiara figured everyone was overreacting. Because she was so hungry, she devoured it.

Sure enough, half an hour later, Kiara barfed into a trashcan. Nobody got mad and everyone thought it was funny. Kiara's stomach didn't think it was funny, so Juan's mom gave her some Mexican sweet bread to nibble on, which helped.

Juan gave her extra hugs and played with her hair until she felt better.

Kiara had bad luck. She got caught ditching.

When she got home, her mom was waiting for her. She was pissed. The school had phoned home regarding the absence.

"You screwed up," her mom berated. "You're making stupid decisions."

"This is so unfair," Kiara said. "Other people ditch all the time. You're lucky I'm not one of those kids. This is the first time I've ever ditched. This was one time and that's it. It's not going to happen again. I promise."

"Where were you?" her mom demanded. "Is this Carolyn's fault?"

"No, leave her out of it."

"Is it a boy? Is it Cole?"

"No, it's not Cole." Kiara's cheeks reddened. "His name is Juan."

"Juan?" Her mom's eyes narrowed. Comprehension settled over her face when she realized that Kiara had a boyfriend. "You are not allowed to date, young lady."

Kiara grunted but said nothing.

"Do you hear me?" Her mom got inches from her face.

Kiara turned away. "Mom, you don't understand."

"No, you don't understand. Stupid decisions can change your life. Trust me, I know."

"Fine, Mom." Kiara closed her eyes. "I won't date. Are you happy?"

Her mom took a slow breath. "Go to your room. You're grounded."

"Mom—"

"I said, go to your room."

Kiara walked away. She could've confided in her mom, shared details of Juan and their relationship. But why would she? What was the point in talking to someone who clearly didn't want to listen? Her mom never wanted to talk; all she ever wanted to do was yell.

Juan would be a secret from then on. At least *he* made Kiara feel wanted.

42

Climbing Trees

Now THAT FALL WAS WINDING DOWN in their second year of high school, Kiara, Carolyn, Nicole, and Jenny sat around their lunch table—they currently controlled two-thirds of the real estate—and discussed getting more involved on campus with activities. Because it was a new high school without many clubs, they decided to create one.

"Let's do a community service club." Jenny notched up the enthusiasm. "My church serves food at the homeless shelter and brings meals to the elderly. It's good to help others."

Thank God that both her mom and Carolyn's mom finally allowed them to quit the church after earning the Sacrament of Confirmation. What Kiara's mom thought she had confirmed—her faith in God—was quite different from what Kiara actually confirmed—her freedom from the church.

Even so, Kiara was glad Jenny had found a supportive group at her grandparents' church.

"Alright, let's start a community service club," Kiara said, surprising herself by taking the lead. Jenny beamed at her. "Not only will it supposedly look good for college, at least we'll do something good for society. Let's find a club advisor."

And so began the hunt. The twentieth teacher they asked finally agreed. Rather than start from scratch, she explained that there were already large adult organizations like Kiwanis that sponsored high school clubs. After school the girls sat in their advisor's classroom to brainstorm ideas. Their advisor suggested Kiara and her friends be the founding members to bring one of those clubs, like Key Club, on campus. They'd get more support that way.

"Sounds like a smarter way to do it," Kiara said. "Any objection to a Key Club?"

There was none. Kiara was nominated to be president, Carolyn chosen to be the secretary, and Jenny wanted to be treasurer. Nicole refused to take a board position but would be willing to participate as a member. Who would be vice-president?

Kiara brought it up to Juan before school. He wrapped his arm around her waist and pressed her body close to his so he could plant kisses on her neck.

Kiara pushed back. "Do you want to be my vice-president?"

He pulled her close. "I can be a lot of things for you."

Kiara removed his hands from her waist and stepped back. "I'm being serious."

Juan laughed. "Clubs are silly. Community service is court-mandated for criminals. I'm not a club type of guy." He kissed the back of her hand. He made eye contact and smiled. "I'll support you, if it means spending more time with you."

Kiara went to English class sad and angry and disappointed. When she stepped in and found a substitute teacher, she took the opportunity to slide into an empty seat alongside Cole.

"To what do I owe the pleasure?" Cole grinned.

"I want to copy your homework." She smirked.

"You've never been a cheater before. Besides, English has always been your thing." He elbowed her playfully in the side. "Read any good books lately?"

"No time anymore. You?"

"Nah," he said. "Have you finished writing your novel yet?"

"Your expectations of me are quite high," Kiara said. "I have a favor to ask."

"Asking me to co-write a book with you is probably unwise." He laughed.

Kiara rolled her eyes. "We're starting a service club. Do you want to be vice-president?"

Cole raised his eyebrows. "And serve under you, Madam President?" He did an exaggerated half bow. "It would be my sincere pleasure. Plus, I love that idea of serving the community. I'll help you out in any way possible."

"So, co-writing a book with me ... Is that option still on the table?"

One of the first orders of business, according to Jenny, normally carefree and silly but taking her treasurer position seriously, was to fundraise. They needed money to plan service projects. How could they raise money without having any money to begin with?

Kiara, Cole, Jenny, Carolyn, and Nicole, who, even though she hadn't taken a board position, attended every board meeting, sat around and brainstormed ideas.

"Sell candy?" Jenny said.

"Nope," Kiara said, "that requires money."

"Car wash?" Nicole said.

"No, we need school approval."

"Beg for money?" Cole said.

"No, Cole," Kiara said, "that's funny but we can't do that."

"The holidays are coming up," Carolyn said, "so why don't we sell mistletoe? It's free to pick off trees, and we'd be doing the trees a favor anyways. We need baggies and ribbons."

Brilliant. They made plans to drive up to Big Rock Creek together. Carolyn had a driver's permit and an appointment to take her driver's test in late December. They agreed not to tell their parents her in-legal-limbo status. Cole called shotgun on account of being the tallest of them.

"I brought some big black trash bags," Carolyn said.

"Let's go to my house after," Kiara said. "We can break it up into sprigs and tie ribbons around them." Her mom would either be at one of her jobs or in her room, so they'd have the house to themselves.

Nicole brought a container of frosting that she swiped from her kitchen cabinet so they could snack on a sweet treat on the way there. They drove along the winding road past the Abbey, and slowed when they approached the oak trees with the top-heavy clusters of mistletoe.

After they parked and got out of the car, they peered up at the tall trees and realized they had a problem. Someone was going to have to climb up there and knock the bunches off the branches to get it.

Jenny and Nicole said no way; they volunteered to pick up the pieces that fell to the ground and put them in bags.

Carolyn said she was doing the driving and couldn't risk getting hurt and they all felt that was more than fair.

Simultaneously, Cole and Kiara said, "I'll do it." They agreed it was safer for them to climb up together.

Carolyn stepped aside to have a smoke while they began their ascent.

Kiara and Cole scouted for a tree that had enough bunches that were low enough that they wouldn't have to get out on any unstable limbs, and that had bottom branches hanging close to the ground to provide them access.

"I didn't know you climbed trees," Kiara said as she stepped on the step Cole created with his hands to boost her up.

After she was on the first sturdy branch, Cole pulled himself up, and took her hand to steady himself.

"I guess there's a lot you don't know about me." Cole smirked. "And for the record, this is the first time I've seen you climb a tree."

They made their way higher and higher up until they were close to the first bundle. At this point they needed a rest to regain strength, or at least Kiara did.

From their vantage point, they could look down on the others who appeared to be having fun talking and joking around.

Cole, at her eye level, met her gaze. "I hear you have a boyfriend now."

"What?" She leaned against the trunk. Kiara couldn't see his eyes. "Oh, Juan? Yeah."

"I broke up with my girlfriend," Cole said, after a few moments.

"Why?" She had lost track of which one he was allegedly dating; if the rumors were true, Cole had gone through half a dozen beautiful girls from a variety of backgrounds.

"She wasn't smart enough, or kind enough, or honest enough. It wasn't fun, and I think I've figured out that a relationship is supposed to be fun."

Kiara considered how things were with Juan. They weren't always fun; he wasn't too bright when it came to school—she, taking Advanced Algebra 2, tutored him with some basic pre-algebra stuff she did in middle school. And his sense of humor was crude. And he was getting a bit pushy with her to go further sexually.

She was okay with kissing, but he pushed to make-out and touch her in places he promised would feel pleasurable. Instead, she felt shame and disgust. Each time he slid a hand underneath her sweater or down her shorts, she smacked his hand away. Then he rubbed her over her clothes which wasn't much better. He didn't comply when she told him to stop.

She didn't reveal any of this to Cole. She stared at him and waited for him to speak.

"I miss hanging out with you," Cole said.

"Me, too." She widened her eyes. Was that okay to say? She had a boyfriend, after all. Besides, they were only talking about hanging out as friends.

Cole had the biggest grin. "I guess we better get some mistletoe."

Neither of them had removed mistletoe from a tree before. Carolyn shouted up directions. Kiara tried to wiggle it free. The bunches were far heavier than she could have imagined. It wasn't like a pile of leaves; it was a dense mass.

"Heads up," Cole called down. He pulled and pushed at the top of the bunch, until it snapped off and fell to the ground with a loud thud.

"Here, Kiara." He reached for her. "You do the next one."

She smiled at hearing him say her name. "How?"

"Come up here. I'll help you." He stepped back to another branch to make way for her. He gripped her hand and guided her around him. "Hang on tight to the branch and wiggle the mistletoe back and forth until it comes loose."

"Okay." Kiara glanced down; it was a long way to the ground.

"Don't worry. I got you." Cole rested a hand on her back. "Go ahead. You can do it."

His hand felt warm and comforting. She yanked at the bunch and tossed it down.

"Wow." She smiled back at Cole. "That felt satisfying."

"Right?"

After that, they took turns.

It was fun, like the days of making igloos out of sugar cubes, or building bridges and hot air balloons. Her worries lifted. She forgot about Juan for a while.

Jenny, Nicole, and Carolyn shouted for them to stop because they had more than enough and it was a lot of work getting them into the bags and that they were having to break it up to make it fit.

Cole called down that because he and Kiara did the climbing, that they would take a break while the others bagged. They said that was fine.

"So, what do you look for in a boyfriend?" Cole leaned his body between the crux of two branches. The sun was starting to set, and with them being in the middle of two hills, darkness was coming on fast.

"One who asks me out." Kiara turned away. She dropped her shoulders. Juan had asked her out, not Cole.

"I see."

She picked at the bark of a branch. "What do you think of Juan?"

Cole shook his head. "You can do better."

"What's that supposed to mean?"

"I'm keeping my mouth shut, because the last time I spoke my mind, you didn't talk to me for months. And, honestly, I don't want to go through that again."

"I didn't mean it back then. We were kids. You know me better than that."

"And you know me, so I think you already know how I feel."

How could she respond to that? Kiara's heart sped up and she took shallow breaths. Even though a part of her wanted very much to keep talking about this, and maybe to do so while lying against his chest, she said nothing. Oh, how she wished it were Cole's arms and not Juan's who held her at home. Shame bubbled in her chest, and she blushed.

"What comes next for us?" She quickly added, "After high school."

"College, of course," Cole said.

"Are you going to go away?" she asked.

"Why would I stay?"

"I ask myself the same thing all the time," she said. "It's scary to think about leaving. Where do I go? How do I get there?"

"Neither of our parents went to college. We have to figure it out on our own." He scooted closer until his leg brushed against hers. "We can help each other though."

The sun was fully down, and the outline of Cole, and the trees, darkened.

Cole noticed it, too. "Let's climb down. I don't want you to get hurt."

He climbed down a branch and paused to direct her hand and foot placement. Then he went down another level and repeated that until he was able to jump down off the last branch. He turned and held out his arms and she jumped into them. He set her down and they brushed themselves off.

The others were dragging the heavy bags back to the car. Cole rushed over to help.

After the cargo was smashed down enough to safely be stored in the trunk, they piled in the car.

"Nicole," Cole said. "Why don't you sit up front? It's only fair."

Nicole, nearly as tall as he was, didn't object.

Kiara sat in the middle in the back. Cole climbed in next to her, his body squished between the door and hers. Their legs and knees and arms touched. Neither of them could move since they were sardined in there with his broad shoulders.

She had so much more fun with him than Juan; with Cole, she could be herself: silly, smart, and honest. With Juan, things were so serious, and she dumbed herself down in order to build Juan's confidence.

On the way home, along the winding road and down through the foothills, Nicole groaned. She was miserable. In pain, she contorted in her seat.

"She's car sick," Jenny yelled. "Stop the car."

"Please, don't puke in my car." Carolyn pulled over on the side of the road.

Nicole stumbled out and violently threw up in a ditch. None of them could figure out what happened until Carolyn looked down on the floorboard.

"You licked frosting off your fingers, huh?" Carolyn asked. "After bagging mistletoe?"

Nicole nodded.

"Great. You just went and poisoned yourself."

43

The Outsider

THEY GOT BACK TO KIARA'S HOUSE in time to watch Tom hop into the backseat of a car backing out of the driveway.

Cole leaned close to Kiara. "Tommy hangs out a lot with Dave, huh?" Cole was the only one who still referred to Tom by his old nickname. "At least you're not fighting anymore."

"Because he's never home," Kiara said.

Once they got inside, Nicole ran into the bathroom and threw up.

"Do we have to get her to the hospital?" Cole asked.

"Maybe?" Kiara turned to Carolyn. "What do we do?"

"I'll check on her." Carolyn went and knocked on the bathroom door. "Nicole? I'm coming in."

"Shit." Kiara flopped on the couch. "I hope she doesn't die."

"I doubt that." Cole sat down and brushed a hair from her face. "Don't worry."

A few minutes later, Carolyn and Nicole reappeared. "I got her some water. She needs to keep drinking water to flush it out and stay hydrated."

"I'm fine." Nicole wiped her eyes. "Let's do the damn mistletoe." After that, she didn't throw up again and was able to keep down a few crackers.

Together, they prepared cute bundles of mistletoe, all except Nicole who decided she'd be happy if she never saw another piece of mistletoe in her life. She lay down on the couch curled up in a ball. The rest of them took handfuls of little bags and put a sprig of mistletoe in each bag.

Carolyn made sure everyone washed their hands, and emphasized that they must warn all customers that this was poisonous and to keep them in the sandwich bags. To make sure of that, Carolyn tied a ribbon tightly around the bag and knotted it and told them all to do the same. They placed the sealed bags in baskets to sell at school.

Cole held a bag over his head, grinned at Kiara, and playfully raised his eyebrows up and down. She shook her head and slugged him in the arm. He pretended it hurt and asked for an apology hug, which she gave him. No matter how brief it lasted, having Cole's warm arms around her felt amazing.

Fortunately, as the evening continued, Nicole recovered. Her accidental poisoning passed like a stomach flu. Carolyn said she was lucky.

Back at school, Juan helped Kiara carry around the basket as long as she handled the sales, which at least was nice enough of him. It was annoying that he kept holding a bag of mistletoe over his head and prompting her for a kiss after every transaction.

Within the day, they sold out.

On January 17, 1994, the earth shook in a massive way. Down below, in the San Fernando Valley, the shaking only lasted less than half a minute, but the 6.7 magnitude quake managed to mark its place in history as the most destructive one since the deadly 1906 earthquake in San Francisco. It occurred on a previously unknown thrust fault line. Portions of two major freeways collapsed, tens of thousands of homes were destroyed, and close to 100 people lost their lives.

The only saving grace was that it happened at 4:30 AM on a federal holiday, or, rather than empty, those two freeways would have been packed with thousands of cars, which would have plummeted from the sheer drop-off of the collapsed Newhall Pass 5 Freeway Interchange.

Soon as the sun was up, Kiara called Cole. She got a busy signal. She hung up and the phone rang. Cole had been calling her at the same time. His dad had finally bought them a new TV, so Cole saw the destruction as did Kiara.

"Mom called one of my uncles who lives in the valley," Kiara said. "His house made it, mostly, other than a crack across the ceiling and down a wall, but his exterior brick wall, and every dish and glassware he owned, were destroyed. He cut his foot running across the room."

Kiara and Cole sat quiet on the line, speechless from the destruction—extensive damage at California State University Northridge, collapsed parking structures, crumbled apartments that smashed carports below and flattened cars, over 80,000 commercial properties and houses destroyed, multiple hospitals that had incurred irreparable structural damage, plus the fires, and the chaos.

A couple hours later, Kiara phoned Juan to ask if he was watching the news. He said his mom mentioned it, and every time he walked by the TV, they replayed the same images.

"Kinda sucks for those people, but I'm glad it's not us," Juan said. Then he added, "There's one more reason for you not to go to college. Or at least not there." He laughed.

Kiara felt ill and wished she could punch him through the phone. Instead, she said she had to go, hung up, and called Cole.

That afternoon, Tom meandered into the living room and sat down next to Kiara on the couch. He pointed to the TV. A helicopter camera panned over a collapsed section of the freeway overpass and retold the tragedy of the motorcycle cop, Officer Dean, who fell to his death.

"Dave's dad drove over that just last night," Tom said.

Kiara's eyes widened. "Are you serious?"

"Yeah, pretty unbelievable, right?" Tom said. "I can't stop thinking about it."

"Or that cop," Kiara said. "Can you imagine? And the people in the apartments."

"Never know when you're going to die." Tom stared at the TV.

Kiara looked at him. She couldn't imagine something like that happening to Tom. She wanted to hug him but didn't. He used to crawl up on her lap and she'd hold him and comfort him. Things weren't the same. He was bigger than her.

Kiara sat in her room that evening and gazed out her bedroom window, which she had been spending increasing amounts of time doing. Sometimes, she'd watch the leaves move on the scrawny sycamore tree in her front yard which had, despite the odds, continued to grow.

When it was dark, she stared at the stars and at the bright light reflecting off the snow at the top of one of the San Gabriel mountains. That was Mountain High, the ski resort where many of the kids at her high school went. It was not only close by, but you could get cheap lift tickets. She was too terrified to try skiing, especially with her balance challenges, besides which, they didn't have the money for the clothes or gear.

The blinding glow in the darkness, a white light in the heavens, was a beautiful sight.

When the power went out one night that winter, and their mom wasn't home, Kiara and Tom made a fire in the fireplace by themselves. As their mom had done numerous times, they shoved crumbled newspaper and twigs underneath large logs. Tom used the poker to reposition it all. Kiara struck a long fireplace match to light the tinder. She pumped the bellow to fan the flame. Soon, a fire roared to life.

When the fire dimmed, they added logs. The bellow fanned the flames.

Then the fire died down and started smoking and nothing they tried helped.

"Do we have lighter fluid?" Kiara asked.

"How should I know?" Tom said. "I can't see a damn thing."

"Light the kerosene lantern."

Tom fiddled with it. "It's not working."

"How hard can it be?" Kiara said. "Here, give it to me."

They had trouble lighting the lantern because the wick was too low or too high, so they gave up on that for the moment, and the flashlights, like usual, were nowhere to be found.

Underneath the kitchen cabinet Tom found a bottle of some type of cleaning fluid—not that they were cleaning much at all since their grandma left and their mom quit the daycare. In fact, things had gotten so bad around the house that the week before, Kiara and Tom took the mounds of dirty dishes piled all over the kitchen sink and counters, from the dining table and the living room table and floors, and dumped the whole lot into the bathtub.

They simply had nothing to eat on because they were out of paper plates and the dishes smelled and were covered in a variety of molds: green and white and black and brown. They poured dish soap over everything and filled the tub with hot water and let everything soak overnight. They sprayed everything off with the shower, and had to repeat the process with more hot water until all the crusty food and mold was soft enough to scrub off.

Even when the dishes were clean, there wasn't much to put on them. They sorted through expired cans in the walk-in pantry and grabbed a box of off-brand macaroni and cheese that was edible after they scooped out the weevils that floated to the top when they boiled it.

Tom produced the container of fluid and squirted it into the fireplace. A fireball flew up into the chimney and the flames turned blue. They screamed and jumped back in surprise. After that calmed down, the fire was going better.

"What the fuck was that?" Kiara asked. She held the bottle in the light of the fire to read the label. "This isn't lighter fluid. It's cleaner."

"It worked, didn't it?" Tom smirked.

Rather than smack him, she grinned. "I have an idea." She set down the poker.

They grabbed another cleaner and squirted the fluid into the fire, a can of this, an aerosol of that.

Look at the orange flames! Green that time. Did you see the purple?

Like children in the wild, they lost all sense of reason and jumped around the living room taking turns dousing the fire with chemicals, until one fireball shot back out of the fireplace at them. They screamed and lunged out of the way.

The smell was foul and made them cough. They opened the windows to air it out. Tom's arm hairs had been singed.

That was the end of that. They promised each other not to do it again. And swore each other to secrecy.

At school, Kiara noticed that the Mexican girls snickered when Kiara walked by holding Juan's hand. She asked him what they were saying and he shook his head to ignore them.

Then she heard it: *pinche güera* or fucking white girl.

"That's bullshit," Kiara said. "I'm going to say something to them if you won't."

"Don't bother," Juan said. "They're just pissed that I'm dating a white girl."

"Because you're Mexican?" she said. "What the fuck? Are they going to jump me or something? How is this okay?"

"Just ignore them. Even Mary doesn't care."

"Easy for you to say. I'm the one they're calling a bitch."

Kiara couldn't wrap her head around that one. She avoided walking around those girls by herself, because she was scared of these girls with the penciled-on eyebrows, thick foundation, bright lipstick, and big hoop earrings. Kiara hadn't been afraid of her safety like that before.

She confided in Juan. "What if they beat me up? A girl got arrested last year for knocking a girl unconscious on the concrete ... over a guy."

Juan laughed. "Don't worry. Some girls say stupid stuff."

The girls called her *puta* and other nasty words. Juan was her first boyfriend. She didn't deserve that. Did his family say these things behind her back?

Juan invited her to go to another family birthday party at his house which meant a *piñata*, delicious food—carnitas, beans, rice, and tortillas—lots of little kids, and prying family members asking her if she spoke Spanish and how long she had been dating Juan and if she wanted kids of her own and if so, how many.

One of Juan's aunts handed Kiara a baby, one of many in the family.

Kiara hoisted the baby up around her waist. He whimpered, so she handed him back.

"Ah, you have good hips." The aunt nodded. "Those are good birthing hips."

"What?" Shocked, Kiara walked away while Juan's aunt laughed. Kiara felt uncomfortable in her own skin. Juan said it wasn't a big deal.

Juan got jealous of Cole. He asked Kiara to spend less time talking with Cole before and after class, and more time with him. That seemed like a fair request, since Cole had done that to her with his first girlfriend.

At lunch at school, Juan lured her away from the lunch table and led her to dark, secluded corners and kissed her and groped her over her clothes. She got tired of it and told him so. He shrugged and did what he wanted anyway.

Her friends were starting to sour on Juan a bit. They didn't say much but rolled their eyes when he came around or when she said his name.

"What's the problem?" Kiara said one day when Juan wasn't there. "He loves me. He tells me that all the time. He writes me sweet love letters."

"Mm-hmm," Carolyn said. "Right."

"What's that supposed to mean?" Kiara put her hands on her hips.

"You haven't heard the rumors?" Jenny asked, wide-eyed.

"What rumors?" Kiara looked from one to the other.

"She's not going to listen," Nicole said. She stared at Kiara. "He's talking to and flirting with other girls."

"He said that rumor's not true," Kiara said. "The Hispanic girls just don't like me dating him, because he's Mexican and I'm white."

"I told you she wasn't going to listen." Nicole shrugged at Jenny and Carolyn.

"Why would he lie to me?" Kiara said. "He wants to marry me. Obviously, he wouldn't be saying that if he was interested in other girls."

Maybe her friends were jealous that their boyfriends weren't talking marriage. Besides, Juan couldn't cheat on her because he was always with her. He loved spending every moment with her. He loved her. And she loved him.

At another family party at Juan's one night, his uncle got drunk and belligerent in the street. It took half a dozen family members to get him to shut up and get in the house, and Kiara realized they all—Juan included—drank a lot of beer. It made her uncomfortable, but he wasn't the only one. She thought of Stephanie, Jessica, and Heidi, and all the party kids at school.

And then there were the conversations with Juan's mom who was increasingly finding time to talk with her whenever Juan left the room.

Juan's mom made them French toast. He took a shower while Kiara finished eating. His mom stood nearby in the kitchen and scrubbed at the cast iron pan.

"Why are you always so stressed out?" his mom asked.

"I'm not," Kiara said. She put her last bite in her mouth.

"I notice you always worry about school. Relax." She rinsed off the pan. "You know, things don't always go as planned."

"What do you mean?"

"Life may disappoint you if your dreams are too big."

"I don't agree." Kiara glanced around the corner. When was Juan going to get out of the shower?

"Just realize." His mom picked up a dishcloth to dry the pan. "There are more ways to be happy than going off to school constantly stressing and worrying."

"I'm going to college."

"I understand. I wanted to go to college, too, when I was younger, but I had Juan and his brother and family is more important." She set the pan back on the stove. "Juan is a hardworking guy. He'll make a good husband and a good dad."

She wished she could tell her friends about this super awkward conversation. She couldn't find the time to talk to them in private: Juan was always there.

Another time, when Kiara was over at Juan's house, she mentioned to him that it made her uncomfortable that he had a calendar of naked women pinned to the wall over his bed. She insisted he take it down. Juan got mad and screamed at her. With tears in her eyes, she retreated to his living room where, unfortunately, his mom was sitting.

"Well," she said to Kiara. "Sometimes guys are dogs. That's how it is."

"No," Kiara said, "that's not okay."

"That's how it was with Juan's dad." She smiled. "Let things go. He loves you. Stop worrying so much."

None of this sat well with Kiara. Juan had been pulling her away from her friends, and he was always at her house, or she was always at his, and so she still hadn't gotten the chance to talk to her friends about it yet.

Besides, what would they say?

44

Innocence Lost

CAROLYN, JENNY, NICOLE, AND KIARA spent a lot more time with their current boyfriends over the summer. Carolyn and Nicole each got their drivers licenses—neither Kiara nor Jenny had the money for a car or insurance, so they didn't bother.

Sometimes they'd get together and one of them, or their boyfriends, drove to a park to talk and make out. Kiara's friends didn't bring up issues with Juan anymore, and Kiara didn't want to make them hate him, so she decided to keep her concerns to herself.

Kiara spent the night at Carolyn's house several times, which involved waiting for Carolyn's two younger brothers and her parents to fall asleep, stuffing pillows under the covers, and sneaking out of Carolyn's bedroom window so Carolyn could visit her boyfriend, Trevor.

Carolyn led Kiara on a midnight stroll through the neighborhood. Guided by the moonlight, they snuck around her front gate, through Trevor's chain link fence gate, trampled across his backyard, and climbed in through his window.

Kiara sat around while the two of them, along with several other friends who showed up, smoked weed from a bong. She tried it once, but her throat burned so intensely that she couldn't at all understand the appeal. Was she doing it wrong? For her, sleep deprivation was enough to give her an out-of-body experience and she'd giggle over nothing. When Kiara told the others she didn't need the weed, because she was *high on life*, they laughed for much longer than the joke called for.

The suffocating smell made Kiara cough. She declined their offer to share their stash and opted to sit outside by herself in the dark, cold night. She stared at the stars until her face was numb from the cold and it was time to head back.

On another occasion, Trevor and one of his friends snuck into Carolyn's bedroom to share a joint. She lit incense and the woodsy sandalwood and fragrant jasmine covered the scent. To be polite, they offered to Kiara. She declined. Plumes of incense swirled and crawled up through the air. Maybe Kiara was getting a mild contact high.

Tom, ready to start eighth grade, was hardly home. He spent so much time at Dave's that Kiara wondered if he was going to move in.

Once Dave and his dad came to get Tom and the boys ran into Tom's room to get his things, Kiara was stuck in the living room making small talk with Dave's dad. His eyes lowered to her breasts and lingered there, a hungry look on his face. It made her nauseated. She wanted to disappear. She crossed her arms over her chest, which is when his eyes noticed her face.

She told Juan. He said she was attractive so naturally guys were going to check her out and to take it as a compliment. She disagreed, because compliments shouldn't carry humiliation.

When Kiara wore a skirt or dress above her knees, and sometimes even if she was wearing sweats and a tight top, guys gawked at her in public. When this happened, Juan raised his head higher, a rooster parading his chick around.

She didn't like that, either. Not that she wanted him to make it worse by making a big deal out of it, but to at least acknowledge how gross it made her feel, especially when the men were two or three or even four times her age.

Juan wrote letters on lined notebook paper and folded them into hearts. He handed them to Kiara when he'd walk her from one class to the next. She unfolded the hearts discreetly in class to read them. Juan professed how much he loved her and how happy she made him. Kiara smiled and a warmth came into her cheeks.

She didn't get the chance in class to write back. How did Juan find the time to pour out his heart to her in writing while sitting in class listening to lectures or doing work?

She collected the paper hearts in a bag at home. If she couldn't sleep at night, she'd pull out the bag to reread his notes.

When Kiara wasn't with her friends, Juan monopolized the rest of her time. He asked to come over when her mom wasn't home. She didn't want to risk getting caught. He insisted they wouldn't. They made out in the living room. If

Tom came home from Dave's or her mom arrived early unannounced, Juan quickly left out the sliding glass door.

Once her mom came home early from work because she was ill. Juan was in Kiara's bedroom. When the key turned in the front door, Kiara panicked. She shoved him into her small bedroom closet. As soon as her mom shut her door for the evening, Kiara snuck him out.

They didn't have to sneak around at his house, on account of his mom openly endorsing anything the two wanted to do. She even, not so subtly, offered them condoms, and didn't mind Juan's calendar of naked women, or that he watched porn on the TV in his bedroom.

None of this felt right to Kiara. Juan brushed off any of her concerns and told her she was overreacting and to not be so childish.

"Don't be uptight," Juan's mom told Kiara. "At your age, I was already a mom."

When Juan's brother came back from bootcamp to visit, Mary asked Kiara to spend the night. After Mary's parents were asleep, she and Kiara climbed out the window, tiptoed around the back of the house, slowly unlatched the chain link gate, and hurried down the road in darkness. Juan and his brother lived down the street.

Mary tapped on Juan's window—his brother's room faced the street and was too obvious—and Juan let them in. Mary disappeared into the brother's room, while Kiara fell asleep on Juan's bed. She awoke to see him at his desk writing her a love note. When he found her awake, he serenaded her with the song "You Are So Beautiful to Me." With a warm smile on her face, she fell back asleep in his bed. It was those little moments that brought her joy.

The following week, Juan complained to Kiara. "I wish we didn't have to hide our relationship." He tucked a strand of her hair behind her ear and traced her chin with his finger. "I want your mom to get to know me. Can't we tell her?"

"I don't know." Kiara had zero desire to communicate with her mom.

"Sneaking around isn't right." He took her hands in his. "Especially if we're going to have a future together."

Kiara got butterflies in her stomach. He really did love her. "Okay, I'll tell her."

That night, Kiara stood in the kitchen while her mom prepared spaghetti.

"Mom." Kiara took a deep breath. "I have a boyfriend, and he wants to meet you."

Her mom glared at her then turned away without saying a word.

Kiara sighed. "Mom, stop it. I'm trying to talk to you."

"What's there to talk about?"

Rather than scream at her mom, Kiara shook her head and went to her room. It was no use. Why did she even keep trying to have a relationship with her mom?

Juan offered to come over to help her mom with yard work. Kiara made introductions. Her mom didn't say much.

Juan tried to make a good impression. The following weekend, he helped to straighten up the garage. Her mom thanked him.

Juan's mom invited Kiara and her mom over for dinner so they could meet. Juan's mom was super nice—even Kiara's mom said so—so, Kiara's mom began to be okay with her dating Juan. Juan even befriended Tom. He brought Tom gifts: baseball cards and comic books. To Kiara, that meant her relationship with Juan was pretty solid.

"See?" Juan said to her one night while he kissed her neck. "I told you your mom would like me if she met me."

Kiara had to admit he was right.

Juan intertwined his fingers with hers. "What if one day we get married and have kids of our own?"

Kiara stared into his brown eyes and noted his shy smile. "Maybe I don't want kids."

"You say that now," he said. "It's different if we have our own." He touched her cheek. "Little you's and little me's running around. Wouldn't that be cute?"

Kiara imagined herself being a part of his fantasy. She could wake up next to Juan every morning and kiss him good night and they would sit at the dinner table—just the two of them.

"We'd be so happy together." He kissed the back of her hand. "And I'd still bring you flowers and write you poems and sing you songs. Is that okay with you?"

"As long as you keep doing all those things. Those are nice."

"I'd be proud one day to call you, my wife." He wrapped his arms around her and embraced her in a hug. "I love you more than anything."

"I love you, too." She melted into his arms. She'd never had someone love her so much. She *felt* loved. And this, more than getting out of the desert or away from her mom, was enough.

As the weeks continued, whenever she wasn't at Juan's house, he was at hers. He was increasingly not taking no for an answer when it came to putting his hands under instead of over her clothes. Each time, he assured her it's because he loved her and that's what people do when they love each other.

Juan listened in on her calls if she phoned a friend while he was over. He told her it was rude for her to talk on the phone while he was there. She could see his point. She stopped calling her friends.

Juan gushed when she wore dresses, because he said she looked hot in them, and he told her what he wanted her to wear when they left her house or whenever they went somewhere; she was flattered he cared so much and complimented her all the time.

Kiara's mom changed and told Kiara she couldn't go over to Juan's house as much because her room was messy or she had to do chores. It felt like when her mom kept Kiara away from Carolyn. She told Juan, so he came over and helped her do all those things, and so Kiara's mom lost on those objections.

One night her mom called her into her room and said she wanted to have a talk.

Kiara didn't like the sound of that. She sat down on her mom's bed and stared at the TV which was running the home shopping network on mute. Her mom sat up and awkwardly put an arm around Kiara's shoulders.

Kiara's skin bristled at the touch.

"I should bring your brother in here, too." She called out to Tom who appeared and stood in front of them, blocking the TV. "Have a seat. I want to have a talk with the both of you."

Kiara glanced up at Tom. He shrugged and took a seat next to her.

"Do you both know about sex?"

Kiara almost choked on her own spit. "Mom. You do know that I'm sixteen and Tom's thirteen?"

"Well?" Her mom leaned over to Tom who stared intently at the ground. "Okay. I know I should've had this talk with you both a lot sooner. I want you both to know how important it is to not have sex before marriage."

"Wouldn't want to piss off God," Tom said.

Kiara couldn't stop herself from laughing.

"Knock it off you two." Her mom alternated between a stern lecturing voice and a fake syrupy sweet one. "I had sex when I was engaged to your dad and I regretted it. I mean at least I was engaged, but still, you can't take that back. I wish I had waited. I don't want you two to make the same mistake."

No one moved or said a word after that. They sat there frozen in place.

Tom broke the silence. "Are we done? Can I go now?"

After her mom indicated the torture session was over, Kiara and Tom raced for the door. Kiara hardly ever spoke to her mom, and this half-assed sex talk made her feel dirty and gross.

Kiara and her friends entered their junior year; Juan was a senior. What would happen when he graduated? Would they stay together?

Carolyn and Trevor continued dating even after he graduated, so anything was possible.

Kiara still had Cole in almost all of her classes but he maintained a distance. He waved at her and smiled but walked past her. Kiara brushed it off, because Juan was waiting there for her outside after almost every one of her classes to escort her to her next class.

Nicole, Jenny, and Carolyn shared most of the same classes with Kiara, although they debated dropping some of the honors classes in their senior year. No one made any decisions yet because that felt so far away.

On their one-year anniversary, Juan told Kiara he had a surprise for her. When she got to his house, he had her close her eyes, and led her into his room. She opened her eyes to a nearly empty room. Juan had cleared most of his furniture out. A table was set up with a tablecloth, and nice dishes, and candles. He did all this for her?

Juan's mom entered with homemade Chinese food. His mom did all this for *Kiara*?

Juan handed her an old Cabbage Patch doll.

"I remember you said you always wanted one," Juan said. "You couldn't get one because they were too expensive."

"Oh my gosh, that's so sweet." Kiara held the raggedy doll in her hands and kissed him. No one had ever given her a gift with so much thought behind it.

Juan got down on one knee and pulled a diamond solitaire ring out his pocket.

"Kiara, would you marry me?" He gazed up into her eyes.

Marry him? *Marry?* Kiara sat there speechless. Butterflies jumped in her stomach.

Juan smiled up at her.

"We're so young," she finally said.

"You're almost seventeen. I'm almost eighteen."

"Which is too young."

"We don't have to get married now."

"I'm going to college after high school."

"Maybe." He shrugged. "There's a community college in Lancaster."

In her heart, she was conflicted. The gesture had been so grand and his efforts so earnest, she felt that they would be the happiest people in the world together. She could even consider having little you's and little me's with him. It would be the fairy tale ending she'd hoped for.

Inside her head a little voice that she'd been shushing since the day she met him, screamed at her to say no.

She panicked. How long had he been kneeling there? She needed to answer him.

Juan sensed her indecision. He took her hand in his. "I want you to have this. Let's call it a promise ring. I saved up money to get it for you because I love you. I want you to be my wife. How does that sound to you?"

"To be your wife?"

"And for me to be your husband." He kissed the back of her hand and gazed up at her. Even his eyes were smiling.

Husband? Wife? Kiara's stomach fluttered and she bent her head, her cheeks warm.

"I promise I will take care of you," he said. "You won't have to worry anymore."

His voice lulled her. It was like a movie—all the candles and preparation for their anniversary dinner, and the Cabbage Patch doll and the diamond ring.

"Will you promise that when you're ready to get married, we can get engaged?" Juan asked. "More than anything, I want you to wear this ring for me, for us."

The small diamond shone and reflected rainbows of light, and she did love rainbows, so she said yes, she'd wear the promise ring—she wasn't clear on what the promise would be—and let him slip it on her finger. While it was shiny, the weight was heavy.

Kiara dreamt that night about their evening. She twisted the ring around her finger. She could get used to wearing it. She could get used to the idea of being engaged.

Getting married and having kids with someone who loved you so much wouldn't be so bad. She and Juan didn't throw things at each other like her mom and dad used to do. Juan's mom adored her, more so than her own mom. His mom said how much she'd love to have grandchildren. Kiara's mom never said anything like that.

Juan's family welcomed her at their parties and into their home.

She heard Juan's voice telling her how he loved her more than anything.

Maybe she could be happy out there with Juan. She could be his wife.

By spring, Juan got more aggressive sexually; 'no' no longer meant no in the same way with him. Eventually, Kiara relented and let him undress her and go all the way. She didn't understand all the fuss, because sex didn't feel good—it hurt. There were no fireworks or sparks, like her grandma's romance novels said there would be. Juan said that's because they had to do it more.

Kiara worried she could get pregnant. Juan said she shouldn't worry, because they would get married if that happened. That put her somewhat at ease but anxiety balled up in her stomach at the thought of having a baby.

After that, Juan changed. He bragged about her beauty to his friends. He told her, instead of asking her, when they'd hang out and where. For her seventeenth birthday, he bought her lingerie. Kiara hated it, but didn't want to be rude, so she thanked them. Embarrassed, Kiara hid the lingerie in the back of her sock drawer.

Many days at his house, while he did chores, or helped with his younger siblings, Kiara sat alone in his room—Juan had claimed his brother's room—and stared out the window at the massive weeping willow in his yard. She loved the delicate leaves that shook and danced in the wind. They made the most glorious sound that reminded her of the Abbey.

One day in the spring, Kiara asked Juan if they could climb up the willow.

He eyed her strangely and agreed reluctantly. She thought of Cole, and his boyish eagerness to climb trees, and his adventurous side. This felt different.

Juan climbed up first and helped pull her up. They climbed several branches higher and got comfortable. He leaned against the trunk, while she straddled between two branches.

She closed her eyes and felt the breeze on her cheeks, and listened to the leaves rustling by her ears. She breathed in nature and a calm washed over her.

In this moment of bliss, she felt Juan's hands on her thighs and his lips against hers.

"Can't we sit here and enjoy the tree?" she asked, pushing him back.

"Why?" he asked. "What's the point?"

What's the point? Cole would have never asked her that question.

"Why don't we enjoy this moment?" she said. "Or maybe think about the future?"

"What's there to think about? Oh, I forgot to tell you something."

"What?" She was afraid to ask.

"I can't graduate," he said. "I failed a bunch of classes. I don't have enough credits."

Her jaw dropped. So, all those times he was writing her love notes, he wasn't doing anything in class? What the hell? This wasn't a situation she had ever considered happening.

He shrugged. "It's not a bad thing. They said I can stick around for a fifth year. That means we can graduate together." He brushed his hand across her cheek. "As long as you help me with my work. You're so smart. You know how I am with that stuff."

She stared at him but said nothing. Was this really happening?

"And the best part," he added, "we'll get to spend a lot more time together."

Great. Dating a fifth-year senior. She'd be mortified to face her friends at school. A little voice in her head screamed for her to run, run away, run far away.

"I need your help," Juan said. "I have to turn in a project, so I can pass with a D."

Kiara, on the other hand, had all A's and B's in her honors and AP classes. She remembered Cole's biting words: *You could do better.* Thinking of Cole made her long to be with him at that moment, to tell him everything that was happening, to hear what he had to say.

Did Kiara want to marry Juan? Maybe. It was such a huge life-altering decision. Deep inside, she knew what Cole would say. He'd tell her she was out of her mind and that she should focus on school and college and getting out of the desert.

Juan loved her though, and she loved him. Wasn't love more important than anything?

Juan asked Kiara, "Are you going to help me?" with more impatience in his voice.

Kiara nodded. She didn't want to. She narrowed her eyes and clenched her jaw.

"I'm bored," he said. "I'm going inside. Stay up here as long as you want." He jumped down and left her up there alone.

That's when she realized her mom was right about one thing—Kiara regretted having sex with Juan, but not for any type of religious reason.

45

Suffocation

KIARA STEPPED OUTSIDE HER HOME and caught a pungent whiff of onions. In the fields across from her, agricultural fields grew alfalfa and onion crops. Watering wheels attached to long rusty pipes made their way from one end to the other and kept the crops alive. Even on the hottest of days, pumped-in water brought life to the desert. Without constant care, the crops would wither.

If Kiara dropped a cup of water on the ground, it wouldn't be long before the cool liquid evaporated in the heat. She wondered who thought it was a good idea to water the desert.

Back when they moved in over ten years ago, her mom planted those six fruit trees—apples, pears, and peaches, and made it Kiara's chore to hand water each one every day with a hose; she remembered most days. The dirt sucked the water dry.

Kiara initially watered with hope for fruit. The trees remained barren. Why bother? The desert had determined they weren't going to grow. Her mom said they needed more time. Kiara doubted it. She figured they wished they had a new home and weren't stuck in the desert.

Then, after a round of storms that summer, one of the pear trees did blossom. On discovering this, Kiara went out and watered them every day. Sure enough, the blossoms turned into baby pears, and she kept watering, excited to watch them grow.

They didn't get much bigger. They did, however, change colors. Her mom said that meant they were ripe, so Kiara picked a tiny pear and took a bite—or at least tried to. The pears were all rock hard and bitter, nothing like a pear should be.

The leaves on the other trees dried and shriveled. Their limbs lost their green and they stood there—empty shells of their former life.

Kiara identified the cause of death—suffocation in the desert. She wondered if she would be the next casualty.

Kiara still had it in her mind that she was going to college, partly because her mom kept saying that, and partly because Cole—in the extra minutes they could talk in class—repeated that they'd both go away to college like in the movies. They'd live in dorms and study on grassy hills under trees and everything would be green and beautiful.

How much was everything going to cost? She heard she could maybe get financial aid. Would it be enough for her to live far away?

Carolyn, who had been acting more withdrawn for the past six months or so—she wouldn't say why—had gotten a job out in Lake LA at Burger Basket. She encouraged Kiara to find a place to work, too.

So, Kiara searched for a job, a real job, not an occasional babysitting one. Minimum wage was $4.25 an hour and she calculated that if she worked twenty hours a week for her last year in high school, and saved most of it, she could have over $4,000 saved up. Maybe she could buy a used car with that money, after she could afford to get her driver's license. She passed her permit test, but nobody took her out driving; she couldn't learn to drive without practice.

Because she didn't have a car yet, Kiara couldn't work in town and had to inquire at the few stores and restaurants out there in Lake LA. Burger Basket wasn't hiring, so she couldn't work with Carolyn, which they agreed would've been fun.

Kiara was competing against everyone else in Lake LA who didn't have a car, which was most people and so she wasn't having an easy time of it. She read books about how to get a job, and figured out how to type a resume on her mom's typewriter. She added her GPA and the honors and AP classes, and took her resume to the businesses and asked to talk with managers—Cole's advice—and that at least got her a job application and an interview at Pizza Factory.

The owners—an older couple—were impressed by her grades and her classes, because it was rare out there. They figured she'd learn quickly. She was shocked when she got the job.

Juan was happy, because he said now, she could buy pizza with her employee discount; she didn't want to spend her money, but he wasn't offering to pay.

Kiara didn't do too well during her first two weeks. Everyone, most of whom were only a year or two older than her, encouraged her and said she'd get the hang of it.

After a month, everyone there realized a few things: Kiara was too uncoordinated to toss a pizza, too slow to prepare food on account of trying to make everything perfect, and too clumsy to bring food out to tables without spilling on the customers.

Her saving grace was that she could do basic math, was honest, friendly, and nice to look at. That meant she got to answer the phone, take orders, and work the register. Once in a great while, she got tips for it, too—especially from older men who might have misinterpreted her friendliness. In that way, it worked out and Pizza Factory gave her three or four five-hour shifts per week once school started up.

Sometimes, they got behind on the orders, and Kiara had to help make the food. The guys at work were nice and patient with her even when she took forever to evenly space out pepperoni in a circular pattern. When Kiara helped make sandwiches, the girls got frustrated at her ineptitude and said she needed to hurry up. How could she get it done any faster without forgetting the mustard or the right number of tomatoes or slices of cheese and meat. Wrapping and cutting? Not her strong point, either.

Could she do anything right?

Juan said maybe she could get another job. They agreed she'd have to learn to drive first. He had an old car. It was a stick shift and often had to be push-started, meaning someone would push it a bit down the street, while the other person flipped the ignition and popped the clutch to jerk the car back to life.

After Kiara stalled out at a couple stop signs with the cars behind them honking, Juan told her he'd take his mom's new car out instead. He wasn't going to tell his mom though.

As the weeks went by, Kiara reminded him, and he kept forgetting. Finally, he said he'd take her out driving.

The sun was starting to set so that made her nervous. He showed her how to turn on the headlights, and he had her drive straight down the main road into town, Palmdale Boulevard.

Even though Juan had her stay in the right lane, she was terrified when cars drove up alongside her. Then, without warning, he shouted at her to make a right turn. There wasn't a street light but, in the darkness, she took the next right. That's when she read the entrance sign for the 14 Freeway.

Her heart pumped hard and she screamed, but she had no choice, because she was already on the on-ramp.

"Jesus Christ. Shut up, all right?" Juan shouted. "Just stare straight ahead, focus, and press down on the gas pedal."

She gripped the wheel and entered the right lane. A car behind her honked and flashed their headlights, before switching lanes, accelerating, and cutting her off. Other cars sped by to her left.

"Speed up!" Juan yelled. "You're going too slow! Hit the gas pedal harder."

Her stomach cramped and churned. Her pulse raced. Her breathing quickened.

"Where are the turn blinkers?" She whimpered. "Are the lights even on?"

"Oh my God," Juan said. "You're being fucking ridiculous. Of course, the lights are on."

"I don't know what to do!" Kiara shouted, her voice cracking. Would they die out there?

Juan started laughing.

Kiara jerked the car off the next exit and after they were off the freeway, she pulled over into the dirt shoulder. Gripping the steering wheel, she cried, a heavy, heaving, panicked cry. If she had crashed on the freeway, she could've killed them both.

When she lived in the big two-storied house with the waterfall, her mom threw her into the pool to teach her to swim. Kiara flailed and cried, and flapped her arms and legs in fear to get to the side of the pool. Her mom said that was a good way to teach her to swim. It was a lie.

Kiara was so traumatized she didn't step foot into another pool until middle school when her short-term best-friend Tessa taught her to swim in a public pool up in town. Tessa said it was mean what her mom had done, and dangerous, too.

This moment in the car felt like being thrown into a pool without floaties.

"Oh, quit whining," Juan said. "Get out, switch places, and I'll drive the rest of the way home since you're being such a baby."

Kiara, tears hardening on her face, walked around to the passenger side, secured her seat belt, and slunk down in her seat. She felt suffocated, like life was being sucked out of her.

As Juan drove, he kept laughing at her and said, "Well, guess what? Now you can drive."

He was wrong. And she was feeling what she thought might be hatred for him.

46

No Direction

CAROLYN DROVE KIARA, NICOLE, AND JENNY into town to the mall to get glamor pictures done after they took their senior pictures. Hanging out with her friends instead of Juan was a welcome change for Kiara.

They sat at a table in the food court at the mall. Kiara took a bite of her Subway turkey sandwich and stared at her friends. They all looked so much older, almost adults.

"I wish we could do this more often," Kiara said. "Why is everyone so busy?"

"Besides work?" Carolyn asked.

"I got a job at the hospital," Jenny announced. "It's more of a volunteer thing. I'm a candy striper and help the nurses out. I'm so excited though. I've decided I want to be a nurse." She paused and winked. "Plus, I met some guy there who came into the ER."

The others pushed her for details. Jenny kept her lips sealed.

Kiara felt envious that Jenny had decided on a course for her future. Kiara had no clue.

Unfortunately, Kiara didn't get another chance to lounge around the mall with her friends. Nobody was available, tied up with boyfriends and life.

Kiara had hoped to have her senior year to herself, but Juan was still there, a fifth-year senior, which embarrassed her. She was stuck sitting at the edge of the lunch table while he discussed his favorite things—besides her—hockey, concerts, and cars.

Outside of school, Carolyn only hung out with Trevor who had graduated a year earlier. She had become distant from the group lately; the more she withdrew, the more she smoked, and the less she spoke.

Jenny's relationship with the mystery patient ended and she hooked up with some guy none of them had met. He lived with a twin brother and they lived off the grid in the remote foothills somewhere. She didn't say much else, except that one of them got arrested.

Arrested? Kiara couldn't fathom. That was a world away from hers.

Nicole flipped between boyfriends—with her beauty, she was never alone for long. And Kiara ... Well, she had Juan.

Tom entered Littlerock High as a freshman. Kiara didn't go out of her way to find him—she had learned her lesson back when he was a kindergartener who was too cool to be seen with his big sister.

Tom had chosen drama as his elective and she caught glimpses of him hanging out with the other drama students, many of whom dressed in black more often than not. She wondered how he was doing, but he avoided her.

So, when he came home from school one day and burst into her bedroom, she didn't know what to think.

"Guess what?" Tom announced, a huge smile on his face.

Kiara shrugged. "What? You have a girlfriend?"

"Yeah, that'll never happen." Tom rolled his eyes. "Anyways, I got a role in Macbeth."

"As what? I didn't even know you auditioned."

"Ross, Lady Macbeth's cousin. Misty said—"

"You know her?"

"Why wouldn't I? She's in Drama. She's *so* good. She got the lead role. She encouraged me to try out, so I did." He struck a dramatic pose. "You're looking at the next Hollywood star."

"Calm down, Mr. Famous." Kiara smiled, proud of him. "That's awesome though. Congratulations."

Still beaming, he raised his eyebrows. "Are you going to come see the play?"

"Me? You want me to go?"

"Well, why else would I ask? You should come see the cooler version of you."

"You're such a dork. But, yeah, of course I'll go."

A month later, after many long practices, Tom handed Kiara a flier.

"The play is this Friday," Tom said. "Are you still going?"

"Why wouldn't I?" Kiara said. "My brother is a star."

Tom shook his head and grinned.

Juan had no interest in watching a school play. Carolyn and Trevor agreed to come to "support the arts." That meant Kiara had a ride and was able to enjoy the production. Sitting in the new theater, Kiara was in awe of the huge stage and the gorgeous, velvet curtains. At the end, she got access backstage because of Trevor's connections.

She quickly found Tom.

"You were great," Kiara said. "I had no idea."

"You mean it?" he said. "I think I found my calling."

She shook her head and held out her arms. To her surprise, he took her up on the hug. She squeezed him then let go.

"I'll be back late," he said. "Hanging out with the guys for a while…" He paused and lowered his voice. "Thanks for coming."

What he didn't say out loud, but she heard, was, "Thanks for coming because Mom didn't show up." By this point, both Kiara and Tom had the mutual understanding that their mom's absence probably had more to do with her being depressed than anything else. Regardless, the results for them, especially for Kiara who bore the brunt of her mom's irritation, were the same.

⬥

Kiara tried her best to listen to homeroom announcements read through the classroom speakers. It was hard to hear over her chattering classmates, and the teacher didn't make much of an attempt to quiet them down either.

They announced dates for college applications and an ASVAB test, neither of which she understood. In her Calculus class, she approached Cole, still her usual source of information, and asked him.

"I think we need to apply for college, too," he said. "Why don't we go to the counseling office to ask?"

"Sounds good. Let's go during break. What is—"

"The ASVAB is a military aptitude test," he said. "I'm taking it."

"Why? You're joining the military?"

"I don't plan to. You get feedback on strengths for possible jobs to choose from. I don't know what I want to do yet. I thought it couldn't hurt to get more info."

"Like the dumb test the school counselors had us take in class?"

"Oh, the one that, along with a bunch of other random shit, said we could all be janitors?" Cole laughed his usual lighthearted laugh.

She couldn't help but giggle along with him, whenever his laugh floated her way.

As soon as the bell rang for break, Kiara gathered her things and followed Cole out the door. There, waiting for her, the same as every day, was Juan. He smiled, gave her a hug, and handed her a heart shaped note. She told him what she and Cole planned to do, and Juan said he'd go along. Cole mentioned the ASVAB and Juan said maybe he'd sign up, too.

In the front offices, a couple of college banners hung overhead for UCLA, Berkeley, and USC, and other colleges she had never heard of.

Juan signed up for the military test. He said he'd wait outside because the college stuff was boring and didn't matter to him.

Kiara and Cole spoke with a guidance counselor. The woman acted both flabbergasted and excited to have anyone come in to request college information.

"You have less than thirty days to apply for college before the deadline," the woman said.

Kiara and Cole were both surprised at how quickly that was approaching. November had only started. College seemed so far away.

"Don't forget to send in your SAT scores," the woman reminded them.

"How do we do that?" Kiara only vaguely remembered taking the SAT in the spring with Cole. They had signed up only because their Trigonometry teacher—the same fighter pilot one who taught them Geometry in ninth grade—advised the two of them to take it.

The counselor handed them applications—and said she'd only handed out half a dozen—for the California State Universities and for the University of California ones, all public colleges they could attend. They'd have to live in dorms, which was expensive.

"You can apply for grants, based on grades and income, and maybe get loans," the counselor said. "You have to fill out the FAFSA and report your parents' income on the form."

Kiara's stomach sank. Send SATs, fill out applications, apply for FAFSA—was this worth it? What if she didn't get any money and couldn't afford college?

"Don't worry," the counselor said. "You're both on the free lunch program and you'll probably get Cal Grants and Pell Grants."

Kiara and Cole gave her a blank stare.

"That's money you don't have to pay back. It's free."

Kiara shook her head. She had a hard time believing anything was free. There were usually strings attached, at least in her experience.

Cole seemed to be taking mental notes on all this.

The instructions and options swirled around Kiara's head, not in it.

"I don't want to be stuck living at home for another couple years, so I'd rather not go to AVC." Cole winked at Kiara. "I'm sure Kiara feels the same way."

The counselor paused. "Sit here for a minute. I'm going to pull up your transcripts." She came back a few minutes later with papers in hand and a smile on her face. "Oh my. You two are in the top fifteen students out of nearly 400 in your graduating class. Unfortunately, we don't weigh your grades here. At any rate, you both would qualify for Cal-grants based on your GPA."

The woman stared directly into Kiara's eyes and continued. "That's free money you don't repay. You both need to get accepted, which, of course, isn't guaranteed, even with your SAT scores and GPA. You're competing against a bigger world than the AV out there."

It was overwhelming. Applications in hand, neither Kiara nor Cole left feeling prepared for the uncertain future.

"We're on our own with it all," he said, "since neither of our parents have any experience with the whole process."

Kiara turned to Cole. "If you come over to my place this weekend, can we try to fill out the applications together?"

As they stepped around the corner, they found Juan chatting with a group of girls nearby.

"Won't Juan get pissed?" Cole raised an eyebrow.

"He'll probably be there, too, so it'll be fine."

Cole shook his head, mumbled something under his breath, and walked away.

Juan said they had plans that weekend because his mom was throwing a birthday party for one of his cousins and all of the family—aunts, uncles, grandparents, and cousins would be there. He said everyone would ask questions if she didn't come, so Kiara agreed to go.

She rescheduled with Cole a couple of weeks later and he said that was fine, but they couldn't put it off much longer.

The day came to take the ASVAB and Kiara thought there must be trick questions, because honestly, it was too easy, not like the AP exams she and Cole were taking and passing in English and US History, and, hopefully soon, Calculus.

The hardest questions were the mechanical ones and she had to think *right-tighty* and *lefty-loosey* to imagine directions of one gear against the other, and figured she did alright.

When the results were released, the calls and letters started coming in; Kiara had scored in the 99th percentile. She was bummed she didn't get 100% until Cole told her that wasn't possible. The Coast Guard and Navy and Marines and Army and Air Force reached out to her.

Kiara thought it would be cool to be a fighter pilot like their math teacher, but with her bad eyesight—even with corrective contact lenses, she was told she was ineligible, so that idea fizzled out.

She threw around the idea of the Navy or Air Force to Juan and he thought that was hilarious, and told her there was no way she'd make it through boot camp.

Cole said she could do it if she wanted to, but he didn't think she'd like it much. They agreed to apply to colleges. They hadn't chosen which ones—neither of them had ever visited any, and she didn't know what she wanted to study, or how it would all work, or who would help her move or anything.

She asked her friends. Carolyn and Jenny said they were going to start at AVC then transfer—Jenny held firm she'd be a nurse; Carolyn wasn't in a rush to make career decisions because she and Trevor were planning a future together.

Nicole, on the other hand, said she was going to start modeling even before graduation. Several photographers had approached her at the mall and offered to take free headshots.

All the girls agreed she had good odds of making it, because if she wasn't beautiful enough before, she had only continued to blossom and seemed to belong on a runway—Juan agreed, too. Kiara frowned when she caught Juan staring at Nicole's breasts.

Kiara brought it up later. "I don't like the way you're checking out Nicole."

"Don't get jealous," Juan said. "It's okay to look at someone who's pretty. Guys check you out all the time."

Kiara felt a knot in her chest. She said she wasn't mad. It was a lie.

Kiara sat alone in her room that night and read through the college applications. It was daunting. She'd have to write an essay for the UC application, and even though she loved to write, the idea paralyzed her. Her mom was absolutely no help. Every time Kiara asked her what to do and if she should apply, she shrugged and retreated to her room. She did give her a copy of her taxes to fill out the financial aid paperwork at least.

Kiara tore up the UC application and threw it away.

"You did the right thing by not bothering with the stupid essay," Juan said. "Are you even sure college is the right thing? You can stay home if we have kids. You don't have to worry about all this dumb shit. We can get married after graduation."

She didn't think she wanted to. From the years of babysitting and taking care of Tom and having kids thrust in her face every time Juan's family had a party, she was tired of kids. She was starting to feel tired of Juan, too. Why couldn't he encourage her to try harder, to do more?

A big ball of confusion settled in her stomach. None of her options for the future felt right. She turned it over in her mind for hours but was no closer to any decision.

It was easier to stop thinking about it.

47

Wild Night

IN THE FALL, thousands of tumbleweeds throughout the Mojave Desert break their roots free from the dirt and tumble their own way across the desert without aim or direction. Eventually some pile up into long trains that roll across the land with more power and destruction.

Driving along a two-lane highway in the fierce fall winds may mean dust storms will cloud visibility; the granules audibly slam and scrape against the paint of the car; roaming gangs of tumbleweeds smash into vehicles and get caught in truck grills. Cars slow, pause, and time their acceleration and passage across the roads based on the rolling waves of weeds. A scene from the Westerns, without horses.

Heaven forbid you catch yourself outside unprotected in their path. There isn't much to do to save your skin except run out of the way and dodge them as they come. People can't direct tumbleweeds, the Russian thistle, which rush at you without discrimination and mow you down. Every year it's the same. You can't fight it, just learn to live with it.

To Kiara, life felt like that, too. She was caught in a tumbleweed storm.

Juan said Kiara was working too hard on school and stressing about applications, so he suggested they go to a party out in the desert. A couple of teenagers would be setting up big tents out there to stay the night and it was going to be wild, he said.

Nicole had a boyfriend they all liked. Then he dumped her. She wouldn't talk about it. They didn't press for the details.

Juan encouraged Kiara to invite Nicole to come along, and so she did.

They followed a couple of other trucks down a windy dirt road; they had to go slow to avoid the deep pits and peaks in the rough path. The idea was that the long drive down these remote dirt roads was worth it because the sheriffs out there didn't patrol the county lines much, the ambiguous border between LA and San Bernardino counties.

Kiara and Nicole whispered they were having second thoughts because they were getting out so far from civilization, and it was dark, and were they even going the right way?

As they drove around some short rocky hills, Kiara laid eyes on a huge bonfire. White tents flapping in the wind reflected light from the moon and the car's lights.

They pulled close to some other trucks and parked. Kiara stepped out. She didn't recognize most of the people and there were dozens and dozens of people hanging out laughing and drinking. She realized this wasn't her type of crowd. Nicole agreed.

Juan approached them with a bottle of gin and a lime. "Hey, I've got something for you both to try."

Kiara sniffed the bottle and made a face. "No thanks."

Nicole smelled it and did the same.

"It's not so bad. Watch." Juan took a swig and bit down on the lime. "How can you judge it if you haven't tried it? Nothing bad's going to happen. It's not as if you're going to get in trouble out here."

"Fine," Nicole said. "Fuck it." She grabbed the bottle and took a gulp. She puckered and almost spit it out. Juan handed her the lime and she sucked hard on it and wiped her mouth.

Juan held the bottle out to Kiara. "Nicole did it. It's your turn."

Kiara thought there wouldn't be harm in trying it once. And she didn't want Juan to think Nicole was braver than her.

The moment the clear liquid hit her mouth and slid down her throat, everything burned. She choked it down, grabbed the lime and tried hard not to throw up.

Juan teased them both to keep trying to compete with each other to drink more.

After a few more times, Kiara felt like puking, so she stopped. Nicole seemed emboldened and took a few more swigs.

Neither one felt any different for a while, and Juan went and talked to some people by the bonfire. He returned with a couple of beers. He had already downed half a bottle.

Kiara took a sip and hated it.

Nicole wanted a Pepsi. There wasn't any of that to be found. She took a few sips of the beer and decided, because she was thirsty and there was no water around, that she'd drink a little bit more.

Ten minutes later, everything changed. Both girls felt woozy and dizzy. Kiara staggered a few feet away. Was this what it felt like to be buzzed or maybe drunk?

Juan got a little flirty, winking at Nicole and putting his arms around both of them. Nicole rolled her eyes. For some reason, she thought it was funny. It wasn't funny to Kiara. She tried to call him out. He told her she was imagining it. She wasn't.

The evening blurred. Dancing by the fire. Flickering flames. Black sky with pulsing stars. Music and shouting and laughing. Kiara's vision swirled and distorted reality. Bodies pressed together. Girls snickered at Kiara and Nicole as they stumbled over rocks and fell onto the dirt a couple times. Guys leered at them from behind Juan's back.

They stayed half the night out there. None of them slept.

Exhausted, Kiara and Nicole carried their sleeping bags into a party-sized empty tent. Behind Kiara's back came a retching sound. She spun around in time to see Nicole puke onto her sleeping bag. She grabbed Nicole by the arm and yanked her outside.

Within minutes, Kiara was in a field holding back Nicole's hair while she threw up into the bushes.

Kiara yelled at Juan. "This is your fault." Her words slurred together.

"Don't be so uptight." Juan scowled. "Fuck this." He left them there and headed towards the group by the fire.

By the time they all got back home, Nicole swore she'd never hang out with Juan again, and Kiara said she was done with parties. Whenever Juan came by their lunch table, Nicole walked away. Kiara remembered Juan's hands all over her and Nicole. She balled up her fists and narrowed her eyes at him. He acted as if nothing was wrong and said it was all in her imagination. She knew it wasn't.

Cole came over as promised and he and Kiara both filled out and mailed in their college applications to three California State Universities—San Diego, Long Beach, and San Luis Obispo, all far enough to move away. Kiara felt nothing but relief to be done with it.

The next day, Juan said, "I'm glad that the whole thing is over with."

"What's that supposed to mean?" Kiara asked.

Juan shrugged it off and changed the subject.

When he pushed her against the wall and kissed her neck, Kiara got to thinking that it might be nice not only to get out of the AV but to get away from Juan.

But how? Moving far away into a dorm? By herself? Without him?

Change is hard. Doing the same thing as before is simpler.

Maybe Kiara needed to stop fighting life, stop swimming upstream, relax—as Juan would say—and go with the flow.

48

Things Left Unsaid

AFTER THE TWO-WEEK WINTER BREAK, Kiara's friend Mary returned, like the rest of them, but she was different. Normally, Mary had a thin figure. Now her belly protruded. It clearly wasn't weight gain.

"The baby's due in spring." Mary fidgeted with a bracelet on her wrist.

"What are you going to do?" Kiara felt panicked for her.

Mary bit her lip. "Try to finish high school—"

"In the pregnant minor program?" Kiara asked.

"Not sure. Maybe I'll get my GED." Mary blinked back tears. "There goes college and all my plans. What was the point of all those honors classes? My life is so fucked up."

"What about…" Kiara paused. "Are you getting married?"

"To Juan's brother?" Mary crossed her arms, refusing to even say his name. "That asshole? He broke up with me after boot camp. When I told him I was pregnant, he stopped answering my letters. Mother fucker. If I ever see him, I'll kick him in the fucking nuts."

"Oh my God," Kiara said. Would Juan do the same to her if she ever got pregnant? *Love her then leave her.* "That's horrible. I wish there was something I could do."

"My parents want to move down to the valley with me and the baby. Get a fresh start."

Although the other girls, Kiara included, were intrigued by the baby bump—Mary let them place their hands on her abdomen when the baby kicked—they feared the condition was contagious. Mary, now a social pariah, hung out with a girl who'd had a baby the year before.

Sure enough, the contagion spread. Carolyn swore Kiara, Nicole, and Jenny to secrecy. Carolyn asked Kiara to drive her "down below" to get an abortion. Kiara agreed.

During the long drive, Kiara asked, "Why are you doing this? Does Trevor know?"

"Well, of course, it's his."

"You've been together for two years, right? And you said you're both talking about a future together. Why do it?"

"Two and a half years. I'm not that far along." Carolyn paused. "I'm still a kid. We're not ready to raise one."

"You don't want kids?"

"Not yet. After I graduate, maybe. First, we're going to move in together, get married, get better jobs, a house, and after that, maybe get pregnant the right way—on purpose."

At the appointment, Kiara entered the waiting room with Carolyn. It had soft lighting and warm colors. Carolyn filled out paperwork on a clipboard.

"Are you okay?" Kiara paced.

"Yes," Carolyn said. "You can go wait in the car."

So, Kiara did. She helped Carolyn back into the car afterward.

"Do your parents know?" Kiara asked during the drive home.

Carolyn gazed out the window and shrugged.

"Won't they find out?" Kiara asked.

"I doubt it."

"Is there something you're not telling me?"

"There's a lot I keep to myself."

"But we're friends."

Carolyn nodded.

"Well," Kiara said. "I'm here if you ever want to talk."

Carolyn took a deep breath. "I need a cigarette."

Kiara didn't inquire further. Carolyn had a shitty day. Still, why had she asked Kiara to take her on such an important appointment if she didn't trust her enough to confide in her?

Kiara didn't know what to say or do, other than drive. Her friends were drifting further and further away, Carolyn and Mary, too. All alone was a lonely place to be.

Carolyn watched out the window while the clouds, Joshua trees, and hawks blurred by. "I'm glad I did it," she finally said. "It's like a weight has been lifted off my shoulders."

Kiara nodded.

"Drop me off at Trevor's grandma's house, please," Carolyn said. "I'll come by and get the car from you tomorrow."

"Trevor's grandma?" Kiara asked. "What do you mean?"

"It's a long story and I'm too exhausted to tell you now." When they got to the house, Carolyn gave her one last hug. "Sorry for snapping at you. It's my dad I'm pissed at. He can go fuck himself. But, anyways, I appreciate you helping me out."

"That's what friends are for."

"Yes, friends forever." Carolyn slipped out of the car and disappeared into the house.

The girls agreed the school should've taught more lessons on pregnancy prevention and fewer on abstinence. Birth control options would've been helpful to understand, especially for teens growing up in a rural community where there was pretty much nothing to do except drink alcohol, smoke weed, and have sex.

During spring break, Kiara planned to host a big sleepover with her friends—perhaps the last time they could all four be together before the end of the school year.

The Thursday prior, Kiara's mom yelled from her room, "Kiara, get in here right now!"

Kiara cringed. What was the problem? Tom hadn't tattled in years, so it shouldn't be that. Kiara trudged into her mom's room.

Her mom was sitting up in bed, her face bright red.

Kiara held out her hands. "What?"

Her mom tossed a paper at her. It didn't go far, fluttering to the ground.

Kiara picked it up—it was her third quarter progress report. She glanced down the column of classes: A in English AP, B+ in physics, A in ceramics, A- in civics, C+ in AP Calculus. Not bad, considering how burnt out she was in school. She had gone down to five periods this year so that she could pick up more hours at Pizza Factory.

"What the hell is that?" Her mom pointed her finger at Kiara.

"Good grades?" Kiara smirked.

"So, help me, young lady," her mom threatened. "You better get your grades up."

Kiara glanced over at her mom's bedside table where she spotted Tom's progress report. She snatched it up before her mom could stop her. Tom's grades left something to be desired: English honors B-, Geometry C, Biology C-, Spanish 1 C, Drama A+, Health C- with an "in danger of failing" notation.

"How the hell do you get a C- in health?" Kiara wondered aloud.

Her mom grabbed both papers. "Mind your own damn business."

"It *is* my business. Tom is as smart as me, he always has been, but he doesn't care. Me? What about me? I've never gotten a C before in my whole damn life. You grounded me in tenth grade when I got my first B. My first B. How hypocritical—"

"You're grounded." Her mom tossed the papers onto her table for emphasis. It was hardly effective.

"Oh really?" Kiara asked. "And where's Tom? Oh, that's right. He's spending the night at Dave's house. On a *school* night."

"Your sleepover is cancelled, you little brat. Go to your room."

Kiara rolled her eyes. What did her mom think, that she was still a kid? Kiara left the room and slammed her mom's door shut. Then she went into her own room and slammed that door shut, too. How was any of this fair? Kiara spent her own money and brought home dinner from work. Was that appreciated? Hardly.

Screw the double-standard. No fucking excuse. God, how Kiara wished she could run away. She had half a mind to call up Juan and make plans to elope. She *could* move in with him.

Kiara spent most of her spring break staring at the scrawny tree outside her window and blaring music like

"What's Up?" by 4 Non Blondes, "Cumbersome" by Seven Mary Three, and "Creep" by Stone Temple Pilots.

Kiara returned to school apologetically. They had all been looking forward to the sleepover, what might have been their last opportunity for one.

"Where's Jenny?" Kiara asked. "She's always here."

"Well, yeah," Nicole said. "Better than being at home."

Juan came up to the table and wrapped an arm around Kiara's waist.

Carolyn nudged Nicole. "Want to go for a smoke?"

Nicole nodded and the two of them disappeared to the field.

Two more days passed without Jenny.

Even after being friends for several years, Kiara viewed Jenny as an enigma, hiding trauma behind her bubbly smiles and infectious laughter. Even while hanging out with Juan, Kiara couldn't shake the ominous sensation she had in the pit of her stomach.

On the fourth day of her absence, Kiara, Nicole, and Carolyn freaked out.

"What if something happened?" Kiara asked.

"No one is answering her phone," Nicole said. "Usually her grandma does."

"Why don't we drive out to check on her?" Carolyn asked.

On the way, Carolyn explained that Jenny and her grandparents had cut contact with Jenny's mom who was still addicted to drugs. Nicole filled in more details for Kiara's benefit: Jenny had been molested by at least one of her mom's boyfriends when she was in middle school. Social Services got involved. After that, Jenny moved in with her grandparents.

Carolyn pulled the car into Jenny's driveway; there weren't any other cars there. They rang the doorbell and pounded on the door. No one answered.

They sat in the car for half an hour debating what to do.

"What do you think happened?" Kiara asked. Panic set in.

"No fucking idea," Carolyn said.

"Maybe she got involved with the wrong guys," Nicole said. "I mean, come on, living off the grid? Some of these guys lately have been pretty shady."

"Should we call the police?" Kiara asked.

"What good do you think that's going to do?" Nicole said.

"Let's leave her a note," Carolyn said.

They tore out two pieces of notebook paper and wrote Jenny messages and begged her to call them. They left their names and phone numbers on the notes and tucked one into the side of the garage door. They left the other under the doormat coated under a thick coat of dirt.

Carolyn drove them back home in silence.

Jenny never returned to school.

They came up with wild theories: maybe her druggie mom kidnapped her, maybe she ran away from home, maybe she had secretly gotten addicted to drugs, maybe she got kidnapped, maybe her grandparents' house was foreclosed on and they moved without warning—this was the least believable theory since there wasn't a foreclosure note attached to the door.

They made a few other attempts to contact her by stopping by her house. Nobody was there. The curtains were drawn and it was dark, vacant of people.

They realized their helplessness and gave up. After that, nobody mentioned Jenny because her absence hit them hard. It was awful.

Jenny was gone.

49

Giving Up

COLE AND KIARA KEPT CHECKING in with each other about college—had they been accepted or rejected? Kiara could deal with rejection. Being stuck in limbo was frustrating.

In talking with their classmates, they learned a handful had gotten acceptance letters from private and public schools. Most of the others in their honors and AP classes were going to start out at AVC and said they'd transfer.

Then the letters came.

Cole and Kiara made a pact not to open the letters until they were together.

After school on Friday, Cole came over to her house. Juan wasn't there; he said he had to help his mom with something and that he'd be over later. Kiara had a heavy weight in her stomach. A little voice rang alarm bells; as usual, she ignored them.

Cole and Kiara sat on her carpeted bedroom floor. They each had three letters addressed to them from the three universities that they applied to.

"Let's open them at the same time," Kiara said.

"Wait, before we do, what's the plan?" Cole asked.

"What do you mean?"

"Should we make a pact?" Cole raised an eyebrow.

"We're not in a cult."

Cole put a hand on hers. "I mean, if we get in, should we go to the same school?"

Kiara's heart fluttered and she let the warmth of his hand melt into hers.

"I'd like to," she said. "I hope we get into the same schools."

"Or that we get accepted at all." He smiled at her.

They held up the letters from San Diego State University. They carefully ripped off the top and pulled out the letters. Cole pumped his fist in the air and Kiara squealed. They had been accepted. Then CSU Long Beach: another yes. Cal Poly San Luis Obispo: waitlisted.

"Oh my God!" she squealed. "We did it." She wrapped her arms around him in a huge bear hug; he wrapped his arms around hers. She stayed in his arms for a moment longer breathing him in. "Which one are we choosing? San Diego or Long Beach?"

They pulled out a map and compared both locations.

"Long Beach is in between LA and San Diego, so maybe that's better?" Cole said.

"I love that it has the word beach in it." Kiara smiled and flopped down on her bed. "I'm so damn tired of this desert. I can't wait to live by the beach."

Cole held up the letter. "It says we need to respond before the end of the month to accept the offer."

Kiara's phone rang. It was Juan. When he heard Cole's voice in the background, he got quiet for a second before screaming through the phone.

"I knew you were cheating on me, you stupid whore." Juan's words were slurred. "Well, guess what? Me, too."

Kiara's jaw dropped. *Was he drunk?* "What the hell are you saying?" Kiara asked. "Calm down. We're opening up college letters." Not that he would ever understand.

"You're still planning to do that?" Juan's voice dripped with loathing. "I thought that was to stroke your ego. You're so stupid that you live in this fantasy world. You think you're going to move away by yourself? Who's going to help you? You don't have a penny to your name. Maybe you feel better about yourself if they say they'll take you. Let me tell you something, it's so they can suck even more money out of you. Don't be naïve."

The more he spoke, the smaller she felt. Why didn't she just hang up? After he was done, he apologized for yelling at her and said he'd still come over if she could forgive him, and they could talk it over then.

"Fuck you," Kiara said, tears running down her cheeks. "You're an asshole."

Juan laughed. "Whatever. This other girl's hotter than you anyway. Have a nice life."

He hung up on her. *Other girl? Hotter?* She dropped the phone to the floor, grabbed the college letters, crumpled them up, and threw them into the trash can.

Cole stared at her for a few seconds. "Kiara ..." He reached for a hug.

She shoved him away. "Just go," she said, her chest heaving from the tears. "I want you to leave. Go do whatever you want. I want to die. I wish I wasn't alive."

Cole brushed her long brown hair aside. "Kiara, I ..."

She screamed, "Just stop, Cole! You don't understand." Kiara wished she could tell him how much she hated Juan, how she should've listened to Cole, but Cole had let this all happen. He didn't fight for her. She had wasted so much time with Juan—time she and Cole could've been together—time gone forever. With her eyes clouded by tears, she stared at Cole—the boy she had always loved. What did that matter? Nothing good would ever last.

She stood and paced, while Cole sat on the carpet next to the space she left behind.

"Kiara, don't do this again." Cole had tears at the corners of his eyes. "Kiara, please—"

"Go home. Leave me the fuck alone."

Kiara burst into tears and ran outside to her backyard swing set. She sat there alone on the creaky swing and let night fall. She scratched at her wrists until they bled. The scar from when she ran into the Joshua tree felt more present than ever.

She wanted the pain to stop.

50

Poison

AMONG MANY FEARFUL CREATURES in the wilds of the desert are Mojave green rattlesnakes, bark scorpions, black widow spiders, camel spiders, and potato bugs—the latter two mostly because they strike fear into your heart when you happen upon them; the former ones because they can inflict painful bites with toxic venom that can be debilitating and, in some cases, fatal.

The smallest of these dangers is also one of the deadliest: the female black widow spider has a jet black, glossy body and characteristic red hourglass on its underbelly which serves as a warning to not provoke it, and she eats her mate.

Black widow webs are messy; they cling to dark corners outside homes and in garages and in cluttered wood and junk piles; they love to lay white fuzzy egg sacs under lawn furniture and in old tires.

Kiara was familiar with all of these, having found a scorpion under a rock in her backyard, a potato bug crawling on her bare legs in her living room, heard the warning of the rattler in the fields, and had to overcome the territorial claim black widows had over her garage.

When she had to do laundry, she first examined the area around the washer and dryer for their webs, then for the spiders themselves. One time, desperate for clean clothes, she ran the wash cycle. She needed to transfer the clothes to the dryer, but that would put her in danger of a large black widow. She cautiously approached. The spider did not retreat. Without any better option, she grabbed a can of Aqua Net and sprayed the spider. It flinched which shook its web. It did not retreat. Kiara kept spraying until eventually it got stuck in place. She transferred her clothes safely into the dryer.

Kiara felt cornered, like with the black widow spider. Despite her best intentions, life wasn't going to work out as she had hoped. She had to know when to back away and let it go.

Without Juan there, she was relieved, so why did she feel so empty and sad and lonely?

That's when she discovered her mom's boxed wine in the fridge. First, a tiny cup, then a juice cup, then a water glass. She tried to be careful to space it out to not raise suspicion and she hid it from everyone, including her friends.

That was until Nicole was over one night and caught her drinking; Nicole admitted she'd been doing the same on account of her dad who she said was trying to ruin her modeling career.

They couldn't keep sneaking liquor from their parents. Nicole had already learned that all they had to do was flirt with some guys near a liquor store.

A middle-aged man blushed at the attention, went in and bought them what they requested—cheap vodka and Boone's Farm Strawberry Hill wine. Nicole and Kiara took the booze back to Kiara's house to get drunk while her mom was working up at the Abbey.

Senior year was almost over, and Kiara simply didn't care about anything anymore. She had no boyfriend, she wasn't speaking with Cole, and she had decided not to go away to college. What was the point? Juan was right—how could she have been so foolish to think she could afford to move out on her own without help?

Nicole said she'd been partying a lot lately and that she'd found a new hangout—a pool hall up in town. When the employees weren't looking, Kiara and Nicole sipped cheap beer out of the thirty-two-ounce plastic beer pitchers, the kind Kiara served to customers at the pizza place. Kiara had hoped to quit her job and go away to college.

As Juan's mom used to say, plans change and sometimes life dishes you out disappointment.

At the pool hall, Kiara and Nicole connected with a group of young adults—a few had already graduated high school; some had dropped out years earlier. It was a mixed group—black, Hispanic, and white—and nobody had any beef with anyone.

Kiara and Nicole got better at shooting Eight Ball thanks to tips and guidance from their new friends. The guys wrapped their bodies around the girls from behind, to guide their pool sticks and improve their shots.

In the evenings, anyone under twenty-one was supposed to leave. The manager Tyree knew Kiara and Nicole and didn't care. Sometimes he'd come by and shoot pool with them and their new cool crowd, all of whom were friends of his.

One Sunday night, after they played a couple games—neither Kiara nor Nicole ever had to pay for drinks or games because everyone always covered the costs for them—they were invited to go chill with everyone at Tyree's house. Kiara no longer told her mom where she was going or when she was coming home, so she said, sure, she'd go.

Nicole pulled her aside. "I can't go."

"Why not?" Kiara whispered.

"My dad will kill me if I'm not home tonight." Nicole flung back her hair. "Go without me if you want."

"I thought we were sticking together." Panic bubbled up in Kiara. "What happened?"

"Never mind. It's a long story," Nicole slumped her shoulders. "I can drive you home. Or, you can stay. Your choice."

Nicole left; Kiara stayed. She felt uncomfortable without Nicole; for the first time, Kiara was alone with a bunch of people who she realized were strangers. But, why did that matter? Kiara didn't give a shit anymore.

A dozen of them caravanned from the pool hall in Palmdale to Tyree's place in Littlerock. It was an older house with peeling paint and a battered garage door. There was junk scattered in the front yard and a rusty car on blocks in the driveway.

They parked halfway off the street, halfway on the dirt, and went in. The inside was dark, lit by a couple of mismatched lamps, and the shag carpet matted from years of neglect. Ashtrays filled with butts adorned tables around the living room. Most of the people seemed to have a usual place, either sitting on one of the three stained couches or on the floor leaning against the furniture. Kiara squished in between two husky guys, both who reeked of cheap beer and cigarettes, in the middle of a couch that sagged down to the frame under their weight.

Tyree introduced Kiara and the others who hadn't been there before to his wife and his four-year-old son.

Kiara was surprised Tyree was married and had a kid already; he was only twenty-two, the general age of most of them, give or take a couple years. She, on the other hand, at eighteen, was the youngest, other than his preschooler.

The manager called his son over, "Hey, go get daddy a beer. Hurry the fuck up."

The kid ran off and returned with a can.

"Go get some more for daddy's friends," he said. "Did you hear me? Get more. Come on, daddy's not fucking around. Go get more of daddy's juice." He laughed.

While the kid ran back and forth passing out cans of beer, Kiara observed the others and their reactions. Everyone was oohing and aahing about how adorable he was and how cool that he'd bring them beer.

It hurt Kiara. She thought of all the kids she used to babysit and how the little ones his age used to love coloring and playing with toy cars, how they'd beg her to read them bedtime stories. *This* little kid was fetching beers. Kiara no longer was in the mood to drink.

One of the young women called out Kiara's reaction, and told her to stop being so uptight and just chill. Another one agreed and asked Kiara if she was a goody-two-shoes. Kiara cringed. She hadn't been called that in a long time.

"Nah, it's not that," Kiara played it off. "Been drinking all night. My head hurts. I'm freaking tired."

That got them off her back, and they found her a spare bedroom with a mattress on the floor and told her she was welcome to spend the night. She lay there on a sheet of questionable cleanliness. In the living room, a couple guys raised their voices until the women told them to "calm the fuck down."

Watching Tyree's little boy bringing beer was a reality check for her. How had she descended into the company of the desert folks—high school dropouts—without a future? Was this the life she wanted for herself? She didn't know what she wanted. At that moment, she knew what she didn't want—to become like this.

Nobody was in any safe condition to drive her home; she curled up and slept as best she could with a blanket that reeked of stale cigarette smoke. She was cold and shivered. Another girl came in and asked to share the bed, and so that created some body heat and Kiara fell asleep.

When the sun rose and shone through the window, Kiara woke up and shielded her face from the painful brightness. She quietly tiptoed through the house—everyone was asleep on couches and on blankets on the floor and most would probably have a hangover. As it was, Kiara hadn't drunk enough water and her head pounded.

Finally, she found a wall clock and realized it was 7 AM and it was a Monday; she had school today and no way to get there. She knew better than to call home.

Back in the bedroom, she heard the other girl stirring; she'd been the one who drove her there from the pool hall the night before. Kiara didn't remember her name.

"Hey," Kiara whispered. "I'm late to school. Is there any way you could drop me off? It's not far from here."

The girl stretched and wiped her eyes open. "School? What are you talking about?"

"Littlerock High School."

"Oh, shit. You're still in school? Fuck. I didn't know that." She agreed to take her. "We have to sneak out because nobody wants to be woken up early. I don't want any trouble."

There Kiara was, walking in five minutes late to her first period AP English Literature class. Her hair was finger brushed and she wore the same short skirt and top that she had on the night before. Her cheeks reddened as she slunk down in her seat and bowed her head.

In the fresh air-conditioned classroom, Kiara realized her sweat reeked of alcohol and her wrinkled clothing exuded cigarette stench. She discreetly borrowed a stick of deodorant from a baseball player—she didn't dare ask gossiping girls—which somewhat covered the other smells. She wished she were invisible.

Without her backpack, she had to borrow pencils and paper all day and became acutely aware that students were staring at her and snickering. They eyed her short skirt, and their lips mouthed all-too-common words.

Kiara blinked back tears. She refused to make eye contact with anyone that day, even her friends. She escaped out to the field during lunch and sat by herself.

She decided she didn't belong with the desert rats. Maybe she didn't belong with the smart kids, either. Maybe she didn't belong anywhere. Maybe, like the tumbleweeds, she'd be doomed to aimlessly wander.

51

The Poppy Fields

AT SCHOOL, AN EXCITING OPPORTUNITY CAME UP—
the chance to fly in a small plane—for *free*. Local pilots were
hosting an event and volunteered to give a limited number of
high school seniors the chance to experience the gift of flight.

Too many students wanted to do it, so the school said they
were going to use a lottery system and anyone who was
interested needed to have their parents or guardians sign the
waiver, and then turn in the application and hope for the best.

To make an awkward peace with Cole, Kiara approached
him and asked him if he was going to apply. He stared at her
with unease as if deciding whether or not to respond.

"These are ..." Kiara squinted at the flier. "Biplanes and
Cessnas, super scary."

"People fly all the time," Cole said.

"I've never flown before." Kiara gave him a weak smile.

Cole sighed and shook his head at her. "I guess we're doing this."

"Doing what?"

"The usual. Acting like nothing happened."

That was the way at Kiara's house. How should it be any different with Cole?

"This is different." Kiara glanced back at the paper. "People fly in huge jets; this is an unpressurized cabin."

"All right," Cole gave her a sideways glance. "Let's do this. Let's go sign up."

Kiara followed him to wait in line to get an application.

The next week, the school posted the list of the *chosen ones*. Kiara was selected.

"That's amazing." Cole gave her an awkward hug. "Aren't you excited?"

"No, I'm terrified." She peered up at him. "Why don't you take my place? Please?"

"I can't," Cole said. "My parents didn't sign the waiver."

"What?"

"Dad was drunk and Mom refused to go behind his back on this one."

"Can't you forge it?" Kiara searched his face for the emotions she knew he was hiding.

"This isn't PE class and we're not freshmen, so, no, I don't think that's a good idea."

She shifted her weight from one leg to the other. "What if the engine falls out and I die?"

"Not likely. When has this opportunity ever come up? Never. Kids like us don't get these kinds of chances. When will you get another shot at something like this?"

Kiara stared into his green eyes. Many things had changed. Cole's sense of adventure never did. She knew he wanted to fly, and she wanted nothing more at that moment than to give him the chance to do it.

"You have to go," Cole said. "If for no other reason than to come back and share every little detail with me so I can live vicariously through your experience."

Eventually, he convinced her to accept the opportunity to go up in the plane.

Once she was buckled in, and the plane taxied down the runway, she realized it was too late to back out. Another girl got to sit in the co-pilot's seat up front and Kiara buckled up in one of the two back seats. Each was given a headset to put on which blocked out some of the loudest noises.

The propeller whipped around loudly and the engine whizzed as they ascended into the clear blue sky. Kiara's stomach got left behind on the runway.

The plane banked to one side. From her window, she watched the ground below them; neighborhoods disappeared as they headed north.

The pilot spoke to them and pointed: they were approaching the Antelope Valley Poppy Reserve in Lancaster.

Far in the distance, bright orange dots scattered across the brown and green desert fields. They flew closer and colors unfolded in front of them, a mosaic of yellows, purples, and bright orange, a color set off even brighter by the contrast of the clear blue sky. The hills were blanketed with beautiful orange, separated only by brown trails that snaked through.

Kiara couldn't distinguish the individual buds which bloomed on this spring day—the ruffled petals that opened and leaned into the sun, the waves of flowers undulating in the breeze. The aerial perspective was magnificent. She was in awe of the beauty of the desert seen in a way she had never experienced before. There were only sprinklings of poppies near her house that added a splash of color. This was an ocean, a bright orange ocean.

The pilot leveled out the plane and swooped in the opposite direction as he looped them back around. That's when the nausea hit. Kiara took measured breaths and focused on the horizon and tried not to puke in the backseat.

Even when her feet were back on land, the aftereffects of nausea lingered for hours.

After her mom drove her home and left for her weekend job, Kiara phoned Cole.

"Now that I'm finally not going to barf," Kiara said, "do you want to hear about it?"

"I do," Cole said, "but not over the phone. I'd rather hear about it in person."

"Do you want to come over now?"

She could hear him smile over the phone. He said, "Yes, I do. I'm on my way."

When he arrived, Cole had a knapsack with him. "Can I take you up to the water towers for a picnic?"

"What? No barbed wire?" She smirked. "Are we too old for that?"

Cole made eye contact with her. "I think we're definitely too old for those games."

It was hot, and the wind was picking up. They decided they should wait until it cooled down a bit and they settled into the worn-out couches in her living room, careful to avoid the hard plywood under the cushions—a recent addition to the décor.

"I wish I could've gone flying," Cole said. "My dad's such a jerk, and my mom lets him be that way. I honestly can't wait to get out of there."

"Do you worry what will happen to your sisters when you leave?"

"Not really." He shrugged. "What can I do about it? I'm the oldest and he's always been hardest on me. He treats me like I'm not even his real son."

Kiara was quiet for a moment. "Did you return the card to accept your place at college?"

He reached for his bag and pulled out some papers. "I wanted to wait for you to accept."

"I threw mine away. Remember? It's too late for me."

He slid a crinkled paper across the table.

"What's this?" she said.

"I tried my best to straighten it out," Cole said.

"My application? You saved mine?"

He nodded. She jumped up and wrapped her arms around him and squeezed tight. He pulled back a little to tuck loose strands of her hair off her face and behind her ear. He softly petted her head and smoothed her hair down her back.

"Is my hair tickling you?" she asked.

He shook his head and smiled. Kiara leaned her head on his chest. Cole held her there and kissed the top of her head. She wrapped her arms around him tighter and didn't ever want to let go.

After a while, Kiara sat back up and Cole gazed at her and brushed his fingers against her cheek. They locked eyes and she turned away, embarrassed.

She jumped up to her feet, took a risk and reached for his hands. Cole let her pull him up. Was she being too forward? Did he want her to do that? She waited for his reaction.

"Where are we going?" He smiled, his face full of warmth and comfort.

"Let's take that picnic," she said.

"First," he said, "we put these in the mail. And I have something for you." Cole reached into his bag and pulled out a gift-wrapped box and handed it to her.

"What is it?" The box was the size of a brick and weighed as much as one.

"Open it."

Kiara tore off the blue wrapping paper. She slid her fingers along the edge of the box to break the tape. She reached inside and pulled out a snow globe with spruce trees covered in snow. She shook it and white granules swirled and floated down.

"Remember your poem?" Cole scooted closer to her. "You're no longer trapped in the desert snow globe."

"That's so sweet of you. I love it." Kiara blinked back a tear. "We did it together."

Within a few minutes, they dropped the letters in her mailbox and headed down the street towards the buttes. Cole reached for her hand and pulled her in a different direction.

"Let's go to our old school," he said. "I'll race you there."

He jogged slowly until she, with a grin, sprinted past him.

By the time they got to the front of the school, they were both panting for breath.

The gate was locked.

They exchanged a knowing glance. He tossed his jacket over the top of the chain link, and, like old times, they scaled the fence and jumped down the other side.

In the deserted playground, the afternoon sun slid lower in the horizon. With the same thought in mind, they gravitated to two swings and sat side-by-side. She pumped her legs and he did the same and they flew through the air, legs reaching high, and swung back again.

They stopped and sat there, their toes swirling circles in the sand below their feet, and their fingers intertwined, holding hands for the first time.

Kiara took a deep breath and closed her eyes.

The future wasn't looking so dark, after all.

52

Powerful Silence

BLUE, GREEN, AND SILVER—their three school colors. Graduation was upon them, and Cole and Kiara were among a dozen students given silver graduation gowns, an honors designation. Together, with their classmates in the blue and green robes, they represented the Littlerock Lobos.

Nicole and Carolyn were given silver robes, too, although Nicole refused to wear hers and announced she wasn't going to attend the graduation ceremony.

"I don't care about all that," Nicole said. "I don't want my parents there."

"Why not? I want you to be there," Kiara said.

"Well, I'm not going."

Kiara vowed to convince her to go. Carolyn intervened and said to leave Nicole alone, to let her make her own decisions.

At the stadium in town, they were assigned seats. Carolyn was on the left of the aisle while Kiara and Cole were seated on the right.

Kiara leaned around the students in between them and smiled at Cole, knowing this wouldn't be the last graduation for the two of them. She pictured strolling alongside him, both of them in black robes, at their college graduation after they earned their Bachelor's Degrees.

Neither had decided which career to pursue and would enter with undeclared majors. Maybe they'd study business and open up a business together or land jobs at the same company. They didn't discuss marriage or children or houses like she and Juan used to. Instead, their conversation focused on the endless possibilities of a future outside of the desert.

Cole had to leave right after the ceremony; his parents wanted to beat the traffic.

Kiara's mom gave her a hug and a card and some flowers. "Congratulations, sweetie. I'm so proud of you. You're going to get to do so many more things in life than I ever could."

"Thank you." Kiara returned the hug with suspicion.

Her mom nudged Tom forward. He handed her a card. "Congratulations."

"You can give me a hug," Kiara said.

Tom rolled his eyes but allowed the hug. He was even taller than she remembered. He looked like a man. Where had the time gone?

"You'll have to come visit me at college," she told Tom while they walked back to the car. "I promise I won't make you play Barbies."

Tom smirked. "Well, only if I get Ken." He made the motion of ripping off the head of a doll with his teeth.

She shook her head. She'd forgotten that. It was funny how something that once had provoked so much anger in her could become a faded memory, an inside joke.

On the way home, Kiara stared out the window. Her mom didn't say anything about her graduation. She didn't explain how she felt or what exactly she was proud of.

Her mom cleared her throat. "I've been meaning to tell you. I got a new job." She glanced over to make sure they were both listening. "A lovely couple I met at the Abbey own a Christian bookstore in town. They hired me to do their accounting and said they're going to train me to be a manager. Isn't that great?"

"You won't have to work your other jobs?" Kiara asked.

"Well, for a while I need to still work at the Abbey. At least this will be a reliable full-time position. And soon, I'll only have to work one job, because they're paying me more than I've been making. This is honestly the best thing that's happened in a long time."

Best thing? What about Kiara getting into college? Guess that didn't matter.

"That's great, Mom," Kiara said. "I hope it works out."

Maybe her mom would find happiness at the new job. Either way, Kiara wouldn't be around to notice if anything changed; after all, she'd be with Cole.

As the weeks of summer dragged on, Kiara went through a range of emotions, most notably uncertainty for the future. How was she going to pay for school? She sat down in the living room one evening to discuss it with her mom.

"God will help us find a way," her mom said.

Kiara rolled her eyes. "Is God paying my tuition and housing? I guess I'll have to figure out how to get a loan or something."

Her mom looked pained. "You'll figure it out." She scooted closer to Kiara and rested her hand on Kiara's knee. "I'm proud of you."

Kiara flinched at her mom's touch. She didn't believe her. If she was proud of her, she had a funny way of showing it.

Over the next couple of weeks, Cole got quieter.

"Something's up," Kiara said. She straddled Cole and pinned him to her couch. "Tell me, mister. What's bothering you?"

He sighed. "My parents are guilting me out about leaving and not staying to help with my sisters."

"That's bullshit," Kiara said. "You're coming with me."

"I doubt they're even proud of me." Cole turned away.

"Well, I'm proud of you." She grabbed his chin and turned his face towards her. They locked eyes. She stuck out her tongue at him. "And isn't my opinion worth waaay more?"

Cole wrestled her off and reversed their positions, so that he had her pinned to the couch. "Well, Missy, that is definitely true."

He placed a kiss on her cheek—her skin flushed with warmth. He stood, reached for her hand, and pulled her up. Her stomach pinballed in excitement.

Without another word, he wrapped her in an embrace and kissed the top of her head.

She closed her eyes. She had a desire to wrestle him back to the couch, or maybe to her bed. She took a deep breath. No, it was better to take it slow and not regret anything like she had with Juan. Besides, if something was good enough to last forever, it was best to savor each step like enjoying each small lick of ice cream.

They counted down the days…five more weeks before they both had to pack up their belongings to venture out into the world. In the meantime, there was so much to be said between them, so much Kiara wanted to tell Cole. When they sat together, in the silences between words, more was understood than any words could ever express.

After the mail came the following week, Kiara ran inside holding a letter as if it were burning in her hands. Her heart raced. She phoned Cole.

"It's from the financial aid office," she said. "Did you get your letter?"

"No, not yet," Cole said. "What does it say?"

"I didn't open it yet."

Silence on the other end before he spoke. "Well? … Do I need to go over there and open the letter for you?" It wasn't said in the snarky way of Juan, but with encouragement—to say in the silence that no matter what the letter offered, they would overcome any challenge together.

Kiara slid her finger along the top to break open the seal.

The words blurred together. She shook her head and read it aloud to Cole.

"That's fantastic," Cole said. He hooted.

"It is?" Kiara asked. "What does it mean?"

"They're giving you Pell Grants and Cal Grants," he said. "It means you no longer have to worry about paying tuition or books."

Kiara wanted to scream with joy until she remembered the other cost. "Cole," she said, "What about the dorms? How am I going to pay for that?"

"I'm sure there's a way with those subsidized loans."

Neither of them understood the particulars.

Another afternoon with Cole in the books, Kiara returned home to an empty driveway.

Her mom was often at one of her three jobs; however, it was night, and her mom no longer worked evenings. She didn't have close friends and never went on dates—perhaps this was another source of her unhappiness? Regardless, her absence raised suspicions.

Her sense of foreboding increased as it got closer to ten and neither her mom nor Tom were home from wherever.

She phoned Cole, and they both went through various scenarios. He tried to calm her. He suggested maybe she contact Tom's friend Dave to see if they were there. Turns out that she didn't have to. A beep sounded in her ear and she recognized Dave's name on the caller ID—they had gotten a new cordless phone that had too much static, which required her to constantly click on the channel search button to try a slightly different frequency. At least it had caller ID.

"Hey, it's Dave," he said. "Is Tom there?"

Kiara said he wasn't.

"That's weird," Dave said. "He said he was coming over a couple of hours ago."

That's when that little voice screamed at her.

"I don't know where they are," Kiara's hand shook and her voice quivered.

Dave put the phone down for a minute, then said he and his dad were going to drive the route that Kiara's mom would've taken. He guessed that maybe the truck broke down. He said he'd call her back to let her know if they found them.

Kiara convinced herself that was a good possibility; their truck had been getting old.

There weren't pay phones along the road, which is how they usually communicated. If she didn't have enough change to make a phone call, she and her mom had a system whereby she'd make a collect call and, in the recording, when it asks who's calling and to, "please state your name," after the beep, Kiara would quickly say something like "come-pick-me-up-at-school" or "be-home-late." When her mom answered the phone at the other end, she'd listen to hear *who* was calling then declined the collect call. When the operator came back on the line, they'd tell Kiara that the collect call had been declined—rather than no one answered. This is how Kiara confirmed the message had been sent and received.

Tonight, no calls had come through—collect or not.

Kiara reasoned they may have had to walk a long way to a house to call for a tow truck, and tow trucks, much like police and ambulances, could take thirty to forty-five minutes to get out there. Still, Dave said they left two hours ago.

Kiara clicked back over to the other line and updated Cole.

"I'll stay on the line until Dave calls back," Cole said.

They didn't have much to say other than conjecture what could've caused the truck to break down—hopefully it wouldn't need a new transmission or engine because that would hit her mom hard financially.

Fifteen minutes later, with still no call back, there came a loud knock on her front door. She set the phone down to answer it.

There was Dave and his dad at the doorstep, their faces somber.

"Kiara," Dave's dad said. "There's been a bad accident."

53

Alpha and Omega

KIARA WAS AFRAID TO ASK Dave or his dad for more information and they didn't offer any. She climbed in the front passenger seat, and they headed down the road in silence.

When they got around the curve in the main road—David lived on the Lancaster side of Lake LA—they came upon flashing lights. A tow truck and police car were there.

Kiara ran out and almost tripped on a rock in the darkness. Emergency lights and headlights shone directly on the wreck.

Her mom's pickup truck, or what was left of it, was a crumbled twisted mess of metal.

Dave's dad approached a cop. After they spoke for a minute, the officer took Kiara aside.

"A car pulled out in front of your mom. According to witnesses, they didn't even stop at the stop sign before slamming into your mom's vehicle, flipping it, and sending it rolling over into the bank on the side of the road."

Kiara, shocked, cried out, "Mommy! Tommy!"

Blue and red lights flashed. The cop put his arm around her and led her to his cruiser and sat her in the backseat with the door open while she sobbed.

"The fire department used the jaws of life to pry open the truck to get them out of there. They were transported to the hospital. We had to air evac them down below to the nearest trauma center. I'm sorry, honey. I'm sure they're doing everything they can. They were banged up pretty badly, but both were alive when they left here." He set a hand on her shoulder. "Can we call your dad?"

She shook her head, tears streaming down her face. She couldn't breathe. The lights, blue, red, blue red, white headlights, everything blurred together.

Behind the officer, Dave's dad explained there was no one else to call. It was just Kiara, Tom, and their mom.

Or maybe just Kiara.

The officer pulled Dave's dad to the side, out of Kiara's earshot, and had a talk.

They came back around.

"Kiara," Dave's dad said. "Dave and I are going to drive you down to the valley. We got directions to the hospital. The cop radioed dispatch to tell the hospital we're on our way."

Her chest heaved and she sobbed.

Dave wrapped his arms tightly around her until she stopped crying; her tears soaked his shoulder; his tears soaked hers.

"I'm worried, too, Kiara," Dave said.

The ride down below was silent. No one said anything other than, do you need some air? Or, what's the next turn? It was over an hour but felt like ten. She wished the car would go faster.

She spotted the hospital tower. They pulled up to the emergency room entrance.

Kiara stood at the front desk. They told her to take a seat and wait for the doctor.

Fresh tears ran down over the dried ones. Every once in a while, a sniffle came to the surface. She sat there alone. Dave and his dad were silent, sitting nearby.

When the surgeon came out, his words faded into the background ... broken bones and fractures ... something punctured ... blood loss and head trauma ... surgery ... critical condition.

The doctor put a hand on Kiara's shoulder. "Don't worry. They're lucky to be alive. We're optimistic they'll both make a full recovery."

"Can I go in?" Kiara wiped her eyes. "We drove all the way down here. I want to see my mom and Tom."

"I wish I had better news," the doctor said. "Your mom and brother aren't awake yet." He turned to Dave's dad. "It would be upsetting for her to visit them tonight in the ICU. I suggest you go home and come back in a couple days. You can call the hospital anytime to talk to the staff and we'll give you an update." He turned to Kiara. "How does that sound, dear?"

She didn't know whether to be angry at the condescending tone, or to appreciate what may have been spoken to her out of mercy.

Over the next few days, everything in the world turned to haze. Kiara stayed home alone and fed herself with whatever scraps she scrounged up from the pantry. Cole was there. Then he wasn't. Dave was there. Then he wasn't. She called her grandma. Then her grandma and uncles called. She let the machine record their messages.

Dave's dad drove her back down after the doctors said they could have visitors. When she arrived, Kiara was led back into both hospital rooms. She hurried through the doorways and couldn't hold back from kissing Tom on the cheek and hugging her mom—something she hadn't done in a while—and telling them both how much she loved them.

Tom was up in spirits enough to joke around and ask if the car was going to live. Kiara showed them Polaroid photos and the story in the AV Press. The driver of the Buick steel boat of a car who hit them had been arrested on drunk driving charges. No one recognized the name. It was someone from out of the area who lived down below—an uninsured motorist.

The next time Kiara got to visit, she brought two Snickers bars and went into Tom's room first. She sat in the chair next to his bed. What should she say? He had bandages around every part of his body. Why couldn't they have stayed close like when Tommy was little, hiding under the covers with her in their old house? Did he remember any of that?

She clasped her hands together and stared at the ground.

"Hey, sis," Tom said. "Are you going to give me the candy, or are you here to pray the rosary?"

"What?" She shook her head and tossed him the chocolate. "You're ridiculous."

"Jokes are the way to survive, right?" He unwrapped one Snickers and took a bite. "Leave the rosary praying to mom."

"You didn't turn to Jesus after the miracle of your survival?"

Tom bit off another piece. He spoke with his mouth full. "The miracle is that you're still here visiting us. Let's be honest." Another bite. "I've been a pain in the ass. I'm sure you've had a little joy at seeing me like this."

"Not at all. It hurts me as much as when you got your head hit with the baseball."

"And you carried me home."

She studied his face. "You remember that?"

"Yeah. I remember a lot of things." He shrugged. "Why do you think I'm never home? That way you don't have to keep protecting me. If you only knew half the crap that I've gotten myself into... well, let's just say I'd be in the hospital, because my overprotective sister would try to murder me."

Tears welled up in her eyes. She reached over and embraced him. Her tears wet his arm.

"Don't get all mushy on me." Tom leaned back. "They already gave me a sponge bath."

"The nurse?" Kiara sat up and wiped her face. "I hope she was cute."

"Yes, *he* was." Tom opened the second Snickers bar. Another bite.

"All right. I'll leave you alone." Kiara smirked. "Shall I tell the nurse you need anything?"

"No, it's better when I look helpless."

"Oh my God." Kiara rolled her eyes. "See you when you get out of here."

She made a quick stop at her mom's room and was relieved to find her too groggy from the pain medication to talk.

Within a couple of days, Tom and her mom were both transferred to a rehabilitation facility in Lancaster to recover. They estimated her mom would require several more weeks before going home. Tom would be released hopefully by the end of the week.

Dave and his dad decided that after Tom got discharged, they'd take care of him until Tom could walk unassisted. Maybe he could even move in with them until senior year.

What about her mom? Kiara could call the college and ask to defer entrance for a semester, or maybe a year if she needed it. She could get a better job to help her mom pay the mortgage until her mom could return to work.

When a certified letter came to the house addressed to her mom, Kiara opened it and discovered her mom had been hiding a pretty big secret. Kiara read the letter a second time. Her mom was more than four months behind on their mortgage and the bank had been mailing her foreclosure warning letters.

Kiara phoned the bank and explained the situation. She relayed the story of the car crash. Could they make an exception? The bank didn't care. They said sorry, but her mom owed them too much money. The best they could do would be to hold off for a couple more months.

News of the accident spread throughout the church and their community. People showed up at Kiara's door bringing food and asking what they could do for her mom. Kiara was too ashamed and in shock to admit the house was in foreclosure.

After they discharged Tom, he moved in with Dave and his dad.

Kiara visited her mom. She brought her some flowers and a get-well card. She also brought the letter from the bank. She wasn't sure how to approach it. She didn't want to get her mom upset while she was still trying to get better.

Her mom thanked her for the card and flowers then turned her attention back to the TV.

"Mom, there's something else." Kiara slid the letter over.

Her mom glanced down at it. "I already know."

"When were you going to tell me?"

"Tell you? What does it matter to you?"

Kiara's jaw dropped. She said nothing.

"Your brother is the one I'm worried about. You'll be off doing your college thing."

"My college thing?" Kiara said. "No thanks to you."

"What do you expect from me?"

Kiara stared at the IV tubes and monitors and the bandages. "Nothing. I never expect anything." She stood to leave. "I'll be back tomorrow. Tell me if you need anything."

"Okay." Her mom held her arms open. "Come give your mom a hug."

Kiara obliged.

She paused at the doorway and glanced at her mom, engrossed in the TV.

Tom settled in at his friend's house. Kiara's mom was discharged from the skilled nursing and rehabilitation center. She was able to move with assistance from a walker. She had gotten hurt worse than Tom who still had a leg cast, some pins in his leg and hip, and used crutches.

Kiara's mom returned home, for as long as the house would still be their home.

Without having been able to work either of her jobs: cooking for the weekend retreats at Saint Andrew's Abbey or her new full-time job at the Christian bookstore, she was shorter on money than ever. She had never been good at budgeting or maintaining emergency savings.

It wasn't long before the electricity was shut off. Her mom couldn't afford any food, and the fridge was useless without power, so Kiara brought pizza home from work, got a Styrofoam cooler to keep it in, and lit the kerosene lanterns.

"What are we going to do?" Kiara asked. She'd been sharing her mom's bed to save from having to use up the kerosene to light two rooms. Besides which, it got cold at night.

"Well, I have to figure things out," her mom said. "Watch over Tom to make sure he's all right. That's the most important thing. This is a lot of change for him. He's on his own. I love him and wish I could do more to help him. We both need to be by his side."

Kiara dropped the pizza crust on her paper plate. "Why won't you love me? You love Tom. I deserve to be loved and cared for, too."

Her mom sat still for a moment, seeming to consider Kiara for the first time.

"Answer me," Kiara pleaded. "I'm here by *your* side. I've always been by *his* side. When have you ever been by *my* side?"

Her mom burst out in tears. "You don't know what I've gone through. I had you young, got pregnant then married, shunned by the church, my mom, my dad, my brothers. Everyone was so disappointed in me."

Kiara stared at her. Maybe that's why her mom and grandma didn't get along?

Her mom reached for her. "I'm sorry if I never knew how to show you love… I did the best I could, damn it. Maybe it wasn't good enough. I didn't want you to screw up your life like I did." She took a deep breath. "I wasn't shown love… always taken for granted that I was fine, to grow up, suck it up, and raise my brothers."

Kiara shook her head and held out her hands. "Well—"

Recognition washed over her mom's face. "Oh my God. Please forgive me."

Her mom reached over to hug Kiara who stiffened in her mom's arms. Her mom squeezed tighter. Kiara stared at the shadows on the ceiling and the piles of laundry on the floor.

Kiara reflected on her mother's words. Had her mom shown Kiara love? Her mom loved others unconditionally—Tommy, Carolyn... and Cole.

Kiara pitied her mom, but this was no excuse.

She sat there motionless in her mother's embrace, staring at the wall. She didn't feel much inside except sad.

The next morning, Kiara's mom told her the owners of the Christian Bookstore had a proposition for them, so they went up to town to meet with them.

When Kiara stepped inside the store, she was hit with the smell of incense and candles. Rows upon rows of glass shelving held knickknacks, statues, books, and Christian paraphernalia. Statues of the Virgin Mary and crucifixes on the wall reminded her of her grandma.

A short, stout woman with wiry glasses, a necklace with a gold cross around her neck, and tight gray curls—almost like the horrid haircut her mom forced on her years ago—approached. The woman pushed up the sleeves of her flowered blouse and wiped her hands on her jeans.

"You must be Kiara." She reached out her arms for a hug. "I'm Patty."

Kiara smiled and walked into her arms. Patty exuded warmth and kindness, quite different from the coldness she experienced in her mom's embrace.

"Well, dear, it's lovely to meet you." With a wide smile on her face, Patty motioned to Kiara's mom. "Oh, Marcy. Glad you're walking again... sort of. Why don't the both of you come on down here to the back room." She turned her head. "George, they're here."

A man with more hair in his gray beard than on his head came around the corner. His button up shirt was tucked into his pants, but hung over his belt, and he walked with a slight limp. He had deep smile lines around his mouth and his kind eyes.

"So happy to meet you, darling," George said. "Marcy, I can't tell you how thankful we are to see you. Hallelujah, God answered our prayers." He gave Kiara's mom a hug and nodded to Kiara. "Your mom is an incredible bookkeeper. She straightened things up around here. We thank the Lord for bringing her to us and for saving her and your brother."

"Amen," Patty said. "Ain't that the truth. We've been offering up prayers for your family at the church." She led them into a small room that served as both office and breakroom with a kitchenette. "Here, please have a seat. Can I get the both of you anything?"

Patty knew their house was going into foreclosure and that Kiara was accepted to college. She understood Kiara's mom wasn't well enough to work. She and her husband were foster parents. Most of their kids were adults. Some still lived at home. They had a large house down below. She and George would be happy to make room for Kiara's mom to recover there until she could get back on her feet financially.

They both turned to Kiara.

"Your mom is so proud of you," Patty said. "The one thing she wants more than anything in this world is for you to leave the desert behind and go to college."

Kiara blinked. If her mom wanted this so badly, why not tell Kiara herself?

Patty and George exchanged a knowing glance. Had Kiara given her mom a dirty look? Is that what they saw? Oh, God, Kiara hoped she hadn't.

"Darling, can you come with me for a moment?" George asked.

Kiara followed him to a small office that had another desk. He opened a drawer, brought out a photo album, and displayed it on the desk. He pointed around the room and invited her to explore. Kiara followed the motion. Frames dotted every wall. Inside every frame was a picture of Kiara, Tom, or Kiara and Tom. George nodded.

"This is your mom's office," George said. "We've heard so much about you and your brother. You mom finds every chance she can to tell anyone all of the amazing things the two of you have done. She loves you *both* so much."

Kiara flipped open the album. She'd seen the pictures before—awards ceremonies, plays at school, her eighth-grade speech, Kiara holding a trophy in this one, blowing out candles on a homemade cake in the shape of a dog, hand sewn costumes from before the divorce...

Kiara shook her head. "I don't understand."

"Sometimes it's hard to see what's outside the frame when you're the one in the picture." George smiled. "Your mom was always the one outside the frame taking the pictures. And there are a lot of pictures." He chuckled.

Kiara's jaw dropped.

She followed George back to the kitchen.

"I don't want to leave my mom and Tommy behind." Kiara surprised herself by the words. Tears welled in her eyes.

Patty and George were insistent.

"Your mom will help you get some student loans for the dorms, but if you ever need anything at all," George said, "don't be shy in asking. Patty and I will get it for you."

"Besides," Patty said. "Honey, you'd have nowhere to stay if you don't go off to school on account of your mom losing the house."

"Don't worry. God will watch over you and your brother," George said. "He has a plan for all of us. Patty and I count our blessings that we're in the position to help your mom."

"Which in turn," Patty said, "will help you. We'll be praying for your success in school. We mean it. If you need anything at all, we'll make sure you have it."

Kiara glanced over at her mom. Her mom nodded and wiped tears from her eyes.

Was this really happening? Was Kiara really going to leave Lake LA? She'd never been so lucky in her life. She was afraid she'd blink and it would disappear.

"I don't even know what to say." Kiara rushed up and gave them both hugs. "Thank you both so much." A deep sense of gratitude stirred from within.

She spun around and, for the first time, Kiara found her mom. She wrapped her arms around her in a tight embrace and cried.

Maybe she'd been wrong about church. The teachings of God, whether or not God taught them, mattered. People who followed "God's teachings," as did Patty and George, were good people; People who followed God but *not* His teachings, like the three witches, were not. Sometimes it was hard to tell the difference.

Perhaps her mom had been misguided at times, or maybe her depression and life circumstances caused the confusion, but whatever the reasons, her mom was still one of the good ones—one who would sacrifice for her daughter's success.

That settled that. Kiara would leave the desert.

She found herself eager to tell Cole. Then, she wondered why after all of this time, he was still the first person she wanted to tell everything to.

54

Distance Between Us

KIARA DROVE TO THE LOCAL MARKET with Carolyn to pick up some food—it was too far to head into town and cost too much in gas while they were both trying to be careful with money.

As the electric doors swished open, Carolyn held out her arm to stop Kiara.

"Turn around," Carolyn said.

It was too late. Kiara had already seen it. Juan had his arms around a tall, thin blonde. Kiara recognized her as a cashier at the store. Carolyn told her to wait in the car while she picked up a few things off the shopping list.

Kiara stared out the car window and watched Juan and his new girlfriend walk out. He led her around the corner where he squeezed her butt, pushed her up against the wall, and they kissed for a few minutes. He moved his lips up and down her neck like he used to do to Kiara.

Even though she hated him in many ways and he hurt her, this hurt her, too. Kiara's heart stung and she stared at them. Thankfully, Juan didn't see her.

Carolyn got back in the car. "I know it sucks," she said. "He's the lowest form of scum on this Earth, Kiara. You need to remember that."

"Easy for you to say," Kiara said. "You've got Trevor."

"At the moment, he's all I got."

Kiara paused. "Why? What's going on? There's a lot you haven't been telling me."

"When you come back out to visit, I'll explain the whole story." Carolyn nodded. "I've got to dangle a carrot to get you to visit. Otherwise, you'll go off to college and never return." She pointed out the window. "Besides, this is the perfect time to remember how much you hate Juan, so you never end up with another creep like him. While you're at it, send prayers to that girl. She's going to need it."

Kiara told Cole. He said it was understandable for her to feel that way about Juan.

Cole suggested they take a walk up to the water tower. Perhaps that would clear her head.

He leaned against a boulder; his legs spread wide enough for her to sit in between and lean back against his chest. As he stroked her hair, Kiara felt calmer and her stress dissipated.

They looked down over the town, the Joshua trees tiny in the distance. Kiara vaguely remembered when they had bloodied her arms. The scars were faint. They had left their mark on her, like everything else in the desert.

"I'm not going to miss it," she said. "What about you?"

Cole quieted and stopped petting her hair. He wrapped his arms around her.

"Kiara," he said. "I don't know how to say this, so I'm just going to come out and say it."

There was that little warning voice in her head. She held her breath.

"I'm not going," he said.

"What?" Kiara turned to face him. "Did I do something? Why don't you want to go?"

In all the years she had known Cole, he never sobbed. Not when his father was in a drunken haze, or when life had slapped him around. Now, he not only had tears in his eyes, but his chest heaved. "That's not it at all. I want nothing more than to go and be with you."

She had tears in her eyes, too. "I don't understand."

"I didn't want to tell you." He wiped his eyes.

"Cole." Kiara turned around, her face inches from his. "Whatever the reason, we'll figure it out together. Isn't that what you always say?"

"My dad wouldn't give me his tax info. He was holding it over my head." Cole sighed. "I couldn't fill out the FAFSA financial aid form. I can't get money to go."

"Can't you forge his signature?"

"That's not going to work. I don't have his taxes."

"Can't you find the papers without him knowing?"

. "That's just it." He shook his head. "Mom said he hasn't filed taxes in years and probably owes the government money."

Kiara's heart sank. "Are you kidding me? And they never told you?

"The last time he got a refund he blew it on beer and cigarettes."

Kiara wrapped her arms around his neck. "What the fuck is wrong with him?"

"I ask myself that all the time." Cole embraced her in a hug. "I don't know why he's an ass. Maybe he's trying to kill my future because he couldn't make anything of himself."

"We can still go," she said. "Can you get a job? I'll help you pay for it."

"I can't make enough for tuition and housing without financial aid. I'm sorry. You know I want that more than anything else in the world. But I can't, and it's killing me, Kiara. The fact that I can't be with you every second and every moment absolutely kills me."

"Why does the world hate us?" Kiara asked. "It isn't fair." She dared to dream of a life beyond the desert and life had handed her disappointment. Her heart ached.

The sun sank lower, dragging a rainbow curtain of colors behind the Joshua trees.

"I'll get a job," Cole said, "go to AVC, save up money, and transfer in two years."

"That's fine then," Kiara said. "I'm staying, too."

"This isn't making it any easier. Trust me, I've been dreaming about this, about us, for a long time. You need to do this for you, not me. You owe it to yourself."

Despite his arguments, she held firm. She stared into his green eyes, the same green eyes she noticed at the dry lakebed so many years ago.

"We'll both go to AVC," Kiara said. "I'm not going away without you."

Cole tucked a strand of hair behind her ear. "You have the money to go. You have to go."

"I will not. I've lived the past twelve years without saying what I wanted to say—what I should've said a long time ago."

He watched her intently.

She placed her forefinger on his chest. "Cole... if you've been listening to my silence through all these years, then you already know this." She closed her eyes and took a deep breath. "What I'm trying to say is…" She opened her eyes and stared into his. "I love you."

"I know." Cole wrapped his arms around her. "Oh, how many times I've wanted to say those words to you. I love you, Kiara. I've loved you for a long time."

"I know." She looked up at him.

He cradled her head in his hands, leaned forward, and pressed his lips against hers.

She closed her eyes as a warmth washed over her. Cole tasted like peaches and musky aftershave. He tasted like the boy who had listened to her when nobody else did, who climbed trees with her, and above all else, had believed in her.

He pulled back and they locked eyes. He had that same boyish grin.

Streaks of vibrant oranges and reds filled the sky behind him. She locked this perfect moment into memory, nuzzled her face against his, and planted kisses across his cheeks.

He kissed her again, harder. She breathed him in.

She playfully pushed him onto the ground, snuggled alongside him, and rested her head on his shoulder. He wrapped his arms around her and pressed their bodies closer.

This is what love is—not jealousy and control, but joy and bliss.

Pinks and purples in the sky faded into navy blues beyond the silhouette of the buttes.

"I want to live the rest of our lives together and grow old together," she said. "It doesn't matter where, even if we stay here forever."

"Ever since we were kids," he said, "we promised to escape the desert."

She nodded. Her eyes adjusted to the darkness. The moon and stars illuminated the night sky. She traced the big dipper with a finger. "Remember the constellations you showed me?"

Cole sat up. She rested her head onto his lap. He brushed his fingertips lightly across her cheek, down her chin, and across her lips. Her skin tingled with his touch.

"What if you do stay?" Cole asked. "What then? We'll never leave the desert. We'll become bitter and unhappy. I don't want that for us."

"That's not going to happen."

"Of course it won't." He stared into her eyes. "Because you're not going to stay, even if I have to drag you down there myself. I'll never forgive myself if you don't go."

Kiara rose to her feet and brushed off the dirt.

She took a shallow breath and turned away. "This wasn't how it's supposed to end."

He got up and reached for her. "What are you saying?"

She whispered, "You're not going to transfer. This is it. If I go, everything ends here."

Cole gave an exasperated sigh.

"Kiara, no matter how many times you've pushed me away, or how many times I've had to step back and let you make your mistakes, after all of that, you think I'm going to walk away and give up? I promise you. I'm getting out of here, too. It may take me a little longer."

Kiara's skin got cold and she shivered. Her teeth chattered.

"Come on." Cole rubbed his hands up and down her arms. "We have to get you inside. I don't want you getting sick."

He wrapped an arm around her and held her close as they walked back to her house.

"I don't want to wait two years to be with you," she said.

"Kiara. Just go. It's only two years." He squeezed her. "Just don't climb too many big trees down there without me."

They reached her front porch. She turned to face him but stared at his shoes instead.

"I can drive you down there on Sunday," he said.

"No, I can't see you before I leave if this is how it's going to be. You know that."

"I understand." He held her and stroked her hair. She pressed her face into his chest, tears wetting his shirt. He pulled back and lifted her chin. He wiped the tears from her eyes, his thumb lingering on the hollow underneath her eye. "Hey."

Smiling tearfully, she said, "Hay is for horses."

He shook his head and a smirk crept onto his face. "You're doing it again."

"Doing what?" she asked.

"You're crinkling your nose, which is absolutely adorable."

Kiara's blue eyes met his gaze. Her stomach fluttered at the kindness in his face.

Cole bent down, wrapped his arms around her, and their lips met in a final sweet kiss.

He gave her a tight embrace and whispered in her ear, "Don't forget about me."

"Impossible."

He stepped back, slipped his hands into his pockets, and walked away.

Kiara entered her dark house, shut the door, then cracked it open to stare at Cole's receding shadow in the moonlight. She watched as it grew smaller and, eventually, disappeared into the desert darkness.

Author's Note

I'm glad you've gotten the chance to meet Kiara and Cole, and their friends and family. What happens to Kiara and Cole? I assure you that by the end of the series, you'll know. *Dare to Dream* is the first book in the *Desert of Dreams Series.*

Check out Reac*h for Hope (Desert of Dreams Series Book 2),* Carolyn's story!

What was the inspiration behind this series?

The tagline of the *Desert of Dreams Series* says it all: Trauma. Resilience. Hope. Everyone has their own story.

Growing up, I didn't know many people who had "normal" childhoods. Most of my friends, much like my characters, survived trauma that presented itself in many forms—neglect, as well as physical, mental, emotional, and sexual abuse.

While being a latchkey kid may have been typical in the 1980s and 1990s, abuse and neglect should never be normalized. Ever.

It's amazing how a great psychologist, counselor, or therapist can help people work through trauma and develop resilience, so that we can overcome the worst of the worst.

Keep hope alive, because as my friends will tell you: it does get better. And there are good people out there. Trust me... there are. Hold on to those friendships.

Acknowledgements

Thank you to my mom for always believing in me and supporting me as a writer. Being a single mom wasn't easy. It wasn't the path you would've chosen. I attribute much of my strength to you and the sacrifices you made.

Leo, thanks once again for being the perpetually perfect partner for me and for sacrificing many board game nights for these books. Thanks for the constant encouragement and for reading the same chapters over and over again...last time I promise...haha.

Thank you to Jenny Orci for your tireless help during the writing and revision process—you're a skilled writer whose opinions I hold in the highest regard. Kiara appreciates you helping her find outlets for her rage.

Thank you to Ken Elliott, another talented writer: you're such a good sport with my early morning questions. Thank you to Lisa Park for the time and energy you've devoted to read and discuss the plot... I promise I'll put together a nonfiction desert book one of these days in my usual snarky voice.

To my fellow desert rats who managed to get out and get educations: You the bomb. Yeah you, too, Sarah C.. Thank you to my childhood friends—you're my chosen family. Louis Diaz, my original Google Search engine, we will continue to one up each other to the end (Am I winning?). Maria Leighton, I admire how you're able to find hidden fields of desert flowers off remote dirt roads—wait, where are we going?

Thank you to my Beta Readers: Sarah Goyette—your intuitive insights and eye for historical regional accuracy is unmatched—thank you for saving me on the frog vs. toad debate (see book 3); Thank you for keeping me in the game, Haley Lynn—slow burn love story for the win! Thank you to Audrey and Kevin for offering a teen's perspective in the early stages of this project.

Thank you to my cover designer, Fiona Jayde Media: I appreciate all of the time and energy you spent in bringing these covers to life. A huge thank you to my editors, especially the talented Jennifer Silva Redmond whose countless hours of advice and suggestions helped me to craft a better story. I hope I've made you proud. To the SCWC family: you make me want to be a better writer.

This book isn't just for young adults. Those of us who have lived through a messy childhood or survived trauma at any point in our lives can find comfort in knowing we're not alone in that experience.

I won't call out names, but, after talking to others about this book, people whom I've known for years have opened up and shared some shocking dark secrets about their past and family trauma. Hey, if you're reading this, you know who you are. You are survivors. Be proud.

We've struggled through experiences that had to either make or break us. I'm thankful we didn't break.

To all the teens and adults out there just trying to survive, you are stronger than you realize. Be brave enough to reach out and ask for help if you need it. I'm cheering you on.

Discussion Questions

1. What is a healthy vs. unhealthy relationship?

2. What are warning signs of physical, mental, emotional, and/or sexual abuse? When should you seek help? Who is a safe person to go to if you need help?

3. What can you do if a friend confides in you that they've experienced trauma and/or abuse?

4. What are your views on sex, drugs, and alcohol?

5. How can you be a good role model for others and stand up for yourself safely?

6. How can we build resilience to overcome life's challenges?

7. What are your dreams in life? What do you hope to achieve?

If you or someone you know is struggling with their mental health or is in crisis, please reach out for help. In the US, you can call or text the National Suicide and Crisis Lifeline at 988.

About the Author

For thirteen years, Amanda LaPera grew up in the small rural community of Lake Los Angeles, where, much like her characters, she was disappointed to learn there wasn't a lake and everything she planted died. She and her friends survived, buoyed by resilience and determination. Now her hobbies include watching hummingbirds in her yard surrounded by trees, playing board games with her husband, taunting her sons, and appeasing her dogs. She has sworn off succulents, because she believes they belong in the desert.

Amanda LaPera is a national award-winning author. Her book, *Losing Dad, Paranoid Schizophrenia: A Family's Search for Hope,* won a Silver IBPA Award, was a *BookLife Prize* quarter finalist and a *Readers' Favorite* Awards finalist. Her sequel *Finding Dad, Paranoid Schizophrenia: An End to the Search* was a finalist in the IAN *Book of the Year Awards.* She teaches English and is a member of the California Writers Club and the Southern California Writers Association.

To be notified of new releases and exclusive offers, sign up for her newsletter at **www.amandalapera.com.**

Connect:

Instagram: @desertstoryteller

Facebook.com/amandalapera

Facebook.com/desertofdreamsbook

linkedin.com/in/amandalapera

Also by the Author

Fiction

Young Adult Coming-of-Age — *Desert of Dreams Series*

Desert of Dreams Series: Coming-of-age standalone books connected by friendship, time, and place. Surviving difficult family amidst a small-town landscape during the 1980s and 90s.

Sway with the Wind: A Prequel Novella
(Desert of Dreams Series)
Anne's story takes place 20 years earlier!

Dare to Dream
(Desert of Dreams Series Book 1)
Kiara's story

Reach for Hope
(Desert of Dreams Series Book 2)
Carolyn's story

Embrace the Truth
(Desert of Dreams Series Book 3)
Misty's story

Allow in Light (Desert of Dreams Series Book 4) - Nicole's story coming soon!

Mend the Heart: The Final Story (Desert of Dreams Series Book 5) - Jenny's story coming soon!

Nonfiction

Psychology Memoir – *Losing Dad Series*
A poignant true story of how a father's sudden late-onset mental illness and homelessness impact his entire family.

Losing Dad, Paranoid Schizophrenia: A Family's Search for Hope (10th Anniversary Edition)

Finding Dad, Paranoid Schizophrenia: An End to the Search (the sequel)

To order books: